The Collected Romantic Novels of Penelope Aubin Volume 1

The Collected Romantic Novels of Penelope Aubin Volume 1

The Life of Madam de Beaumont

The Strange Adventures of the Count
de Vinevil and His Family

The Life and Amorous Adventures of Lucinda

and

The Noble Slaves; or, The Lives and Adventures of
Two Lords and Two Ladies

Mrs Aubin

LEONAUR

The Collected Romantic Novels of Penelope Aubin
Volume 1
The Life of Madam de Beaumontt
The Strange Adventures of the Count de Vinevil and His Family
The Life and Amorous Adventures of Lucinda
and
The Noble Slaves; or, The Lives and Adventures of Two Lords and Two Ladies.
by Mrs Aubin

First published under the titles
The Life of Madam de Beaumont
The Strange Adventures of the Count de Vinevil and His Family
The Life and Amorous Adventures of Lucinda
and
The Noble Slaves; or, The Lives and Adventures of Two Lords and Two Ladies.

Leonaur is an imprint
of Oakpast Ltd

ISBN: 978-0-85706-950-4 (hardcover)
ISBN: 978-0-85706-951-1 (softcover)

http://www.leonaur.com

Publisher's Notes

The views expressed in this book are not necessarily
those of the publisher.

Contents

Contents

The Life of Madam de Beaumont

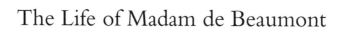

Contents

Preface to the Reader

The air has infected some of the neighbouring nations with the plague, and swept away the astonished inhabitants by thousands; but in our nation it has had a different effect, it has certainly infected our understandings: a madness has for some time possessed the English, and we are turned protectors, exceeded the French in extravagant whimsies, and parted with our money as easily, as if we had forgot that we were to live a day longer; we are grown false as Jews in trading, Turks and Italians in lust, Libertines in principle, and have more religions amongst us, and less sincerity, than the Dutch. The knavish part of us are employed at present in getting money; and the thoughtless, which are the major part, in searching for something new to divert their spleen: the tales of fairies, and elves, take with them, and the most improbable things please best.

The story I here present the public withal, is very extraordinary, but not quite so incredible as these. This is an age of wonders, and certainly we can doubt of nothing after what we have seen in our days: yet there is one thing in the story of Madam de Beaumount very strange; which is, that she, and her daughter, are very religious, and very virtuous, and that there were two honest clergymen living at one time. In the Lord de Beaumount's story, there is yet something more surprising; which is, that he loved an absent wife so well, that he obstinately refused a pretty lady a favour.

These circumstances will, I suppose, make the truth of this story doubted; but since men are grown very doubtful, even in those things that concern them most, I'll not give myself much trouble to clear their doubts about this. Wales being a place not extremely populous in many parts, is certainly more rich in virtue than England, which is now, (as at time of first publication), improved in vice only, and rich in foreigners, who often bring more vices than ready money along

11

with them. He that would keep his integrity, must dwell in a cell; and Belinda had never been so virtuous, had she not been bred in a cave, and never seen a court.

Wales has produced many brave men, and been famed for the unshaken loyalty of its people to their princes, and bravery in fights scorning to how their necks to slavery, or be conquered; why may it not produce a woman virtuous and wise, as the men are courageous?

In this story I have aimed at pleasing, and at the same time encouraging virtue in my readers. I wish men would, like Belinda, confide in providence, and look on death with the same indifference that she did. But I forget that this book is to be published in London, where abundance of people live, whose actions must persuade us, that they are so far from fearing to die, that they certainly fear nothing that is to come after dying; some of these not speaking good English, will not, perhaps, read this; I shall therefore refer them to their own countries for virtuous examples, and present this story to the true-born English, and Ancient Britons, to whom I wish increase of sense and virtue, plenty of money, good governors, and endless prosperity.

Penelope Aubin.

Chapter 1

Not far from Swansea, a sea-port in Wales, in Glamorganshire, there dwelt a gentleman whose name was Mr. Lluelling; he was descended of a good family, and had a handsome estate of about 500 *l. per annum*, all lying together in that place, on which he lived comfortably and nobly, doing much good; a man whose generous temper, and good sense, made him beloved by all that knew him: He had been once a Member of Parliament, travelled in his youth, bred at the university, and in fine, was a most accomplished gentleman. It is not therefore to be doubted, but that he had many opportunities of marrying, but he always declined it, and seemed, though ever gallant and complaisant, yet indifferent to the fair sex; he was thirty-six years of age, and wisely preferred a country retirement before noisy courts, and business; his person was very handsome, and his conversation and mein perfectly genteel and agreeable.

This gentleman, in the year 1717, one evening, in the month of May, was walking alone by the sea-side to take the air, and passing over some little hills, came at last to the top of one much higher than the rest, where standing still to view the lovely prospect of the neigh-bouring fields and valleys, which were now all in their greatest pride, adorned with lovely flowers, and various greens; he saw just opposite another hill, and in the side of it a door open, before which there stood a maid of such exquisite beauty, and shape, and in a habit so odd and uncommon, that he was both extremely surprised and charmed: he stood still, not daring to approach her, left he should surprise, and make her fly from him. She seemed very thoughtful, but at length, looking up, she saw him, and immediately retired, shutting the door after her.

He continued musing for some time, and having well observed the place, returned home, resolving to go back thither early the next morning; he passed that night without once closing his eyes, such strong impressions had her beauty made in his soul, that he thought of nothing but the bright vision.

At break of day he rose, forbidding his servants to attend him, and hastened to the hill, from whence he descended into the valley, where he sought for a convenient place to conceal himself at some little distance from the cave, resolving to watch the opening of the door, and observe what past there. Having found a low tree, he climbed up into it, and did not wait long before he saw a proper lad come forth with a basket on his arm; he went towards the town, as if he were going to fetch provisions: soon after a maid servant came out with a broom, and swept before the door of the cave, dressed in a red-petticoat, a French jacket and coif; and in some time after she went in, he saw a lady in a rich nightgown, and nightclothes, something in years, but very beautiful, attended by the young virgin he had seen the day before, who was dressed in a cherry colour silk petticoat, flowered with silver, a white satin waistcoat, tied down the breast with red and silver ribbons, her neck was bare, and her hair was carelessly braided, and tied up in green satin ribbon: upon her head she wore a fine straw-hat, lined with green and gold, and a hatband suiting: she appeared to be about fourteen, was fair as Diana; her eyes were black, her face oval, her shape incomparable; she wore a sweetness and modesty in her look, that would have charmed the coldest breast, and checked the boldest lover from proceeding farther then he ought. Their habits, speech, and mein, spoke them persons of quality, and foreigners.

'Come my dear child,' said the lady, 'let us take a walk over the hills this sweet morning, 'tis all the diversion our sad circumstance permits us to take.'

'Why, Madam,' answered the fair Belinda, for so was the young lady called, 'can there be any pleasures in the world exceeding those this sweet retirement gives us? How often have you recounted to me the miseries and dangers that attend a life led in crowded cities, and noisy courts: had you never left the quiet convent for the world, or changed your virgin state, how happy had you been. Our homely cell, indeed, is nothing like the splendid places I have heard you talk of; but then we are not half so much exposed to those temptations you have warned me of: nothing I dread but only this; should Providence take you from me, I should be so sad and lonely, that I fear my heart would break.'

'My child,' the lady answered 'our lives are in the Almighty's hands, and we must still submit; you can't be wretched whilst you are inno-cent, and I still hope your father lives, that we shall meet again, that we shall leave this dismal place, return to France, and live to see you hap-pily disposed of in the world. 'Tis now fourteen years and six months since we have lived securely in this lonely mansion, a tedious task to me; you know I dare not return to France a second time, having been once betrayed, and with much difficulty escaped from my enemies hands: I want only some faithful friend that could go thither for me.'

By this time they were past on so far, that Mr. Lluelling could hear no more; he came down from the tree, and followed gently after, soon overtook, and thus addressed himself to them:

'Ladies,' said he,' be not surprised, I am a gentleman of this place, one who am able to serve you, my estate and heart are at your com-mand; sure I have been very unfortunate in being so long ignorant of my being near you. I have overheard your discourse, and am come to offer myself and fortune to you.' Here he threw himself at Belinda's feet: 'To this fair creature, said he, 'I dedicate the remainder of my life; I and all that's mine shall be devoted to her service. Speak, lovely maid,' said he, 'whose eyes have robbed me of a heart, may I presume to hope?'

Belinda, much confused, looked first on him, then on her mother, remaining silent, seized with a passion she had been a stranger to till that moment: the lady well perceiving it, answered thus;

'Rise, Sir, since Heaven, who has till now preserved us from all discovery, has permitted you to see us, and, as I conjecture, more than this time, so that it would be in vain to forbid your coming where we are; I consent to accept the friendship which you offer, not doubting but you are what you appear, a person of birth and fortune.'

He bowed, and taking Belinda by the hand, said, 'Madam, you shall find me all you can wish; let me now have the honour to wait of you home to your cell, and there we may be more at liberty to talk.'

The ladies consenting, they went back together to the cave, the inside of which was most surprising to Mr. Lluelling; there he found five rooms so contrived, and so richly furnished, that he stood amazed. 'In the name of wonder,' said he, 'Ladies, by what enchantment or art was this place contrived, from whence is this light conveyed that il-luminates it, which seems without all covered over with earth, and is within so light and agreeable?'

The lady answered, 'When you have heard our story you will be satisfied in all. At our landing on this place, we found a cave, or little cell, but not like what it now is; the seamen belonging to the ship that brought us here, contrived and made it what you see; the damask beds, *scrutores*, and all the furniture you find here, I brought with me from France: the light is from a skylight on the top of the hill, covered with a shutter and grate, when we think fit to shut day out; a pair of stairs leads to it in the midst of the rooms which you see lie in a kind of round: the building is contrived an oval, part lined with some boards, to defend the damps from us; but yet in winter 'tis no pleasant dwelling.'

'Madam,' said he, 'I have a seat, and more convenient house that shall be proud to receive you, and I shall not cease to importune you, till you grace it with your presence; I shall therefore deny myself the pleasure of staying with you longer, and fetch my coach to bear you thither.' At these words he took leave.

When he was gone, the old lady, looking on her daughter, spake thus to her; 'Now, my dear child, what ' do you think. Providence provides us here at last a friend; and, if I am not deceived, a husband for you: What think you of this gentleman?'

'Alas! Madam,' she replied, 'I know not what to think, I wish I had not seen him; for if he proves deceitful, as men, you say, often do, sure I should be unhappy.'

They continued this discourse, breakfasted, and before noon saw Mr. Lluelling return with a coach, and servants, to fetch them to his house to dinner; he wisely left his coach on the farther hill, and came alone to them: his importunities were so great, they could not refuse him; so staying only to dress, they went with him. The ladies' habits, though not made after the English mode, were rich, and such as were hardly ever seen in that part of Wales, being what the lady brought from France with her. When arrived at his house, they were entertained in a manner suiting the noble nature and hospitality of the antient Britons; nothing was wanting to show the master's respect.

How much the young lady was surprised, it is almost impossible to imagine, since she had never been abroad before, or conversed with any stranger. After dinner, Mr. Lluelling carried the ladies into a drawing-room, where the pictures hung of his ancestors: stately, and so furnished was the place, it might have taken up some hours to have viewed it with delight. Here wines, sweetmeats, and tea, were placed, and the servants withdrawing, he seated the ladies, and himself, and then said, 'Now, Madam,' addressing himself to the mother, 'may I, without offending, beg to know your quality, the adventures of your life, and the true cause of your dwelling in the obscure place I found you.' 'Yes,' answered she, 'your curiosity is just, and I readily agree to all you ask.'

Then she began the narrative of her life in this manner.

Chapter 2

I was born in Normandy; my father being a French nobleman, his name was the Count de Rochefoucault: my mother was an English lady, who came over with the unfortunate Queen of England, wife to King James II. to whom my mother's father was a loyal, and faithful servant, though a Protestant: He was a lord, but could give no fortune with my mother, but her beauty and virtue. My father being at court at Paris, and visiting at St. Germains, there saw, and fell in love with her, in the end married, and brought her to his seat in Normandy. I was born the first year of their marriage, and by my mother secretly bred up a Protestant; we talking together in English, which she taught me; for which reason I was not much esteemed by my father's family, when it came to be known.

When I was ten years of age, it pleased God to take away my dear mother, whose virtues had made her dear to all that knew her; but my father's grief was such, that it overcame his reason, and in a short time threw him into a deep consumption, of which, to my unutterable grief, he died, leaving me, his only child, an orphan of but twelve years of age, he left me a great fortune in lands and money, in the care of three Catholic noblemen, his own relations, whom he strictly enjoined to take care of me, and never force my inclinations in anything, or force me into a convent; but no sooner was he laid in the ground, but they shut me up in a monastery of Poor Clares, as they pretended to have me convinced of my errors in religion, but, in truth, with design to wrong me of my fortune.

Here I continued a year, being very kindly treated by the abbess and society, who were most of them ladies born of good families, and perfectly well bred; amongst these was one, whose name was Katherine, daughter to Monsieur de Maintenon, the governor of Normandy. With this young lady I contracted a strict friendship; to her I opened all the secrets of my heart, and we loved so tenderly, that we were inseparable: we lay together, and she had told me all her griefs, confessing she had, and did still love, a young gentleman who was a colonel and relation of her mother's; which coming to her father's knowledge, who was related to the king, and, a man very ambitious, had so offended him, that he had sent him away to the army, and forced her into this convent. This lady had an only brother, who was called the Count de Beaumount, who was young, gay, handsome, witty; and in fine, everything that's charming; his soul was noble, and full of truth and honour.

This young lord came frequently to the grates to visit his sister, whom he tenderly loved: by this means he saw, and loved me; his conversation charmed me, and I quickly found I more than liked him: in fine, he declared his passion, and I at last yielded to fly with, and marry him, on condition that his sister should go with me. Nothing now was wanting but an opportunity to effect our design, which we did in a few days, in the manner following: The count went to the gardener who used to look after the monastery garden, and with gold bribed him, to get another key made to the garden gate, with which my lover entered when he pleased, concealing himfelf in one of the arbours till my companion and I came to walk.

We soon agreed on the day, and hour, when we should escape; the evening of the appointed day, he brought a chaise with fix horses, to a village near the convent, and in the dusk came in it to the garden gate, which was the hour we used to be at Vespers: I and Sister Katherine feigning ourselves not well all that day, got leave to be absent from prayers; this gave us an opportunity of getting to the count, who received us with transport: he carried us in two hours time to the Chavalier de Alancon's house, which was twenty miles off; there we alit, and were received gladly: this gentleman was father to the colonel whom Lady Katherine loved, and therefore was glad of this opportunity to oblige the Count de Beaumount, hoping it might be a means to procure his son's happiness, who was his only child, and whom he loved excessively: the count having also promised me to consent to his sister's marriage, had made choice of this gentleman, as most proper to assist us in this affair.

Here having changed our habits, and put on others which the count had provided for us, we were entertained with a splendid supper; after which, the count pressed me in so passionate a manner, to make him happy, by marrying him that night, that I condescended to his request, and the *chevalier's* chaplain made us one. The next morning the Chevalier de Alancon sent away a servant express to the army, to give his son notice of Lady Katherine's escape, and that he should come immediately home *incognito* to marry her. The Count de Beaumount that evening returned home to see how our flight was taken, and how his father resented it, promising a speedy return to us; which he soon did, for the next morning he came back, and acquainted me with all that had past.

'My father,' said he, 'no sooner saw me enter the room, where he was sitting with some noblemen at *ombre*, but he rose, looking fiercely upon me, and addressing himself to them, said, "*Messieurs*, I beg leave to withdraw with my son for a few minutes."

I followed him into his closet, where we no sooner entered, but he shut the door, and said; "Son, I am highly troubled to think that you have done a deed so unadvised, so rash, and I fear ruinous to yourself, and disgustful to me: are you married without my consent, and to a heretic? what will the king say? Could you not find a wife of our own faith and family? but you must rob a convent for one? Where is your deluded sister? Have you matched her too? Alas! alas! my son, what grief and confusion will you bring upon us?"

'My surprise was so great to see my father so calm, that I could scarce answer; but throwing myself at his feet, embracing his knees, I implored his pardon, and his blessing, saying, "My honoured lord, and father, the lady I have married, is our equal both in birth and fortune; virtuous, young, and will, I doubt not, be everything you can desire: let not her religion, which is not a fault in her, but the misfortune of her education, make you prejudiced against her, I shall soon prevail with her to be what I am; if not, our children shall be bred as you desire: she was no nun, but wrongfully detained there by her guardians, who will no sooner hear who she belongs to, but they will resign her fortune; and now, my lord, compleat my happiness, permit me to bring my bride to pay her duty, and receive my sister, who, both by promise and affection, is engaged to the brave Alancon, a young gentleman whose worth excels all titles, who will be to you another son, and make her happy."

'"Rise son," said my father, "I will endeavour to be easy."

'At these words he took me up, and opening the door, returned to the company, I following; he said nothing of my marriage to them: in the morning I paid my duty to him in his chamber, and told him I was going to fetch you to him; he bid me go.'

This news overjoyed us all, and the *chevalier*, my Sister Katherine, the Count de Beaumount, and I, taking coach; went to the castle, where my father in-law received us with such goodness, and with an air so obliging, that I was amazed: an apartment was immediately assigned me, the same my mother-in-law had in her lifetime. Our wedding was kept as became our quality, and in few days I had the satisfaction to see my dear sister, whom I tenderly loved, made happy as myself, being married to the colonel, who being come post to his father's, was by him brought to us, and married in my father's presence with full consent. And now we appeared to be the happiest family in the world: my guardians no sooner heard of my marriage, but they waited on my father and husband, and in few days delivered my fortune into their hands.

For some months my father treated me with all the kindness imaginable; when it began to be whispered that I was with child: then my sister began to importune me, when we were alone, to change my religion, which I evaded to answer to, as much as possible, beginning to suspect that she was put upon so doing, and this made me very thoughtful, and apprehensive of some misfortune.

One morning my father-in-law entered my chamber, and with a very serious air began to talk to me in this manner: 'Daughter, I have been very indulgent to you, and do now assure you that I love you extremely, of which I can give you no better proof than what I am going to propose to you: You have been bred in an error, and your religion is false; I have provided those that shall instruct you in the truth, and I expect that you hearken to them, and embrace it; and if you mean to live happy, and be dear to me, you must be a Roman Catholic, otherwise the king has commanded me to part my son and you. I have said enough, I hope, to convince you that it is absolutely necessary that you comply with my desires.'

At these words he went out of my chamber, leaving me in great confusion and disorder. At this instant my dear lord came in from walking in the park, and was much surprised to find me in tears; he clasped me in his arms, and pressed me earnestly to tell him what was the cause of my grief.

'Forbear, my dearest,' said I, 'do not ask many questions, we must be parted, and be wretched, the king will not permit you to caress a poor orphan, and sleep in the arms of a heretic; I must change my faith, or lose all that is dear to me upon the earth: hard choice!'

He wiped away my tears, kissed and comforted me all he was able, using all his eloquence to persuade me to comply; and I must confess it was more difficult to me to refuse him, than all the world; not racks, nor flames, could move my soul, so much as one of those tender things he said to me: and now I was daily visited by learned priests, and such who, as relations or friends, thought themselves obliged to assist in my conversion; but having been educated in an intire abhorrence of the Church of Rome, I gave little heed to their arguments, and resolved to continue firm to the opinion I had been bred in, which they soon discovered, and took my silence for obstinacy: with which, acquainting my father, they so wrought with him, that he grew to hate me, and believed nothing could be done with me whilst my lord was present: he therefore resolved to part us, hoping by this means to shock my resolution, and make me yield to his desires.

In order to this, he procures a commission for a regiment of horse for the count his son, with a letter from the king, commanding him to repair to his command immediately: this his father delivered to him, telling him withal, that he had provided him an equipage, and all things suiting his quality, and that he must not fail to be ready by the next morning to be gone.

This news was, as you may imagine, like a sentence of death to us both: as for my part, fearing to declare my grief, left it should encrease the count's, I remained silent, and restrained all but my tears, which flowed incessantly. This sight so moved my lord, that at last he resolved to expose himself both to the king's and his father's displeasure, rather than leave me; but upon reflection, I dreaded the consequence so much, of so rash an action, that I proposed an expedient: 'My dear lord,' said I, 'my mother's brother in England, the Lord —— will no doubt gladly receive and take care of me; send me thither, with part of our fortune, there I shall enjoy my religion without molestation, and be safe from all my enemies, till you return; which Heaven grant may be soon, and to both our comforts.'

This proposal he with much reluctance agreed to, and the next morning told his father that he could not consent to part thence under seven days, in which time he would take care to remove me out of France, being fully determined not to leave me in my enemies power; which the old lord was forced to yield to, finding it was in vain to oppose him, and being glad that we should be separated so far asunder. The Count de Beaumount was resolved to see France no more till his father died, designing that I should go to meet him in Flanders, by the way of Holland, so soon as I should have lain in; he therefore called in all the ready-money he could raise, which he turned all into gold, and borrowed some of his friends, giving me jewels and money, to the value of fifty thousand crowns: he hired a vessel at St. Malo's putting aboard of it all the rich furniture of my apartment, and all my clothes and linen; and at last my sister and he brought me aboard, my father-in-law having first took leave of me, and again made me large offers, if I would turn Catholic, and stay in France, which I modestly rejected; and the wind being fair, in this fatal vessel my dear lord and I took leave of each other.

And first I embraced my dear sister, who took our separation so heavily, that I believe it hastened her death, which happened not long after; and then my lord, with eyes full of tears, took me in his arms, where he held me some time before he was able to speak, then said, 'Farewell, my dear Belinda, may guardian angels guard you, and the dear pledge you carry with you; may God defend you from the danger of the sea, and bring you safe to land, and to my arms again; judge by yourself what pangs I feel, and spare to torture me by saying more.'

I could not answer him one word, but fainted in his arms: my sister urged him to be gone, saying, it would be wiser to depart, than continue the tragic scene; which he would not do till I revived, and then I faintly said, 'My Lord, farewell, remember we are Christians, born to part, let us as such support our afflictions, and live in hope to meet again, if not here, yet in Heaven. Farewell.'

He repeated his embraces, and at length yielded to go. The ship set sail for England, designing to reach the port of London; but as we were at sea, the wind veered about, a dreadful storm arose, and with much difficulty the ninth day of our being at sea, we made this point of land, and in the evening got ashore near the cave where you found us: there we looked for some place to secure ourselves and goods in, and found this cave, which doubtless had been contrived by some hermit in antient times, and was the work of past ages; it was all ruinous, and covered over with weeds, but the seamen soon cleaned and fitted it up as you see; I liked the place for its privacy, and revolved to tarry here till I could write to London, to my uncle, whom I very well knew and loved, he having been several times in France to visit my mother.

The captain of the ship went to Swansea, bought provisions, sent away my letters, and in some days we received an answer, little to our satisfaction; I trembled when I opened the seal, seeing the direction in a strange hand, and found it was writ by a gentleman who was something related, as it appeared, to my uncle; who receiving my letter, answered it, informing me my uncle was long since dead in Scotland, being forced to fly England, all his estate being seized by the government on account of his loyalty to King James, and carrying on designs for his service; therefore he advised me to return to France, and not venture to come to London.

Upon this news, I resolved to continue in the cave, with my two servants, my maid, and a boy, whom I had brought from France, Maria having been a servant to my mother, and a native of England; the boy Philip was preferred by my uncle to my mother's service, when he last visited her in France; for which reason I always took care of these servants, and thought they would be most proper for my service here, speaking the language.

And now, in few days, the captain having bought what he wanted, and repaired his vessel, set fail for France again, to give the Count de Beamount an account of all that had happened to us; but, to my great misfortune, the ship (as I have been since informed) foundered at sea, so that my lord could never be informed what was become of me. Here I was brought to bed of this daughter by a country midwife Philip fetched from a village hard by; and having in two years no news from France, I resolved to venture back thither myself: so I took the boy with me, leaving Maria with the child, and in a small vessel, which I found at Swansea, and hired to carry me over to St. Malo's, I got passage, leaving Philip at Swansea, to return back to the cave, he being only fit to fetch provisions, and what the maid and child wanted.

At my landing at St. Malo's, I went to a friend of my husband, whose house we were at, at my leaving France; there I got a man's habit, and so disguised, took a post chaise for the Chevalier de Alancon's, where being safe arrived, I discovered myself, and was received with all demonstrations of friendship; and here I learned that my dear sister was dead of a fever the year I left France; that the Count de Beaumount, having the news of the ship's being lost, and hearing nothing from me, came back from the army to his father's, and concluding me dead, fell into a deep melancholy; at last quarrelled with his father, resigned his commission, quitted the French service, and was gone for Sweden, where he had obtained the command of a regiment under the King of Sweden, who was engaged in a war with the Czar of Mufcovy, and that, no news had been heard of him since.

'This,' says the *chevalier*, 'has so incensed your father-in-law against you. Madam, whom he looks upon as the principal cause of this his great misfortune, in losing the comfort of his son's presence, that I would not for the world he should find you here, for I know not what his passion would transport him to do; I therefore advise you to get back to St. Malo's as soon as possible, and return to England; I will do all that's possible to send word to the count of your safety, and the place of your residence.'

After supper I went to bed, much distracted in my thoughts: the next morning early, I set out again for St. Malo's; but at noon, entering into an inn to refresh myself, I was seized for a spy, carried before a magistrate, who soon perceiving I was a woman, and, in fine, knew me, and immediately confined me in his house, till he sent to Monsieur de Maintenon, who by the next morning arrived at St. Malo's, and coming into the room where I was, accosted me in this manner: 'So, Madam, I think myself very happy in seeing you once again in France, you have made me one of the most unfortunate fathers m the world; I have by your means lost an only son: you fled hence for conscience, and I, to satisfy justice, shall confine you here the rest of your days.'

He gave me no time to answer; for I was pinioned, and put into his coach, with four of his servants to guard me: nor did they suffer me to rest, or eat, for twenty four hours, in which time we stopped but twice to change horses. At length they brought me to a ruinous old castle, near the sea-side, where they left me in the hands of a man, whose grim aspect spoke him a gaoler; this man, his daughter, and wife, were all that dwelt in this dismal place; they drove me up into a room that was in the top of an old tower, and there locked me in, like a wild beast in a den: and here I sat down and reflected on my condition.

★★★★★★

Here Mr. Lluelling interrupted the lady, saying, 'Madam, thank Providence you are now here, and at liberty; come, we will defer to some other time, to finish this dismal story: supper is upon the table, let us eat and forget all past sorrows, tomorrow I will beg to hear the rest.'

So presenting her his hand, he led her to the table. After supper the ladies would have taken leave, and returned to the cave; but he so importunately desired their stay there, that they at length consented, and were lodged in an apartment altogether suitable to their quality.

Chapter 3

In the morning the ladies were waked by a concert of music, playing under their window; with which the young lady was much delighted, having never heard anything so charming, or of that nature before.

'Madam,' said she, 'what an agreeable part of the world are we come into? Why did you not sooner bring me into company? What a ravishing thing is society? For Heaven's sake do not return to our unwholesome lonely cave. We want not a fortune to pay for all the conveniences of life, why should we fly company? We are in a nation where you have no enemies to fear.'

The old lady smiled, saying, 'Alas! My child, you little know what you have to fear, and what mighty cares attend a married life; though I hope God will, in pity to my sufferings, make you happy, and grant you a long series of years free from misfortunes.'

At these words a maid servant entered the chamber with Maria, who was come to attend her ladies, and to inform them that Mr. Lluelling begged the honour of their company to breakfast: they dressed, and went down into a parlour they had not seen the day before; and here the Lady Beaumount was surprised with the sight of her mother's picture, amongst many others, which were all drawn by the hands of celebrated masters; 'My God,' said she, 'how came this lovely picture here? Alas! my dear mother, little did I think ever to see that face again!'

Mr. Lluelling, interrupting her, said, 'Madam, that lady was by my father courted, and beloved so dearly, that when she left England, he seemed to have lost all he valued, fell sick, and soon after died; my mother having left him a widower, dying in childbirth of me, whom he left an orphan about three years old. This melancholy account I have had of his death, but little thought I should have seen a daughter of that lady's, or shared my father's inclinations, in loving one descended from her. Fair Belinda,' said he, turning to the young lady, 'do not by a cruel absence from me, kill me too.'

Belinda blushed: 'Believe me,' said her mother, 'she is much inclined to stay with you; and if all your actions correspond with what we have already seen, I shall never desire to take her from you.'

At these words he bowed, saying; 'May I be hated by Heaven and you, and may she scorn me, when I cease to love, to honour, and take care of you and her. Madam, till now, I never loved, my heart has been indifferent to all the sex; but from the moment I first looked on that angel's face, where so much innocence and beauty shines, I have not asked a blessing in which she was not comprehended; make her mine, and I have all I wish on earth.'

Here tea, chocolate, and coffee, was brought in, so they turned the discourse.

After breakfast they walked into the gardens, and being come to a lovely banqueting-house, they went into it, and sat down. Here Mr. Lluelling importuned the lady to finish the story of her misfortunes: 'Madam,' said he, 'I left you in a dismal place last night, pray glad me with an account of your deliverance thence.'

'I will,' said she; so continued her relation in this manner.

Chapter 4

Being left, as I before told you, imprisoned, and all alone, faint, hungry, and bereft of all comfort, I did, as most people do, when their own prudence can help them no farther; looked up to God, whose power can never be limited, and from whom only I could expect my deliverance: lifting up my hands, I cried, 'Now, my God, help me; I am perfectly resigned to thy will, accept my submission, encrease my faith and patience, in proportion to the evils thou hast decreed me to suffer; be to me food, liberty, and a husband; and to my child a father and mother.'

Here a flood of tears interrupted, I could speak no more, after which I grew calm, found my faith encrease, my fears abate, and my soul seemed armed for all events. Thus, Sir, I experienced that great truth, that we have nothing more to do, to be happy and secure from all the miseries of life, but to resign our wills to the Divine Being; nor does Providence ever appear more conspicuously than on such occasions. I fell soon into a sweet slumber, which in few hours so refreshed me, that I awoke a new creature. About ten in the evening, the wife and daughter of my gaoler came into the room, bringing me some sour cider to drink, and a piece of bread: a poor repast, alas! after such a fatigue as I had undergone! but I took it cheerfully, and thankfully. The women seemed to compassionate me, and after an hour's discourse; they both wept with me; they were persons of mean capacities and education, but were not altogether void of good-nature and humanity.

Here I remained for two long years, and was delivered by a strange accident: My food being very mean, and my grief great, I soon fell into a languishing sickness; at length the good woman informed her husband, that she believed me near death, and therefore thought it concerned their consciences to fetch a priest to me; which he consenting to, the daughter was sent for a friar, who was curate of the parish. The good man, whose outside was mean, as his inside was rich, soon came; but believe me, sir, his understanding and goodness was such, that it might justly have preferred him to a mitre; his name was Father Benedict; he was the son of a lord, and had refused all dignities, purely out of his great humility, for which reason he chose to live in this obscure place. He approached me with such compassion in his looks, as encouraged me to hear him without prejudice: I was then so weak I could not rise; he asked me many questions, how I came there, why I was thus confined; and being truly informed of all, spoke of my father-in-law with much dislike: 'God forbid,' said he, 'our faith should be propagated by such detestable means as these; Madam, I am sensible of your wrongs, and will deliver you, or die in the attempt.'

He never urged me farther as to my religion, but advising me to secrecy, not thinking the women proper to repose confidence in; he came every day to visit me, bringing in his bosom wine and meat to comfort and strengthen me, which, with the reviving hopes of liberty, soon restored me to health: and now he studied how to compleat his good work, by getting me thence, which he thus effected: He came to me one afternoon, bringing another brother of his order with him, who had a double habit on; in this religious disguise I dressed myself, and Father Benedict going into the room where the gaoler's wife and daughter were sitting, who, at his coming, as usual, left my chamber; he held them in discourse whilst Father Anthony and I went down, and past the gate by my gaoler, who civilly bid us goodnight.

I was conducted by this good father to a little hermitage on the top of a hill near the convent he belonged to: Father Benedict came soon after to us, and here we consulted what to do; they agreed that I should stay there for some days concealed, that then Father Anthony should go with me to Grandvil, from whence he should send me to England, that being a sea-port less frequented, and consequently less dangerous for me, than St. Malo's. I stayed in this hermitage five days, they bringing me food: no search was made after me, because the gaoler fearing to be ruined, when they missed me, went away to Monsieur de Maintenon, and told him I was dead of a spotted fever, and they were forced to dig a grave, and throw me into it the same night, for fear of infection; of which news he was very glad, and Christian burial being not allowed to heretics, he did not regret the manner of my burial, but rewarded the gaoler, who returned joyful to his miserable home.

The good Father Anthony and I, set out for Grandvil; my cowl and frock, with a long pair of beads tied to my hempen girdle, made me appear a perfect Capuchin: We arrived safe at a convent, where, being refreshed, we went to the port; there we found a Guernsey ship just ready to depart for Southampton; and here the good priest, to compleat his generosity, gave me a purse of gold to pay for my passage, and assist me to get to my home: he gave me many blessings at parting, and I returned him innumerable thanks, promising ever to pray for him and Father Benedict, which I am bound to do. I arrived in England on the 17th of March, 1707-8, and from Southampton hired horses and a guide to this place; at the post-house, I parted with and discharged the man and horses, and walked to my dear cave, where my child and servants received me with such transport, as if I had been risen from the dead: and here I resolved to stay the remainder of my days, unless Providence, by some miracle, restores my dear lord to me, of whom I have never been able to get any tidings, not daring to return to France again.

★★★★★★

'Madam,' answered Mr. Lluelling, 'I will be the person who shall do you that service, be pleased only to consent to remain in my house, where you are from this day mistress; send for your furniture from the cave, and make this, which is far more commodious, your abode, and I will forthwith to France, to learn all that is possible of your lord.'

The ladies accepted with joy his offer, and now he passed some days agreeably with them, whilst all things were getting ready for his departure to France, In this time he studied both how to divert them, and secure the young lady's heart, with whom he longed to talk in private, hoping to be satisfied what sentiments she had of him; to do which, he fought a fit opportunity.

Chapter 5

The young lady was now, by the little God Cupid, rendered more thoughtful than usual, and loved to retire from company, often frequented the grove, and shady walks. One evening, some ladies whom Mr. Lluelling had brought acquainted with his guests, were playing at cards with the Lady Beaumount, Belinda stole into the garden to walk alone; her lover, whose eyes watched all her steps, soon followed.

'Now, fair Belinda,' said he, 'Fate has given me the happy moment I have so long wished for; here we are alone, no spies to overhear: Ah! tell me, charming maid, what may I hope? Am I beloved again? Or must I die unblessed? Though I must be all my days the most unhappy of mankind, if you refuse me that fair hand; yet believe me, lovely virgin, I would not force your inclination for an empire, nor occasion you one moment's uneasiness, though to enjoy you, which would be to me the greatest bliss my soul could know: speak, and let that charming mouth pronounce my doom.'

Belinda quite unpractised in the cunning arts of her ingenious sex, her face over-spread with Blushes, answered, 'Sir, the passion of love, I think, I am a stranger to; but this I own, I have a grateful sense of all the generous treatment we have received from you: I don't dislike your person, nor disapprove your passion, if sincere, but do not think myself of years to chuse a husband; my mother must dispose of me, for she has both wisdom and experience, 'tis her commands must guide my choice.'

'Ah! must I then,' said he, 'owe that to her commands, that I would only owe to you? Say, should she command you to receive another in your arms, would you consent to see me wretched, cursing my fate, and dying at your feet, and make another happy with my ruin?'

'Press me no more,' she cried, 'you have urged me to a point I cannot answer to.'

At these words she fainted in his arms; joy and fear, at that instant, did so divide his soul, he knew not what he did: he took her in his arms, and bore her to his own chamber, laid her on his bed, and there, in transports, viewed her reviving beauties, saw the roses return to her pale cheeks, and her eyes open to behold the man she loved; and here he gained a promise from her to be his. Here they joined lips and hands, for fate had joined their hearts before, and bound themselves in sacred vows, to be forever true to one another; then he, reflecting on his indiscretion, led her to her chamber, where, repeating his protestations and embraces, he left her.

Full of joy he rejoined the company, where he appeared so gay and cheerful, that it was easy to imagine something more than usual had happened to him. In some time, the company taking leave, the Lady Beaumount asked for her daughter, and was told she was not well in her chamber; thither the lady went, and found Belinda so disordered, that she was much surprised, but could not guess the reason, till Maria, who had seen from the window Mr, Lluelling carry her in his arms into the house from the garden, whispered her lady, which filled her with such suspicions, that she was almost distracted; she desired Belinda to go down to supper, and take the air, thinking it wiser to conceal her thoughts, than ask questions, hoping to discover by their behaviour what had passed.

No sooner did Belinda enter the parlour, where her lover waited their coming to supper, which was then upon the table, but his eyes sparkled, and her colour changed, and both trembled; at supper his eyes were continually turned upon her, and hers cast down; he seemed more tender and officious than ever, she more shy. After supper they walked into the garden, and here Mr. Lluelling thus put an end to the old lady's pain: 'Madam,' said he, 'you are, I am certain, too clear-sighted, not to have observed something in my looks and behaviour this evening, that must inform you, that the charming Belinda and I have had an interview alone, much to my satisfaction, nor do I doubt but somebody has whispered it to you already; I saw at table how you watched our eyes and looks, and to prevent all suspicions that may ruin our peace, I tell you, she has this happy day made herself mine, and tomorrow morning, if you bless me with your consent, we will be married; for I cannot leave Wales before I have secured my charmer from the temptations she might be exposed to in my absence, which, when a wife, she will be freed from.'

The old lady gladly consented, and the next morning they went privately in the coach to a village, where the ceremony was performed to the satisfaction of all parties. The next day it was public talk, and Mr. Lluelling showed his joy, by treating all his country relations and tenants for ten days together; all which time he kept open house. In this juncture there came down from London, to pay him a visit, a young gentleman who was his cousin-german, and had long wished his death, no doubt, because he was his heir, if he died without issue.

This young man, Mr. Lluelling had always loved and bred up as his son, having bought him chambers in the Temple, where he, like most gentlemen of this age, had forgot the noble principles, and virtuous precepts, he brought to town with him, and acquired all the fashionable vices that give a man the title of a fine gentleman: he was a contemner of marriage, could drink, dissemble, and deceive to perfection; had a very handsome person, an excellent wit, and was most happy in expressing his thoughts elegantly: these talents he always employed in seducing the fair, or engaging the affection of his companions, who doted upon him, because he was cunning and daring, could always lead them on to pleasures, or bring them nicely off, if frustrated in any vicious designs.

His name was Mr, Charles Owen Glandore: this gentleman was received by his kinsman with much joy and affection; he assured him he should not be slighted or forgotten, though he was married; he brought him to his lady, recommending him to her favour. And now the time approached when Mr. Lluelling was to go for France, all things being ready; he thought none more proper than his kinsman (who had by this time gained the lady's esteem) to take care of his affairs in his absence, he therefore desired him to stay, till his return, with his wife, and mother-in-law, who would by that means be eased of some care and trouble; and so taking leave, in the most tender manner, of his charming bride, he set sail for France, in a small vessel which he hired on purpose to go for St. Malo's, and wait his return, proposing to be back in Wales in a month or six weeks' time.

Chapter 6

Mr. Lluelling being now gone, Mr. Glandore, his young kinsman, had the pleasure of entertaining the ladies, and frequent opportunities of being alone with Belinda: his kinsman's fortune was all at his command, and having unfortunately cast his eyes on her, whom he no sooner saw, but he loved; he strove to gain her affection, and charm her virtue asleep, by all the arts imaginable: he dressed magnificently, gave them new diversions every day, was gay and entertaining, studied how to gratify all her wishes; and in fine, was so assiduous and tender of both the ladies, that had Belinda's heart not been pre-engaged, he would certainly have gained both that and her mother's consent. Being now grown intimate and familiar with both, Belinda did not scruple sometimes to walk with him in the gardens, grove, and fields; and when her mother was engaged with grave company, courted these opportunities of slipping out with him, whom she believed honourable and virtuous as herself, and loved as a brother.

He being perfectly skilled in the arts of his subtle sex, resolved never to discover his base design to her, till he was well assured she liked him, and a fit opportunity offered in a place where he might ruin her, without being prevented; for he was resolved to enjoy her, though by force, and determined to run all dangers rather than miss of what his headstrong passion persuaded him he could not live without. He knew the time was but short before Mr. Lluelling would return, and therefore he must be quick in executing what he designed; he had a servant whom he had left in town, who was a pimp to all his pleasures, a fellow who was wicked, bold, and in fine, such a one as was fit to carry on any vicious or base design, secret and proper for his vile purpose: him he sent for; he came down, and they contrived the poor Belinda's undoing.

At the bottom of the grove, which was a quarter of a mile distant from the house, was a fine summerhouse; hither one evening he led her, whilst her mother was engaged at cards with some ladies who were come to visit her.

When Belinda and he came to the grove, he persuaded her to go up into the summerhouse, into which they were no sooner entered, but he shut to the door, saying, 'Madam, be not surprised, but hearken to what I am going to say, and answer me.' Here he threw himself upon his knees; 'Charming Belinda,' said he, 'I love you, I even die to possess you; oblige me not to use force, where I would use only prayers, make me this moment the most transported, the most happy man alive, or else I must convey you to a place where I shall make you comply, and perhaps make us both wretched: here we can have opportunities without being discovered, and may enjoy one another without public scandal and noise; but if I take you hence, I must live with you in obscurity, and if we are discovered, kill your husband in my own defence and yours; or dying, leave you to his reproaches, and public disgrace. You are, I know, with child, and therefore need fear no discovery.'

Here he drew forth a pistol; 'Look not round about,' said he, 'for help, death stands between this door and him that dares to enter; I have those at hand that make all safe for me to act.'

Belinda, who had now no other arms but prayers and tears, to defend her virtue withal, threw herself at his feet, saying, 'Oh! cruel, faithless man, what joy can you receive in the ruin of a person who can never be lawfully yours? Consider the sad consequence of such a deed, which you will doubtless repent of: By Heaven, I'll never give consent, and if you force me like a brute, what satisfaction will you reap? I shall then hate and scorn you, loath your embraces, and if I ever escape your hands again, sure vengeance will overtake you; nay, you shall drag me sooner to my grave, than to your bed; I will resist to death, and curse you with my last breath: but if you spare me, my prayers and blessings shall attend you, nay, I will pity and forgive you.'

'I'm deaf to all that you can plead against my love,' he cried, 'yield, or I'll force you hence.'

'No,' says she, 'I'll rather die; now, villain, I will hate you: help and defend me Heaven.'

Here he seized her hands, his man at the same instant entering, gagged and bound her; then they blindfolded her, and Mr. Glandore carried her down, putting her into a coach, where, drawing up the canvasses, he held her in his lap, whilst his man drove them over the hills across the country, with design to reach a village fifty miles distant, where Mr. Glandore had procured a place to receive them; being an old ruinous castle, where none but an old man and his family resided, who spoke nothing but Welsh lived on what was produced about the place, and never saw a market-town, so that he could keep her there without fear of discovery. To be enabled for this, he had taken a considerable sum of money of his kinsman's in the coach, and had besides some fortune of his own: they changed horses on the road twice, all things being before provided, and travelled all night, he taking the impudent liberty of kissing her as he pleased.

About five in the morning they were in sight of this dismal place; here he stopped the coach: she being swooned away in his arms, he unbound and gave her some wine; but before he could bring her to herself, he saw four men in vizards, well mounted, coming up to the coach, which made him leap out, to be upon his guard: his guilty conscience made him tremble, for though he was brave on other occasions, yet now he was not so; Heaven that had permitted him to act this villainy, still protects innocence, and had prepared its judgments to overtake him. These men were robbers, who lived concealed in these desolate mountains; they went to seize him, he resisted, his man coming down to help his master, was shot dead, and in the dispute the unfortunate Glandore was killed.

During this scuffle, the unhappy Belinda revived; they dragged her out of the coach, which whilst they were rifling, a company of clowns, who were going to a fair, about twenty miles thence, with horses to sell, came up, at whose approach the thieves fled. By these honest countrymen the lady was relieved, but they could speak nothing but Welsh, so that she could not make them understand one word: one of them got up into the coach-box, and drove the lady to his landlord's house, where he gave an account of what had past: the son of the gentleman was at home, but his father was elsewhere; he was a very accomplished young gentleman, well bred, handsome, about twenty years of age: he and his father, who had in this place purchased a small estate, lived very private, for reasons that shall be hereafter declared: he was known by the name of Mr. Hide.

He received the young lady in a manner so courtly, that it was easy to guess he had been educated in palaces, and conversed with princes; having treated her in the highest manner with wine and food, he begged to know who she was: she prudently concealed her name, family, and all the transactions of her life, telling him only that she was coming this way with her brother, who was the unfortunate gentleman, whom the thieves had killed, and came from Swansea, to which place she begged he would send some of his servants back with her, and it would be the greatest favour he could do her. This he promised to do, but, alas! the blind God had already wounded his breast; he gazed upon her with transport, and resolved not to part with her on any terms.

The coach being cleaned and put up by the servants, they found the sum of gold Glandore had put up in the seat, and honestly brought it to the lady, who genteelly gave them five guineas to drink: this largess, the greatness of the sum, which was fifteen hundred pieces, and her habit, made Mr. Hide conclude she was some person of distinction; which the more inflamed his desires to know who she was. He entertained her magnificently, but put off from day to day her departure, saying she must stay till his father came, and then he would wait on her home himself. She too well guessed the reason of his prolonging her stay, and having so lately escaped from the hands of a desperate lover, was dreadfully alarmed at this new misfortune: he behaved himself with such modesty and respect, that she could not complain, but still she feared it was like Glandore's cunning, only to procure an opportunity to undo her: she was wholly in his powers having none but servants in the house, who spoke nothing but Welsh; this made her very reserved. At last he declared himself to her, as they were sitting together after dinner, the servants being all withdrawn:

'Madam,' said he 'Providence that brought you hither, did it, I hope, for both our happiness; I no sooner saw you, but my soul adored you; I am by birth much nobler than I appear to be, our years are agreeable, I will omit nothing that can gain your affection, nor think any pains too much, or time too long to obtain you. Charming fair, why do you fear and avoid me? why treat me with such coldness and reserve? Am I disliked, and must I languish, sigh, and beg in vain? Never can I cease to love you, till I cease to live; permit me then to hope, if not, I am resolved to die a victim to your disdain; forbid me not to follow you, for I must disobey, I cannot bear your absence, nor consent to live, and see a happy rival possess you.'

Here he seized her hand, and in a great disorder kissed it.

'Forbear Sir,' said Belinda, 'I never can be yours, I am already married, and with child.'

Here she related to him, how Glandore had stolen her away.

At these words a deathlike paleness over-spread his face, a cold sweat trickled down his cheeks. 'My God,' said he, 'it is enough; Madam, I will no more importune you, fear nothing from me, virtue and honour are as dear to me as you; since you cannot be mine, I ask no more, but that you'll stay and see me die, and not detest my memory, since vice has no share in my soul.'

Here he fainted, and was by the servants carried to his chamber: Belinda wept, her heart was young and tender, and the honour he had shown, touched her soul so nearly, that she much lamented his misfortune, and could not consent with ease to let him die; therefore she strove with reason to assuage his grief, and cure his passion: but in vain, he fell into an intermitting fever, and grew so weak, that he could not rise without help, yet would every day be taken up, and brought into the parlour where she sat. And here we must leave them, and return to enquire after the Lord Beaumount and Mr. Lluelling.

Chapter 7

Mr. Lluelling arrived safe at St. Malo's, July the 30th, 1717, and went, as the Lady Beaumount had directed, with a letter to the gentleman's house, where she had been received at her being in France, but he was dead; so that he was obliged to go thence without much information of what he wanted. But it being now a time when France and England were at peace, he had nothing to fear; he went therefore directly to Coutance, and there lodged at the best inn, where he enquired for the Governor Monsieur de Maintenon: they told him he was long since dead, but the young *marquis*, his son, was still alive, but had quitted all his employments, being retired into the country.

'Is he a single man?' said Mr. Lluelling?'

'Yes, Sir,' said the innkeeper, 'he is a widower for the second time, having buried his second lady about two years ago; he has a daughter of his wife's by a first husband, who is one of the beautifullest children, and will be the greatest fortune in this province.'

Mr. Lluelling was impatient to see him, so stayed no longer there than that night: the next morning he set out with his two servants which he took along with him from Wales, and arrived that night at a village which was about three miles short of the *marquis's* seat: it being late, he stayed at the village that night, and the next morning went to the *marquis's*, whom it was no easy matter to speak with, for he was denied to all company, but some particular friends. Mr. Lluelling sent him word, by his gentleman who was called to him, that he came from Wales express, to bring him news of some persons whom he would be much overjoyed to hear of.

The *marquis* no sooner received this message, but he came down and received him in much disorder; he was dressed in mourning, and looked like a man half dead: 'My Lord,' said he, 'I doubt not but I shall be welcome, since I come from your virtuous Lady Belinda, she lives, has a daughter, who is my wife, to present to you; such a one, that you may glory to be the father of.' Here he presented him a letter from his wife, at the sight of which, the tears ran down his face, and he fainted away, joy having so overpowered his faculties, that they lost their power to perform their functions.

Mr, Lluelling supported him till he recovered, and then he broke out into these passionate expressions: 'My God, am I alive! do I wake! Can this be true! Is my Belinda, my joy, my all, still living? Is the precious pledge of our mutual affection born, and preserved to this day: Oh! mitigate my transport, or strengthen my faculties! Do I here find a son?' Here he embraced Mr. Lluelling. 'Oh! welcome, welcome, ten thousand times; I want expressions to speak my gratitude to my God and you.'

Here they sat down, the *marquis* called for wine, and now Mr. Lluelling related to him all the adventures that had befallen his lady since their parting: but when he related Monsieur de Maintenon's cruel usage of her, the *marquis* wept. 'And now, my lord,' said Mr. Lluelling, 'I should be glad to know your story, but we will defer that to some other time; 'tis joy enough to me that I find you here alive.'

The *marquis* answered, 'That story will serve to entertain us in our journey to St. Malo's, and voyage to Wales: I must now order my affairs to go thither, for my impatience to see my dear Belinda, and my child, is such, that I can think of nothing else.'

Mr. Lluelling was entertained here so magnificently, that he was even surprised. The young lady, daughter-in-law to the *marquis*, whose name was Isabella, was so beautiful and witty, that Mr. Lluelling thought her equal to his wife: she was then thirteen, and the *marquis* was very fond of her, she begged to accompany her father, to see her new mother and sister, and at last prevailed to go with them. In few days all things were ready for their departure, the servants were ordered to repair to the *marquis's* seat at Coutance, to be ready to receive their lady; the whole country rang of this strange adventure: the *marquis* set out, attended by only two of his own servants, and Mr. Lluelling's two, with the Lady Isabella, and her woman: they arrived at St. Malo's, and the next morning set sail with a fair wind for Wales, in the vessel that attended Mr. Lluelling.

And now being aboard, he importuned the *marquis* to relate his adventures in Sweden, which he willingly condescended to, and began the narrative of his misfortunes in this manner:

Chapter 8

You have heard how, my father and I quarrelling, I left France, supposing my dear wife dead; and considering him as the principal cause of her death. I had continued with him about six months before I resolved to be gone; I was fallen into so deep a melancholy, that I was regardless of everything, but fearing my death, he so importuned me to reassume my usual cheerfulness and gayety, that at length he obliged me to discover my resentments, declare the reasons of my being uneasy in his presence, and resolution to continue no longer in France. I had writ several letters to my wife's uncle, but receiving no answer, I concluded him also dead, and therefore ordered all my affairs to depart for Sweden, determining to seek a noble death in the field, under that glorious monarch, the last King of Sweden. I took no more but three servants to attend me, having remitted money sufficient to purchase an employment, and answer my expenses.

I no sooner arrived at Stockholm, but I obtained the command of a regiment, and after having courted death in many skirmishes and bloody battles, I was unfortunately in the last that brave king fought with the *Czar*, taken prisoner; my whole regiment, and the greatest part of the army, being destroyed, I fell full of wounds amongst the slain: but upon the Mulcovites stripping the dead, they found some signs of life in me, and judging by my habit that I was some person of distinction, they carried me to a tent near the general's, where they dressed my wounds, and with cordials brought me to the use of my reason again, to my great grief. I continued so ill and weak, for three months, that they had small hopes of recovering me: in this time I was removed to a town called Toropierz, where the general had a country-seat.

In this place I was very civilly entertained, the general having taken a great liking to me, and here he much persuaded me to enter into the *Czar's* service, saying, that being a native of France, and no subject of Sweden, having paid for my employment there, he thought I was under no obligation to the King of Sweden, and that his master should engage me to his service, by giving me a command under him.

I answered, that having voluntarily drawn my sword in the King of Sweden's defence, honour obliged me never to quit it; that I was highly obliged to him for his generous offers, and should upon all occasions return the obligation. He smiled, seeming to applaud my resolution, but told me he should, he believed, find an advocate that should prevail with me, otherwise he should set a ransom so great upon me, knowing my worth, that he believed he should have the pleasure of my company long; and since he could not engage me to serve his prince, he would, if possible, prevent my fighting against him.

At these words he took me by the hand, and led me to his wife's apartment, where were his two sons, and wife, with his only daughter, a maid of fourteen years of age, beautiful as nature ever formed; she was tall, slender, fair as Venus, her eyes blue, bright, and languishing; her hair was light brown, and every feature of her face had a charm; but, son, her conversation was enchanting, as I afterwards experienced. The general presented me to his sons, two lovely young men, whose looks and habit spoke their worth and quality. 'Here children,' said he, 'is the bravest enemy our emperor has; a man who is so dear to me, that if you can make him our monarch's friend, you will oblige me in the most sensible manner; use all your utmost skill to gain him.'

Then he took Zara, his fair daughter, by the hand, presenting her to me, 'Here is the dearest thing I have in the world,' said he, 'I give you leave to love her; nay, will bestow her upon you, to secure your friendship: if her eyes cannot prevail, our eloquence cannot succeed.'

Here he left us, and from this day I was caressed by all the family; and Zara, the charmingest advocate that ever sued to gain a heart, tried all her arts, she danced, sung, dressed, and trying to ensnare me, unfortunately lost herself, for, alas! she loved me, and had not my whole soul been filled with the bright idea of my Belinda, it would have been impossible for me to have resisted her charms.

At length I generously told her, as we were sitting alone in a drawing-room, it being the cold season of the year, when we were obliged to sit in warm rooms; 'Charming Zara,' said I, 'it would be cruel and ungrateful in me, not to deal ingenuously with you; I own you are the most lovely, the most accomplished maid my eyes ever saw, there is nothing wanting in you to make a man compleatly happy you have wisdom, beauty, and virtue, and God never made any work more perfect: but, alas! Fairest of your sex, I am a man unworthy of that affection, which given to another, would set him above monarchs; my choice was long since made, my heart is a captive to one like yourself, who was my wife; one in whose arms I slept more glorious and content, than Eastern kings; a lady who is no more, yet one whose memory is so dear to me, that I am grown insensible to all your sex: her bright idea fills my mind, in dreams I'm nightly happy, pursue her shadow, and embrace her heavenly form; and when awake, still long for death, in hopes to meet her in the glorious regions where the happy souls shall meet again: look then no more upon a wretch, who can make no returns to your invaluable bounties.'

Zara beheld me all this while as one amazed, the roses forsook her cheeks, and finding I had done, she thus began: 'Unfortunate Beaumount, are you enamoured of a ghost? Must the dead rise to rob the wretched Zara of your heart? Why did you not forewarn me e'er I was undone? Ye Powers, why does my vengeance stay to stab the wretch that is a witness to my folly; I never loved before, she whom you loved is buried in the grave: Can you consent to sacrifice me to her ghost? Can you enjoy a shadow? Consider e'er you bid me die; I will not live and be despised.'

'Forgive me Heaven,' said I, 'may a thought like that ne'er enter your soul; may Zara live, and be most happy, gladly I'd die to save your life, but cannot make a second choice.'

Here we were interrupted, and after this she shunned me, and for some months kept much within her chamber, grew sick, and altered, which much alarmed the family; and I confess, my thoughts were much confused; sometimes I thought to marry her, and run all hazards to make her happy: but then Belinda might be still alive, and then I were undone, and my peace loft forever.

One morning Barintha, Zara's governess, came hastily into my chamber: 'Sir,' said she, 'if you will ever see my lady more, come now, for she's expiring.'

I followed her, and found Zara in the agonies of death; she fixed her dying eyes upon me, grasped my hand, and faintly cried, 'Farewell, cruel, but faithful Beaumount, *adieu*; I go to seek the ghost of her that murders me; I loved you, could not live without you, and therefore drank a poisonous draught last night to free me; forgive me, Heaven, since life was insupportable: ah! pray for me, dear cause of my sad fate, I'm going I know not where.'

Here her tongue faltered, her agonies encreased, and in few moments she expired. At this instant my grief was such, that had I not been a Christian, I had surely ended my life and misfortunes together; I kissed her pale face and lips a hundred times, wept over her, and then retreated to my chamber, threw myself upon my bed, refused to eat, and by next morning was seized with a violent fever, which robbed me of my reason for some days, at the end of which, my disease being something abated, I saw Zara's two brothers enter my chamber, with four soldiers; the eldest loaded me with reproaches for his sister's death, to which I was unable to reply through weakness. at last they took me out of my bed, pinioned me, and set me upon a horse, the four soldiers riding by me as a guard: they went with me over dreadful mountains and hills, whose tops were covered with snow, and after three days, and two nights travelling, in which time they never entered any house or inn, but laid me bound upon the ground, whilst the horses fed and rested, giving me brandy, bread, and meat, out of their knapsacks; we at last arrived at an old tower on the borders of Muscovy, where they delivered me into the hands of a gaoler, who lodged me in a close damp room, loading me with irons, Here I remained ten months sick, and had not God's Providence preserved me miraculously, I had doubtless died.

Three months after my arrival, a young gentleman was brought prisoner to this dismal place, by order of the *Czar*, who having much gold to fee the gaoler, had the liberty of walking up and down the prison; we conversed together, he much pitied my misfortune and ill treatment, and promised to procure my enlargement, either by his interest with the general, or force. His friends who solicited for him at court, being unsuccessful, gave him notice that his case was desperate: upon which we took a resolution to kill our gaoler, and fight our way out.

Accordingly the next morning we seized him as he entered my chamber, and having knocked him down with the bar of a door that we found in my room, we dispatched him took the keys, and rushed by the gentries who kept the out-gate; and not knowing where to go, we fled over the mountains towards a wood in Tartary, to which he guided me, where none but robbers and outlaws lived. My fetters much hindered my speed, being extremely weak, but fear gave me strength so that we reached the wood before night, believing it more safe for us to put our lives into the hands of thieves, than our merciless enemies. Here we laid down under a tree to rest, not being able to go farther, and slept some hours, though in danger of death every minute, from the wild beasts who went howling about the woods for prey, or more barbarous men; but God kept us, and awaking, we thought we perceived, at some distance, a light.

Necessity, being in great want of food, made us venture to the place. We saw a little cave, in which a venerable old man sat reading by a lamp; we entered, saluting him in the Muscovite language, with 'God save you, Sir, take pity of us who are fled from our enemies, out of a prison, destitute of food or comfort, grant us a retreat for a few days, or at least a few hours; we are Christians, Catholics, and one of us a native of France?'

At these words the old man rose from his seat, embraced us, and stirring up the embers, made a fire, and gave us wine and bread, telling us we were welcome: we informed him whence we came, the causes of our confinement. At last he turned towards me; 'Countryman,' said he, 'tell me what family you are descended from, what province you were born in.'

I informed him, then he caught me in his arms as a man lost in wonder. 'My lord,' said he, 'I have sought you long, and can disclose wonders to you; my name is Anthony, I am a Capuchin Friar, who saved your lady's life, and came to Muscovy on purpose to seek you out.'

Here he recounted to us how Belinda came to France in search of me; how my father imprisoned her! but e'er he could finish' his story, a band of Tartarian robbers entered the cave, seized us, and he importuning them for us, was unfortunately shot by one of the barbarous villains. They tied us back to back, and carried us some miles farther into the wood, where there were about a hundred of them encamped; and now we were again prisoners: here they lived with their women all in common, lodging only in tents, and chiefly supporting their lives with robbing all passengers that came near the wood; yet though barbarians, we found some humanity amongst them; they gave us plenty of food, took off my fetters, and offered us our freedom, if we would consent to live with them; which we accepted, and for some days were obliged to ride out with them, at the head of twenty or thirty Tartars, where we robbed, getting considerable booty from some Persian merchants, who were going to Muscovy with rich merchandize. The Tartars were so well pleased with our behaviour and conduct, that they gave us what we pleased of the plunder: by this means we were trusted with good horses, which, though small, yet were fleet as the wind.

We did not design to stay here, but fought an opportunity to escape, which Providence favoured us withal in this manner: One morning, at break of day, we went out with a party in search of a caravan that we had information was to pass by that road; it consisted of about fifty merchants, passengers, and soldiers of several nations, who were coming from Persia to Mulcovy with merchandize. We no sooner saw this company coming up, but the Tartars began to shrink; they saw their enemies well armed and numerous, and did not think themselves strong enough to attack them: we set spurs to our horses, leaving them in this consternation, and calling to the foremost of the caravan, in a suppliant manner throwing down our arms, desired to be heard.

Seeing us but two, they stopped, and upon our declaring our-selves friends, received us. We then gave an account of our adventures with the Tartars, and enquired if any of them were going to Sweden or Germany: there were two gentlemen and their servants going to Hungary; these we went along with, leaving the rest: and the young Mulcovite lord, not knowing how to provide for himself, I offered to carry him with me to France, and there take care of him, which he gladly consented to.

Being arrived in Hungary, having now but little money left of what we brought with us of the plunder we got amongst the robbers, we were obliged to sell some rich diamonds we had saved, and hid in our clothes; and with this money we procured ourselves horses, with a couple of servants to attend us, and so set out for France, whither I was now determined to return, being wearied with the many misfortunes I had met with abroad: and at the end of six weeks we arrived safely at Coutance, where I found my father dead, and all my relations and friends overjoyed to see me. I was sorry my father died e'er I had seen him, to have asked his pardon for my rashness in leaving him, though he was to blame; yet I believe God punished me for my disobediences, and 'tis to that cause that I attribute all my misfortunes in Muscovy.

Being now settled in my father's estate, and posts of honour, by the king, to whom I paid my duty at my first arrival in France; he received me with his accustomed goodness, reproving me gently for leaving his service, saying, 'My lord, love is an excuse, I own, for doing many rash inconsiderate things: I don't approve your father's proceedings with your wife; but I and your country had done you no wrong. 'Tis true, your father used my name, which was not well done, but I protest I was ignorant of all, till since your departure from France; and had you addressed yourself to me, be assured I would have made you easy and happy. I here give you all your father's posts of honour, and doubt not but you'll as bravely and faithfully discharge the trust I repose in you, as he did.'

Here the king embraced me, and during his life, I was so happy to have his favour. I now thought only of my Belinda, and examining all my father's old servants, discovered the castle where she had been imprisoned; I went thither, found the gaoler dead, but his wife and daughter told me she died there of a spotted fever, fearing to confess the truth, that she had escaped from them. I writ to St. Malo's to my friend, at whose house she had been; he was dead, and I could learn no news of her there.

Thus I remained two whole years in suspense; at last tired with the importunities of my friends, I resolved to marry again. It was now nine years since I parted from Belinda, and I concluded it was impossible that she should be still alive, and I hear nothing from her; nor had I any hopes till last week, when a friar came to me, who is just arrived from Muscovy, where he had seen Father Anthony before, I met with him in Tartary, and he told me he related to him the cause of his coming thither thus; That Father Benedict soon after he returned from Granville, where he had sent my wife away, falling sick, enjoined him to go to Sweden in search of me, in case he died, which he did soon after: and this was the occasion of my meeting that good father in the wood, who learning in Sweden that I was in Muscovy a prisoner, came thither, but could not discover where I was, so retired to this dismal place, where we found him; where he begged in the neighbouring villages, his holy habit securing him from injuries.

But I concluded, not being able then to get any information of her, she was dead; and in compliance with my friends importunities, married a lady who was a young widow, of a great family and fortune, having only this lovely daughter: but, alas! I found myself so miserable now, that I cannot describe the tortures of my mind. I never entered my bed with this lady, but I shivered; she loved me tenderly, but I fancied Belinda's ghost pursued me; every place where she had trod, each room, brought some new thing to my remembrance: I talked and started in my sleep. In fine, though I did all that I was able to conceal my distraction, all the world perceived it; and my wife, who was a lady of great wisdom and goodness, and most unfortunate in being mine, was so sensibly touched, that she fell into a consumption, and after having languished for two years, all means proving unsuccessful to preserve her, she died.

47

In her last agonies, as I was weeping by her, for indeed I highly respected, though I could not love her with passion, and omitted nothing that could oblige or help her; she pulled me to her, fixed her lips on mine, then sighed deeply.

'My dear lord,' said she, 'I thank you, you have done more for me, than for your loved Belinda; the constraint you have suffered upon my account, is the greatest obligation; I am now going, I doubt not, to rest, and hope to meet you again in glory; let my child be your chief care; and if the tender affection I have borne you, merits anything, show your esteem of me, by your love to her. I die, 'tis true, by having had too deep a sense of your misfortune, in not loving me but, my lord, believe me, 'tis with pleasure that I leave the world, since it will set you free: could you have loved me, as you did Belinda, I should have been desirous to live long; but since you cannot, I wish to die.'

Here she again embraced and kissed me, then turned to her confessor, who stood on the other side the bed; 'Father,' said she, 'I have now done with the world, and all its weaknesses; I'll grieve no more for mortal things, but fix my thoughts on Heaven.'

We all withdrew but the good father, and in about an hour she departed, leaving me most disconsolate for some months I kept my chamber, and then resolved to retire, and quit all public business; I went to the king, took my leave of him, recommending the Muscovite lord to him, to whom he gave a company of dragoons: then I retired to my country-seat, where you found me.

Thus the *marquis* finished his relation; they past the remainder of this day, and the next, very agreeably. In the evening of the fifth day, the sky began to darken, the wind blew, and about midnight a dreadful storm arose; at length the pilot was obliged to quit the government of the ship, and let her drive before the wind. At break of day they found themselves in the Irish Seas, and not far from land; their rigging was all torn, their mast shattered, and it was in vain for them to attempt going for Wales, before they had repaired their vessel, and refreshed themselves; therefore they made in for land, and cast anchor at Wexford, in the county of Rosse, in Ireland. They went ashore with the captain, and lodged at an inn whilst the sailors refitted the ship.

Chapter 9

In the time of their stay at Wexford, they were curious to see the country, and the *marquis* and Mr. Lluelling frequently rid out to view the adjacent towns and villages, leaving the young Lady Isabella with her servants. One evening they lost their way returning home, and wandering about, found themselves near a wood: it was almost dark, and they knew not whither to go; they therefore made a stand, consulting what to do. At last they espied an old man with a candle and lanthorn coming towards them, in very poor habit, and a beard down to his breast. 'Honest man,' said Mr. Lluelling, 'can you direct us to some safe place to lodge in tonight? Or put us in the way to Wexford?'

'To Wexford, Sir!' said he, 'you cannot reach that tonight: in the morning I'll put you in the way; but for tonight, if you'll accept a lodging in my poor cottage hard by, you are welcome.'

They gladly accepted his offer, and followed him into the wood, though something afraid, lest he should betray them into the hands of robbers, of which there are many times gangs that retreat to such places. At length they came to a poor clay cottage, where a boy stood at the door; the good man bid them alight, which they did, taking their pistols in their hands, the boy taking their horses: they found the place near, and nor destitute of necessaries; the man entertained them handsomely, bringing out venison-pasty, wine, and dried tongues.

'Gentlemen,' said he, 'eat heartily, and spare not; we'll drink the king's health before we part.'

The *marquis* and Mr. Lluelling began to imagine there was some mystery in this man's living here, and were upon their guard; they appeared very merry, and guessed by their host's behaviour, that he was a man of quality. When they were well warmed with wine, they all began to be free, the old man toasted the king's health, they pledged him. 'My lord,' said Mr, Lluelling, 'methinks 'tis almost as good living here as in France, or Wales; Faith, I can't treat you better when you come to Swansea.'

At these words, the stranger looked upon them, saying, ' gentlemen, are you natives of these two places? They are both well known to me.'

Here they were interrupted by the boy, who informed his master some friends were come; he presently stepped to the door, where they heard the sound of horses feet: after some time he returned to them, saying, 'Gentlemen, I beg pardon for leaving you, but it was to take leave of some friends who are going for France?' It was now midnight, and he genteelly said, 'Gentlemen you are weary, will you be pleased to go to bed?'

They finished their bottle, and were conducted up stairs, to a room where they could but just stand upright for the ceiling; but the softness of the bed, and fineness of the sheets, made amends: however they could not sleep, their minds were so filled with curiosity to know who this man was. They talked all night; the *marquis* mentioned Belinda several times, and Isabella, saying, 'My dear child will repent her leaving France, and be much concerned for us this night.' This their discourse was overheard by the old man, who lay in the next room; they heard him up early, and rose: coming down stairs, they found breakfast ready for them.

'Now gentlemen,' said their host, 'I must be impertinent, and ask some questions before we part: I last night heard one of you name Belinda, and find you are lately come from France; I had a sister of that name, who dying, left a daughter, of whom I would be glad to hear some tidings: Come you from Normandy?'

'By Heaven,' said the *marquis*, embracing the old man, you are the L—— the uncle of my dear Belinda, that charming virgin, fate made me the happy husband of.' Here they sat down, recounting, in a pathetic manner, all their adventures: the *marquis* concluding, said, 'And now, Sir, tell us what Providence brought you here.'

'Sir, said he, I will: My loyalty to my prince brought me under some misfortunes, at last I was forced, with my only son, to fly to Scotland; there we lay concealed a while, till I had received a great sum of money, that I had taken methods to have remitted to me. From thence we hired a small vessel, and sailed for Wales, where I thought I should be secure from all discovery; there I changed my name, purchased a small estate, and have lived happily, though obscurely, ever since, making several voyages to France, hither, and elsewhere, upon business to serve my friends. I came to Ireland some months ago, and chose this place to reside in, my habit, and my servants, making us pass undiscovered; the gentlemen you heard me speak to, are gone to take shipping, and I design to go for Wales with the first opportunity.'

'We will go together,' said Mr. Lluelling, where we shall fill our expecting wives hearts with joy.'

They parted, the L—— not thinking it proper to go along with them by daylight, sending his boy to guide them to Wexford, where they arrived to the great joy of the Lady Isabella, who had been almost distracted for fear her father and brother-in-law had been killed. In few days after, the ship being ready, the *marquis* and all the rest went aboard, with the L—— who came to them disguised; they set fail for Swansea, where they soon arrived in good health.

Chapter 10

Mr. Lluelling conducted the *marquis* and the L—— with the young lady and servants, to his house; where being arrived, he saw the servants look upon one another, and a general sadness and silence seemed to reign in every face and room, 'Where is your lady, and her mother?' he demanded.

None answered.

At length, 'Sir,' said a boy trembling, that had been bred in his house, 'my lady is stolen away, as we suppose, by your kinsman Mr. Glandore; we have heard nothing of her this month and more: the old lady has taken it so to heart, that she has kept her bed ever since, and is more likely to die than to live.'

'Show me to her,' said Mr. Lluelling, 'and let us join with her in sorrow. My God,' continued he, 'where shall we find faith in man? Can neither the ties of blood, friendship, interest, nor religion bind men to be just: but alas! he lived too long in that cursed town, where vice takes place of virtue, where men rise by villainy and fraud, where the lustful appetite has all opportunities of being gratified; where oaths and promises are only jests, and all religion but pretence, and made a screen and cloak for knavery; a place where truth and virtue cannot live. Oh! curse on my credulity, to trust so rich a treasure to a wolf, a lustful Londoner?'

He would have gone on, if the *marquis* had not interrupted him, begging him to be patient, and at least procure his happiness, by bringing him to Belinda. To her chamber they went, where she was lying in her bed so weak, that it was even dangerous to let her know her happiness. The *marquis* threw himself upon the bed by her, weeping, and embracing her in his arms, cried 'My God, I thank thee, that my longing arms again do hold my dear Belinda; spare her, I beg thee, some few years longer to enjoy the mighty blessings thou hast granted us: look up, my dear, and bless thy ravished husband with a tender look, let my soul leap to hear thy well-known voice, and thy tongue tell me I am welcome.'

'Am I alive! and do I wake!' she cried, 'do I behold my dear lord again! it is impossible! let me behold him till my eye-strings crack, and my life ends in rapture; what thanks, what returns, can I make to heaven? Let all my faculties exert themselves, and all united praise my God.'

Here she fainted, joy having overcome her wasted spirits; cordials were brought, and she was recovered from her fit, and then she began to weep. 'Alas! My lord,' said she, 'were I able, I would ask you a thousand questions, but I hope now to live and enjoy your dear company again; but we have lost our child, dishonourably stolen. Ah! Son,' said she, turning to Mr. Lluelling, 'you were deceived, and left a villain to supply your place.'

At these words she saw Isabella: 'What fair virgin,' said she, 'is that, my lord? Have you more daughters? And has some other woman slept in your dear arms?'

'My dear,' said he, 'I have been married since we parted, believing you were dead; but the lady was so happy as to die before I was blessed with the knowledge of your safety: this is a daughter of hers, by a former husband; she is as dear to me as Belinda, and I brought her, to present her to you, as the greatest blessing Heaven can send you, next my life, and Belinda's safety.' Then he turned to Mr. Lluelling; 'Fear not, my Son,' said he, 'I will find and fetch "Belinda back, if yet alive, and use the ravisher as he deserves.'

Then the servants were all called up, and examined; they informed them of Glandore's being seen with her in the summerhouse, and of some places where they were seen together on the road; so they concluded she was carried northward, and the L—— said, 'My estate lies that way, nephew, if you please to stay with my niece, my kinsman and I will go together; we know the roads and country, and shall soon trace the robber to his den, I doubt not.'

The servants said they had rid all about the country, but could get no intelligence where they were.

The next morning, the Lord —— whom we must henceforward know to have gone by the name of Mr. Hide, for he was father to the young gentleman who had Belinda in keeping, set out with Mr. Lluelling and three servants, well armed, and went the road to his house, which was in Merionethshire, near the River Wie; they got information on the road of the coach, and so continued to go towards Mr. Hide's, where they found young Mr. Hide dangerously ill: he received his father with all joy and affection, and after some discourse, related to them the adventure of the young lady's being brought thither, with the manner of her being rescued from Glandore, and his, and his servants being killed by the highwaymen. Then Mr. Lluelling, impatient to know where she was, interrupted him, asking to see her.

'Are you then, said Mr. Hide,' the happy man to whom Belinda is wife? Why do you ask me for her? I sent her home to you three days since, in your own coach, guarded by three of my servants, not being able to persuade her to stay here, till I was either dead, or able to see her home myself.'

At these words Mr. Lluelling was even thunderstruck; he looked on the Lord —— 'Am I then, said he, 'born to lose her? What can become of her now?'

'Doubt not,' said the young gentleman, 'Heaven will preserve her; such perfection, such virtue and beauty, angels attend upon; I am undone forever by the sight of her, before I knew she was another's I adored her, and now die a victim to her charms: her virtue I never attempted, but honoured and protected her, hoping to die respected of her; and though 'twas worse than death to lose the sight of her, yet I consented to our separation, and sent her away; since which I find my illness encreased, and hope my end is at hand.'

Mr. Lluelling looked upon him with jealousy and rage: 'Is Belinda,' said he, 'so unfortunate, to raise me a rival in every man of worth that sees her: Why did she not rather die in the retreat I found her; let me but find her once again, and she shall never quit my sight; I'll guard and keep her with such care, that all my lustful sex shall never be able to seduce, or steal her from me.'

Here the old lord interposed: 'My friend and kinsman,' said he, 'you wrong your lady and my son; Why do you rave? Has he not done nobly by you? If he loved her before he knew that she was pre-engaged it was no crime, but his misfortune; and his honourable treatment of her since, renders him highly deserving your compassion and esteem. Come, let us wisely search for her, and return to your home, where she, by this time, may be arrived. Come, my son, vanquish the frailty, of your mind, and then your body will recover; Belinda has a sister, fair as herself, a horse-litter shall be provided to carry you with us to Swansea, there company, and the lovely Isabella, will, I hope, compleat your cure, and make you happy.'

All things were strait got ready for their return thither, where being arrived, there was no news of Belinda. And now we shall leave them to go in search of her, and give an account of what had happened to her.

Chapter 11

Belinda being on the road with her attendants, about ten miles from Mr. Hide's the coach going gently over a dangerous mountain, was met, and set upon, by a band of ten robbers, who stopped the coach, and killed one of the servants, and two of the horses; took the other two servants, whom they bound hand and foot; then they pulled Belinda out of the coach, and searching that, found the sum of 1490 *l.* in gold, Belinda having used only ten pounds of the money Glandore had brought in the coach, which ten pounds she had given Mr. Hide's servants, and the clowns that rescued her. There was one amongst the thieves that seemed to be much respected by, and commanded the rest. He put Belinda into the coach again, and going into it himself, bid her be silent, and no harm should come to her.

One of the thieves got up into the coach-box, and with the four remaining horses drove the coach down the mountain into a deep valley; then he drove to a wood about two miles from that place, and being entered into the thickest part of it, they stopped, took the horses out, and left the coach: the captain leading Mrs. Lluelling, they came to an old ruined stone building, where an old church was remaining, and part of the house.

Here these robbers lived, it being a place desolate of all inhabitants, and long since abandoned: here they locked the two servants they had taken prisoners into a room, and then pulling off their vizards, they saluted Mrs. Lluelling, and told her she was welcome: But, good Heavens! what a surprise was she under! when she saw the captain of the robbers' face, and knew him to be a young gentleman whom she had once seen at Mr. Hide's with letters, and had been by him caressed in an extraordinary manner; he soon perceived she knew him.

'Madam,' said he, 'you will not be half so much surprised as you now seem to be, when I tell you, that I no sooner saw you at Mr.

Hide's, but I loved you; I am a man nobly born, but unfortunate; we are all gentlemen, most of us outlawed, except three really thieves, whom we are joined with. We have for our royal master's, and religion's sake, been ruined; our estates, or our fathers, which was our birthright, confiscated; we have tried to get our bread abroad, but like the poor cavaliers, were looked on as burdensome wherever we came.

'Thus made desperate, since Lewis the Fourteenth died, we returned to England, we had most, of us a being when first we came, but our friends are since impoverished: our spirits are great, therefore we have chosen this desperate way to maintain ourselves. At the harmless country peoples, where we lodge in couples, we pass for Jacobites, and honest Tories, great men disguised, &c., and when we have got a good booty, and are flush of money, they imagine we have received supplies from abroad. News we often do indeed receive from foreign parts, but money never: we would, if a change came, venture into the world again, and live honestly.

'We never murder any man, or rob a poor traveller; we hold correspondence with some servant or other, in every gentleman's family in the country, and seldom miss of intelligence where great sums of money are stirring, This place is our rendezvous, here we divide our plunder, and then we separate. You see, madam, the confidence I repose in you; I believe you are a lady of quality; I admire your person, I am not your inferior in birth, and therefore since I have purchased you with the hazard of my life, hope you will grant me the possession of your person with reluctance; I will maintain you nobly, and run all dangers to preserve, provide for, and please you.'

Here one of his companions entered, saying, 'Sir, dinner is ready.' He took her by the hand, she not daring to resist, and led her to a large room, where was a table spread, and great store of cold meats, with plenty of wine: she was placed by the captain at the upper end, and now he and his companions gave a loose to joy; mirth and good-humour reigned. Belinda could not eat, her soul was filled with all the dreadful imaginations of ruin and misery; but after they had eaten plentifully, they all withdrew to sleep, and she and the captain were left alone: he pressed her earnestly to yield to him, but she refused him with such soft words and resolution, that he forbore to treat her rudely, trying to win her to his embraces gently for though necessity had made him a robber, yet it could not make him a brute; he had been well born and educated, and retained some remnants of honour.

At night he left her there, and went out with his band, leaving with her two women, who were in appearance servants to them: to these she addressed herself, saying, 'You are women, your hearts must be tender and pitiful! I am a wife, brought hither by misfortune, torn from a fond husband, and a doting mother. Oh! help me in this great distress, assist me to escape, and bring me to them, and you shall be rewarded to your satisfaction.'

The eldest of the two replied, 'Madam, we gladly would, but cannot serve you; we are strangers in this place like you; we were brought here by force, blindfold and taken far from hence: 'tis now eight months since we were brought to this sad place. Here we have been ruined, and are made subservient to the lust and humour of these desperate men; we both were gentlewomen born in France, though we speak English: this is my niece, I was a single woman, had no relation whom I thought so well deserved my love as she. I had a handsome fortune, and we lived together; and having some business to go for England, I took her, with me: we took along with us our necklaces, rings, clothes, and what we had most valuable to appear in, with money to defray our charges.

'The vessel we came over in, was bound to Southampton, but a storm drove us upon this coast; we got into Swansea, and from thence hired horses to carry us cross the countries thither, with a guide. In the way we were set upon by this band of robbers; they stopped us, took us off our horses, carried us, our boxes, and all off along with them, and brought us to this place. Our guide they bound, and left behind, and now threaten us with death, if we attempt to leave them, Alas! We know not where to fly to, this place is destitute of all inhabitants; besides, some of our band is always watching near this wood: we are strangers to this country, have no friends here to make inquiry after us; we came only to trade, which I often did, and so learned English, and now despair of ever seeing our native land and friends again.'

This story nearly touched Mrs. Lluelling's heart. 'Find a way for our escape, said she, 'and I will procure your safe return to France.'

Here she related to them all her own adventures, at which they seemed astonished; but when she named her father and mother, they fell a weeping, and embracing her knees, declared that they had been servants to her grandfather, the governor of Normandy, the eldest having been many years housekeeper to her grandmother, the Marchioness of Maintenon.

'My dear lady,' said she, 'what would I refuse to do to serve you? I will set you at liberty, or die in the attempt.'

Here they consulted what to do, Mrs. Lluelling resolving not to stay there all that night, fearing the men's return. There was in the chapel many disguises, with which the robbers used to conceal themselves; of these they chose three, which were old ragged coats, shoes, hats, &c. being beggars' habits; they took soot and grease, and made an odd kind of pomatum to rub their faces and hands; and thus accoutered, with long oaken sticks in their hands, they ventured into the wood, leaving the dismal dwelling, empty of human creatures. They went on, trembling at every noise or rustling of the trees, seeking a path, but could discover none: they still went forward, till they had passed through the wood, and then they discovered the open country, where they could discern nothing but dreadful high barren mountains, and lonely valleys, dangerous to pass: they had no food with them, nor any money, for the robbers never left that behind them in that place.

Thus they wandered over the mountains till night approached, weary, and faint for want of food; and when it grew dark, they could go no farther; back they neither dared, nor would return. Belinda had a soul too noble to submit to gratify a villain's lust, 'Come my companions,' said she, 'let us lie down on the cold earth, and trust that Providence that still preserves those that put their confidence in it; 'tis better far to perish here, than live in infamy and misery: 'tis true, our bodies are enfeebled by the want of sustenance, but sleep will refresh our tired spirits, and enable us to prosecute our journey; recommend yourselves to God, his power is all-sufficient, and when human means are wanting, can supply our wants by miracle.'

Here she fell upon her knees, and cried, 'My God, encrease my faith, pity our distress, and send us help: but if thou hast decreed us to die in this place, support us under the mighty trial, and give us grace to be entirely resigned to thy will, and send thy angels to receive our souls.'

Her companions remained silent, admiring the constancy of Belinda, who seemed then scarce fifteen; they laid down and slept profoundly, weariness making them rest, though under the most racking apprehensions of the greatest dangers. At break of day they arose, but knew not which way to go.

Thus they wandered three days and nights: the evening of the third day, they discovered, at a considerable distance, a small town; but now, alas! they were no longer able to stand. 'My merciful God,' cried the almost dying Belinda, 'must I perish now, when help is so near? Why do my fainting limbs refuse to bear me to that place, where food is to be had, and drink to quench my raging thirst, which water will no longer do? My craving stomach sickens with the cold draught, and casts it back again.'

Here she fainted, Lisbia and Magdelaine, for those were the women's names that accompanied her, looked ghastly upon her, and fell down by her.

Thus the Almighty tried her faith and patience, but designed not she, who fled from sin, should perish: a she-goat, with a little kid, at her recovering from her trance, stood by her; she catched at it with her eager hands, the goat fled, but the kid she laid hold of, calling to her companions to assist her, and with a knife she had in her pocket, she stabbed it. They licked up the warm blood, and eat the raw flesh, more joyfully than they would dainties at another time, so sharp is hunger! Refreshed with this, they slept that night much better, though it was now pinching cold, it being the latter end of October.

It snowed hard towards morning, which so benumbed their limbs, that they were not able to walk; and here they sat eating their strange breakfast of raw flesh, till it was almost noon, making many vain attempts to rise and walk: but then the sun breaking out, they made a shift to creep along towards the town. But, alas! when they thought they were almost there, they met with the River Wie; they saw no bridge or boat, and it was impossible for them to get over it on foot: they went as far as they were able by the riverside, ready to sink down at every step; at length they sat down, and wept sadly.

Belinda believing herself near death, her constitution being more tender and delicate than the French women's, with a weak voice thus exhorted them: 'My friends,' says she, 'I need not tell you that we are all born to part, and die; I believe our time is short, and that in few hours we shall be released from the miseries of this life: how necessary is it for us then, to improve those few hours Providence gives us, to prepare for eternity? My life has, I thank God, been passed in retirement; I have not been exposed to the temptations of the world, yet have I not been free from errors: you have lived long, I beg therefore that you would apply yourselves earnestly to Him that must condemn, or save us, out of whose mighty Hand none can deliver us; and remember that now is the moment, when eternal happiness is to be obtained or lost.'

Here she could proceed no farther, but fell back in a swoon. At this instant a poor fisherman brought his nets down to dry them on the shore; and seeing three poor men together, two of them weeping over him that was lying down, he drew near, and overheard their complaints. The man spoke but bad English, but he understood it much better; he found the person dying was a woman disguised, because they wrung their hands, and lamented her, crying, 'Our dear lady is dead, what shall we do?'

The good man looked about to see if his boat was coming in, which he had left his boy to bring thither, which at that instant brought it to the shore; the good man leaped into it, and took out a bottle of brandy, which he quickly brought, and poured some of it down Belinda's throat, at which she recovered; the two women drank likewise. He told them his house, though a poor one, was but a mile farther, and invited them to it; but, alas! they were not able to walk thither: he and his boy were obliged to help them into his boat, in which he carried them to his cottage, where they were kindly received by his wife, to whom the fisherman told how he found them; the good woman warmed a bed, and got them into it, giving them good hot broth. And now being much refreshed, Belinda told her who she was, and that she lived at Swansea.

'Alas! Madam,' said the good woman, 'you are a great way from home, but I will send my husband thither, to give your friends notice.'

'He shall be well rewarded,' said Belinda.

The next morning the fisherman set out for Swansea, and Belinda fell very sick; Lisbia and Magdelaine recovered soon, but she remained so weak, that she could not walk. In five days the fisherman reached Mr. Lluelling's, whom we must now return to speak of.

Chapter 12

Mr. Lluelling, the Lord ——, and his son, being arrived at Swansea, and finding no news of Belinda, they took all the methods possible to find her out, but in vain. Mr. Hide was so weak that he could not accompany his father, and kinsman, who rid out every day in search of Belinda; the *marquis*, who could not part one hour from his dear lady, and the lovely Isabella, kept him company: her charms soon touched his soul, and he at last began to imagine, that if Belinda was found again, and happy, he could be so with her sister. Isabella grew insensibly to be fond of him, her virgin heart that never felt love's flame before, was warmed, and everything he did, was charming in her eyes: he now was able to walk into the garden, and though very weak, was well-bred, obliging, gay, and entertaining.

The *marquis* was extreme fond of him, and was pleased to see the growing affection betwixt Mr. Hide and Isabella, nothing was wanting but Belinda's presence, to make this family compleatly happy: and now the fortunate moment came, they so much wished for; the fisherman arrived, and gave an account of her being at his house with two friends, with the manner of their coming thither: but, good Heavens! what transports filled Mr. Lluelling's and her mother's soul? It was late at night when this news was brought, and impossible to travel by reason of the snow and darkness, yet it was with difficulty that the *marquis* restrained his son from venturing.

In the morning they set out at the break of day, the *marquis*, Lord ——, and Mr. Lluelling, in the coach and six, with five servants, and the fisherman well horsed: the old lady would fain have gone, but her weakness was such, that she, Mr. Hide, and Isabella, were constrained to stay at home. In three days Mr. Lluelling, and the rest, arrived at the cottage, where he was blessed with the sight of his dear Belinda; she was in bed, very weak, but when she heard his voice, she started up, and when he came to the bedside, threw her arms about his neck, and both remained silent for some moments, whilst tears of joy shewed their affection: then he recovering, said a thousand tender things, such as fully expressed his fondness. Her father next embraced her, saying, 'See here, Belinda, your transported father, who never saw a day like this! now my God has crowned my age with blessings, exceeding expectation, and almost belief. What thanks are we obliged to render our Creator, for the mighty blessings he has this day bestowed upon us?'

She bowed, but being faint, could scarce reply, when Mr. Lluelling, looking tenderly upon her, said 'Alas! my Belinda, may I hope that I shall sleep again within those arms? Has no vile ravisher usurped my right, and forced you to his hated bed? Has not that lovely body been polluted with his cursed embraces? Though I believe your mind still pure, and that your soul loathed, and abhorred the damning thought; yet forgive me, if I tremble at the dreadful idea of so cursed an act, and long to know the truth.'

Belinda, lifting up her eyes, looked on him with disdain; 'Are you my husband?' she cried, 'Do you know me? And can you believe me capable of so vile, so base a crime, as yielding up my honour to a ravisher? No; I would have preferred the cruellest death to infamy; or if by force compelled, would never have let the impious villain live for to repeat his crime; or I would have urged him to destroy me, pursued him with reproaches, till with my blood he should have bought his peace, and washed away my stain: believe me, I am innocent as when you took me first a virgin to your bed, and your suspicions are unkind.'

Here she fainted, he held her in his arms, asking pardon for his rashness, and with fervent kisses sealed his peace upon her lips and hands. And now they thought of removing her to Swansea, this was a place not fit for her to stay in, physicians, and all things wanting, could not here be had. He had forgot to bring clothes and linen thither, and till she was to rise, took no notice of hers, and her companions habits; but when he saw Lisbia bring her beggar's coat, and other accoutrements, he, and the *marquis*, and Lord ——, were much surprised, and diverted; and indeed it was a pleasant sight to see her, and her female attendants, so dressed, enter the coach.

And now nothing remained but to reward the honest fisherman and his wife; Mr. Lluelling gave them ten pieces of gold, a sum they had never been masters of before in their whole lives; he told them if they would come to Swansea, he would give them a house to live in. They returned him thanks, but said they had lived in that cottage thirty odd years, and had rather continue there; but if he would give their boy Jack a new fisherboat against he was married, which was to be shortly, they should be bound to pray for him to their live's end. He agreed to their request, bidding the fisherman come to Swansea, and chuse such a one as he best liked, and he would pay for it: so they parted thence, and in three days came in safety to Swansea, where Belinda was received with excessive joy by her mother, and the rest.

Isabella admired her sister's beauty, though somewhat changed by sickness, when she saw her dressed in her own clothes. Habits were given to the women her attendants, and none but Mr. Hide feared to look upon her; she turned towards him smiling, 'My generous lover and friend,' said she, 'look not upon me with such disorder; believe me, your treatment of me was so generous and noble, that had I not been disposed of, nor known Mr. Lluelling before, I declare, Mr. Hide should have had the first place in my esteem: but here is another to be disposed of, my charming sister, who has, in my eyes, superior charms give her that heart which I must now refuse, and make her happy. Speak, my dear sister,' said she, 'shall he be heard? and do you not think him worthy your love?'

Isabella blushed, and the *marchioness* answered, 'Her father and I approving it, I dare answer for my dear Isabella, she will be guided by us.'

Mr. Hide made a low bow.

'My lord,' said he, 'may I presume to hope so great an honour as seems here designed me?'

'You may,' answered the *marquis*, 'I shall be proud to call you son.'

From this hour Mr. Hide paid his addresses to Isabella, and content reigned in every face, and now Belinda gave an account of all that had happened to her, from her being taken by the robbers, to her arrival at the fisherman's.

Two days after her return home, the two poor servants that were taken by the thieves with her, and left locked up in a room, when she fled from the ruinous house in the wood, came to Swansea, and told how having found themselves there alone, and hearing nobody stir, or come to relieve them for two days and a night, they resolved to force their way out, at all adventures; and searching about to find the best place to make their escape at, one of them pulled a great stone out of the wall, at which they both crept out: they saw nobody, and rambled all about the house, and ruined church , there they found several boxes and trunks, but most of them empty: examining more curiously, they found a trapdoor in the chancel, which, lifting up, they ventured to go into a vault, where was much treasure, as plate, jewels, money, and clothes; they took as much as they could well carry in their pockets, and departed, going over the mountains till they thought they were safe, and there they lay that night. The next day, knowing the country, they went home to their master, Mr. Hide's house, and from thence came to Swansea, to give him an account of all.

Upon this information, and Mrs. Lluelling's, Mr. Lluelling resolved to send to the high-sheriff, and raise the county, to apprehend this gang of thieves; but Belinda entreated him to spare the captain of the robbers.

According to his desire, the sheriff gave orders, and Mr. Lluelling heading the hue-and-cry, Mr. Hide's servants guiding them, they went directly to the wood, where they apprehended two of the meanest of the crew, that is, two real thieves; who informed them, that the whole band returning thither two days after Belinda's escape thence, and finding the two women, and Mr. Hide's two servants gone, they feared being discovered, and had therefore changed their lodgings, and retired to a place more secret, and almost impossible to be discovered, taking part of their treasure with them, and were resolved to go off to sea, if they were too closely pursued to live longer there; and had left them behind to give intelligence. They said moreover, That they had looked narrowly upon most of the mountains for Belinda and the women, and missing them, hoped they had perished in some of the dismal valleys, or tumbled down from some precipice, and killed themselves.

'Our captain,' indeed, said one of them, is a brave gentleman, and stormed dreadfully at us, saying, he would give his life willingly to save the lady, and that if we did not find, and bring her safe back, he would kill us: which we little regarded; for though we let him at present head us, and command, 'tis only because he is boldest, and will venture where we don't care to go: but should we be taken and imprisoned, we should not scruple to hang him, or any of his friends, to save ourselves.'

'Villains that you are,' cried Mr. Lluelling, 'if possible, I will save him, and hang you.'

They were pinioned, and the house and church searched narrowly, where some plate and clothes were found, and afterwards put into the sheriff's hands, to be restored to the owners, upon public notice given, and their appearing; and after much search, being able to discover no more of the thieves, Mr. Lluelling dismissed the assistants, and returned home, the two thieves being first lodged in the county goal. Some days after, a man brought a letter, directed to the French *marquis*, Monsieur de Maintenon; he gave it to one of the servants, and departed: the *marquis* opened it before the family, and read the contents, which were as follows:

My Lord,
It is with the utmost confusion I inform your Lordship, that I am the unfortunate Sir C. O. known here only as captain of a band of robbers, amongst whom are Mr. T. B. Sir A. D. the two A—rs, and two gentlemen more, unknown to you. I am perfectly sensible of the danger and sinfulness of this wretched course of life I at present follow, and would gladly leave it for any honest way of getting bread. I throw myself at your feet, to implore your pity and pardon for the rudeness I offered Belinda, which I heartily repent of. I knew your generosity and goodness, and revolve to put my life into your hands, by coming to you; and if you think me worthy to live, dispose of me as you please, I will follow you into France, and draw my sword no more, but for yours, and my master's service: if you condemn me to death, send me to a prison, and you will take away a life, that, whilst I continue in sin, must be burdensome to
Your Devoted Friend,
and Old Acquaintance,
C. O.

Chapter 13

The *marquis* was much surprised at reading this letter, knowing the gentleman very well: he asked Mr. Lluelling, his lady, and Lord —— advice; they all agreed that they would, if possible, save him and the rest. The next day the captain of the robbers came, and Mr. Hide embraced him, and so did the *marquis*, Mr. Lluelling, and L——; they had the diversion of his relating to them all his dangerous and bold adventures: he lay there that night, next morning Mr. Lluelling went to the port, and hired a vessel to carry him and his companions to Spain, the *marquis* giving him letters of recommendation to some great men there, who were his friends, He made him deliver up all the things of value he had left in his hands, of his robberies, and part of Mr. Lluelling's money, and gave him bills for a handsome sum of money to support him and his friends, till they could be provided for in the army, which they desired to be received into: this the *marquis* generously gave out of his own pocket, with some gold for their present occasion, till they came to Barcelona, the bill being drawn on a merchant there, with whom he held a correspondence.

The rest of the unfortunate gentlemen, who, by their captain's advice, were all near at hand, went aboard the vessel, to which the *maqruis*, Mr. Lluelling, L——, and Mr. Hide, went with the captain, and there they supped merrily, and parted; the *marquis*, and his son, L——, and Mr. Hide, returning home. Next morning the ship sailed with a fair wind, and Wales was delivered from a band of gentlemen thieves, and the unfortunate gentlemen from hanging.

And now nothing remains to compleat this family's felicity, but Isabella's marriage with Mr. Hide, which in some days after was consummated; this wedding was very splendid, all sorts of innocent diversion, as dancing, feasting, and musical entertainments, compleated the festival. The country-people had their share in it, and much pleased the ladies with their odd dancing and songs: the Welsh harpers came from all parts of the country, blind and lame, and the halls echoed with the trembling harps. The *marquis*, who had heard the most harmonious concerts of music in Rome and France, confessed he had heard nothing more diverting, or seen an entertainment where there was less expense, or more true mirth; saying, 'Were the Welsh language as agreeable and musical as their harps, I should love to hear them talk, and prefer it to French?'

The *marquis* and his lady resolved to continue here till Mrs. Lluelling was brought to bed, which she was in the March following, on the 17th of which, she was happily delivered of a son. After she was up again, the *marquis* thought of returning to France with his lady, but desired he might have his little grandson and his nurse with him; the L—— and Mr. Hide likewise resolving to go with him, and settle there, sold their estates. Mr. Lluelling and Belinda offered to accompany their father and mother, and spend the summer in Normandy. And now it being the year 1718, on the 2nd of May they went aboard a ship they had hired to carry them, and arrived safe on the 9th, in the evening, at St, Malo's, from whence they set out for Coutance, and in few days arrived at the *marquis's* seat, where they were entertained nobly. The two French women, Lisbia and Magdelaine, went joyfully to their home, returning many thanks to the *marquis* and ladies. Mr. Lluelling and his lady, found France so charming, that they continue there.

Thus Providence does, with unexpected accidents, try men's faith, frustrate their designs, and lead them through a series of misfortunes, to manifest its power in their deliverance; confounding the atheist, and convincing the libertine, that there is a just God, who rewards virtue, and does punish vice: so wonderful are the ways of God, so boundless is his power, that none ought to despair that believe in him. You see he can give food upon the barren mountain, and prevent the bold ravisher from accomplishing his wicked design: the virtuous Belinda was safe in the hands of a man who was desperately in love with her, and whose desperate circumstance made him dare, to do almost anything; but virtue was her armour, and Providence, her defender: these trials did but; improve her virtues, and encrease her faith.

Such histories as these ought to be published in this age above all others, and if we would be like the worthy persons whose story we have here read, happy and blessed with all Human felicity; let us imitate their virtues, since that is the only way to make us dear to God and man, and the most certain and noble method to perpetuate our names, and render our memories immortal, and our souls eternally happy.

The Strange Adventures of the
Count de Vinevil and His Family

Contents

Preface to the Reader

Since serious things are in a manner, altogether neglected, by what we call the gay and fashionable part of mankind, and religious treatises grow mouldy on the bookseller's shelves in the back-shops; when ingenuity is, for want of encouragement, starved into silence, and Toland's abominable writings sell ten times better than the imitable Mr. Pope's *Homer*, when Dacier's works are attempted to be translated by a hackney-writer, and Horace's *Odes* turned into prose and nonsense; the few that honour virtue, and wish well to our Nation, caught to study to reclaim our giddy youth; and since reprehensions fail, try to win them to virtue, by methods where delight and instruction may go together. With this design I present this book to the public, in which you will find a story, where divine Providence manifests itself in every transaction, where virtue is tried with misfortunes, and rewarded with blessings: In fine, where men behave themselves like Christians, and women are really virtuous, and such as we ought to imitate.

As for the truth of what this narrative contains, since *Robinson Crusoe* has been so well received, which is more improbable, I know no reason why this should be thought a fiction. I hope the world is not grown so abandoned to vice, as to believe that there is no such ladies to he found, as would prefer death to infamy; or a man that, for remorse of conscience, would quit a plentiful fortune, retire, and chuse to die in a dismal cell. This age has convinced us, that guilt is so dreadful a thing, that some men have hastened their own ends, and done justice on themselves. Would men trust in Providence, and act according to reason and common justice, they need not to fear anything, but whilst they defy God, and wrong others, they must be cowards, and their ends such as they deserve, surprising and infamous.

I heartily wish prosperity to my country, and that the English would be again (as they were heretofore) remarkable for virtue and bravery, and our nobility make themselves distinguished from the crowds by shining qualities, for which their ancestors became so honoured, and for reward of which obtained those titles they inherit. I hardly dare hope for encouragement, after having discovered, that my design is to persuade you to be virtuous; but if I fail in this, I shall not in reaping that inward satisfaction of mind, that ever accompanies good actions. If this trifle sells, I conclude it takes, and you may be sure to hear from me again; so you may be innocently diverted, and I employed to my satisfaction.

Adieu.

Chapter 1

In the year 1702, the Count de Vinevil, a native of France, born of one of the noblest families in Picardy, where he had long lived possessed of a plentiful estate, being a widower, and having no child but the beautiful Ardelisa, his only daughter, finding his estate impoverished by continued taxations, and himself neglected by his sovereign, and no ways advanced, whilst others less worthy were put into places of trust and power; resolved to dispose of his estate, purchase and freight a ship, sail for Turkey, and there settle at Constantinople, to trade: being induced so to do, from the perfect knowledge he had of those parts, having been in his youth for above ten years with an uncle of his, who was consul there for the French factory, and carried him along with him to show him the world.

Accordingly he turned all into ready money, except some lands, which being entailed he could not sell; and those he intrusted in the hands of the Count de Beauclair, his sister's son.

Having thus ordered his affairs, he purchased a ship called the *Bon-Avanture*; and having loaded it with goods proper for the Levant, he went aboard with the fair Ardelisa, and a youth, who being an orphan, and heir to a considerable estate in Picardy, was left to his care. This youth was Count of Longueville, then about seventeen years of age; a young gentleman of extraordinary parts and beauty: he was tall, delicately leaped, his eyes black and sparkling, and every feature of his face was sweet, yet majestic; he was learned beyond his years, and his soul was full of truth and ingenuity; he had received from the best education the best principles, was brave, generous, affable, constant, and incapable of anything that was base or mean.

These qualities rendered him dear to the Count de Vinevil, who looked on him as his own son, and was pleased to find that Ardelisa and he grew together in affection as they grew in age. She was then fourteen, and the most charming maid nature ever formed; she was tall and slender, fair as Venus, her eyes blue and shining, her face oval, with features and an air so sweet and lovely, that imagination can form nothing more compleatly handsome or engaging. Her mind well suited the fair cabinet that contained it; she was humble, generous, unaffected, yet learned, wise, modest, and prudent above her years or sex; gay in conversation, but by nature thoughtful; had all the softness of a woman, with the constancy and courage of a hero: in fine, her soul was capable of everything that was noble. There needed nothing more than this sympathy of souls, to create the strongest and most lasting affection betwixt this young nobleman and lady; they loved so tenderly, and agreed so well, that they seemed only born for one another.

The evening before the Count de Vinevil lest his castle to go for Turkey, he called the young Count of Longueville into his closet, and spake to him after this manner: 'My lord and son,' said he, 'I am, you see, going to quit my native country, and to trust the faithless seas with, myself and all that is mine: I am going amongst Mahometans, to avoid the seeing those, who have been my vassals, lord it over me; but, my dear child, I am most unwilling to hazard your life, or involve you in whatever misfortunes may befall me.

'You have a noble fortune to enjoy, great relations, such as can, with ease, procure you such an honourable post at court, or in the army, as may give you opportunities of using, to your king and country's glory, those admirable qualifications Heaven has bestowed upon you; which I have not been wanting to improve in you, nor omitted anything that could make you such, as I desired to see you: and, believe me, no news will be more grateful to me in my exile from France, than to hear that you are great and happy. Now then, my dear child, let me prevail with you to consent to our separation: stay here, and be as blessed as I wish you; and if I die in Turkey, and leave Ardelisa an orphan, let her returning find in you such a friend, as you have found in me.' Here he stopped.

The young count, whom respect had till now kept silent, throwing himself at his feet, and embracing his knees with tears, replied, 'My lord and father! what have I done to merit your displeasure, that you should propose such a thing to me? Can you believe me capable of an action so base, as to abandon you and Ardelisa to whom my soul is devoted, out of whose presence I would not live, to gain the Empire of the Eastern world? No, my father, your fortune shall be mine; we will live and die together, nothing but death shall ever separate us. Ardelisa shall be my charge, and I will be to her a lover, husband, and father; and to you a son, in the strictest and most tender sense. Urge me no more to leave you, my soul is filled with horror at the thought.'

The old count taking him up in his arms, embraced him with transport; 'Forgive me, my son,' said he, ''twas the excess of my affection made me fear to hazard the life of what I loved so well; may Heaven prosper our voyage, and reward you with a long life and safe return to France, when I am gone to rest: And may Ardelisa make you just returns, and be to you as great a blessing as you are to me. Let us now go to take our repose, and with the rising-sun, we'll set out; all things are ready, the wind is fair, and in another country we will try to improve that fortune we shall never be able here to better.

The next morning the good old count, young Longueville, and the fair Ardelisa, left the castle, attended with many friends, who accompanied them to the ship, where they were all handsomely treated with a dinner: After which they took leave, with many tears, and good wishes. The old count's servants expressed themselves in so moving a manner, that it would have drawn tears from the most savage heart; nor was there one of them, but did beseech him to let them go with him, though he had taken care to recommend and provide for every one of them, having, left pensions to those who were grown old in his service. He thanked them tenderly, and dismissed them all but four, which were Nannetta, a maid, who had brought up Ardelisa, and governed his house ever since he had been a widower; Bonhome, his old steward and secretary; Manne and Joseph, a young maid and boy, who had been bred up in his family. And now, with a fair wind that evening, they hoisted sail, on the 12th day of March, in the year 1702/3 and, having a prosperous voyage, reached the desired port, arriving at Constantinople, May the 1st.

So soon as they came to an anchor, the old count, who best knew the customs of the place, taking the captain of the vessel, went ashore to visit some French merchants, to whom he brought letters, and to pay the usual compliments to the Bassa of the port, and French consul; leaving the young count with Ardelisa, whom the disorder of a sea-voyage had so much indisposed, that she was scarce able to rise off the bed: 'Now my charming dear,' said the lover, 'we are arrived at a strange country, where we shall no more see Christian churches, where religion shows itself in splendour, and God is worshipped with harmony and neatness; but odious mosques, where the vile impostor's name is echoed through the empty quires and vaults; where cursed

Mahometans profane the sacred piles, once consecrate to our Redeemer, and adorned with shining saints and ornaments, rich as piety itself could make them.

'Alas! alas! dear Ardelisa, what will our father's ambition and resentments cost both him and us? My boding soul seems to forewarn me, that we here shall meet some dire misfortunes: The wealth we have brought with us, may perhaps occasion our undoing; but more, your beauty, should some lustful Turk, mighty in slaves and power, once see that lovely face; what human power could secure you from his impious arms, and me from death! Let me intreat you, as you prize your virtue, and my life, show not yourself in public; let the house conceal you, till divine Providence delivers us from hence.'

Ardelisa, who was from his discourse made too sensible of what she had to fear, shedding some tears, replied, 'My dear lord, I did not dare to tell my father what I thought of this design; but I, like you, have had a dread ever since we left our native land, I shall be wholly governed by you in all things, and rather chuse to confine myself from all conversation, than give you the least disquiet: but, alas! should my father's new undertakings, his trading, occasion your absence from me, what must I do? Or who shall protect me from the *infidels* insolence?'

At these words, she remained silent, a flood of tears interrupting; whilst he folding her in his arms, sighed deeply, and just as he was going to speak, was prevented, by Bonhome's entering the cabin to inform him, that the boat was returned, with a message from his master, that they should come ashore, and that he only should stay aboard, to see the cargo of the ship unloaded: my lord likewise,' continued he, 'desires that you, Madam, will take care to bring, in your own hand, the little cabinet of jewels; you will find him at a French merchant's house, where you are to continue, till my lord has taken a house.'

Nannetta and the young lord assisting, Ardelisa arose, and was led to the side of the ship, and he descending into the boat, received his mistress into his arms and with the faithful Nannetta and Joseph, landed. They were by the seamen conducted to the merchant's house, where they found the Count de Vinevil, and were received and entertained with all the kindness and magnificence imaginable. Here they continued for about a month, in which time a handsome house was taken, and furnished, all the goods got out of the ship, brought ashore, and safely put into warehouses; the greatest part of which goods were quickly sold to the Turks, by means of the French consul and merchant.

The Count de Vinevil, at their leaving his house, made handsome presents to Monsieur de Joyeuxe, his lady, and servants; and he and she had conceived the highest esteem and friendship that is possible for him, his daughter, and the young lord. And now the count settled, and thus acquainted, and assisted, began to be extremely pleased with his voyage and success, and to resolve upon continuing in this place the rest of his days. Ardelisa carefully avoided going abroad, whilst her father, and lover, visited, managed, and dispatched all the affairs with the merchants: but so many *bashaws*, and persons of quality, came to her father's to traffic for European goods, that she could not avoid being sometimes seen. Amongst these, Mahomet, the captain of the port's son, a chief officer in the *sultan's* guards, was so charmed with her beauty, that he became passionately in love with her; and knowing that her father (being a Christian) would never consent to her being his, he concealed his affection, resolving to wait for an opportunity to steal her away, or take her by force.

In the meantime, he sent her several presents of considerable value, by a slave, whom he ordered to watch the young count's going home at noon, and to ask for her before him, and in case he was refused the sight of her, to deliver the present and letter to the count for her. This he did, to render the count and her uneasy, having been informed that he was to marry Ardelisa. These letters had no name to them, but were very amorous, and contained all the passionate expressions in which a lover could declare his passion. This rendered both the old lord, and young, very uneasy; but above all, Ardelisa, who foresaw her ruin approaching. One day the same slave comes as usual, bringing a letter in a silver basket of choice sweetmeats, in the midst of which was placed a gold box, under the letter: this he delivered to the old lord, for his daughter, who now kept in her chamber, and would no more be seen by strangers.

Longueville offered the slave a large reward, if he would reveal his master's name and quality. The slave surlily answered, 'Do you take me for a Christian, that I should betray my trust? A true believer keeps his word. My master, when he thinks fit, will take what he is pleased to love: Ardelisa shall then know her happiness. Till he reveal it himself; not all the wealth, the damning gold, that would procure a set of courtiers great enough to depose a Christian king, or to create two new ones, should seduce me to reveal his secret; though I am sure to fall a victim by his hand, whenever he is displeased, or would divert himself with dooming me to die. Farewell Christian, take care, and blush to think we both despise your faith and you.'

He left them much amazed; they went to Ardelisa in her chamber, and there opening the gold box, they found inclosed the picture of a young Turk, set round with diamonds of great price. Just at this instant the old lord was called by Nannetta to the French consul, who wanted to speak with him; he leaving the room, the young count throwing himself at his mistress's feet, said, 'Now, my Ardelisa, my prophetic fears are verified, now what course shall we take? Why does Christianity forbid me to prevent your ruin and my own by a noble death? Where shall we fly to? Oh! now deny me not one last request; this night, this hour, prevent my dishonour, and let us marry. Stay not, for a foolish modesty, till you are ravished from me; then we may with honour go together, wherever cruel fate shall drive us.'

Here he embraced her tenderly, and she replied, 'My dear lord, I am at my father's and your dispose, I will no longer deny you anything. May Heaven prosper our virtuous union, and preserve my person always yours.'

At these words the old lord entered the room, to inform them what the consul was come about: 'He tells me,' said he, 'that he is secretly advertised, that there is some design of seizing our ship as it lies in the harbour, by means of some Turkish *bassa*, but he can't yet discover who; and counsels me to send you, my son, immediately aboard, with what goods we have proper for the Spanish trade, and that you sail for the first port there, or in Italy, which you may reach in few days, and stay there till I and my daughter can secretly get off with the remainder of our effects, which he will dispose of for us as his own. Now therefore, my dear children, let us resolve what to do; too late I see my rashness, for which I know you must condemn me: but forgive me, and reproach me not, say what's best to be done?'

The young lord answered, 'My honoured father, first make Ardelisa mine, send for the consul's priest, and marry us, that I may not be so wretched to lose her unenjoined. Next let us go aboard in the dead of the night, and leave this fatal place.'

'Alas!' answered the count, 'my son, that is impossible, your first request is just, and shall be instantly complied with; but what you last advise is impracticable. You know no ship can go into this port, or out, but must first pass examination; they will not stop you, but rather will be pleased with your absence. You therefore can with safety carry off what is most valuable of our effects, and stay at some port, to which we will follow you; from thence we will return to France?'

'No, my father,' said the young lord, 'I can't consent to leave you, the consequence of that must be her ruin, and your death; but this I will do, I will this night go on board the ship with our best effects, under pretence of going to trade; thus I shall pass safely out of the port, at some distance from which I will lie at anchor, till you and Ardelisa come to me, which you shall do in this manner:

'Tomorrow in the afternoon you shall borrow the consul's boat, pretending you are going to take the air on the water for pleasure, so you may get an opportunity of escaping to me.'

This the old count agreed to, and the same evening the priest made the lovely Ardelisa wife to the generous Longueville, the time and circumstances requiring haste and secrecy. After supper the servants packed up what was least cumbersome, and most valuable; the consul accompanied the young lord to the *bassa* of the port's house, who easily granted them the passports proper for Longueville's departure with the ship and goods. In the night he took leave of his bride and father, with much concern and disorder: 'Now,' said he, 'my charming Ardelisa, whom Heaven has this happy day made mine, I am going from you for some tedious hours, which I shall pass with an impatience and concern which words cannot express: May angels guard you and conduct you to my longing arms again; but if some dreadful chance prevents our meeting, remember both your duty to yourself and me, permit not a vile *infidel* to dishonour you, resist to death, and let me not be so compleatly cursed, to hear you live, and are debauched.

'My soul is filled with unaccustomed fears; forgive me, Ardelisa, I know your virtue's strong, though you are weak, but force does oft prevail. We are now on the crisis of our fate, 'tis a bold venture that I run to leave you here; but if I stay, we are sure of ruin. To keep you, I must leave you; in Providence is all my hope: if we do meet no more, to God I'll dedicate the wretched hours I shall survive you, and never know a second choice.'

At these words he took her in his arms, whilst she, all drowned in tears, said, 'Why, my dear lord, do you anticipate misfortunes? Why doubt that Providence which has preserved us coming hither, and will, I hope, prevent our ruin? Fear not my virtue, I'm resolved never to yield whilst life shall last. I applaud your resolution, and shall prove I'm worthy you. Go, since there is no other way to save us, and by these fond delays waste not the time fate points us out for our escape, before the vicious *infidel* gets knowledge of our design.'

At this he loosed her from his arms, and, turning from her, wiped the falling drops from his eyes, whilst the old count embraced him with all the tenderness of friendship, and such affection as fathers have for only sons, saying, 'A thousand blessings follow you, my son, and prosper what we do.'

At these words the young lord bowed, and went to the boat, followed by the boatswain only, the captain and part of the men being gone before on board. He arrived safe into the ship, and fell down at break of day, passing the castles, into the road, where he cast anchor.

Chapter 2

And now the sun rising, the young lord began to count each minute, still looking out to see if the wished-for boat appeared; but Providence, that was resolved to try his faith and virtue, determined to separate him and Ardelisa. A dreadful storm arose at noon, so violent, that cables could no longer hold the labouring vessel, the anchors broke their hold, the ship was drove into the open seas, and in few hours lost sight of all the Turkish coast. Eighteen days they sailed, and then got sight of Leghorne, into which they gladly put, to get refreshments, and repair the shattered vessel, which had loft all her masts and rigging.

Here they were constrained to stay to refit fourteen days more; and then, contrary to the captain's advice, Longueville, whose uneasy state of mind it is impossible for words to describe, commanded them to return to Constantinople, leaving; here, with the French consul, the money and goods they had brought: from Turkey, for which place they again set sail; where we shall leave them pursuing their voyage, and return to the old count and Ardelisa. No sooner was the young lord gone aboard, but the Count de Vinevil reflecting upon their danger, told Ardelisa, 'He did not think it advisable for her to stay that night in the house:' So he called Nannetta and Joseph, and bid them go with her to the consul's, whither he would come in the morning, to consult how to accomplish what they designed.

She much intreated her father to go with her; but he answered, 'No, my dear child, it is noways safe for me to leave the house; for should the *bassa* of the port send spies, my presence would prevent their suspecting our design of going away; if you are asked for, I can plead your being in bed, as a just excuse for your not appearing; me they have no reason to hate.'

These reasons made her (though with great reluctance) consent to go without him; shedding a flood of tears, she embraced him, saying, '*Adieu*, my dear lord and father, may the attending angels keep us, and blast our enemies bad designs against us.'

He blessed her, and they parted, never, alas! to meet again, for fate had so decreed. The count and servants busied in packing up what yet remained in the house, Ardelisa having carried only the small cabinet of jewels, with about a thousand *pistoles* in hers and the maids' pockets, they shut all the doors and windows fast, to avoid discovery; but it was not long before somebody knocked with such fury at the gate, that they all stood looking with amazement on one another. At last the count bid them go see what was the matter: The servant, who went to the gate, demanded civilly, Who was there? thinking it might be the young lord returned, or Ardelisa; but he was soon answered by the enraged Mahomet, who having been informed by his slave of what had passed betwixt Longueville and him, was resolved to gratify his love and revenge together.

In order to which, he designed the seizing the ship to prevent their escape, and then caused this rumour to be spread, in hopes it would drive Longueville to fly, with her, that so he might have a just pretence to seize them; but finding he went alone, and that the lady and her father staid behind, he resolved to give them this visit in the dead of the night, not doubting to find them defenceless: and besides, whatever violence he should then commit, would be better concealed, being not willing to occasion a quarrel betwixt his emperor and France; or what was more certain, lose his own life by the bowstring, if justice were required by the French ambassador. To prevent all which fatal consequences, he determined to kill the old lord and servants, carry off the lady, and leave none in the house to betray him. With this villainous intent he came, attended with his bloody vassals, whom the fear of death had so possessed, that they dared not fail to act whatever villainy he commanded. Mahomet bid the servant open the gate that moment, or he would force his way in with fire and sword,

At these words the poor boy fled into the house, to give his lord notice; but the fatal message had scarce past his trembling lips, when they heard the gate broke open, and saw the merciless Turks enter the house; Mahomet crying, 'Secure the Christian dogs; by Mahomet! if one escape alive, besides the lady, your forfeit lives shall answer it.'

At these words they laid hands on the amazed servants, with their drawn scimitars in hand. The old lord, whose noble soul disdained to shrink, stepped boldly to him, saying, 'Insolent lord! what have we done to injure thee? Why are we treated thus? Natives of France, and friends to your great emperor and you; if I, or mine have injured you, you have a right, as well as we, to procure justice on us: speak, what is our crime?'

Mahomet clapping his dagger to his breast, replied, 'do you ask questions, fool? Show me to your daughter's bed, and, with her honour, buy that life, which I, on any other terms, won't spare. Make me happy in her arms, and silently conceal all that shall pass this night, or I will plunge this dagger in your heart, leave nothing here but speechless ghosts, and murdered carcases, then with Ardelisa I'll return to my own palace, and there force her to give all her treasures up to me, and glut myself in her embraces.'

The Count de Vinevil, with a look that spoke disdain and rage, replied, 'No, villain! Ardelisa never shall be thine, not empires, or the dread of any death thy cursed fury could invent, should make me but in thought consent to such a deed; life is a trifle weighed with infamy; the God I serve shall both preserve her virtue, and revenge my death: My daughter is not educated so, and will, I know, prefer a noble death to such dishonour.'

Mahomet enraged, cried, 'Slaves! go, search the chambers, and bring her naked from her bed, that I may ravish her before the dotard's face, and then send his soul to Hell.'

At this the old lord smiled, and lifting up his hands to Heaven, cried, ''Tis just, my God, that I, who have thus exposed my child, should first feel the misery, my rashness merits, but do not let her perish here: preserve her, Great Creator, from the lust and rage of these vile *infidels*, and let thy angels guide her home again; let my blood expiate all my sins, and give me courage in this great extremity.'

At these words the Turks, who had in vain searched all the house, assured their lord, that

Adelisa was not there: 'Die then,' said he, to the old count, 'here I'll begin my vengeance.' At these words the cruel Mahometan plunged his dagger into his breast; at which the old lord fell, crying, 'Mercy my Saviour!' The slaves soon dispatched the innocent servants, who in vain implored their pity; then they proceeded to plunder the house, after which they shut the doors after them, and departed: Mahomet swearing, he would find Ardelisa, or destroy all the Frenchmen in Constantinople.

Chapter 3

Whilst this tragic scene was acting, the innocent Ardelisa, having recommended herself to Heaven, was sleeping in her bed, and dreamt her father called her, in a distant room, to come to him. She fancied she ran thither, and saw him all over blood and wounds, at which he vanished from her; then found herself with strangers in a wild desolate place, where they were in great distress for food, and knew not where to go; she starting, waked, and, in much disorder, finding it was day, she rose, calling Nannetta, who was up already: 'Oh Nanon,' said she, 'I've had a dismal dream, make haste, and send Joseph to see if my dear father's stirring yet.'

The maid was going, when the consul's lady, entering the chamber all in tears, said, 'Dear Ardelisa, I have news to tell you, that a virtue less than yours could not support, now summon all your reason and religion to your aid, and to that God submit, who has this dreadful night preserved you.'

'Alas! Madam, I too well understand you,' she replied, 'my father's murdered.' She at these words fell into a swoon, out of which, with difficulty, they recovered her; returning to life, she fell into such moving lamentations, such extreme, though modest sorrow, that would have made even the cruel *infidels*, could they have seen her, melt, and feel remorse.

The lady comforted her all she could, telling her, she must now think of her own preservation in order to which, the boy and maid must not be seen to stir abroad: 'Says the, Monsieur de Joyeuxe, who living near your father, first heard the dreadful news, just now sent a servant to acquaint us, that your father and you were murdered, with all the servants, and the house plundered; but that nobody could tell by whom. Those that have done this hellish deed, will doubtless lie in wait for you. Let us permit this report of your death to spread, that we may get you secretly conveyed to some distant port, from whence you may get off safely.'

'Alas! Madam,' said she, 'your goodness will expose you and your family to ruin; were I so ungrateful as to accept it, my staying in your house would undo you. No, Madam, God forbid I should involve you in my unhappy fate, it is my ruin the fierce villain seeks, my fatal face has been our destruction. Had I not left my father, we had nobly died together; the only favour I can ask of you, with honour, is, to let me depart e'er I'm discovered: Procure me but the habit of a man, the boy and I will venture to feign ourselves belonging to some ship that now lies in the road; if we are taken, we can only die; if we escape, money shall bribe the captain, where we get aboard, to put us safe into my dear lord's ship.'

' No, Madam,' replied the lady, 'your life's too precious to be risked in such a manner. We have a country-house within thirty miles of this city, at a village called Domez-Dure, thither I will this night send you and your servants; you and Nannetta shall be dressed like men, and Joseph shall black his face and hands like Domingo our slave: so you shall feign yourself very sick, and in our horse-litter shall be conveyed thither; there you may continue in safety, till a fit opportunity presents to get you off: our boat shall about noon go off, and acquaint your lord with all that has happened, and bid him put off to sea, and make away for some other port, where he may, some days hence, drop in with his boat, and receive you. Perhaps, by that time, he whom we suspect to have done this villainy, the Bassa Ibrahim's son, who, it seems, was seen last night attended with his slaves late in the streets, may be commanded hence to the army, and then you may go away safely.'

This offer Ardelisa accepted of, with many acknowledgments, and the consul's lady left the room, to acquaint the consul what they had determined to do, leaving Ardelisa on her bed, overwhelmed with grief. The maid soon packed up the things, men's habits were brought, and she and her lady, who seemed half dead, dressed, and put into the litter, with Joseph walking by the side, so black, that he appeared a perfect Moor. They arrived safe at the country-house, where Ardelisa fell sick, and remained much longer than she expected. The same day she went from Constantinople, the storm prevented the consul's boat from giving the Lord Longueville notice of what was past, and he was drove out to sea, as is before recited.

Chapter 4

Many spies were employed by Mahomet to get intelligence of Ardelisa; and the same evening of the day she went away, the consul's house was searched, under pretence of his servants having concealed a Turkish slave, whom the *bassa* of the port pretended his son had lost; so that it was a great Providence for her, and the family, she was not there. Whilst she lay sick at Domez-Dure, Joseph, the fictitious black, used frequently to go about the town for provisions, and became well acquainted with all the country thereabouts. It chanced one day, that as he was going to a village near the sea, he saw some troops of Turks going along the road; and fearing to be questioned, he retired into a thick wood: which, viewing well, he thought he perceived something like a house; but so covered with trees and bushes, that he could scarce discern it, curiosity made him venture to go farther, and coming into the midst of the wood, he saw a small cottage, into which he entered by a door that stood ajar.

He stopped awhile to hear if any creature moved in it; but finding all things in silence, he entered and there found two little, but convenient rooms, with a little table, three low stools, a fireplace, some earthen-dishes, a knife, fork, and spoon of silver, and a little pot; and in the inner room, a mattress, laid on some rushes, with a quilt and sheets; a box, in which he found some linen, and some books of devotion in the Latin tongue, with a crucifix: but no person being there, he concluded some Christian slave had escaped, and lived there concealed.

The soldiers, as he supposed, being now gone, he returned to the road, pursued his journey, and went home, relating to his lady and Nannetta what he had seen in the wood; adding, 'My honoured lady, should we be pursued hither, it were a most safe retreat for you to fly to.'

Some days they continued undisturbed, Joseph frequently going to the consul's, to learn news of his lord, but in vain. Sometimes Ardelisa tormented herself, with thinking he perished in the dreadful storm; but, on reflection, thought again, some token of the wreck would sure have appeared, being so near the shore. Then she concluded he was drove to sea. But, at length, Joseph going to the consul's, chanced to overtake a slave, who was going the same way; with whom falling in talk, he asked him, whither he was going, and from whence he came?

'From Dormez-Dure,' said he, 'where I have been to view a Frenchman's country-house, and have found what I wanted, for which my lord will pay me nobly.'

I don't doubt these words struck Joseph like a thunderbolt, he, recollecting himself, said, 'Friend, will you drink a dram with me; here,' said he, pulling a little bottle full of good wine out of his pocket, 'come let us sit down under this tree, and rest awhile.'

The Turk suspecting nothing, and tempted with the opportunity of drinking wine, consented; and Joseph, as he lifted the bottle to his head, stabbed him to the heart with his knife: 'Go, dog,' said he, 'go bear thy message to the prince of Hell, there look reward.'

The Turk cried, ''Tis just, Great Prophet! Youth, I envy thee the deed; so should the fool be served that tells his master's secret: much Christian blood I've spilt, and thou hast punished me. Tell Ardelisa, if you do, as I suppose, belong to her, she is not safe at Dormez-Dure; I can no more.' He in few minutes died; whilst Joseph, turning back, fled, to forewarn his lady to be gone.

He had no sooner told the story, but a deathlike paleness overspread her face, and poor Nannetta could not speak: 'Dear God,' cried Ardelisa, 'where shall I fly? what must I do?'

'Madam,' cried the faithful boy, 'this night fly to the cottage in the wood; the slave, prevented from delivering his message, gains us time.'

'But, alas!' said she, 'whom may we find in that sad place?'

'None but a Christian,' he replied, 'for such I'm sure he must be, by what I saw, if anybody lives there now. I will go hide myself in the wood, and wait, to see if any one come in or out, and speak to the person; and if I see any, then return to let you know what is best to be done. Here we must not stay much longer, the dead slave will be found, and some other sent; it is enough that this place is suspected, and God, by my hand, has given us this time to think and escape.'

Having eat something, he departed, leaving Ardelisa much distracted in her thoughts. He had not waited long in the wood, beore he saw a man come forth of the cottage, in the habit of a *Santoin*, or religious Turk, with sandals on his feet, his face pale and meagre; he had in his hand a piece of bread, he lift up his eyes to Heaven, sighed deeply, crossed his breast, and began to eat. Joseph, who at first feared he had been a Mahometan, was now overjoyed; and stepping from behind the tree, where he had stood concealed, threw himself at his feet, saying, 'Christian and friend, fear me not, but let us go in and talk, and I will shew you a way to preserve lives that may be of great use to you.'

At these words the hermit viewed him with much attention; and though greatly surprised to hear him speak, yet as a man, to whom death itself would not be terrible, answered, 'Speak on,'

'Father,' said the boy, ''tis dangerous for us to talk here.' At this they entered the house, where he told the hermit, that a Christian lady, a maid-servant, and himself, begged·to be sheltered there, till they might find means to get off at a sea-port, to return to France.

'To France,' said the hermit, 'Moor, for why?'

'Because we are all natives of that place,' replied the boy.

'Your lady's name,' said the hermit.

'My dear lord was de Vinevil,' the youth replied, 'and I a luckless lad, who here have lost him.' At these words he wept.

'Alas! sweet boy,' said he, 'I knew him well; all that are his, I love, and, will refuse no kindness to.'

The boy, at these words, looking earnestly on him, knew him to be a priest born in Picardy, who went a missionary to Japan about ten years before: 'Father Francis,' said he,' how blessed am I to see you, though in this sad place? How came you here? and by what Providence preserved?'

The joyful priest embracing him, perceived he was no black, and said thus: 'A cruel storm, in our return to France, drove our vessel on this coast, where a few of us were preserved from death, but not from cruel usage: We were but five, and soon were separated; three died, I and my Brother James a Turk brought to Constantinople, under pretence of kindness; then demanded a ransom most exorbitant, which we protesting that we could not pay, he loaded us with chains, threw us into a nasty vault, where we remained, sustained with bread and water, till he feared our deaths. Then he removed us to his gardens in the country, where he made us work as slaves; till, weary of our lives, we resolutely leaped the wall, and fled; and meeting with this wood in our way, staid here to rest:, not being able to go farther.

'My Brother, stripping off his coat, even naked, entered the village begging, to prevent our perishing for food, pretending sanctity and vows to Mahomet, The charitable villagers supplying his wants with food and raiment, he returned loaded to me. Thus were we encouraged to erect this homely cell, with boughs and boards we begged, to shield us from the winter-rains and cold. Thus we lived three months together, when he fell sick, and died; for six months since I've lived by begging as before, but never discovered where I dwell: I go each morning forth, and roam about, or sometimes sit under some tree to rest, but don't return hither till night?'

The boy, thus satisfied, told all that related to his lady; telling him withal, they had much treasure, and that he might, with less suspicion than they, visit the next port, and find a way both to deliver himself and them; and that he expected his lord in a ship belonging to them, of which he should have intelligence from Constantinople.

He answered, 'Child, you need not urge these reasons, since God, who has preserved me here so long, requires that I should assist others in distress. Go, bring your lady hither, and may the angels guide and keep us whilst we stay, and give us opportunity to escape from hence. Be gone; I must, as usual, go my round, and shall be back at night.' He gave his blessing to the youth, and so they parted.

Chapter 5

Joseph returning home, gave his lady an account of the surprising things he had met with in the wood; and she, lifting her hands to Heaven, said, 'Now, my Great Deliverer, whose Providence has provided me this retreat, keep me and mine; guided by thee, I cannot be unfortunate.'

At night they left the house, taking their money and jewels; and getting safely to the wood, found the good father waiting at his cottage-door, who received them with a joy and civility suiting the polite education he had received. He embraced Ardelisa with a concern, that called the blood into his pale cheeks, and shown how dear her father was to him: 'Welcome,' said he. 'Daughter of my dearest friend; this place, and the poor master of it, is devoted to your service.'

Leading her in, he seated her, having a poor lamp burning: He had decked his little cell as well as he could, having, in one corner of the out-room, laid a bed of rushes for the boy and him to lie on; and made a door to the inner-room of plaited rushes, to render it more private, that she and her maid, who wore their men's clothes, might undress; and rise, without being seen. He then reached a bottle of wine, which he had kept there, with some bread, for fear he should fall sick, and not be able to go out some days; with a cup they drank, and, after some discourse, the lady retired to rest.

The next morning the boy and priest went forth early: At noon the lad returned, bringing provisions for three days. They buried their gold in a hole, under their bed, in the inner-room; and their jewels behind the cottage in a hollow tree, covering the box so carefully with leaves and earth, which they filled up the hollow with, that it was almost impossible for others to find them; and in the evening the boy set out for Constantinople, to see if there was any news of his lord and the ship, as also to inform the consul of their departure from his country-house, and new habitation.

The lady and her maid thus left alone, passed the time in prayer and discourse, wherein they conversed so piously, and expressed themselves so excellently, that it is pity the world is not favoured with a recital of all they said: for Nannetta was a maid whose education had been noble, her birth not mean, and indeed Ardelisa owed to her, in great part, the exalted principles and sentiments she possessed, she having had the care of her in her infancy; they eat together, and Ardelisa forgot all distinctions, only Nannetta's respect increased with her mistress's favour. At night they were glad to see the good father return home; he told them, he had learned what ought to fill their souls with fresh acknowledgments to God, who had that day miraculously preserved them.

'So soon,' says he, 'as I entered the village, I found the people all in an uproar, and their eyes and steps were all directed to the house you left, where a band of Turkish soldiers were rifling and searching all the rooms and gardens, headed by a man, who, by the respect they showed him, seemed of no small quality. I staid at some distance to observe what past, and, after some time, saw them depart in much disorder, and he in the utmost rage, swearing by Mahomet, *he would destroy the village if he found you not soon.* The people stared upon one another, and separated. I asked no questions, but, as usual walked forward, seeming to mumble my orisons, and receiving the alms of those who called me. I would advise you, Madam,' continued he, 'not to stir forth of the house some days; I will go to the next sea-port, to see if any ship be there belonging to Spain, France, Holland, or England, in either of which we may escape, after Joseph is returned.'

Ardelisa then besought him to take five pieces of gold, to serve his necessities: 'No, my child,' said he, 'the Providence of God shall provide for me, money would render me suspected, this habit is my passport here, I pray God to keep you in my absence, and prosper my journey.'

They supped, prayed, and went to repose, and before day the hermit departed.

Chapter 6

At the end of three days Joseph returned to his lady, and related the unhappy news he brought after this manner:

'My dear lady,' said he, 'the consul and his lady are in health, are much transported at your safety, and send you word my lord was well some days ago, and is so still, they hope.'

'Is he then alive, and here?' she cried; 'then I am happy.'

'He was well,' replied the boy, 'and was here, but is departed. Madam: his ship was drove so far out to sea in the storm, that he was obliged to make the first port, which proved Leghorne, where the ship was repaired, and victualled again. Thence he returned to Constantinople, but entered not the port, fearing discovery. At evening he sent his boat ashore, ordering the crew to report, when asked, that he was dead, and that the captain of the ship came there only to trade. The coxswain was ordered to go to Monsieur de Joyeuxe's house, to enquire for my old lord and you. They there informed him, that he, you, and all the family were murdered the same fatal night he left you, and that he counselled my lord to get off the coast immediately, and return to France, where Monsieur de Joyeuxe and his family hoped e'er long to see him, designing to return thither next year.

'The coxswain returned to the ship with this message, upon which they set sail, and are doubtless gone home to France. The consul heard nothing of the ship's arrival, till Monsieur de Joyeuxe sent him this account. The consul has sent a letter by the ambassador's packet, which he hopes will meet him in Picardy, to inform him, that you are living, and the consul will take care to inform you of the first opportunity to get off for France: meantime he is ready to serve you in all things, and hopes it will not be long before he shall be able to send you word, that your enemy is gone to the army, and that you may safely return to Constantinople.'

'Alas! my God,' answered Ardelisa, 'when will my sorrows end? Thankful I am that my dear lord still lives, but why did he depart without me? That he lives said I! Alas! Grief has perhaps e'er this finished his life and sorrows, and I have little or no hopes of ever seeing him again.'

Here tears stopped her from proceeding, and poor Joseph and Nannetta strove to comfort her all they were able.

The same night the good priest returned, but brought no news of any ship; to him they related what the boy had learned at the city. He counselled Ardelisa to trust in Providence, and rest satisfied: 'My dear children,' said he, 'this life is attended with nothing but uncertainties, and full of sorrows; the enjoyments of it are short and transitory. In all our affections and friendships here with one another, we should have a future view, and manifest that love, by being instrumental to one another's eternal welfare. Our wise Creator inclined us to love one another so tenderly, with a more glorious design than that of only propagating mankind; it was to render us useful to each other in the greatest concern of life, that of obtaining eternal happiness; whilst this is our aim, no separation can be grievous, nor the death of what we love cast us down.

'He that leads the person he pretends to love into sin, acts the devil's part, and is his greatest enemy. I remember my dead friends as my greatest treasures, which I hope to enjoy, when we wake together; so you Ardelisa must do, and if Heaven denies you the sight of a loved husband here, consider, in a little while, he will be restored to you so improved, that your joy and friendship shall be eternal: this those who live as, and are Christians, are certain of.'

'What Heavenly sounds are these?' said Ardelisa: 'your words convey a balm into my sickly wounded soul, have stilled my passions, and cured my frailty: yes, Father, I submit, and death itself will, I hope, find me well prepared.'

These heavenly conversations they continued daily, and, betwixt the pious Father and the boy, were well supplied with necessary food. Ardelisa and the maid ventured not out at any distance from the house: One evening they were surprised with hearing a hollowing in the wood; they looked upon one another as persons apprehensive of some great misfortune; but the noise coming nearer, the good Father being not returned home, the boy went boldly out, and saw something like a man on horseback. He went up to him, saying, 'In the name of God, what would you have?'

This he spoke in the Turkish language; but the man replied in French, 'Are you not Joseph? If so, bring me to your lady.'

The boy said, 'Who do you belong to?'

'The consul,' said he.

At these words he knew him, and said. 'Domingo, you're welcome.'

The horseman taking his hand, said, 'How fares your lady? Mahomet, her enemy, is gone for the army, a French ship is in the harbour, and I have brought the horse-litter to our country-house, with horses for the good Father, you, and I. Bring your lady thither presently, and tomorrow we'll return to Constantinople.'

By this time they came to the house, from whence the servant returned to the village; and the little family packing up what they had brought, designing to leave one of the consul's servants to wait the Father's return, and bring him to them at Constantinople, departed soon after, leaving the lucky mournful cottage destitute of inhabitants, where they had lived three months without disturbance.

Chapter 7

Full of joy and hopes, they cheerfully walked towards Domez-Dure; but nothing is to be depended on in this world. A great Turkish general, named Osmin, who was going to Constantinople, with many attendants, chose the coolness of the night to travel, as is very customary in the heat of summer, met these poor travellers, ordered them to be stopped, and seized. They told him they were two poor French lads, and the black, who were cast ashore in a boat coming from a ship for provisions, and were making their way to Constantinople, where their ship was sailed for, to go in search of her, or apply to the French consul to be sent home, if the ship was lost, or sailed thence.

This Ardelisa, who was orator for the rest, said; but the charms of her face, and the eloquence of her tongue, so enchanted Osmin, that he resolved to secure her for himself. He told them, they were slaves, run away from their owners, he supposed; however, he would, carry them to Constantinople, and there see the truth of what they said. So ordered they should be chained together, and walk in the middle of his troop, commanding that no violence should be offered to them, or anything they had about them taken away.

They had not gone far before Ardelisa fainted, being unable to support her inward grief, and the fatigue of the march: At which the general was alarmed and feeing the concern her companions were in, guessed her to be the most noble of the three: he therefore ordered her to be put in a horse-litter that attended him; so before day they arrived at his palace, which was at the entering into the city: she, and the boy, and maid were brought in, and locked into a room, where they could only sigh and look upon one another, but dared not talk for fear of being overheard and discovered.

In few moments after they were thus left, the general entered, and addressing himself to Ardelisa, said, 'Lovely boy, or maid, I know not which as yet to call you, fear not: the treatment I shall give you; my heart is made a captive to your eyes, I will enjoy and keep you here, where nothing shall be wanting to make you happy: If you are a man, renounce your faith, adore our prophet, and my great emperor, and I will give you honours and wealth exceeding your imagination: if you're a woman, here are apartments, where painting, downy beds, and habits fit for to cover that soft frame, gardens to walk in, and food delicious, with faithful slaves to wait upon you, invite your stay; where I will feast each sense, and make you happy as mortality can be.'

At these words he clasped her in his arms, and rudely opening her breast, discovered that she was of the soft sex. She, trembling, strove, and, falling at his feet, begged him to kill, or let her go.

'You doubtless are,' said he, 'the beauteous maid, who fled my friend Mahomet's pursuit, for whom he killed your slaves and father; how blessed am I to find you? Your maid, whose tears and blushes has discovered her to me, shall bear you company awhile. I must this moment to the emperor, and shall soon return to sleep within those lovely arms.'

At these words he left the room, and two eunuchs entered, who did lead her and her maid into the garden, and there opening the doors of a beautiful apartment, conducted them in: then leaving them in a lovely room, departed, and soon returned with sherbets of delicate taste, preserved and cold meats, telling them, they should refresh themselves; and showing a rich bedchamber, with closets full of women's clothes, bid them shift, and dress in any of those rich Turkish habits they liked best, none should disturb them. At these words the eunuchs withdrew. Now the distracted maid and her lady, looking upon one another, wept, unable to express their thoughts in words. At length Ardelisa broke silence in this manner: 'Just God! What wilt thou do with us? Direct me now, and help me in this great distress.

'Oh Nannon! advise me: Shall this bold hand destroy the villain when he enters? Sure it can be no sin to save my virtue with his blood? Yes; I am resolved to do it, though I perish. Let his slaves revenge his death on me, and torture me with, all their fury can invent, death's but a trifle in comparison of infamy. Yes; my dear lord commanded me to suffer death, rather than yield to lustful *infidels*, and Christianity enjoins it: Come, let us eat, and, thus resolved, fear nothing. You, my faithful friend, they'll doubtless spare, as being neither young nor beautiful. Pray for me; and if ever you are so happy to see France, and my dear lord again, tell him I have obeyed him, and behaved myself as does become a Christian and his wife.'

She then sat down, looking with such serenity and calmness, as one prepared for all events. They eat and prayed together, and past the night in pious talk, where we shall leave them.

Chapter 8

We now return to Osmin, to show what care Almighty good-ness takes of those who trust in him. The Turk had brought a packet from the grand *vizier* to the *sultan*, the contents of which did so dis-please him, that, according to the barbarous customs of that nation, he wrecked his rage upon the luckless Osmin, commanding him a prisoner to the Seven Towers; where, chained, we leave him to curse his false prophet, and his destiny.

The news of his disgrace soon reached his home; and now the slaves no longer were so careful to watch the doors of his *seraglio*, but, in the morning, left them open; telling the lady, she might have the liberty of the gardens to walk. This was pleasing news to Ardelisa, because she and Nannetta hoped, by this means, to find some way to escape. They thanked the eunuchs who had brought in chocolate for their breakfast; and when they were gone, Adelisa and Nannetta ven-tured into the garden; which was such, as showed that art and nature had there done their utmost, and made it one of the most delightful places eyes ever saw: fountains, and groves, and grottoes, where the sun could never enter; long walks of orange and myrtles, with banks, where flowers of the most lovely kinds, and fragrant scents flood crowded, with pleasure-houses built of Parian marble, and within so wrought and painted, that it appeared an earthly Paradise. Nor did there want large terrace-walks, from whence the eye might be entertained with the full view of that great city, and the noble port, which is one of the most lovely prospects in the world.

They had not walked long here, before they perceived Joseph run-ning towards them; he made a sign to them to retire into one of the grottoes, whither he followed; and so soon as he could recover his breath he embraced his lady's knees, saying, 'My soul is transported, my dear lady, to see you safe; I have news will overjoy you: Last night the villain Osmin was sent by the *sultan* to the Black Tower; amongst the servants I have learned all, and this night will deliver you. I find the servants are very careful of the out-doors and gates, therefore in the night I will set fire to the house, which will put them all into confusion; be you ready to follow me, and I doubt not to conduct you safe to the consul's.'

Ardelisa admired the boy's zeal and love, and said, 'My God, I thank thee; and if I live to see France again, Joseph, you shall know how much I esteem your fidelity,'

They thought it not convenient to talk longer; so Joseph hasted back to the house, being taken little or no notice of by the servants, who were in the greatest concern, expecting their lord's ruin, and consequently a new master, who might perhaps prove more cruel than their old: for it is customary for the *sultan*, when he puts one favourite to death, to give his estate, house, and slaves to another.

The day growing hot, Ardelisa and her maid thought of returning to their apartment to pass the day; when they perceived a lady in Turkish habit, tall, delicately shaped, and a face perfectly beautiful, yet looked melancholy. She started at the sight of them, being in men's clothes, and dressed like Europeans, yet she stood still. At which Ardelisa hasted towards her, and, bowing, spoke to her in French, supposing her some Christian lady, who had, like her, been forced thither: 'Madam,' said she, 'fear not to speak to me, I am, like you, a woman; and if you are a Christian, tell me of what Nation, and how brought here?'

At these words, the lady looking on her attentively, answered, 'Yes, Yes, stranger, I am a Christian, and by birth a Venetian, made captive with many others of our wretched nation, noble virgins, who, like me, have lived too long, being now made slaves to the wild lusts of cruel *infidels*; from which nothing but death can deliver us.'

At these words, Ardelisa embracing her, said, 'Yes; God by me will, I doubt not, this night free us; come with me into that apartment, where I will tell you news, that will not be unwelcome to you.'

They went together, followed by Nannetta, and being seated, Ardelisa told her of Osmin's disgrace, bid her stay with her that day, and at night, she hoped they should be showed a way to escape. 'And now,' said she, 'to make the day seem less tedious, oblige me with the recital of your misfortunes.' To which the lady willingly condescended, and thus began her story.

Chapter 9

My Name is Violetta, I was born in Venice, of a family antient and noble; my father's name was Don Manuel, who did then, and I hope does still, command a man of war for the republic, being honoured with the Order of St. Mark for his great services. My mother is a lady of great goodness and beauty, and descended of one of the most illustrious families of the venetian senators. It pleased God to give them no other children but myself, and one son, who lost his life in that unfortunate day when I was taken.

'He commanded the forces on the coast, and the Turks landing, after a bloody dispute, getting the better by numbers, ravaged the coast; and entering the churches and convents, in one of which my father had placed me to secure me, as most of our nobility had their daughters; they carried us all aboard their ships, with all the treasure their sacrilegious hands had pillaged; and here divided the spoils, presented those of us, whom they liked best, or believed most noble, to the *grand signior* and his favourites: it was my lot to be given to Osmin, and here I have had the misfortune to be kept these two years, being too much esteemed by him.'

Ardelisa interrupting her cried, 'Alas! Madam, are there no more ladies here '

' No,' replied Violetta, 'not at present; there are here sometimes, at least ten more of different nations, some of which are noble as myself, and, in my opinion, more worthy to be loved; but they are all now gone into the country, to a house of pleasure, during Osmin's absence: But as for my part, whether it be that he loves me, as he pretends, more than the rest, or that he fears to trust me hence, I know not; but I was never removed from this place. I have had one son by him, which I secretly baptized, and which it pleased God to take to himself since Osmin went to the army, which is about three months. This is my unfortunate history, I pray Heaven it may end more happily.'

The ladies past the day, with much satisfaction to each other, long-ing for the approaching night.

Chapter 10

Let us now make enquiry after the good priest, who returned not to his cottage till the day after Ardelisa and her servants had left it, being prevented from returning home by the following accident. As he was passing by a wood, in his way home from the sea-side, which he frequently visited, to look out for a ship, he saw a troop of Turks at the head of which was the treacherous Turk, who had used him so cruelly, when he made him and the other good priests his gardeners. He stepped out of the road to avoid being seen, which immediately gave some suspicion to the eagle-eyed Turks, who presently made up to him. This occasioned him to fly from them into the wood, where, looking out for a place to hide himself, he perceived, in the side of a small rising of the ground, a hole big enough for a man to go in at; and, looking curiously into it, saw steps cut in the earth to go down.

His fears inclined him to venture into this place; descending, he came to a door, which was put to, but not fastened; opening it, he entered into a cave, where nature seemed to have played the part of art; it was spacious and clean, a lamp was burning on a table; there stood a large trunk locked, and on a bed of rushes lay a man in a rude habit of beasts' skins, and by him stood an earthen pitcher full of water; he appeared very sick and weak. The good Father drew near to him; at which the man, turning his head, said, with a weak voice, in the Turkish language: 'Stranger, disturb me not, leave me to die in peace.'

The good Father, moved with compassion, answered, 'God forbid I should injure you, I would much rather assist you in all I am able.'

At these words the dying man replied, 'Alas! Turk, thou canst give me no assistance, my Saviour must assist me.'

'Are you then Christian?' said the priest, 'I myself am so; and what is more, a priest: God has doubtless sent me here to you.'

'Then I am happy,' said the penitent; and strait besought him, saying, 'Father, there is bread in that trunk, take it; hear my confession, and make me blessed: let my Lord but visit my soul, and I shall die joyfully.'

The good priest willingly consented, and prepared him for death, as well as the time and place would permit, giving him wine out of a bottle he carried in his pocket; after which he seemed much revived. Then he desired the penitent to relate to him, if he was able, how he came there, and who he was? He answered, 'Father, my strength and life are deficient, in that trunk you'll find a paper, which contains what you desire to know; take that, and what else you will find with it, I thank my God a Christian has it.' Here he returned to prayer, his agonies growing strong, in which he continued till six in the morning, when he died.

The good Father finished his good work, with saying the burial-service over him, and covering him up in his rude habit, and some of the rushes of his bed, went to the trunk, which opening with a key he had given him, he found some very rich linen, and choice books, and a cabinet of great value; which opening, there was a great quantity of gold and jewels, with a crucifix, all diamonds, and, in a corner of the trunk, some church-plate. In the same cabinet a large paper, which, with the help of the lamp, he read, the by his confession he had been partly informed of his life past. The paper contained these words.

Chapter 11

My Name was Don. Fernando de Cardiole, I was by birth a noble Spaniard, and was commander of a galleon; I fell in love with a lady, whose name was Donna Corina, a maid of honour to the queen. She seemed to favour me above all the other pretenders, of which she had many, being a lady of great fortune and beauty; till a young nobleman, who came to court, just returned from his travels, whose name was Don Pedro de Mendoza, made love to her. She grew cold to me, and he rude and insolent; at which, incensed, I watched an opportunity, and had him assassinated: then putting out to sea with my vessel, and not daring to return, steered my course for Turkey; telling the slaves, if they would consent to set me and my treasure, which I had brought on board, safe on the coast of Turkey, I would deliver the ship into their hands, to go where they pleased, which they willingly consented to.

So soon as I came ashore at Gallipoli, I went to the *bassa* of that place, declaring myself a Turk, and offering to discover great secrets to the grand *vizier* of the designs of the Christian princes. I was circumcised, and treated splendidly, sent with great attendance to Constantinople, and there so ingratiated myself with the grand *vizier*, that I was soon entrusted with the command of a ship against the Venetians. There, with the fleet, I did all the mischief I was able, entered and plundered the churches, deflowered noble virgins, and returned much commended, and highly pleased; neither did I fail of reward, being permitted to take what I pleased of the plunder.

I had now a palace of my own, a pension, and *seraglio* of women, and lived in the enjoyment of all earthly delights; but God, who had till now suffered me to go on and continue insensible, awaked my conscience, and I felt such bitter remorse in my soul, that I could take no rest or pleasure. All those things, that I before took delight in, were now hateful to me; after long debates in my own thoughts, I resolved upon what to do: to Spain I could not return, justice would meet me there; shame and guilt forbad me to fly to any Christian country, here my conscience would not let me stay: I determined therefore to leave all my fortune, house, and family, and to retire to some lonely place, where I might spend my days and nights in solitude and prayer; where I might, with penitence, tears, fasting, and prayers, reconcile myself to my offended God. I had a trusty slave, named Ibrahim, who I acquainted with my design of retiring; he found this wood, and contrived the cave you here do find me in; and one evening he brought me hither, with what wealth you here will find, which I reserved to provide for me, if I should live to weak old age.

Once in five days he comes to me, for I have given him his freedom, and enough to live at ease; my fortune and command a favourite Turk enjoys. This servant brings me food, such as will keep; bread, cordials, and dried-fruits, for flesh I never taste, nor wine, 'Tis now a month since he was here, by which I guess him sick or dead. It is now ten days since I was seized with a fever and ague; I find myself so weak, that I am apprehensive I shall die: I therefore write this, that if any Christian finds me here, he may be warned of sinning, as I have done, and may be enabled, by the wealth herewith to procure a happier condition for himself, than I can ever hope for in this world.

Christian, remember you must one day die,
And unto judgment come as well as I.

Chapter 12

Father Francis read this paper with great concern, and, taking the cabinet, left the dismal place, not doubting but his pursuers were gone, and the coast clear; in which he was not deceived: for they having fought for him some time in vain, desisted, and pursued their journey to Constantinople. He got safe to the cottage, but was much surprised to find Ardelisa and her servants gone: one while he imagined they were discovered and seized; but, upon second thoughts, that seemed very improbable. Then he began to think they were gone for Constantinople; he passed that day in much anxiety, and sat musing all night. At last he resolved to go for Constantinople, to the consul's, where he thought, if anywhere, he should hear of them.

Accordingly, early in the morning, he see out, carrying with him the cabinet he found in the Spaniard's cave, and arrived safely at the consul's house; where, having related the cause of his coming, and name, he was kindly received: but neither the consul, nor his servants, could tell what was become of Ardelisa, Nannetta, or the boy. Domingo and the servants, with the horse-litter, were returned from Domez-Dure, having waited there till they were weary, Domingo having first gone back to the cottage, and not found them, 'We conclude,' said he, 'that some misfortune has befallen them going from the wood; but what, we are yet to learn.'

The priest entertained the consul and his lady with an account of all the tragical passages of his life: They spent the evening much pleased with his conversation; but remembering how fatigued he must needs be with his journey, they broke off the conversation, and the consul waited on him to his chamber, begging him to accept of some linen and habit suiting his birth, and more commodious, which he modestly received, with the most handsome acknowledgments: after which the consul retired, leaving him to his devotions.

And now, left alone, he sat down and reflected on the goodness of God, which had at last delivered him from a life of misery, attended with continual fears from cold and hunger, and had brought him safe to Christian conversation, plenty, and a retreat, where he might sleep securely. After returning the due thanks, he shifted, and entered a bed easy and sweet, a comfort his tired limbs had long been strangers to; he wished for nothing now so much as for Ardelisa, and the faithful maid and boy: 'Now my God,' said he, 'show yet more the wonders of thy mercy, in preserving them, if living.' After that he fell into a profound sleep, sweet as the peace of his good conscience.

About midnight he, and all the family, were waked by some persons knocking at the gate, in a manner that spoke the utmost haste or fury; they all left their beds, and one of the servants called to know who was there. Joseph answered, 'It is I, open the gate quickly, I am Joseph.' At these words the servant unbarred the gate, and saw Ardelisa, Violetta, Nannetta, and Joseph: shutting the gate, they went in, where they were received with a joy words can't express. Ardelisa said 'Ask no questions, but put out the lights, for we have left the place we were confined in all in flames; and should any noise be heard in this house, when the city is alarmed, it might render us suspected; whereas now they will conclude us burned, and that will prevent all reports of our escaping.'

The consul consented, and Violetta was with Ardelisa, conducted to a chamber; and the consul; his lady, and Father Francis denied themselves the pleasure of knowing their adventures till the morning. All the family went to bed, but not to sleep; that was impossible for the great noise in the streets, which was occasioned by the fire: for the city of Constantinople has been so many times almost destroyed by that merciless element, that the people are very much alarmed with anything of that nature. Osmin's palace was large and noble, and flamed dreadfully in the garden; and the *seraglio* being fired at the same time by Ardelisa, who left it burning, their departure put the servants in such distraction, that they ran through the streets, crying, 'Fire! Fire!' It raised almost all the city, the consul and his family were early up, and then Ardelisa gave them a full relation of all that had befallen her since her departure from the wood, with an account of all her friend Violetta's misfortunes, whose beauty and wisdom charmed all the company.

A general joy now spread itself through all the family, and Providence seemed to smile; the ladies, priest, Nannetta, and Joseph stirred not forth; and in a few days a French ship being freighted, was ready to sail for France. The consul waited on the French ambassador, to inform him of all, and obtained of him to assist him, in procuring for them a safe passage home. In the consul's boat, accompanied with the consul and his lady, the two ladies, in men's habits, with the priest, maid, and boy, got safe to the ship, with the jewels, gold, and habits they carried with them; and there the consul and his lady took leave of them, with all demonstrations of love and respect on both sides.

This ship was called the *St. Francis*, the captain's name was Monsieur de Feuillade, a fine accomplished gentleman, young, brave, and of a noble sweet disposition. The ladies, so soon as the ship was under sail, laid aside their men's habits, and put on such as became their sex and quality; in which they appeared so charming, that the unfortunate captain soon gazed away his liberty, becoming passionately in love with Violetta. He entertained them with such civility and respect, as showed the esteem he had for them, and spoke the gentleman and the lover.

They set sail the 20th of August, 1705. it being more than three years, since Ardelisa came to Turkey, six months of which time she spent in the melancholy cottage in the wood, and near a whole year since she; saw her lord; and now she doubted not of soon feeing again her dear native country, friends, and relations; but, above all things, him whom she preferred to all things. They passed the time the most agreeably that was possible in which the good Father shared, who was so pious, useful, and modest, that not only they, but all the sailors thought themselves happy in having such a man with them: He was physician to the sick, having great skill in physic and surgery, and could apply fit remedies to both soul and body.

Violetta only seemed melancholy: the loss of her honour, and the dismal impression the way of life she had led with Osmin had made in her soul, no change of condition could perfectly efface; she thought only of retiring to a religious house, to weep for a sin, of which she was in reality altogether innocent. The good priest observed her sadness, and one day took an opportunity, when Ardelisa was gone with the captain and Nannetta, to take the air upon the deck, to speak to her, in this manner: 'Madam, why do you abandon yourself thus to grief, at a time when you are returning to Christians, and your own country; to your noble father, mother, and friends: Your soul should now be ravished in admiration of that Providence, that has so unexpectedly delivered you from the most unhappy condition a lady could be in.'

She lifted up her eyes at these. words, and wiping the falling tears away, said, 'Father, till I saw Ardelisa, I found my conscience undisturbed, I submitted to the fatal necessity of my circumstances; and Christianity forbidding me to finish life by my own hand, I thought I had done all that was required. But that noble lady's heroic conduct has convinced me, I did not what I ought: She never would have permitted a lustful Turk to possess her, but, by his death would have preserved her honour; or, resisting to death, not have survived it. I am no longer friends with myself, and long to hide my face in a convent where tears shall wash away the stains of his embraces: Nay, Father, to you I confess, I even loved him, saw him with a wife's eyes, and thought myself obliged to do so.'

The priest answered, 'Madam, you are deceived: in Ardelisa, who was married to another, it would have been a horrid crime to suffer another man for to possess her; but as you were single, a virgin, and made his by the chance of war, it was no sin in you to yield to him, and it would have been wilful murder to have killed him, or but conspired his death: nay, a sin not to have been faithful to his bed, whilst he is living you ought not to marry, you might have been a means of his conversion; you ought to pray for him, and consider he acted according to his knowledge and education.'

Violetta thanked him, and. seemed much revived.

Chapter 13

They had now sailed six days, when the seventh night it grew dark and tempestuous; the wind changed, and about midnight a storm arose so dreadful, the pilot could no longer steer the ship; so that she drove they knew not whither. At break of day they found themselves amongst the Ægean Isles; the ship had lost all her masts, they had but thirteen hands aboard, when the carpenter going down into the hold, came back with a face that expressed the terrors of his mind; he cried, 'Hoist out the boats quickly, there is five foot water in the hold.'

At these words a death-like paleness spread o'er every face; the captain, ladies, priest, Nannetta, Joseph, and five sailors entered the first boat, taking with them their gold, jewels, some trunks of clothes; biscuit, a vessel of wine, and some quilts, bedding, and salt-meat, what they could possibly put in without endangering the boat's sinking; and then they made away for the island which was nearest, on which they landed safely; but had the misfortune to see the other boat sink, which the greedy sailors had too deeply loaded. The ship floated a little while, and then disappeared, being swallowed up by the merciless waves.

And now being on shore, they were desirous to know where they were; which they soon discovered to be on the island Delos, which lies in the Archipelago, the largest of the Cyclades, once famous for the Temple of Apollo, but now entirely abandoned by the Turks, and desolate of all inhabitants. Here they must remain, till some discovery could be made of a better place to remove to, which they proposed to do by means of their boat; in which, next to Providence, they placed all their hopes. They hasted to bring all ashore, the tempest continuing, and drew the boat on land. And now necessity taught them what to do in a place, where there was neither house nor market. Going up a little, way from the shore, they found two or three ruinous huts, which they entered as joyfully as if they had been palaces. In one of these the two ladies went, with Nannetta, the captain ordering a quilt and some coverlids, the best they had saved, to be put into it; as likewise Ardelisa's trunk, in which was the clothes and treasure belonging to the ladies. Into another hut the priest, Joseph, and he entered , there he placed the wine, biscuit, and meat, knowing he must now husband that, lest they should want before they could be supplied with more.

And now having ordered all things the best that was possible in so unhappy a place and circumstance, the captain and priest went to the ladies, whom they found much dejected, and out of order. They said all they could to comfort them, desiring them to eat something Joseph brought them meat and wine, and the sailors gathered leaves and sticks, and made fires in the huts, being handy, and used to shift. The captain ordered them also some meat and wine, which they eat as cheerfully as if nothing had happened. And now the good Father, feeing the ladies sad, addressed himself thus to Ardelisa: 'Madam, ever since I have had the honour to know you, I have observed something so noble and Christian in all your deportment, that I believed you incapable of fear or ingratitude to God, who this day has given you a signal deliverance from death.

'It is not many hours ago since we expected to be swallowed up in the deep, and thought death stared us in the face, but now the divine power has brought us to firm land, and to a place where, if we are alone, and have no inhabitants to comfort or relieve us, we have no enemies to fear, no inhuman Turks to murder or enslave us; we may here sleep in security. And as for food, Providence, that provides for the wild beasts and birds, will doubtless provide for us; in us, who have had such uncommon and extraordinary proofs of his favour, it would be an unpardonable sin to distrust him now. Summon up then your faith and reason to aid you, and be not cast down.'

These words seemed as cordials to them all; they eat thankfully what was set before them and the captain, priest, and boy returning to their hut, the sailors to theirs, they slept as sweetly as if they had lain in palaces on beds of down.

Chapter 14

The next morning, the sky being cleared up, and the winds ceased, the cheerful sun began to shine; the captain, priest, and sailors walked out of their huts, to view the shore and country: they saw many sea-birds upon it, and plenty of ruins, with some goats and swine, which they supposed cast there by some shipwreck; but so wild, that they fled away as soon as anybody came in sight of them. At last the captain thought it best to send three of the sailors out in the boat, to discover if any place could be found near that more convenient to remove to, or buy provisions at, till some Christian ship arrived to take them in; which, it was probable, would not be long, because this island affords plenty of good water, and is safe for Christians to air goods on, or mend their vessels.

The boat was accordingly got out, and the sailors entered it, the captain charging them not to venture far from that island; but they were either taken, or drowned, for they never returned again with the boat. For some days they lived on what provisions they had brought with them, and the two sailors and Joseph walking daily up and down the island, which is many miles in circumference, gathered up plenty of eggs, which the sea-fowl laid there, and now and then some small fishes, which they catched in some little brooks, which are in the island. But now the biscuit was spent, and bread wanting, they began to despair of the boat's return, which they had everyday expected till now. The ladies, unused to such hardships, fell both sick.

The good Father searched everywhere for herbs medicinal to relieve them; but, alas! so many things were wanting, that they were ineffectual. How could cordials and restoratives be had, when neither wine or spirits could be made? The captain, whose concern for Violetta equalled the passion he had for her, denied himself what was requisite to support his own life, for fear of her wanting; whilst the poor ladies, whom sickness and want had rendered unable to walk, were watched by Nannetta, who was almost as feeble as they. The priest, captain, and sailors did nothing but wander about in search of food: they had brought two musquets, and some powder ashore with them; but that being spent, the guns were useless. They now contrived pitfalls and snares, which they made with twigs plucked from small trees and bushes, which were very plenty by the sea-side; and with these they had pretty good success catching sea-fowls, and sometimes rabbits. These they brought home, dressed, and divided, giving first to the ladies: But, alas! what could this do to sustain the lives of eight persons; Water was all they had to drink.

One evening the boy catched a young goat, and, unable to carry it, tied a string about its neck, and led it home. The dam, with another twin-kid, followed, hearing it bleat. This young goat being brought to the hut belonging to the captain, and tied there, drew the other two to follow her in, and so they were taken. One of the young ones they immediately killed, and feasted upon; the dam they preserved for her milk, and the other kid as a treasure, when they could get no other food. With the milk of this goat the ladies lives were in a manner wholly preserved, the boy feeding her and the kid with what he could get of greens, of which there was no want. And now they all grew so weak for want of food, that they were scarce able to much as to seek for it; Silence seemed almost to reign amongst them, everyone being unwilling to speak his despair to his friend; their hollow eyes were continually directed to the sea, from whence they only hoped relief, nothing but the arrival of some Christian ship could save them from perishing.

The priest, on this occasion, showed himself more than man; he encouraged everybody else, and seemed cheerful himself: and though he eat less than they, yet seemed always satisfied; though his meagre face and leanness showed his decay, yet his tongue uttered no complaint: 'Come, my children,' says he. 'Mortality is subject to misfortunes, the way to Heaven is difficult, but the end glorious; there we shall want nothing: The Almighty's ears are always open to our complaints; trust him, in his own time he will deliver us, or take us to eternal rest. With these, and such like discourses, he comforted them daily.

Chapter 15

One night, as they were retired to rest—for indeed sleep they could not, or at least but little, want of food having made them almost strangers to those sweet slumbers, which are produced by good meat, or wholesome nourishment—they heard a mighty storm, the winds blew, as if nature were in convulsions, and the elements at strife; then guns went off, by which they guessed some ship was near, and in distress. So soon as the daybreak, the boy and sailors ventured out to see what they could discover; and there saw the dismal remains of a shipwreck upon the shore, by the carcases of several drowned men, huge coffers floated on the waters, and some lay upon the shore. The seamen and boy got what they were able, and found some casks of salt-beef, biscuit, rum, and bails of India goods, which showed it was some East-India ship that was lost; they hoped to find some of the sailors, but none were saved alive on that place: by those that lay dead, they guessed them Venetians.

By this time Father Francis and the captain came to them, and gave them their assistance; and now getting home to their huts what they had got, a new life seemed to appear in them. Thus the ruin of others procured their preservation, as is frequent in this world; and one of the vessels of rum being broached, and each taking a dram, with a biscuit, they resolved to return to work, and search all the shore, the sea now ebbing, to see if they could get more, especially food, for treasure was to them useless. That gold, that causes so much mischief in the world, for which men sell their souls, and change their faiths, was here less valuable than a crust of bread.

They succeeded so well, that in five hours they had five barrels of beef and pork, seven of biscuit, three of rum, one of brandy, five of wine, and many rich goods and chests of clothes. Thus Providence, to preserve them, caused the winds and seas to bring them food and raiment. They likewise gathered up many pieces of the ship, planks, ropes, broken masts, sail-cloth, &c. and now they began to think of making a habitation for all the family to dwell together, and nothing but a boat was wanting to make them happy. They in few days accomplished their design of a house; for they made a large tent, with the sail-cloth on poles, with partitions, so that it reached from one hut to the other. Here the ladies could be brought, and seated, to take a little air, and to eat: They had likewise saved some barrels of powder and shot, which was of great use to them; for the men soon got strength enough to walk again about the island, and shot wild-hogs and fowl frequently. Thus they lived for two months.

Chapter 16

One evening Joseph returned from shooting, and told them at the farther end of the island he saw a ship lie at an anchor, at some distance from a creek, into which he saw a boat put. The men came ashore, and about six of them left the boat, and walked up the land towards a brook, as he supposed, for water; and on the ship's stern he could discern a Red Cross, and thence concluded they were Christians. This news made them long for the next morning, when the captain, priest, and boy set out by daybreak, and went to the place, which they reached in three hours time, so much had hope strengthened them; and there found the shore full of seamen, and a tent set up, in which they supposed the captain and passengers were. The priest went up to the first man he found near enough to speak to, and asked him, whence they were.

The man answered 'From Venice.'

'What is your captain's name,' said the Father.

'Don Manuel,' answered the seaman, and the ship is a man of war called the *St. Mark*'

'Now, friend,' said the priest, 'where are you bound?'

'Home, Sir,' he replied.

'Pray bring me and my friend to the captain,' said the priest, 'we are Christians cast on this island, and beg to speak to him.'

'Speak and welcome, gentlemen,' said the man, 'my captain's a noble Venetian, and will treat you generously; a worthier man never sailed the seas.'

They followed him to the tent, and were received with such humanity as surprised them; but discoursing the captain, to whom they related part of their misfortunes, they discovered it was Violetta's father they were talking with. Then the French captain, looking on the good Father, said to the captain, 'Sir, did you not lose a daughter in the last dreadful war with the Turks? A lady the most lovely of her sex, called Violetta?'

'Yes,' answered Don Manuel, 'I did; but why do you mention that?'

'She's here, my lord,' said he, 'and in my care.'

Then the good Father and he related all the manner of her escape: what joy and satisfaction this news was to Don Manuel, the mind can much better conceive, than words express; they dined with him, and, after a noble treat, he agreed to go along with them, ordering the ship to be brought round. In walking with them, he told them, that as he was at sea with his ship, with three other men of war in company, going to meet some Venetian merchant-ships, that they expected from the East-Indies, which they were ordered to convoy home; the storm happened, which had shipwrecked one of those ships, as he was since informed. This tempest parted the men of war, and drove him out to sea, so that he was in great want of fresh water; for which reason he put in here.

They entertained him with Ardelisa's whole history, and so they passed the time, till they reached their tarpaulin palace; into which being entered, they found the two ladies: But when Violetta saw herself embraced by her father, joy so overcame her, that she fainted in his arms; and, recovering, was congratulated by the whole company. And now the ladies and servants seemed so revived, that all sorrow was forgotten; supper was brought in, and nothing spared of the provisions that yet remained, which before they used to divide with care, for fear of wanting. As they were at supper, the first lieutenant of the ship was brought in, to inform Don Manuel, that the ship was come to an anchor near that place. Soon after him came several young gentlemen to compliment their commander, on account of Violetta: this company past some hour, very agreeably, admiring the strange accidents that had befallen them, and particularly their meeting in this place.

Don Manuel, and those belonging to him, returned to the ship; and next morning, returning to shore, passed the day with his daughter and friends, bringing rich wines and sweetmeats to regale them. The seamen halted to water the ship, and to get all things on board belonging to Ardelisa and her family, which they performed in five days; and then the ladies, French captain, Father Francis, Nannetta, Joseph, and the two sailors went aboard the Venetian ship, leaving the desolate island, and their huts, with many things which they thought not worth taking away, which might nevertheless be of great use to any others, who should have the same occasion for them. Ardelisa desired the goat and kid might be brought aboard, which she loved much, because its milk had preserved hers and Violetta's life, and therefore she resolved to carry it to France with her: So it was brought in the boat, being grown so tame, it would follow Joseph like a dog.

They set sail for Venice the 2nd of February, 1705/06 having lived on the island from the 29th August to that time, which was five months and four days; and they arrived safe at Venice in fourteen days, where the ladies were conducted to Don Manuel's house, accompanied by the French captain, the priest, and their servants; and there Donna Catherina received her daughter with the greatest transports imaginable, weeping for joy, the young lady doing the same; a sight so moving, it touched all the company. Here Ardelisa and the rest were entertained magnificently, and not only invited, but even constrained, to continue till a French ship arrived to carry them to France.

Chapter 17

Ardelisa was treated by all Don Manuel's relations, and showed all that was worthy observation in that noble city, whose situation alone renders it a wonder. The French captain, Mons. de Feuillade, was the only person who was not here diverted: He thought only of the approaching separation that was to be made between him and Violetta, to whom he had given a thousand testimonies of his passion, but never made any plain declaration of love, which he was withheld from doing, by these considerations: first, he was not the eldest son of that noble family to which he belonged, being second brother to the Count de Feuillade, who now enjoyed the title and estate.

He had indeed great expectations from the Marquis de Rochmount his uncle, who was his godfather, and had no heir, and was very antient; but then he reflected that Violetta was a lady of the nicest virtue, and would, perhaps, scruple to marry, whilst the *infidel*, who had been happy in the enjoying of her, lived, These thoughts had till now kept him silent; but his passion was too great to suffer him to part from her, without declaring his love: He resolved therefore to take the first opportunity to reveal it to her, which was difficult, by reason of the abundance of company that visited at Don Manuel's and frequent diversions, to which the ladies were invited abroad.

One morning he rose very early, and went into the gardens to walk, being melancholy. after some time he entered a banqueting-house, where he sat down, and was in a profound meditation, when he heard a rustling behind the quickset-hedges, and, lifting up his eyes, saw Violetta alone, very pensive. She passed by, and went up a small mount, upon which there stood a summerhouse, which for prospect, and the painting it was embellished withal, equalled, if not excelled, any in Venice. Into this she entered, and sat down; he immediately followed her thither, and there threw himself upon his knees before her, saying, 'Charming divine Violetta! See here a man who adores you, who has loved you from the, first moment he saw you; and yet, through respect, continued silent, and would not importune you whilst you were unfortunate. You are now returned home, and secured from all future mischiefs; and I, the most unhappy of all men, must, e'er long, leave you; the thoughts of this separation are insupportable. Tell me, divine creature!

'May I hope that you are not wholly insensible of my services? And that you will sometimes remember me with compassion? I am going to my native country, to a place where my friends and fortune are; but; I would much rather stay here and die at your feet, and could wish I had not one moment survived our deliverance from the desolate island, since it is the means of depriving me of your sight, Oh! Speak! Is your soul insensible to love? May I not hope?'

Violetta, much disordered, seemed to ruminate before she spake; and, at length replied, 'Sir, I am neither insensible, nor ungrateful; your affection has been so easy to be discovered in all the kind and generous things you did for me in my distress, that it would be base in me not to acknowledge, That I believe your passion sincere and noble; and the graceful sense I have of it is such, that I will not dissemble with you: Were not my circumstances what they are, I would sooner consent to be yours, than any man's living.'

At these words he kissed her hand with the greatest transport, saying, 'Madam, proceed no farther, let this charming sentence live forever in my thoughts, no circumstance remains to bar me from being happy; do you but bid me live, I shall surmount all obstacles: Your noble father will find nothing in my birth, or fortune to render me unworthy such an honour. You are not pre-engaged, the villain, who possessed that lovely person, had no title to it but lawless force; he neither was a Christian nor a husband; he used you as his slave, and, doubtless, would, whene'er his brutish lust inclined him to a change, have bestowed you on some favourite-slave, to use or poison you.'

Violetta answered, with a flood of tears, 'Yet while this villain lives, honour forbids me to be yours: 'Tis true, he forced me to his bed, but 'twas the custom of his nation, and what he thought no crime, yet he was tender of me; and whilst he lives, my modesty cannot permit me to receive another in my bed.'

'But if he's dead, Madam,' the lover cried, 'then will you give consent to make me blessed; for doubtless he is long since so, the Turkish emperors never failing to send the bowstring to the man with whom they are once displeased. 'Twill not be many days before some vessel will arrive from Turkey, and then you'll be informed of all that's happened, since we left it; till then permit me to declare myself to your father, and to hope.'

Violetta rising, to put an end to the discourse, answered only, 'Importune me no farther.'

He said no more, but taking her hand, conducted her to the house, and returned to the summerhouse, where, for some moments, he reflected, with much pleasure, on what had passed between them. By this time Don Manuel rose, and came into the garden, with Father Francis, who was the favourite of the whole family. The captain joined them, and, after some other discourse, thinking it a lucky opportunity, discovered to Don Manuel in a manner the most respectful and gallant that was possible, the passion he had for Violetta; in which the good priest seconded him, giving him and his family (whom he perfectly knew) such a character, that Don Manuel received the offer very obligingly; telling the captain, if his daughter was consenting, he should not contradict her inclinations. After this Monsieur la Feuillade took the freedom of a lover, often to dance, walk, and accompany Violetta abroad; and all her relations created him as a person they esteemed Don Mamuel's son.

Chapter 18

It was not long before a Venetian ship arrived; the captain of which brought an account of many extraordinary events that had happened at Constantinople since their departure. He said, 'Three days after Osmin's palace was burnt, he, having received the news of it, fell sick, and refused to eat, continuing silent. He fasted three days, and the fourth was found dead in his chains, as he lay on the floor. His body I saw dragged, by the *sultan's* order, about the streets, which his servants afterwards were suffered to take and bury. Some days after the grand *vizier* returning from the army, and being received coldly by the *sultan*, grew incensed against him; and, fearing Osmin's fate, formed a conspiracy, and deposed the *sultan*, setting up Mahomet, his younger brother, on the throne.'

Then he told them, that Monsieur Joyeuxe and his family were returned to France.

The news of Osmin's death gave Monsieur la Feuillade much satisfaction; but Violetta would not be prevailed upon to marry him soon. At length she promised, if he would consent to let her retire for six months into a convent, after that she would comply with his desires. These were hard terms, but he was forced to yield to them, on condition he might visit her there. She however yielded to stay at her father's, till Ardelisa went away; and the lover vowed the six months should begin from the day she received the news of Osmin's death.

As for Ardelisa, though entertained and diverted so highly, she thought each day a year till she saw her dear lord again; and, according to her wish a French ship arrived; which news being brought to her, Monsieur la Feuillade and the priest went aboard; and there seeing the captain, knew him to be Monsieur de Fountain, Monsieur Feuillade's cousin, who was as much, or more, surprised at the sight of them. He embraced them, saying, 'Heavens! did I ever think to see either of you again? Father Francis! What angel has preserved you alive till this joyful day? You, cousin, are thought dead, your ship was reported to be cast away; I have good news to tell you, your uncle the *marquis* is dead, and has left you all his estate and title; you are now Marquis of Rochmount.'

They went into the great cabin, where they drank a bottle of wine with the captain, and then took him ashore; telling him, they would bring him to a lady, at the sight of whom he would be yet much more surprised. They soon arrived at Don Manuael's, where they found Ardelisa waiting their return with impatience; but when she law Captain de Fountain, she was overjoyed, knowing he came from the place where her lord (if living) was. He thought himself in a dream; never was a more agreeable meeting of friends: when he assured her, the Lord Longueville was in health, Ardelisa shed tears for joy; but he told her withal, that he was retired into a convent of Franciscan friars, where, notwithstanding his friends' intreaties, he was determined to stay the rest of his life, if no news of her being yet alive arrived, by a messenger whom he had sent to Turkey, on purpose 'to get a particular account of that unfortunate accident, in which your father, you, and all the family, were supposed to be murdered.'

Here Ardelisa gave him an account of all that had happened to her since that time; as likewise that the consul had sent him letters long since of her escaping in that dreadful night. Monsieur Fountain answered, 'They questionless are come to his hands by this time, but it is six months since I have been in Picardy'

Then Father Francis looking on Violetta, who spoke not all this while, said, 'Madam, we have news for you too, which will not be disagreeable; Monsieur de Feuillade is this day able to make you Marchioness of Rochmount.'

'So Monsieur de Fountain informed her, that the title and estate of the old *marquis* his uncle was given to him. Upon which Violetta looking gravely on her lover, said, 'My lord, Violetta is not a match for a *marquis*, you will doubtless repent of a love so ill placed.'

'Madam,' said he, 'were it possible for me to be angry with you, it would be now; no, had I the Empire of the world, I should dedicate myself and that to your service, and would refuse it, if you were not to share it with me.'

Ardelisa smiled, saying, 'What you refuse the *marquis*, you must grant to me; deny me not the pleasure of seeing you married before I leave Venice the friendship is such between us, that, methinks, you should not let me go to France alone; let us continue to share one fate, and end our lives together; France is a country charming as your own.'

Violetta replied, 'Charming Ardelisa! to whom I owe my deliverance from a life worse than death, Heaven knows how dear I prize your friendship and your conversation; but can I leave my parents? Did not duty forbid me to consent, my heart is so much yours, I should not be able to part with you?'

At these words Don Manuel entered the room, to whom Father Francis told all the news. The ship staid here two months to unlade, and take in goods; at the end of which time, Captain de Fountain gave Ardelisa notice to prepare for her departure to France: and then she so pressed Violetta to marry, that she yielded; and, in fine, Don Manuel and his lady consented that she should accompany her lord to France, where they promised to give them a visit the next spring.

Don Manuel gave her a noble fortune in jewels and bills, and was extremely satisfied with his son-in-law; who was now possessed of a lady, whose temper and person was such as made her a portion of herself, and whose fortune, being Don Manuel's only child, was so great, as might have deserved as noble a husband, if she had wanted part of the excellencies she possessed. This wedding was splendid as their quality, and when they went aboard the ship for France, they were accompanied by all Don Manuel's relations, by whom an entertainment was provided suiting the magnificence of his temper.

We will omit the tender expressions of Donna Catherina at parting with her daughter, with all the acknowledgments Ardelisa made for the noble entertainment she had received, as likewise the good priest, who was much esteemed by all. They all took leave of one another, and the ship set sail with a fair wind, and arrived safe at Calais, July 1, 1706/7.

With what transport did Ardelisa see her native land again! The good Father prostrating himself upon the shore, gave thanks to God for his and their safety. And now they consulted how to go to their homes: Ardelisa resolved, that her arrival should not be made public presently, having a desire first to make a trial of her lord's affection: So they determined to go first to the *marquis's* seat, which was about five miles short of the Count de Beauclair's Ardelisa's cousin, in whose hands the Count de Vinevil had entrusted his estate: they therefore hiring a post-chaise for the ladies, and horses for themselves, Nannetta and Joseph took the road for Rochmount, where they soon arrived, with all the treasure, as jewels, &c, the ladies had saved, and Violetta's father and mother had given her, taking the goat with them. They found the old steward and servants in the house; the Count de Feuillade, the *marquis's* elder brother, having delayed to take possession, or alter anything, till he was satisfied his brother was dead, to whom he was left successor in the title and fortune. But when the servants saw their young lord enter the gate, they received him with such joy as cannot be expressed. He thanked them with much tenderness, and, showing Violetta, said, 'Here I have brought you a lady, who you will find ourselves happy in serving.'

All this while Ardelisa kept her hood over her face, Violetta saying, 'Sister, you are not well, you shall have a bed got ready for you immediately.'

The servants flew to get all in order; the *marquis* conducted his lady and Ardelisa to a noble chamber, where he left Nannetta to undress them, being much tired with the journey; and, leaving order for supper, went in a coach, with Father Francis, to the count his brother.

Chapter 19

The news of the *marquis's* arrival spread so fast, that, returning home, accompanied with his brother, he found the court-hall and parlours full of relations, friends, and tenants; and having caressed them all, he took only his brother upstairs to Violetta. Entering the room, the count knew Ardelisa. It is easy to imagine how entertaining this conversation must be; she gave him the reason why she would be private for that night; which he was so well pleased with, that he agreed to take Father Francis home with him in the coach that night, and to go along with him to the convent to the Lord Longueville the next morning, as she desired: he much admired Violetta, his new sister. The *marquis* was obliged to return to the company below, and in some time most of the visitors took leave, good manners obliging them to withdraw, because it was near night, and the *marquis* come off a journey Some of his nearest relations stayed supper, and so importuned him for a sight of his lady, that he was forced to bring her down to table,

This opportunity Ardelisa took to send Nannetta for Father Francis, who, entering the chamber, she spake to after this manner; 'Father, the great confidence I place in you, makes me desire the favour of you to go to my dear lord; after you have given him an account of my deliverance, of which perhaps the letters have already informed him, proceed to relate to him all that happened to me since, to the time of my being taken into Don Manuel's ship, and there finish telling him, that I there fell sick, and died, requesting you to go to him, if ever you saw France again. And here say all that's moving, as my dying message to him; and well observe his looks and words: and if you find his passion is decayed, cease to importune him farther.'

And here she wept. 'I would not break his peace,' said she, 'or force him to the world again, to be looked coldly on, and loved for duty only; I'll sooner enter a convent, and die silent and unknown.'

'Madam,' said he, 'your doubts are criminal; but you would, I suppose, render him more sensible of his good fortune, by first giving him a glimpse of the most unhappy state, fate could reduce him to: I'll, to oblige you, try his constancy, and doubt not to bring him with me to you.'

He returned to the company, who soon took leave; and then the happy *marquis* with his lady, wishing Ardelisa good repose, retired to an apartment, where the rich furniture surprised and convinced her by what little she had already seen, that France was the most noble country in the world. Here they returned Heaven thanks; and now, freed from all anxious thoughts, being arrived where nothing was wanting to make them happy, they committed themselves to sleep: but Ardelisa could not rest, she talked with Nannetta all the night.

Chapter 20

Next morning the Count de Feuillade, with whom the good Father went, as was agreed, called him, and hasted to the convent; where they found the Lord Longueville much altered, to whom the count spake, after this manner: 'My dear friend, you will wonder doubtless at this early visit but I bring a person with me, who has news of consequence to impart to you he has been in Turkey.'

At these words the Lord Longueville fixed his eyes upon him; 'Father Francis,' said he, 'my God! what do I see? Is, my dear Ardelisa safe and alive? No news but what can comfort me.'

'That I am Father Francis, my lord,' he replied, 'is certain, and I wish I could give you news, suiting your wishes, of your lady, all that relates to her I shall acquaint you with.'

Here they sat down, and he rehearsed all her adventures, and his own; in which the Lord Longueville did not once interrupt him with one question: But when he told the manner of her dying in her voyage to Venice, he turned pale. The good Father hasted to a conclusion and finished in these words: 'The last words, my lord, she spoke, were relating to you, which I omit, because they were so tender, I cannot repeat them with dry eyes, and therefore would doubtless wound your soul: now you must resolve to submit to Providence, and be content.'

'Yes,' answered he, 'I am; my God, I submit.'

Here the drops ran from his swollen eyes, and he could say no more. At length he pursued his discourse, saying, 'Father and friend! I thank you both, and beg you'll witness how resigned I bear the greatest loss that e'er mortality sustained: Be witness, Heaven! how dear I loved her, and since she can be mine no more on earth, this day I'll quit the world: tomorrow's sun shall see me in the humble habit of a friar, these walks shall bound my wishes, and I will know no pleasure but the hopes of seeing her again. Farewell world, and sensual joys, in death I place my hope.'

Here he crossed his arms, a death-like paleness overspread his face, and he fainted.

The count and father, much surprised, called for help; at which the prior, and some friars came and, fetching wine and spirits, brought him back to life. Then they, repenting of the trial they had made, looked confusedly upon one another. At length the priest said, 'Pardon me, Heaven! and you, my lord! this sin; you are imposed upon, fair Ardelisa lives, at her request I made this trial of your constancy: come with me, I will bring you to her.'

At these words he lifted up his eyes, 'Ah! do not flatter me,' he cried, ''tis cruel.'

'By all that's good,' replied the count, ''tis true, she lives.'

Then they brought him to the coach, and told him, as they went along, all that had past in her abode at Venice, and return to France; and being come to the *marquis's*, who was just up, they were received with the greatest demonstrations of friendship. He immediately sent to know if Ardelisa was stirring; Nannetta took the message, and said her lady was not dressed. 'The Lord Longueville is below,' said the servant.

E'er the words were spoke, he came to the door, conducted by Joseph, who had seen him enter the hall, and, throwing himself at his feet, told him his lady was there. He entered the chamber, and seeing Ardelisa on the bedside, caught her in his arms so suddenly, that she scarce knew him: Excess of joy did for some time lock up their tongues, so than they continued silent; but at length they both recovered, and brake forth in words so tender and so passionate, that none but lovers can conceive. The servants all withdrew, and now God had rewarded their long sufferings, by making them happy in one another, A universal joy appeared in all this family, and the Count de Beauclair being sent for, saw this happy couple, and honourably restored his uncle, the Lord de Vinevil's estate, to Ardelisa. Thus these two lords and ladies lived in perpetual felicity and friendship; and Father Francis, with much intreaty, consented to be chaplain to Lord Longueville: Nannetta and Joseph married, and were nobly provided for.

The next spring the *marquis* and his lady had a visit from Don Manuel and Donna Catherina, whom they entertained as became their quality and affection. The same year Violetta blessed her lord with a son, and Ardelisa hers with a daughter, who bear their names.

Thus divine Providence, whom they confided in, tried their faith and virtue with many afflictions, and various misfortunes and, in the end, rewarded them according to their merit, making them most happy and fortunate.

The Life and Amorous Adventures

of Lucinda

Contents

The Life and Amorous Adventures of Lucinda; an English Lady

The custom of former ages to grieve and lament at the birth of their children, and to rejoice and make festivals at their burials, is not so much to be wondered at, when we reflect upon the surprising varieties of fortune, and the inconstancy of that fickle goddess: and although riches and titles seem, in the opinion of the vulgar, to have placed its possessors farther from the reach of her disasters, she often frowns upon these, and we have many precedents of life to convince us, that she sometimes makes it her pastime to humble the most haughty, rich, and aspiring, from the possessions they imagined to enjoy with security, into the most abject and contemned condition. Examples of this kind are so frequent, that there will be no occasion to mention them in this treatise.

Those which have happened to me in the middle state of life which I have passed, will be sufficient to shew the uncertainty of her favours, or the little occasion my parents had to rejoice at my coming into the world. I was born in the famous city of London, my father was the younger brother of an antient family long settled in the north of England, well esteemed, and possessors of a good estate, which they hospitably lived upon. My grandmother came out of the west well born, whom my grandfather married more for love than riches: this reciprocal liking produced a numerous issue, and their being many of them sons, some were sent to the army, some to court; and it was the fate of my father to be sent to this city, and bound 'prentice to an eminent merchant. He was very diligent and well beloved, and soon after the time of his apprenticeship was expired, married a citizen's daughter with a good fortune, and quickly encreased his riches considerably.

They had no other child but me, and great joy there was at my birth, after they had been married six years and almost despaired of children. Whether there was such occasion for their joy, the sequel will shew. They gave me the best education; Masters of all sorts came to teach me to read, write, dance, and all the sorts of needlework then in fashion amongst the young ladies: I delighted most in reading plays and love-stories, and nothing troubled: me so much as where I found a young lady forced by her relations to marry some old rich dotard, when her heart was already engaged in favour of one more suitable in years; This gave me an inexpressible grief, and I could never persuade myself that wealth was of the least consideration, where there was a disagreement in liking.

I was wonderfully pleased that my mother had happened to have given me the name of Lucinda; it founded in my thoughts poetic and romantic, and would much better become a song than Joan or Dorothy. Whether it was given me as a presage of my future intrigues I know not, but it cost my mother no little trouble to have me so christened, and by it I lost the favour of an aunt, who 'tis supposed would have left me all she was worth, had my mother consented to have named me Dorothy after my aunt's name. Alas! I was so foolish that I lamented not for this, and I would not for twice the fortune have been called by so vulgar a name. With such foolish trifles are young people delighted!

Over against our house there lived a rich merchant, who had two daughters that were frequently my play-fellows, and a son whom they called Charles, who was about two years older than I, and being often at the house to play with his sisters, he used to be one; and I began to think our pastime imperfect when he was not of the party. He also, as they observed, was more overjoyed and pleased when I was there. Thus our tender inclinations began, and he now appeared so desirous to oblige and divert me, that his actions gave my father and mother no little satisfaction. Our reciprocal affections increased with our years, and I began now to be sensible of no other pleasure but what his conversation afforded; so soon had love rooted itself in my tender heart. When I was near eighteen, my father's house was continually filled with the young and handsome, as well as the old and rich, who came to court me; but I found not any, in my opinion, to compare to Charles, who entirely possessed my heart. He alone was the object of all my wishes and desires, and the only person that could make me perfectly happy.

Some officious person had acquainted my mother, that the familiarity that used to pass betwixt us, was no longer decent; and that it was dangerous to my reputation to be so often alone with a young man, now we were advanced in years. Thus our frequent meeting as usual began to be denied, and I was in great apprehension would be in a little time quite forbidden: at the intercession of my dear Charles, who was not able to bear the thoughts of not seeing me as usual, I got the key of the back gate to our garden, by which he was to procure another, that by this means we might have the satisfaction of seeing each other, after the servants were gone to sleep.

This happy interview continued for some time, and our inclinations encreasing, I began to think of what consequence such a midnight intrigue might prove, and how injurious to my honour, though I was ever so innocent, it would appear. He who had no design in his heart capable of doing me any injury for his own satisfaction, solicited me for both our securities, to interchange promises of marriage: and to make it more essential, I was obliged to make use of my servant-maid as a confident, where in her presence we vowed to love each other perpetually, and that no force or change of fortune should be capable of hindering us from solemnizing our marriage at the first suitable opportunity.

Notwithstanding this, I was obliged to suffer the disagreeable visits of Roderick, who was very rich, and about forty years of age; and though he was accounted to have wit, his conversation gave me no satisfaction, and I thought nothing could be well said, that came not from my beloved Charles, I endeavoured by my actions, to shew him that my heart was already engaged, that he was labouring in vain, for what it was impossible for him to obtain: but notwithstanding all my fair dealing, he was indefatigable in the pursuit, and I found myself obliged to receive him. My parents were so blinded with his riches, that their doors were always open to him, shewing their designed son-in-law the greatest respect and civility imaginable.

This was often the melancholy subject of our midnight meetings, and Charles was grown almost inconsolable, left in obedience to my relations I should be obliged to consent to marry Roderick: indeed there was some occasion, for not long after this, my mother proposed it to me with severe injunctions of obedience to her commands. I knew not what excuses to make to disentangle me from this proposition, his riches far surpassed what he could expect with me, and his years were not so advanced as to countenance my refusal. My being already contracted to Charles was unknown to them, and I thought it not proper to discover it: my only remedy therefore, was to desire my mother to consider the tenderness of my years, and to bid her not to speak to me of this subject till I had passed a year or two more, which would make me better acquainted with the world, and know how to behave myself in such a solemn state; and that time being expired, if she continued in the same mind, and it was her desire, I should be ready with all obedience to submit to what she should please to command.

She told me it was so much to the advantage of our family, that a delay was dangerous, and that it was the greatest folly not to give an immediate consent. I had no argument of any consequence to oppose her prudent resolutions: being therefore almost in despair, I fell upon my knees, and besought her with tears in my eyes, that she would grant me but eight days to give my resolution, which, with much importunity she consented to. This I thought would afford me an opportunity of consulting my dear Charles about this important affair: I longed for the evening, he came as usual to see me, when I acquainted him with the dismal news, and, that I had but eight days allowed me to frame my resolution of marrying Roderick.

This threw him into the utmost despair; he was so astonished, that for a quarter of an hour he was not able to utter one single syllable, till at length breaking forth in the greatest lamentations, and deepest complaints, 'So then, my dear Lucinda,' says he, 'after all the vows and solemn protestations you have made me, never to have so much as a kind thought for any other, you are going to dispose of what of right belongs only to me, in favour of a parent's choice; What will be the return, think you, of such inconstancy and broken faith? The very apprehension of it almost deprives me of life, and I had rather die ten thousand deaths, than see the only happiness I wish for or desire, in the arms and possession of any other person. How can I endure such tormenting News? But I vow'—and thus he was going on, when I interrupted him by saying:

'How is it possible, my dearest life, that you are capable of thinking me guilty of so much perjury? My conduct towards you ought to have inspired you with kinder thoughts; I deserve not this injurious treatment. Had it been my intentions to enter into any other engagement, I should scarcely have made you a confident of it; No, no temptation can ever make me leave you, and the reason I communicated this to you, was that we might consult together to avoid this disagreeable design.'

He recovered his temper at this discourse; he fell on his knees before me, imprinted a thousand warm kisses on my hands, and returned me with great joy a thousand thanks for the welcome assurances I had given him. The only means that we could think of to remedy this accident, was, that I should fly away with him. We were some time consulting the securest way to effect it, and at last we agreed, that he should expect me in a barge provided for that purpose, at the first stairs below the bridge; where I was to come at the time appointed; and which was to carry us to some other place where we were to remain in secrecy, until the intercession of some of our relations had prevailed with my father and mother to forgive me this fault, and to be perfectly reconciled to us.

My servant maid, who was to accompany me in my flight, was present at this resolution, and afterwards occasioned all the misfortunes that befell me. Roderick in the meantime saw me frequently, and I treated him with more complaisance than usual, that my relations might believe I had no other design but to comply with their desires. The wished for time of my deliverance was approaching, and Charles, who passed not a night without the sight of me, animated me afresh to put in execution our projected design; so that the evening following I took what things were most convenient, as money and jewels of great value, in my own custody; and delivering lace, linen, and the richest clothes in a bundle as much as my maid could conveniently carry, when it was almost dark, we went according to appointment towards the water-stairs, where I perceived a barge, which I imagined was that which my dear Charles had provided for me; and as I was going to ask one of the watermen for the person who had hired the boat, I found myself seized by two men, who by force, notwithstanding the resistance and the exclamations I made for assistance, forced me into the boat, which immediately put out, and rowed away with the utmost haste.

You may guess at the affliction I was in, to find myself in the power of two persons unknown to me, and what to do or how to help myself I knew not. I often called for my servant, but no one answered me; this threw me into such fears and apprehensions, that I could not forbear bursting out into a flood of tears.

When I was in the middle of this lamentation, taking my wet handkerchief from my eyes, I perceived two men near me who were striking fire, and lighted a candle; by the glimpse of it I cast my eyes about the barge on every side, and I could discern no more persons on board than the rowers, the two men that lighted the candle, and the mailer or steersman in the stern. They were all masked, and therefore not to be known by me: I nevertheless took the courage to ask them, What was the reason of this usage, and where was my servant? He that was next me, answered, that what they had done was by the order of their master, and that the passion he had for me obliged him to this treatment, that he would soon be with them to pay me all the civility imaginable; but as for the chamber-maid they knew not what was become of her, having received no orders concerning the taking her aboard.

But what was my insupportable grief, to find myself thus exposed in the hands of persons unknown to me, what would be my fate, or what they intended to do with me, I knew not. I blamed the unfortunate resolution I had taken to leave my parents who were so indulgent to me, I cried out upon the infidelity of mankind; since either by the treachery of one who had gained my heart, and by whose intercession I had undertaken this fatal design, or at least by whose carelessness I was exposed to these dismal circumstances, I was thus brought into inevitable ruin. But alas! 'twas all to little purpose, I had so troubled them with my questions and lamentations, that I could obtain no more answers, telling me they had orders to hold no further discourse with me.

The difference I found between my former condition, the present state I was in, and the misfortunes I was in all appearance destined to undergo, made me suffer a greater dissatisfaction and pain, than if I had been condemned to immediate execution. I flew into the greatest agonies of despair, tore the hair from my head, rent my clothes to pieces, and committed a thousand unaccountable actions, produced from the fatality of my condition; till quite tired with lamenting and complaining, and favoured by the great silence in the boat, I fell into so found a sleep, that I waked not till the barge was arrived at the intended landing-place. Here I was obliged to go on shore, the sun began to display his morning rays, and the pretty innocent birds to sing their melodious notes, when I perceived at the end of a *vista* of shady trees, a spacious and beautiful country seat. The two persons that forced me into the barge conducted me along this walk.

When I was in the house, I looked on every side to discover if there was anything I had seen before, but all was unknown to me. They led me up a pair of stairs, where one of the fellows taking a key out of his pocket unlocks a door, and conducts me into a large room: then making two low reverences they left me alone, turning the key and locking me in.

I went into the balcony, and looked about to see the situation of the place, and if I could remember anything of it. It was yet early, and the sun scarce high enough to shew objects at a great distance; I only took notice of a high lofty edifice afar off, but could not resolve myself to what place it belonged. Whilst I was busy in these reflections I heard a door open, not that by which I entered; and a woman of a middle age presented herself to me in an obliging manner, dressed like a grave citizen, desiring me that since it was so early, I would be pleased to retire to a chamber within, and refresh myself by some few hours repose.

'Oh dear madam,' cried I, breaking out into tears, 'if the prayers of an unhappy creature can move you to any compassion, I beg of you to let me know where I am, and the reason why I am brought to this place.'

I was going to continue my discourse, but my grief interrupted the passage of my words, and I found myself unable to utter another syllable.

'Madam,' answered she, 'you shall soon be acquainted where you are, and for what reason you are brought hither, in the meantime refrain your tears, and be assured that you will be treated with the utmost civility and respect: under this security go in and take necessary repose, for before the middle of the day you will be informed of what you desire to know.'

I found no relief but in my lamentations and complaints, yet considering that it was to little purpose to grieve, I retired into a chamber richly furnished, and threw myself upon a bed that stood in the middle of the room, where tired and fatigued with grief I soon fell asleep. My dear Charles appeared to my imagination, where bathed in tears and making mournful lamentations, he seemed to speak to me in this manner: 'Oh my charming, my dear, my faithful Lucinda, how miserable am I become! I thought I had provided sufficiently for our security, by delivering you from your hateful marriage with Roderick; but to my ruin I find that destiny has deluded my hopes, and your too great credulity has occasioned our misfortunes, and I find myself deprived forever of that happiness which I have searched after, and has cost me so many cares and fatigues even from the tenderest of my years.'

I was just going to demand of him in what was that credulity of mine so blameable. when my drowsiness left me, to represent to me the most hideous and ungrateful object that ever my eyes beheld; it was the old Alphonsus sitting upon the side of my bed, his head resting upon his two hands in the most pensive and melancholy posture that fancy is capable of framing.

Alphonsus was a gentleman of the town, rich, and of a good estate; and although above fifty years of age, love was as busy in his heart as if he had been but five and twenty. He happened to dance with me one night at a ball, to compliment the wedding of a relation, where he fell desperately in love with me; he asked my parent's permission to court me for marriage. But they knowing my aversion for him, made him the civilest excuses they could invent; and he, after this refusal, never coming to our house, I concluded myself quite out of his thoughts, 'Is it you then Alphonsus,' said I, 'that have occasioned my bringing hither? Who could have suspected this from a person of your mature age? What have I done to provoke you to render me the most miserable creature in the world? If I once shewed my aversion to your love, be assured that no confinement, force, or terror, shall ever constrain me to receive it. But if there remain any pity in your heart, towards a person you once pretended to love, I beg of you to compassionate me now; let me be carried to the place from whence you took me, I will freely forgive you the insult; but if you will not oblige me so far, let me at least know where I am, and permit me to find the way myself.'

These words were pronounced with so melancholy and moving complaint, that would have softened any heart but that of Alphonsus; in his it made no other impression but to draw from him the following words with a disdainful smile: That could I think he had me brought hither for no other reason but to send me back so soon? That his design was to endeavour to gain my affection, in this solitary and lonely place, since woeful experience had taught him, that it was impossible to obtain it in so diverting a place as the town, where I was every day besieged with troops of admirers.

'Nevertheless to ease your apprehensions concerning the place where you are, know that the city which you perceive at that distance is London, and the place you are in at present is my country-house, which you may from this moment call your own, if you will consent to marry me: without this condescension, depend upon it, there is no person able to rescue you from my hands; and that in despite of you, you shall be constrained to pass the remainder of your life in this solitude. I give you seven days time to consider upon it; if you are wise, you will rather chuse to be the wife of a gentleman of fortune that loves you to desperation, than to waste and unprofitably consume your youth and beauty, in this solitary and comfortless condition.'

I was not so much troubled at these words, as by the thoughts of what measures Alphonsus had taken to carry me away in this manner; the very same evening, the method and time the same agreed upon between poor unhappy Charles and myself I could not by any means disentangle the intrigue; and therefore I desired he would tell me how he came to know of my design of going away that evening, and the hour appointed where he was ready to take me away.

'I could never have had any hopes of seeing you here, most lovely Lucinda,' said he, 'had not the bewitching splendour of gold contributed to my design: your servant-maid, like *Danae*, had not power to resist so powerful an advocate. know then that ever since I had your father's refusal to give you to my marriage-bed, I have constantly kept a secret correspondence with this maid of yours, with a resolution to run away with you at the first favourable opportunity. It has cost me, I acknowledge, a great deal of trouble, care, and money; but I think all very well employed, since by that means I have you in my power. Last Thursday I received a letter from your maid, wherein she promised me to deliver you into my hands, if I would present her with two hundred guineas; imagine if I had the power to delay one single moment my return to town; where she acquainted me with your consultations, and resolution to fly away with your first lover, the time appointed and the manner how, in order to avoid the hateful marriage with Roderick I observed where the barge that was hired by your lover lay, and ordered mine to put in nearer the stairs. I was the person you took for the master, the two others were my trusty servants, and thus madam you was conveyed to this place; and I wish to the Gods it was as much to your satisfaction, as it is to my happiness and contentment.'

Here amorous Alphonsus broke off his discourse, and left me in as deep a consideration, how it was possible that a young woman in whom I had placed so entire a confidence, whom I thought I had engaged with so many favours and repeated presents; for which I received frequent asseverations that she would serve me faithfully even to the expense of her life; could be capable of betraying me to misery, in this treacherous manner. From this discovery, I concluded that here lay the too great credulity I was blamed for in my last sleep, by the appearance of my dear Charles; and which he told me would be the occasion of all my future misfortunes. These reflections made me so pensive and melancholy, that I had scarcely the use of my senses.

In these troubles and convulsions of grief, Alphonsus left me, and to supply his place, sent to me the same grave woman, that gave me my first reception; she entertained me with such discourse, and talked to me with so much reason, that I found a great abatement in my grief. I began to talk without shedding of tears; and the resolution I had taken rather to die than receive the least nourishment, till I was delivered from this confinement, appeared to me senseless and criminal, and I resolved to accept a small repast in order to re-establish my wafted spirits and vigour; so little are we masters of ourselves, and so prone to inconstancy in our resolutions.

It would not be long before the seven days which Alphonsus had allowed me for my determination were expired; he assiduously visited me, and treated me with the greatest humanity and civility imaginable to engage me to condescend to his desires, but I could not have the thoughts of cohabiting with a person so disagreeable to me, who had forced me from the only happiness I proposed to myself, to constrain me by violence to sacrifice my life to his unreasonable desires. On the other side to pass my life in this solitary place, without any hopes of releasement, to be deprived of all company and conversation, was insupportable; and I foresaw that his hard heart would never relent from his harsh resolution, unless soothed by my compliance. I therefore concluded it my wisest course not to destroy all his hopes, to abate the disdain I shewed in my behaviour to him, and to grant him some small favours; which though no blemish to my honour, I very unwillingly condescended to bestow upon an object so much my aversion: but policy and convenience often compel us to many detestable actions. At these his hopes began to revive, he doubted not to accomplish his design, his air and deportment took a new spirit, his soul was elated, and ready to expire with excess of joy.

Six tedious months I passed in this disagreeable manner, having no other conversation but the old housekeeper and my antiquated lover, with a continual ding in my ears of love and matrimony; the first in hopes of serving her master, and the other to obtain his fruitless desires. It happened, that one day Alphonsus was accompanied hither by one of his nephews; he was young and not disagreeable, as I perceived them from the balcony, as they were coming together along the walk to the house. When they approached within sight, I soon retired, which I knew would be grateful to old Alphonsus, who never desired I should be seen; and threw myself upon the bed, deploring the miserableness of my condition.

I wished a thousand times for the conversation of the young spark, in hopes that his tender years would have moved him to shew more compliance to what I desired. I often thought by what means to bring it about; but every project seemed vain and to little purpose, and I found I was obliged to leave that to fortune, which I found no likelihood of accomplishing any other way.

About two days after this, when Alphonsus was gone to town about some particular affairs, Margaret (which was the name of my female attendant) came as usual to make me a visit, and receive my commands. I found she had some tenderness and compassion for my circumstances and person; and if at any time she entertained me with discourses that were disagreeable to me, 'twas rather in obedience to her old master, than the effect of any ill nature of her own, and she agreeably surprised me, when she began to talk to me in the following manner;

'The great displeasure I have,' said she, 'beautiful Lucinda, to see you consume your youth and beauty in this melancholy state and condition, together with a present of no little value, has prevailed with me to put a letter into your hands; the person who gave it me assures me it contains not anything but what consists with honour, is to your advantage, and he hopes suitable to your inclinations, since it will deliver you from these afflictions. I beg of you to excuse me the liberty I have taken, and to assure me of not making any discovery of it to Alphonsus, otherwise I dare not deliver it; and I wish to Heavens what I have undertaken may prove to your contentment and relief, since the afflictions you endure have, I assure you, as sensibly touched my heart, as if I had suffered 'em in my own person.'

I was impatient to know the whole intrigue, and could not wait for the end of her speech; but immediately promising that all should be kept secret, she put the following letter into my hands.

Having had the happiness, madam, to see you in the balcony, as I was coming in with my uncle, I could do no less than pity the unhappiness of your fate, that confines you here, and subjects you to the unwelcome courtship of old amorous Alphonsus, whose temper I perfectly knew before this bearer informed me of all that passed. I thought it the duty of every young cavalier to offer his assistance to any lady in such extremity, and I therefore send to offer you mine. If you dare rely upon the word of a man of honour, believe that if it be to your inclinations, I will carry you wheresoever you please, without offering the least injurious attempt, either upon your honour or person. If this meets with your approbation, acquaint me with it by the bearer, and I will contrive the most secure means for your deliverance. I expect your answer, and remain,

Yours, &c.

Never any news could prove more, grateful to me: What could be more welcome than a prospect of the liberty I had so much desired? But, to my weakness, I must own there was a farther charm; for I was wonderfully pleased with the person of this lovely youth, and from the first moment I saw him, he was the only man I could like next to my first love; and that I should not think myself unhappy, were I obliged to pass my whole life with him in honourable chains. Curiosity made me enquire of Margaret the quality and circumstances of this youth, with many other things, which the pleasure I received in talking of him, had put into my thoughts. She told me his name was Lewis, the sole heir to his parents, who died extremely rich about four or five years ago; and she gave me such an advantageous account of his obliging temper, humour and disposition, that I already longed for an opportunity to see him: and in these thoughts, so much to his advantage, I returned him the following answer.

> I have received your letter, wherein you assure me of your zeal and endeavours to free me from this miserable confinement. Nothing can be more worthy of a man of honour than to succour a helpless creature of our sex in distress. If your intentions are honourable and suitable to the opinion I have of your disinterested generosity in this affair, let me know the means you propose, and you will find me inclinable to comply with anything consistent with my reputation; and be assured, next to Providence, I shall acknowledge myself most obliged to my deliverer,
>
> *Adieu.*

This I delivered to Margaret, who soon carryied it as intended. In two days I received an answer to it, with the method proposed to execute our design, Saturday night was appointed as the most convenient time, Alphonsus being accustomed to go then to London, and frequently returned not till the Monday after. Accordingly he went that day, as usual, accompanied by most of his servants, after he had locked me up safe in my chamber, as he used to do, so that my old companion had no opportunity to come to me. About the middle of the night I waited with great impatience, in expectation to see by the little light the moon afforded, the arrival of my deliverer; when at some distance I perceived him galloping this way, attended by some servants on horseback.

I was extremely overjoyed to find my wish for liberty so near approaching. Margaret I found was zealous and watchful; she chained up the great dog which was to guard the house, left he should interrupt our flight by his barking, and immediately let down the drawbridge. I had bundled up the clothes and linen which remained, ready for our departure; and tying the sheets together at two of their corners, by that means I let myself gently down from the balcony; which was not so silently performed but that it waked the dog, who made a hideous noise and barking, which unfortunately waked the gardener also, whose apartment was near the house. He came with great haste and fury, armed with a fork, to encounter the thieves, as he apprehended; but soon retired, one of the servants having discharged a pistol with a design to frighten him, which had the desired effect.

We took this opportunity to quit the house; and, when we were beyond the gate, Lewis took me up behind him on the same horse, when Margaret who durst not stay after us, mounted behind the servant.

Thus we rode for the whole night, taking the most private ways, the better to avoid being discovered by Alphonsus, who we were sensible would omit no cost or diligence in the search after us. In the morning we arrived at Stockbridge, having made near sixty miles, where we took some repose, very much pleased to find ourselves out of danger of being overtaken. Fear and dread was banished from my heart, where the kind thoughts I had for my guardian and preserver began to intrude, and my eyes could not refrain from expressing the sense of gratitude I owed to one who had done me such friendly offices, in their languishing air.

This so inflamed him, that in him appeared a manifest content and joy, which discovered the satisfaction and happiness he wished for and expected, could he prevail with me, to enter into the sacred bond of being his forever. He neglected no time, but urged me from that moment, by his obliging manner and engaging deportment, to make him a solemn promise never to contract or marry with any other. My heart spoke very much in his favour; but I thought I was bound by the ties of honour, to tell him what had passed between my first lover, Charles, and myself, now the affair was disconcerted, and should fortune by any of her caprices hinder us from meeting with each other, no other person should ever pretend a right to me, and I should be very willing to gratify him in what he desired.

He assured me that the person I meant was engaged, and he believes married, to another, soon after I fled from my father, at the desire of his relations, in order to break off all future commerce between us; that it was esteemed my inconstancy and wandering inclinations was. the occasion of my flight, which gained his consent with the more ease, so that I might be assured to be at full liberty to dispose of my person to whom I pleased. Upon these reiterated assurances I at last consented, and promised to give myself in marriage to him at the first convenient opportunity and place we should meet with. I left him and went to bed with my old companion Margaret, who entertained me with a discourse most agreeable to me, since it was in praise of my deliverer, for whom she was a welcome and powerful advocate, though I must own it was needless, he having already gained the intire possession of my heart.

The night thus past, we in the morning mounted our horses, as we had done the day before, and continued our journey, but we no sooner were got on Salisbury-Plain, when two persons, with masks on their faces, came up towards us with a design to rob us, the servant who had poor Margaret behind him, spurred on his horse, endeavouring to cover his master and me from the fire of the robbers; one of them discharged his pistol, of which we were afterwards too sensible, when we found the poor old maid dead upon the ground by the shot she had received in her head. The servant had at the same time fired, but unsuccessfully, for he missed his aim. This encouraged the highwayman, who was advancing to attack Lewis, behind whom I sat, trembling and almost dead with fear.

Lewis was prepared to receive him, and champion-like resolved to defend his prize to the last extremity. When he approached within the reach of his pistol, Lewis presented him with two balls, which passed through his body; he soon fell from his horse which galloped away, and the other robber, seeing the fate of his companion, scoured off as fast as his horse could carry him. The danger was now passed, and I began by degrees to recover my senses, when seeing the old maid lying motionless on the ground, I ordered the servant to dismount, and to give her what assistance we were able, towards her recovery: but, alas! she was past relief, and almost cold, the bullet having passed through her head, after it had wounded the servant in the side.

I was extremely concerned at the loss of my poor servant, who had been a great means in my deliverance: I was besides apprehensive lest this accident, and the leaving her upon the place, might bring us into trouble, and discover the whole proceeding to Alphonsus; for this reason we thought it not convenient to remain long here. We took from Margaret the clothes she had on, which were most remarkable, put on her others of mine less known, and ten guineas in her pocket, with a paper to this effect:

Into whatever charitable person's hands this shall happen to fall, they are desired that this unfortunate creature may be transported to the Isle of Wight, where she is very well known, and questionless they will meet with thanks, and a reward from her relations, besides this small gratuity they are desired to accept.

This we thought would amuse 'em, and render them the less inquisitive; and knowing where to hear of the person murdered, would expect to have the whole story from that part; and before there could be returns of the news, we hoped to be in safety and out of the noise. This obliged us to be moving on as fast as the wound my servant had received would permit us to travel, and with great fatigue we arrived that night at Pool in Dorsetshire.

Here it was that I consummated my marriage with Lewis, forced sooner to it than I intended, by the inconvenience I suffered by being alone with two men. A small present tied up the parson's tongue, so that it was performed in private and kept secret, and even the people of the house knew not but we had been long in that condition.

Here we thought it convenient to remain till the servant's wounds were healed. He found he was able to dress himself without the surgeon in about six days time; and there being in the port a Dutch ship freighted ready to return home, we procured the master's cabin, made ourselves passengers, intending to sail for Rotterdam, where she was bound, and from thence transport ourselves either to Florence, Lisbon, or what other place we should think most suitable and convenient to reside at.

The saltwater and the tossing of the boat made me fearful and uneasy, and my hero had scarcely power enough to recompense the pain I endured, or prevent me from censuring myself for the follies

I had committed ever since I left my father's house, and particularly by putting myself in the power of a person scarcely known to me, for whose sake I had run all these hazardous adventures. He did what was in his power to comfort me; he gave me all assurances imaginable of his inviolable passion for me; his words, his behaviour, his concern and every action was an authentic demonstration of it: and, had not that goddess, Fortune, been so noted for her ness and inconstancy, there could be no reason to doubt of the continuance of his love for me till destiny had made a final separation between us.

Holland proved very disagreeable to me; the houses indeed were neat, the prospect of the country various and diverting, by an agreeable mixture of green meadows, cattle, canals, and ships, to please the eye; but the wives were little more than servants to their husbands, and the men so brutish that they were not conversable: traffic and gain was their only aim, and they seemed so fearful of being deprived of the very little they carried about them, that their hands were continually in their pockets to secure it. I therefore pressed my husband to leave this country, and accordingly he was so good, and condescending to my desires, as to take the first opportunity to embark for Leghorn, designing to settle there, or at Florence, where we hoped for more delightful conversation.

At this place we hired an apartment, where we lived contented with our condition. I endeavoured by all my actions and deportment to gratify my husband, and he on his part contrived, and sacrificed whatever was in his power to please me. Our love increased upon the birth of a son which I brought him, and all our care terminated in giving him the best education we were able. This undisturbed happiness continued for the space of three years. I brought him in that time no more children; and, whether that, or what other cause might be the reason of it, I know not, but I perceived his concern and passion for me grew more indifferent every day, and I began to rail at the instability of fortune. He no longer enjoyed the same satisfaction as formerly in my conversation, staid abroad, contrary to his custom, whole days, and sometimes I was forced to pass whole nights without the sight of him. I grew very much troubled at this alteration, I complained to him of his unkindness, and endeavoured to procure a remedy by my prayers and intercessions; but, alas! all my application was to no purpose, and, to my grief, I found his former passion for me was very much diminished, if not quite expired.

This misfortune drew on another; for by continuing this manner of living, he had so squandered away the bills and riches he brought with him, that I was necessitated to dispose of my jewels. I pressed him to go or write to his own country for a supply; but he took no care whilst anything remained. I began to look more narrowly into his actions, to see if I could discover the reason of his leading so disorderly a life; and by great fatigue, bribes and contrivance, found that he courted a French madam.

I was very impatient to see this fresh object of his passion, imagining to myself, that it must be wonderfully charming and engaging, since capable of robbing me of the possession of one who had so often swore to admire me so much beyond the rest of my sex; that it was impossible for him to live without me, and protested to continue in the same sentiments to the end of the world. I therefore one morning left my husband in bed, and went to her house, under the pretence of buying some lace, and French toys, for she dealt in these commodities. Whilst she exposed her ware, I looked with earnestness to discover the charms of her beauty, and I must own it appeared to me very indifferent, though I cannot say, but her air, and manner of speaking, was engaging, I bought but little of her merchandise, and returning home, advised my spouse, that if he was not pleased with my person, he would at least make choice of one more agreeable than that which at present possessed his soul; 'for I have been this morning,' said I, 'at the dirty French woman's to buy some lace, and I find her much more fit for a pedlar of trinkets, than a purchaser of hearts.' He made me no other answer than that I should be quiet and not concern myself with other people's affairs, took his hat and sword, went immediately out, and returned not home in four days.

You may easily guess how this manner of behaviour affected me. What remedy could I possibly apply to it? I could lay the blame to no other but my own folly, for abandoning my father, who had contrived a marriage for me, and had provided a loving husband, with whom I might have lived happily all my life, and enjoyed the comfort of my relations; that now I was sufficiently punished for my undutifulness and disobedience, and when the anguish would end I knew not. I begged forgiveness from the powers above, that they would pardon the folly of my green and unexperienced years, and alter the wandering inclinations of him with whom I had vowed to live forever. It was now the winter-season, and the weather very cold, which obliged my husband to call for a pan of charcoal to warm his chamber.

This had not been made half an hour, when, being in the next room, I heard something fall with a great noise upon the ground. I quickly run in to see what was the matter, and found my husband fallen stupid on the floor; the nauseous fumes had deprived him of his senses, and if no one had come to his assistance, might probable have ended his days. My curiosity made me inquisitive in what he had been imploying his time, and looking about, I found a letter, in a woman's hand, upon the table, with an answer he was writing to it unfinished when the fumes overcame him. My maid was now come to our assistance, we carried him and laid him with much ado upon the bed. I bid her apply the corner of a towel dipt in vinegar to his nostrils to restore his spirits; and snatching up the letter I ran with all haste to my chamber, where I locked myself in, that I might have an uninterrupted opportunity to read it. The woman's letter was to this purpose,

You will bear from the person who brings you. this letter, the reason that hinders me from seeing you before Sunday, I shall be sensible of a great deal of displeasure to be deprived of your company for so long a time, and nothing could make me suffer it, but an indispensable necessity, I should willingly consent to the proposition you made me some days ago, but it is of that importance that it requires a mature deliberation, and ought to be thoroughly consulted. It being securest for us, in my opinion, to leave the country to avoid the search your wife will certainly make after us; my thoughts have continually been employed about it, ever since our last conversation, and are by far too many to communicate to you in writing, Sunday will afford us a more convenient opportunity to confer concerning this affair, and fix upon our last resolution. In the meantime I wish you all happiness and conjure you to continue your affection for one who will faithfully love you as long as she lives.'

Upon reading his letter, I no longer doubted of the reason of the indifference and dislike my husband shewed to my person; and impatient to know what answer my loving spouse would return, I read these words.

I received your letter yesterday with great satisfaction, I kissed it a thousand times, and you may be assured that nothing could be more welcome to me than the assurances you give me of your fidelity and constancy: the interest you have in my hearty easily persuades me to what I most desire and covet, I can scarcely, my dear Cloe, survive so long an absence as Sunday, the thoughts of our future happiness may the better enable me to endure it; and since you approve of that as the most convenient time I shall expect it with the greatest impatience. You need not question an entire disposition to so agreeable a command.: the fear and apprehensions you have of my wife are needless; let nothing discompose you upon that score; for before our departure I will sufficiently secure all occasions of fear from that side, I will acquaint you with the means when next I have the happiness to see you, I have many considerable relations in France—

Thus far had my hopeful husband continued his letter, when the fumes of the charcoal threw him into a swoon, in which he might perhaps have expired, had not I seasonably come with my assistance. When I was sensible of his perfidiousness, I almost repented my endeavours to recover the unfaithful wretch, to live in the arms of another: I was to blame not to let him die in that disloyal action, a fit punishment for so detestable a crime. I put the letters in my pocket ready to produce upon occasion, but this discovery had so overwhelmed me with trouble and grief, that the reflections threw me into a fainting fit.

I know not what happened to me whilst I continued in this condition, but when I came to myself I found I was upon the bed; I opened my eyes bathed in tears, and perceived at my bed's-foot my husband, who seemed to express tender shews of trouble and concern for me: but whether it was produced from my discovery of his infidelity, the tenderness he had for me, or the counterfeit hypocrisy so usual to his sex, I could not determine.

'Oh perfidious traitor,' cried I, 'is this the reward of all the affection I have shewed you since our first acquaintance and mutual protestations? What is become of all those charms you so valued heretofore? Alas! they have lost all their force, and are become incapable of driving the idea of the least deserving, of one whom all but you would despise, out of your heart. Inconstancy has the dominion of it, and heaven knows if I am the first person you have so treacherously betrayed. To have left me in the power of your uncle, had been more humane and kind, than to burden me thus with miserable misfortunes, impossible for me to bear. But if my tears have not power to move you, think on your son, your beloved son, scarce three years old; and let that incline your heart to pity. Who will be a father to him when you are gone? How can you leave your own blood, the resemblance of yourself, thus exposed to the treatment of the savage world?

'I might have reasonably expected a better usage from you, but I have gained by it, at least this dear-bought experience; She who confides in the promises and oaths of faithless man, is sure to be deceived and ruined. Neither can I forbear pitying my worthless rival Cloe, who will doubtless soon be left and abandoned by you; what can she expect from you that have the cruel heart to leave a child, and a tender wife who trusted to your broken oaths, in such a barbarous manner? But know, perfidious wretch, your ill usage, your treacherous dealings, shall not go unrevenged; and by all the Gods I swear that you and your dirty concubine shall soon be sensible of it: Since the two letters I have under both your hands will be a sufficient testimony of your behaviour and infidelity.'

When I had uttered these words, I was putting my hand into my pocket to produce the letters, but found them not there; which made me conclude as it proved, that my spouse had taken them from me. 'Think not,' continued I, 'that your taking these letters from me shall hinder my revenge, for either Cloe or I must die; I will never suffer you to be in the arms of any other, and though you fled with her to the furthest corner of the world, my injuries would carry me thither, and no distance be able to secure you from my revenge, till I had broke the criminal love between you.'

These complaints were attended with such fury and passion, that pitying in some measure my great affliction, and fearing the effects of it, he began to sooth me; he embraced me, kissed me with a fervency, at least well dissembled, begged my pardon with the greatest submission, and vowed to change his way of living, forsake all conversation that should give me any uneasiness, and inviolably keep that faith he had so often vowed to me, and as he acknowledged, I so well deserved.

'I must own, my dear Lucinda,' said he, 'that I could be no less than perfectly blind and stupid when I preferred Cloe's beauty to yours; neither was there anything in her manner and behaviour capable of engaging any one in his senses, who had the possession of you. I can attribute it to no other cause but witchcraft, nothing less could make me guilty of so much folly, so unaccountable an action, as ungenerously to forsake you for so undeserving a creature: but I thank the powers above for discovering our intended flight, the thoughts of it amaze me I but forgive me, my dear, my charming Lucinda; I am convinced of my weakness, dry up those afflicting tears, forget what's passed, receive me into those welcome arms, I shall know for the future how to esteem that happiness, and be assured that for the time to come you shall have no reason to complain of any of my actions.'

Who of all our tender sex could be proof against such promises, and insinuating expressions? My heart had not power to resist, and persuaded that what he spoke came from the sincerity of his heart, I quickly consented to a reconciliation I so much desired; and my eyes, long accustomed to tears of grief, could scarce now forbear paying that tribute to joy. I embraced him, gave him a thousand kisses, swore an utter oblivion of all the injuries he had done me; whilst he reiterated all his protestations and vows of a sincere repentance, and an unmolested possession of his heart to the end of the world. Excess of joy appeared reciprocally in all our airs and actions, and we seemed to enter into a new state of happiness more transcendent than what we enjoyed at our first union. But alas! it is not our lot to have a long and intire felicity in this world! I too soon discovered by his indifference that the distemper was not absolutely cured, this encreased my suspicions and jealousies; I contrived to have him dogged, and found that the faithless creature often went to Cloe's, notwithstanding the promises he made me to the contrary.

I was unwilling to give faith to my informer, without being a witness of it myself; I therefore put on a disguise that I might not be known, and went to the door of Cloe's house: It was in the month of February, the weather rigorously cold, I had waited there two hours in expectation of him; the severity of the weather made me tremble like an aspin-leaf, when Lewis, who came, seeing me in that condition, taking me for a poor woman in want, gave me alms, and bid me go home and buy some wood to warm me, I returned him thanks, the shaking of my teeth with cold altering my voice assisted my disguise; I found there was too much truth in what I had been informed, and returned home very uneasy.

I passed two months without taking notice to my spouse of what I had discovered; when one day, after he was gone out, as I suppose, to see his mistress, an elderly woman, decently and gravely dressed, came to ask for me; I met her in the first apartment, but she desired to speak with me in private: I carried her up into my chamber, where, after we had discoursed of several subjects, she expressed herself in this manner. 'Madam, I hope you will not take it amiss, that at the desire and intreaties of a gentleman, I have presumed to wait upon you; the poor condition you see me in, may serve for an excuse, being obliged to do anything almost for a subsistence and livelihood in an honest way: I am persuaded that the gentleman is too honourable to require anything of you but what decency and good breeding allows'——

I had not patience to hear more, and desired she would tell me quickly what she had to say to me; at this, she took a billet out of her pocket, and prevented it to me, the contents were to this purpose.

> Doubtless, madam, you will think it strange that one who never had the happiness of your acquaintance, should presume to send you a letter; but if you could see to the bottom of my hear, you would soon know the indispensable necessity. I have often endeavoured to check my growing passion, but your charms are too powerful, and I find resistance ineffectual: I know with what caution we are obliged to act where a lady's honour is concerned, I desire not anything that may be injurious to that. All that I beg is, that you will permit me to love you, and to acknowledge myself, madam,
>
> Your most humble servant,
Don Antonio di Castello.

When I had read the letter, I enquired of the woman who this Don Antonio was; she told me a Spanish gentleman that had long resided at this court, of great quality and fortune; that he had always lived with grandeur, and was accounted a generous person, and of untainted honour and reputation; described his person, shape and habit. I told her she might if she pleased carry him back his letter, and desire him not to give himself any farther trouble of this kind, since it would be to no purpose; and I should be obliged to acquaint my husband, to put a stop to his importunity; that I forgave him this fault, because it was the first, but that I could not answer for the event, should he continue to trouble me again. She begged of me not to return the letter, and excused herself from receiving it; that if I would not be so obliging to answer it, she implored me not to offer him the affront to send it back, believing by his expressions that he aimed at no more than what was within the bounds of honour to grant, and what should not in the least violate the duty I owed my husband. In fine, she urged so many reasons, and played her part so well, that not without reluctancy I retained the letter.

I saw the next day a gentleman pass by my balcony, followed by two servants; he was dressed after the same manner she had before described, and I doubted not but it was Don Antonio, especially when I saw him make a low obeisance. My heart trembled at this adventure,

I knew nothing of the manner of courtship the Spanish *dons* used to pay to the married ladies. I observed him attentively, and though I found no disposition in me to love him, I must own his person was not ungrateful to me; he seemed to be about thirty, and his habit and equipage shewed him to be of no mean rank. Don Antonio continued thus to pass by my balcony every day, for at least a fortnight, without making any other advances to gain my love.

This time expired, the woman who brought me the first letter, came with a second, accompanied with a present of great value; which was a large cupid of gold, drawing his bow set with diamonds, the string was a string of pearls, and the sparkling eyes of cupid were represented by two large brillants. I must confess I was perfectly dazzled with the splendour of this rich present; but I durst not accept it, lest it should come to my husband's knowledge, and occasion him to suspect my honesty. Don Antonio in his letter, desired an opportunity to speak with me, but in so humble and obliging a manner, that I could not hate a person who professed to love me, and gave me such convincing proofs of his passion.

I told the old madam, the reasons that forbid me to accept his presents, that I was extremely concerned that Don Antonio should take such pains and trouble to accomplish what my honour would never permit me to grant; that I advised him to place his affections upon some object more deserving of a person of his merits and endowments: and I desired he would send me no more letters or presents, lest in time the consequence might be fatal to me if not to us both.

With this answer, she returned very much concerned that I would not send one more agreeable, or accept of the cavalier's present. For six months after this, the *don* frequently sent me letters, begging for an opportunity to speak with me. I was apprehensive lest they should be discovered, and prove my ruin. I returned him no answer to any, but must acknowledge that his letters did not displease me. My husband continued his lewd way of living, which abated my inclinations for him, and was the reason I discovered not to him Don Antonio's courtship. He was so bewitched to Cloe, that it took up all his thoughts and time; and if an accident had not prevented him, I doubt not he would have left me, and fled away with her to France, according to the before concerted design.

Fate prevented his treacherous intentions, for one morning as I was revolving upon my unhappy condition, he was brought home by two men followed by a confused mob. I soon knew the occasion, he was not able to sustain himself, so dispirited and weak, that his legs were unable to support him; and his face so besmeared and covered with blood, that I could scarce know him. I caused him to be immediately put into bed, and sent for the ablest surgeons; his wounds were searched, and judged incurable, and quiet and rest was the only hopes remained for his recovery. No sooner were the surgeons gone out of the house, but the ministers of justice came in, to enquire into the affair, and the occasion of it.

My husband was obliged to speak, and in this weak condition acquainted them that he had passed the last night at a gentlewoman's house called Cloe, with whom he had kept a correspondence for some time, notwithstanding the exhortations and desires of his wife to the contrary; that he had unfortunately left the key in his chamber-door, and was in the morning in a sound sleep, when he found himself stabbed as he lay in bed; that at this he awakened and knew that it was her brother who gave him this treatment for the dishonour he had done to the family; that he had often waited for an opportunity, but could never meet with any till this unhappy minute.

'I was getting out of bed,' said he, 'when I received another wound, and though I took my sword to defend myself from further attempts, the wounds and loss of blood had made me unable to stand, and I fell helpless upon the floor. He after this, gave me several fresh wounds, and fled out of the house.'

The trouble of uttering this had so abated the small spirits and force remaining, that Lewis fainted away; so that for some time we thought him dead. The ministers of justice left the house, in order to look after the criminal, but they could never discover what was become either of the sister, or the insatiable revenger. He grew weaker every day, no consultation or advice for his recovery was neglected; all proved unsuccessful, and after he had had prepared himself for death, at the end of five days he expired, enjoying his senses to the last, repenting of his ungrateful usage to me., and begging my forgiveness to the last moment.

His last behaviour to me had made such impression, that I grieved very much for his misfortune; I wished I had accompanied him in his death, and heartily forgave him all the injuries he had done me. But, as ill fortune seldom comes alone, this was succeeded by another more afflicting, which was the loss of my son, who soon followed his father. Being thus deprived of all my comfort, the little money remained almost wasted, and nothing but a few jewels left to support me, my condition was reduced to that extremity, that it would have been impossible for me to bear, had not fortune provided for my relief. When Don Antonio had heard of my husband's death, he not only continued, but renewed his applications with greater fervency. It is not difficult to believe that I had now no reason to be displeased at his courtship, the frequent presents he made me, being neither unnecessary, or unacceptable in my present circumstances.

I nevertheless thought it indecent to receive addresses from any other, so soon after my husband's expiration; but the fervent solicitations, and fervent intercession he made to me prevailed so far, that I promised to see him in my house at a time I assigned. Don Antonio overjoyed, came accordingly to visit me the evening appointed. His satisfaction was so great, that it scarcely left him the power to speak, and he treated me with all the respect imaginable, suitable to the opinion and character I had of him. After the first compliments, our conversation turned upon variety of subjects, and was so agreeable to us both, that it continued to midnight before we parted. His discourses appeared to me so full of wit and good sense, and his behaviour so generous and engaging, that my heart began to have no little affection for him. These conversations were kept secret for two months, to avoid the censure of the world, for receiving propositions of marriage so soon after the loss of my husband.

When this time was expired, my new lover made earnest solicitations to me, to accompany him into Spain, his own country; that our marriage should be solemnized when we were gone from this place about a day's journey, where we were not known: and in confirmation of this promise, he presented me with a diamond of great price, and under the writing to this effect, he subscribed his name writ in his own blood. I could not refuse my consent, which made him very industrious to provide with speed everything necessary for our voyage. He acquainted me that the Spaniards were generally so jealous of their wives, that any gentleman who should allow his consort the freedom they permit in other countries, or give them even the opportunity to speak with any other person, would be despised for their folly and loose oeconomy; and therefore that I might not be punished with this required reservedness, or he censured for his unwariness, or loose conduct, he desired I would accompany him in this voyage dressed in men's clothes; that being obliged to go by sea, this would yet be the more requisite.

He therefore provided for me a man's habit, rich and fashionable, with all things suitable. The garb, I fancy, had inspired me with manly resolutions; I had no timorous thoughts, was resolved at least to counterfeit the young hero, and applied myself diligently to attain their airs. My knees at first knocked too close together, and my gate was too mincing; but custom made me step more boldly, and in a little time I could strut and cock my hat as well as the best, and force out a necessary oath to adorn my discourse. Thus equipped, I embarked with my spouse. I passed for a relation of Don Antonio, and there was no one in the ship who suspected my being a cavalier. When the winds had swelled our sails, and our vessel began to scud away, to pass the time more agreeably, I desired Don Antonio to divert us with some tale of love, of which I knew him to be well stored, and able to deliver it to us to the greatest advantage: The captain of the vessel, and the company made him the same request, and he condescended to entertain us in the following manner.

Conjugal Duty rewarded, or, the Rake reformed

In Saragosa, a famous city in Spain, had long inhabited the antient family of the Alvarez., the most esteemed both for their worth and large possessions, of any in the kingdom of Arragon, Of this line was Don Sebastian, one of the most affable and most accomplished young gentleman in that country. He, like the rest of the young noblemen, spent his time in courting variety of young ladies; no particular beauty having yet the influence to fix his inconstant heart, he made an equal application to all. Gallantry was his only diversion, and the nights were passed in serenades, scouring about in masks and disguises, according to the custom of the place.

In the midst of this career he happened to see a young gentlewoman, whose beauty and behaviour seemed to him extraordinary. He was so charmed with her appearance, that he fell desperately in love with her. He followed her home to her house; and taking particular notice of it, that he might not forget the place, he, like other lovers, emitted not to pass often every day by her window, in hopes of the happiness to see the object that had engaged all his thoughts. The day that afforded him not this opportunity was esteemed the most unlucky, but when he was so fortunate to have a sight of her, if she cast but one look upon him which he always interpreted to his own advantage, he thought himself the happiest creature imaginable.

After he had passed some time in these fashionable vanities, finding his passion still increasing, he began to enquire after the condition of the young lady, and understood that her father who had been a goldsmith, was dead for some years; that she had a mother living there, with two brothers who were of the same trade; that she had the reputation of being very virtuous, was much esteemed, of no despicable fortune, and by many courted for marriage.

Don Sebastian was more enflamed at this good character. To obtain the possession of her he made all his endeavours: He addressed and complimented her with letters, tempted her with the richest presents, and omitted not anything that might conduce to effect his design. The lady was proof against all these temptations, and at the end of this course, which he continued for four months, he found himself unable, with all his stratagems, to take this impregnable fortress. He resolved therefore to make his attack after another manner in hopes of better success, and concluded to try if addressing to her in a civil manner, and speaking to her himself, might be more powerful towards the softening her obdurate heart.

He took the first opportunity, when seeing Panthea at the door; 'Madam,' says he, in the most humble and respectful manner, 'I hope you will pardon me if I take this favourable moment, to assure you that the passion I have professed for you in my letters is real and sincere; that I have loved you with the greatest violence ever since the first sight; that you are the continual object of my thoughts, and I commit no action, wherein you have not a concern. Without you it is impossible for me to live; 'tis you that make my destiny, and as you command I am either to be happy or miserable. These are affairs too important to be neglected, and I hope may prevail with you as an excuse for my taking this method to acquaint you with my condition. I hope you will be more favourable to this declaration, than you have been to the letters I sent you, and not condemn a person to be the most miserable of mankind for loving you at this extravagant rate.'

His actions were so conformable to his expressions, and accompanied with so many sighs, uttered in so agreeable a style, that no one who heard him could doubt of the sincerity of his intentions.

'We know Don Sebastian,' said Panthea, 'that you are perfectly master of the art of persuading; your person, as well as your behaviour, are framed for it, and many of our sex have no doubt been sensible of it to their cost. If report be to be credited (you will excuse me the freedom) after the rambling life you are reported to have led, they must be stupid who take this discourse of yours for any other than jest and raillery I neither think it pride or disdain that hindered me from answering your letters, the compliments in them were much beyond what I deserved. I must acknowledge the vanity of supposing myself beloved, was not displeasing to me. What we desire, we are too subject to believe. My weakness was not yet so great, as to condescend to return you an answer to your letters. To have given encouragement to a passion I had no farther proof of, would have been injurious to the honour and decency of our sex, well knowing how little you cavaliers value an easy conquest.

'I therefore summoned all my forces to resist these powerful attempts; and, thanks to my stars, I still possess, and ever shall, fortitude and prudence sufficient to guard me from these temptations, though seconded by your presence, where you confirm those protestations and tender expressions you have so often made use of in my favour. But, to shew you that my heart is not capable of ingratitude, upon condition that what you require is not beyond the bounds of honour, I give you leave to love, and will return it with a virtuous and honest friendship: yet be certain, that whenever you move in the least beyond these limits, you shall never see me more; and, notwithstanding the difference of our qualities, be despised as an invader of my honour, and an enemy that only aims at ruining my reputation, and good name.'

At these words Panthea's mother, who had overheard this discourse, advanced: 'Sir,' said she, 'the folly of my daughter, and the manner of expressing her innocent thoughts, not accustomed to entertain persons of your rank and quality, must appear to you ridiculous.'

'On the contrary, Madam,' cried he, 'when I came here first: I thought not to have staid a moment, but her discourse has such a mixture of wit and good sense, uttered in so obliging a manner, that it is I think impossible for me to go. Her expressions are fresh chains, and her words gather new charms and sweetness, as they come out of her pretty mouth. Virtue and beauty are not always linked to quality: Your pretty daughter possesses both, and though not of so high degree, of so exalted birth, a cavalier of the highest rank may be proud of her conversation , when adorned with two such valuable jewels.'

After much discourse of this kind Don Sebastian took his leave for this time. He continued his visits for fourteen or fifteen days, in hopes of accomplishing his intentions; and though he was well born, rich, not unacceptable to the generality of the ladies, and, as he thought, not hated by Panthea, finding that he laboured in vain, that all his endeavours were to no purpose, that he sighed without any hopes of the return he expected to extinguish his flames, which were continually encreasing, he resolved to try another course, which was to send the mother six thousand crowns, with a farther promise to give her daughter a considerable portion when she should think fit to marry, in case she would comply and gratify his passionate desires. The mother and the daughter were both incensed at this affront: They abhorred the being thought so vile and mercenary as to part with that honour for a little dirty dross, which had been so carefully preserved; they therefore returned his letter and present in the greatest disdain, and bid the messenger tell him, that he might keep his money to ensnare some other heedless ladies, but that she was too sensible of the value of honour and virtue to be taken in such weak toils.

This repulse but the more enflamed Don Sebastian: He knew not what to do, to live without her was impossible: he resolved to have her at any rate, and therefore, although there was a great difference between the riches and the quality of the families, yet her beauty, her honour, and her virtue, had raised her so much above the low stock from whence she proceeded, that he flattered himself she would be esteemed a match not disequal or disesteemed by the most elevated rank; he therefore concluded to marry her, in case she would give her consent, and to this end making her a visit.

'Panthea,' said he, 'I know not if you will forgive me the attempts I have made upon your honour; it is not my least joy that I have found you able to refill my solicitations: your virtue, joined with the charms of your beauty, have gained, my lovely Panthea, the possession of my soul; they are a sufficient portion for anyone, and much more to be es-teemed, than quality and riches where they are not. I therefore come to make you all the reparation in my power, to shew my sincerity, and confirm you in the opinion of the inviolable passion I have for you, by offering you my fortune and person, by becoming your husband. If you will consent to it, you shall find me the most faithful and the most loving that nature ever produced.'

These words were very pleasing to Panthea: 'I know not. Sir,' says she, 'whether this is a new stratagem to inveigle me: I am sensible of the difference of our conditions, and your condescension in it may well countenance my suspicions; but if what you say is really your intention, I shall receive the honour you will do me with all acknowl-edgments of gratitude, and endeavour to convince you by my behav-iour that a person may be happy, though not married to one of an equal rank and quality.'

In confirmation of his promise, Don Sebastian presented her with a diamond-ring, which, after two or three kisses, he put upon her finger, desiring her that the affair might be kept secret till he had acquainted his relations with it: in the meantime she might advertise her mother and brotherly of his design, and that he would himself procure a priest to celebrate their marriage.

The ceremony was performed the next morning, in the presence of her mother, the two brothers, a servant-maid of theirs, and a trusty valet who belonged to Don Sebastian, The whole day was spent in feasting, merriment, and joy, at Panthea's marriage; the bridegroom notwithstanding thought it an age before the wished-for evening, the happy season wherein he was to reap those longed-for joys he had with such indefatigable labour so often attempted, came. Big with expectation he hastes to bed, rifles the bridal treasure, and with repeated pangs often renews the amorous chase, resolved to make a full repast of what he had so long desired. Towards the morning the fury of his appetite abated, he grew more temperate, and began to think of his interest.

'My dear Panthea,' said he, 'I think myself the happiest creature in the world, and prefer my Panthea before all the treasure of the universe; but you know, my dear, that we must not quite neglect the management of our affairs, which required that this marriage should be kept a secret for some time, till all was settled to my intentions: that till then I shall be obliged to lie every night at home.'

That it was more his unhappiness, he assured her than it could be hers, and desired her not to take it amiss, since it was for both their advantages; that he would visit her every day, and, when he had not the satisfaction to be with her, she should be the object of his thoughts and wishes; that, he had provided for her a bill of a thousand crowns to supply her present occasions, and would take care to furnish her from time to time with whatever she wanted. She told him the absence of what she so much esteemed, must needs be very grievous to her; that her only comfort would be to think it contrary to his desires, and the effect of his prudence only, often so great an enemy to love; that she hoped she had the sole possession of his heart, and in that view was very willing to submit to anything he should think fit to command; that she should every day expect him with impatience, and desired him to omit no opportunity that would permit him to come with convenience to her welcome arms. In this amorous state they parted, and he frequently renewed his visits with the same ardour and inclination.

These frequent visits were taken notice of by the neighbours, who began to censure the young lady's conduct and deportment, and reflected upon the mother and the brothers for suffering so scandalous a correspondence, to the prejudice of their sister. They lamented that a young person, who had so carefully preserved her reputation and character untainted to the age of twenty, and who was so esteemed for her virtue and behaviour, should have the weakness and unhappiness, to be enticed into a dishonest conversation. Panthea was not ignorant of these reports; but knowing her own innocence, and believing she should soon have an opportunity to clear her reputation by the discovery of her marriage, she took but little notice of it. She nevertheless often desired her spouse to take her home with him, to avoid the scandal and calumny which the neighbours cast upon her; but he gave her such soothing answers, that that she consented rather to bear the blame and censure of the whole world, than give him the least occasion for displeasure; resolved to sacrifice all her actions to his contentment and satisfaction.

The passions that engage mankind, especially if violent, seldom continue long. 'Twas thus with Don Sebastian, the ardency of his love began to lessen, he often looked upon his Panthea, and found not in her those bewitching charms he used to think her mistress of; this made him incline to repentance for his unwary marriage. In his cooler reflections he thought the inequality of the match injurious to the honour of his family, that it would be to his prejudice to have it discovered; and therefore abstained from visiting her so frequently, and only at those times when his inordinate desires prompted him to it. Thus the poor Panthea was forsaken, he forgot his often repeated vows and promises, the duties of a married state, and fell into his old course of living. Amongst the variety of ladies he courted, the daughter of Signor Mendoza, one of the most antient families in Arragon, fell desperately in love with him; they being both rich, and of equal quality, the relations soon agreed, and the marriage was soon solemnized with great pomp and splendour.

The consummation being past, Don Sebastian went home with his wife to her father's house; where, whilst the honeymoon lasted, like other husbands, he parted his time in content and satisfaction: but it being impossible that this news could be long kept from the knowledge of Panthea and her relations, some busybody or other soon acquainted them with this dismal news; no grief could be more excessive than that which they received at these unhappy tidings; how to proceed they knew not, the priest that solemnized the marriage, that tied the fatal knot, was unknown to them,' both as to person and habitation. To commence a process against two such wealthy and powerful families, afforded a very uncertain promise of success, though a certain and inconceivable expense attended it: that it would be the most prudent way to be quiet for some time, the better to consult what means was to be taken, the most likely to prevail, and remedy their sad condition. This was the resolution of the relations; Panthea's pain and lamentation was more piercing.

'Oh poor unhappy Panthea,' said she, 'how miserable art thou grown, thus basely used by thy faithless, thy once dear Sebastian, tied by the sacred bonds of marriage to be only thine: but alas! what links, what chains, have strength enough to bind insinuating, false, and faithless man! Off from my head ye treacherous locks: these curls helped to contrive my ruin, to ensnare and charm the man that has undone me; the poison is turned upon myself, and I alone the sufferer, down on the ground, and twirl yourselves into a fatal line, to end the wretched life of poor Panthea. If there be a line, a single feature, in this once admired face, it is a traitor, a conspirator, and has helped me to the wretch that has undone me; with these nails I'll dig, and bury them in the bloody Furrows of my cheeks, as deep as the treachery of my faithless husband.'

She was thus going on, her hair tore off from her head, her clothes in pieces on the ground, and her bleeding face teamed with scratches; when the mother and the brothers forced into her chamber, to give her all the comfort they were able. This melancholy sight almost distracted them, they were before too sensibly touched at the disgrace, but this was still more pointed; and what could be more afflicting than to see the only comfort they enjoyed, thus overwhelmed with grief?

'Oh my dear child,' said she, 'cease to complain we own you have reason, but 'tis not in our power to conduct our fates, we must submit to what the Gods decree, and fruitless are our mournings and complaints; this excels of grief is baneful to your health, destructive to the fair form that nature gave you, and breaks into those solid bounds of prudence you have hitherto maintained. Is it so great a miracle to find a faithless man?

'Alas! my child, there are millions in your case; you are not single in this misfortune, the very person who thinks herself so happy in the possession of him has more occasion to complain, he has cheated and deluded her, made her a prostitute, and robbed her of her honour by a trick; but yours, my dear Panthea, is safe and spotless, delivered by due form of law into the hands of him your first possessor, and consecrated by a holy priest. Let the malicious world say as they please, this we all know, thy mother, brothers, and thy tender conscience can testify the sad, and the sole right to him is only yours. A time will come I hope, my dear, when we shall be able to justify your cause in spite of all his grandeur, bring him repenting to your arms, and ask your pardon with a true contrition; but if our right is to be swayed by greatness, there are those in Spain that for a small reward will do us justice, and revenge our wrongs.'

'Oh pray torment me not' Panthea cried, 'you add new fuel to my grief, Sebastian is the vilest wretch of all mankind, base and unworthy of a kind thought; but yet he is my husband: I'll bear my wrongs with conjugal obedience, preserve my innocence with patience, keep my sacred vows, and love the villain to the last. Leave me to grieve my hapless fate alone, I am too miserable for conversation, you but disturb me; excuse me, my dear mother, for my afflictions make me incapable of knowing what I do or say.'

Upon this, they thought it proper to leave her, ordering the maid who was present at the marriage, to stay near at hand, and to watch her carefully, lest she should offer some violence to herself. After she had lamented in this manner for some time, she began to be more appeased, and sometimes would enter into a conversation with her maid; the subject was always the loss she had in one whom she loved so tenderly, endeavouring still to say something in his excuse, and would have willingly persuaded herself that it was the force of his relations, rather than his own inclinations, that had occasioned this ill treatments The servant was of another opinion, she thought it was owing to his wandering humour and ill morals; that she could never forget such an injury, and were it her case, whatever might be the event, no less than the sacrifice of his life could satisfy her revenge.

These discourses were often related to the mother, who was desirous to know how her daughter proceeded in her resentments. She was surprised at, and admired her forgiving temper, wondering how one proceeding from Spanish parents, could be endued with such mildness and goodness: she thought this was to be valued in itself; but in the meantime, how should the honour of the house be salved? If whole families have been murdered for a single look, or an unwary action, what would they think of them who had been so notoriously and publicly affronted, without making a suitable return? This made it necessary to clear their reputation to the world, and should she want one to revenge the injuries of the family, she would be the fatal instrument herself rather than suffer this stain to taint and blot their fame.

When she saw her daughter, she used to entertain her with such discourse which was ungrateful to her temper; and this dispute betwixt forgiveness and revenge, commonly ended in a little quarrel. The brothers and the servant were of the same inclination with the mother; so that there was four against one in this combat. This tender creature was so constantly assaulted every day in this kind of argument, that she was obliged at last, for her quiet, to give her seeming consent towards the prosecution of their bloody design. They had agreed, to make their revenge more notorious, that Panthea, who had been once the mistress of his heart, should make use of those engagements that used to allure him to his happiness, to invite him to his fatal end; and to this purpose they desired, that she would write a kind letter to him, assuring him of her forgiveness of what was past, and that if he would but make her sometimes so happy to afford her his company, it would give her a satisfaction, without which she was not able to live: that if he came according to this invitation, there should be two *bravoes* ready to receive him at the end of the street, and give him an entertainment suitable to his deserts.

This treacherous behaviour appeared very detestable to the honourable Panthea, she would rather have lost her life than have consented to it: but reflecting that their cruel disposition would by some means or other revenge themselves upon this injurer, at a time when perhaps she knew nothing of it, she entered into their measures, and gave her seeming condescension in the following lines.

> The cruel injuries you have lately done me, my dear Sebastian, are not sufficient to blot the memory of you out of my tender heart. The reflection of former joys revive in my soul, and I ardently wish for their continuance: I heartily forgive you, upon the agreeable condition that you see me often; you are too great a treasure to be possessed by one alone, and 'tis a folly to think to keep that to oneself which is the blessing of the whole sex. Fail not to come to me on Tuesday in the dusk of the evening, I can live no longer without you, the maid shall be ready as usual to let you in at the back door, where you shall find a welcome that will convince you how entirely you possess the heart and soul of   Your Panthea.

This letter was approved, she carried it in to seal, and enclosing in it another still more kind, it was delivered into the maid's hand; who had orders to give it with all privacy to Don Sebastian at his own house. In the meantime the *bravoes* were hired to be in readiness, in case the stratagem should take, to assault and murder the *don* as he approached the door. Solemn promises and engagements had past, and everything was provided to execute the attempt. The maid knocked at the *don's* door,' which was opened by a footman, who enquired her business; she told him she must speak with his master, for it was on so important an affair, that she could not deliver; her message to any but himself.

He called his master, and the maid put the letter into his hand; he opened it, and read it over and over. guilt and joy often altered his countenance whilst he read, but the latter seemed to have the transcendency; and he told the maid that her mistress must excuse, him, if he returned not an answer in writing; he had now no convenient opportunity, but he would not fail to come and visit her at the time she had assigned, and with a great deal of joy pay all the arrears of love he was in debt to her. He had often wished to renew this intrigue, the person of Panthea appeared charming after this respite; and he (being a lover of variety) wanted another amusement to pass his time the more agreeably. As he was returning into his house, he drew forth the letter to have the pleasure of reading it again; and found his surprise had made him forget to read the enclosed, which dashed his wanton hopes, and was to the following effect:

> I was obliged to write the letter that enclosed this, upon the command of my relations; who contrived it to revenge the injuries you have done us. My heart is not so warm to invite you to my despised embraces, nor my temper so cruel to tempt you to this treacherous snare. As you value your life, forbear to come, for near the house will be placed two hired villains to dispatch you upon your approach. Thus I take care to save that life which has destroyed mine; but if it be not love, I think it at least the duty of
> Your faithful, though abused wife.

At this he grew pensive and thoughtful, the prospect of the pleasures he proposed to himself were vanished, and he found himself, in danger of paying very dear for those he had obtained by his deceitful practices. He could not but reflect upon his own baseness and perfidiousness, and it shocked him extremely to have his honour so far surpassed by one of a meaner extract, as to endeavour generously to protect that life which had so inhumanly treated her. This revived the covered embers of his love, and by its kindly warmth hastened its growth into value and esteem. He began to loath himself for his treachery to her; Oh that his fickle heart in view of interest, had never tempted him to this second marriage! He wished a thousand times, that the contents of the first letter had been the sense of her heart, and the last the contrivance only of her parents, to break the continuance of the intrigue.

Upon this he reasoned for some time, but all the arguments which his desires could invent, were too weak to conclude anything in favour of his wishes. To go himself he concluded would be dangerous, and a foolish rashness, when thus forewarned. He was doubtful whether the whole might not be fictitious, and a stratagem contrived to draw him into some further mischief which he did not yet conceive. The force that was to assault him was but weak, two villains only, who, accounting for the badness of their action, could not be esteemed above the match of one sturdy resolute fellow, backed by a cause so just; he therefore acquainted a trusty servant he had, of the design there was to assassinate him the next evening, when he should go to such a part of the town; that two persons had undertaken to perform it, that he was resolved to discover the villains, and the bottom of the design; and therefore had pitched upon him as one on whom he could depend: That having this notice, and being well armed, both offensively and defensively, he had not much occasion to fear; for at some distance there should be two or three servants more placed, to assist him in case of extremity; and that his reward should be proportionable to the danger he underwent, and to the great service it would do him.

The servant readily obeyed his master's commands, was proud of the confidence he put him, and pleased with the hopes of a considerable gratuity. The evening approaching, he puts on his master's coat of mail, proof against sword or dagger, arms himself with his long *toledo*, and its dagger behind; and left any of these should fail, he puts a stiletto, and a pocket-pistol into his pocket. It was convenient to take a dirk lanthorn to discover the faces of the assassinators, when they should be either taken or killed; and that it might not hinder his dagger-hand in his defence, he contrived to hang it to one of the breast-buttons of his doublet. This equipment he thought sufficient for his defence. And at the time appointed he thus sallied out; at some distance followed his master, with a servant or two who knew nothing of the affair, to see the event.

According to the letter, when this single person, who was dressed in the clothes Sebastian used to wear, approached the corner of the street, he was vigorously assaulted by the two villains; their thrusts were all to no purpose, the coat of mail was not to be pierced by their violence, and the servant soon laid them both dead, or wounded, at his feet. Don Sebastian was now satisfied of the reality of the design, and leaving his servants came up to view their faces. He believed them to be Panthea's brothers, who intended to glut their revenge, and repair their injuries, by this attempt, and this provoked his curiosity; but he found it otherwise, and immediately retired home with his servants to avoid all further enquiries.

The old woman, who heard the bustle, was pleased with the thoughts of her premeditated revenge, not doubting of the success; but when she went out to fee the tragical effect, she was very much disappointed to find her two villains lie wallowing in their own blood upon the ground, whilst the object of her fury was gone safe away: and what yet vexed her more was, that she found herself obliged to treble her reward to these assassinators, to prevent them from discovering who had hired them to this wicked attempt, and to help to discharge the expense of their cures, if any could be obtained.

When she came back, she repined with her daughter at their disappointed design, and the escape of the villainous wretch who had ruined their reputation; but all the return that she could gain from the good Panthea, was, 'How vain is it for us to pretend to give rules to Providence, whose decrees they reserve in their own power? Whether they are to our happiness or misfortune, it is our duty to submit with patience. The succeeding in so black a crime would have encreased our guilt, and drawn a greater vengeance on our heads. Secure and guarded by our innocence, we enjoy the pleasures of a quiet conscience, and wait till fate shall please to change our dooms, and give us unexpected happiness.'

In the meantime Don Sebastian was returned home, the joy of having escaped so tragical a scene, so well concerted, and attended with such probability of success, and the being indebted for his deliverance to a person he had treated so inhumanly, and from whom he was sensible he merited another return, occasioned various vicissitudes in his mind. He abhorred himself for his former ingratitude, acknowledged that this action must proceed from the highest pitch of duty and inclination; her form, her beauty, her behaviour, were far beyond those to which he had yielded in her prejudice. With what excuses could he palliate his baseness? Or, if this should be known and published to the world, the general censure would condemn him unworthy of the honour of his ancestors, to part with his probity for a new face, whose charms a short time would change into indifference; whilst the black stain of so vile an action would endure forever, was a rash unwary bargain, and hateful to her memory.

These kind thoughts of her began to revive the glowing embers of his former passion; and though he had no reason to complain either of the person or deportment of the lady, with whom he was at present engaged, he wished it had been possible to have untied the fatal knot, or rather, that he had never been so unlucky to have consented to it. But this was to no purpose, a patient submission to his present fate was necessary, and a resolution to bear his chains contentedly, till fortune should be pleased to ease him. He resolved to cast no more blots of this kind upon his honour, but to live up to the rules of honesty, and be a perfect good husband for the future. He behaved himself with all the tenderness imaginable, whether real or counterfeit I cannot determine, to his present lady; and the endearments were so reciprocal, that a happier couple, in the estimation of the world, were not to be found. Nothing was wanting to compleat the joy of the parents, but the blessing of an heir to continue the line. The father lived not to fee his hopes thus gratified, for he died before his daughter had been married nine months.

Sebastian was now sole patron of the house, at liberty to do what he pleased, and no one with authority either to spy into or controul his actions. This altered not his courage, his repentance was sincere, and his resolutions fixed and unalterable, he still proved the most kind and loving husband. Fortune seemed to be pleased with his behaviour; for four months had scarcely passed when she broke off his uneasy chains, by dissolving the second marriage, as a reward of his perseverance. His spouse had inadvertently taken too plentiful a draught of lemonade cooled in ice, when she had been overheated by long walking in her garden amongst her orange-trees, when the sun was too high in the horizon: this threw her into a fever, and in a few days she expired. He was now master of all, he could do no less but grieve for the loss. He had enjoyed the possession of a charming woman, who, as he had no reason to doubt, loved him. He was become lord of a great fortune, absolutely now at his own disposal.

But alas! upon what conditions were they become his? He had cheated the departed fair one of her honour, he had deceived and robbed her indulgent parents of their inheritance, who had thus generously rewarded him for his perfidious villainy. He had no claim, no right to anything, had been long married to another; and instead of this mistaken goodness, the most keen revenge ought to have been his lot. These considerations very much disturbed his thoughts, and when he had solemnized the funeral with the greatest magnificence and dismal pomp, he revolved in his mind all means possible to repair his shattered honour, and to do justice to the injured family. When a decent time for mourning was expired, he frequently sent messengers to Panthea, to acquaint her how Providence had favoured his wishes; and that now, being disengaged from any other tie of honour, he had nothing more at heart, than to manifest his gratitude for that generous action of saving his life; and endeavour to deserve her forgiveness by his integrity for the time to come.

He therefore desired she would consent to have the ceremony of marriage again performed and solemnized: she returned him for an answer, that certainly he had not well considered what he desired, for it would be to his dishonour; and she unworthy of his bed, if the censorious world should have reason to blame her former conduct towards him; that if he had no more regard to his own reputation, she would never agree to anything that should in the least sully it; and had that value for her own, to chuse rather to live unhappy and innocent, than to brand her virtue by rendering her former marriage doubtful; but if his value and esteem for her was so great as to remove all censure from her spotless virtue, and acknowledge those sacred bands which had so long been celebrated between them, her honour and her inclinations could have no pretence to refuse what he desired, and she would fly with pleasure to his arms, the same forgiving loving creature, forgetful of all wrongs, and banish from her breast the unwelcome thoughts that spoke not in his favour.

He could not but applaud her nice taste of honour, and made all necessary disposals to salve his reputation in his former way of living, and make as ample reparation to the injured, as was possible. The family he had last married into, was almost extinguished; he therefore, with great pains, found out the next heir, who was at a great distance upon whom he settled the inheritance of the estate that belonged to his ancestors, and was given him in marriage. The ready money which he had received, most of which he had hoarded up and improved, having a plentiful fortune of his own, he laid out in pious uses; he sent rich presents to Panthea, her brothers he provided with good employ-ments in the government, the mother was treated with the greatest duty and respect, the house new, and richly furnished for her own abode, and the palace to which Panthea was to be brought, was made magnificent to the greatest degree.

All care was taken to satisfy the curious and distrustful, that the marriage was formerly celebrated; and those who suspected Panthea's virtue, were mistaken censurers. The unkind usage she had suffered made her shine the brighter, and every mouth began to open in her praise. Mirth and content seemed the only employment of both par-ties; and the only expectation now was, how sufficiently to demon-strate their universal joy, when Panthea should be conducted home to her repenting wishing bridegroom.

The end of the rake reformed.

Don Antonio had proceeded thus far in his story, when he found himself interrupted by the unwelcome sight of a privateer of Barbary, who made all his endeavour to come up with us. Our ship was in a general consternation, for we were not strong enough to engage him with any hopes of success neither being heavy laden could we propose great safety from our flight. We nevertheless used all means to make it as swift and speedy as possible. But the wind forbearing to swell our sails, there happened an unlucky calm, and we were obliged to lie still. The captain, the other officers, and Don Antonio had the decks cleared, and everything disposed in order to give the Barbarians a warm reception, resolving to defend ourselves to the last drop of blood. We had but six pieces of cannon on board, and these we man-aged to the greatest advantage, returning every discharge the enemy made with one of our broadsides.

The engagement lasted for some time, and it was difficult to deter-mine whether the attack or the defence was executed with the great-est vigour; the officers ran from side to side to animate the mariners, and where the greatest danger was, there Don Antonio was always present. I followed him from place to place, was always next to him; and I, who not long before was ready to die at the sight of a naked sword, was now inspired with undaunted courage, began to contemn death, and slight the greatest danger: of such power is custom to rec-oncile us to the greatest extremes, fear was quite banished from my heart, and no one who had been a witness of my behaviour, would

180

have suspected me for any other than a finished hero.

The *corsair* seeing we were resolved to defend ourselves to the last, doubled their fury and attack. They had made so many shot into the body of our vessel, that she began to leak considerably; we discovered where she took most water, and with our diligence stopped her leak, the captain believing that the Barbarians would at our brave defence despair of taking us. There might have been some grounds for this conclusion, had not an unlucky accident happened; a chance shot brought our main-mast by the board, and by its fall killed the valiant captain, and five of the bravest sailors, who were near him. This misfortune encreased the general consternation in the crew, and they had scarcely the heart to labour sufficiently to pump out the water the ship received at her leaks, but weary and discouraged were inclined to save their lives in slavery by a surrender, rather hazard an honourable death by a brave and resolute defence.

All the pains that Don Antonio took to encourage 'em were useless; they threw down their arms, and concluding that the ship would suddenly sink, and no other remedy in view, they chose to submit to the mercy of the Barbarians, rather than undergo their certain fate from the merciless waves. Upon this, crying out for quarter, the privateer soon boarded us, and several of the privateer's men entered our vessel. The single resistance of Don Antonio would have been very insignificant; he could not bear his hard fate, and his greatest anguish and trouble was for me who was always by his side. Thus agitated, he was going to knock his own brains out against the side of the ship, when we found ourselves surrounded by a file of the privateers, from whom I expected immediate death.

They on the contrary offered us quarter, imagining by our rich clothes, that we should be able to give a good ransom for our liberty, could they take us alive. Don Antonio refused to take quarter, and continued to defend himself so vigorously that they durst not approach him. So that finding it impossible to take him alive, the captain of the *corsair* ordered one of his ship to shoot him, the vessel filling continually with water, and a longer delay being dangerous. According to command the sailor fired his musket, the shot took place, and the brave Antonio fell dead at my feet.

Being thus deprived of all my hopes of all the comfort I had, I resolved to revenge myself of the villain who had given him his death, and running to him with my drawn sword, I gave him a cut in the shoulder, and as I was going to renew my blow, those who were behind me, seized me, soon rested the sword from my too feeble arm, robbed me of the death I wished for, and made me their prisoner. The captain soon carried me into his own vessel, when they had scarcely plundered our leaky vessel before I saw her sink. I was immediately stripped by the captain's order, and glad to put on one of his coats, which though it fitted me not so well as I wished, was more agreeable to my present condition.

When the Barbarians had divided the plunder they found in our vessel, and the prisoners were secured under a strong guard, they put out all their sails, and made the best of their way for Algiers, where we arrived in a few days; from thence we were carried to Constantinople to be sold. My only consolation was, that they had not discovered my sex, being more willing to undergo any slavery they should enjoin me as a man, than be forced to submit myself as a woman to their libidinous desires.

We had not been long at Constantinople before we were carried to the place they call *Bestistan*, that is, the market where they sell their slaves, as we do our cattle and horses in England, There were many that demanded of my conditions, and ability; they made me leap and run, to see if they could find any defects in my limbs; but the person to whose lot I was fallen, putting too great a value upon me for my youth and figure, so much beyond the others, and which he imagined would raise my price, it was long before he could meet with a chapman. At length a rich merchant, who was pleased with my person and appearance, offered him four hundred crowns for me; the market being almost over, and fearing he should not meet with so good a chapman, the bargain was concluded, and I was to be delivered to the merchant at his house. I was accordingly carried to the merchant's, and the captain received the money for which I was purchased.

Now began my first experience in slavery, and I very much lamented my unfortunate condition. I had heard before of the hardships and severities these poor creatures are obliged to undergo, and I represented to my imagination a scene of the greatest misery, but my expectations were a little relieved, when my new patron carried me into his apartment, shewed me the several cabinets, china, and plate in it, and told me that my office should be to keep this apartment, and what was in it, nicely neat, and clean; and provided I acquitted myself well in this employment, he would expect no other service of any kind from me. I was very well pleased with my light task, and believed I had strength enough to perform it to his satisfaction. I instantly applied myself to execute his commands, and he was pleased with my first endeavours.

The bell rung as a signal to call us to our dinners, and I was conducted by one who (as I understood afterwards) was our cook into a large *portico* or hall, supported with pillars, where the slaves were accustomed to eat. But who can express the surprise I was in, and the trembling that seized me, when amongst the number who belonged to my patron, I found Charles, my first lover? Neither the habit with which he was clothed, the abatement of the sweetness of his countenance by his continual slavery, or the long beard he was obliged to wear, could disguise him from my knowledge. If my astonishment was great, his was yet more extraordinary, for I found his eyes fixed upon me, and alterations in his face that shewed the confusion of his mind.

After some time when he had welcomed me into their society, he asked me of what country I was, and what was my name. I told him my country was Great Britain, that I was of the family of the Johnsons, and going to Spain upon some affairs of consequence in the company of some merchants, we had the misfortune to be taken by the Algerines who plundered us of all we had, and sold us as slaves at the next public market. This was what I thought fit to say to my fellow-slave, to disguise my sex from him, and to confirm the rest of the slaves who heard our discourse, in that opinion, it not being yet a convenient time to discover my condition to him. His eyes were unmoveably fixed upon me all the time we were at dinner, and being now time to refresh ourselves with repose, he approached me, 'I wish,' said he, 'that since destiny had doomed you to slavery, that you had been sold to some other master; for when I look upon you, methinks I see that engaging face, that has been the fatal cause of all my misfortunes and misery.'

I could return him no answer, the overseer, or person whose duty it is to take care of the slaves, coming at that instant, ordered me to go along with him. He conducted me into a chamber next my patron's, and shewing me some straw in a corner of it, 'that,' says he, 'is the place where you are to sleep and repose yourself.'

I bowed to him in return of thanks, but sleep was all that night a stranger to my eyes, the thoughts of what I must suffer by the loss of Don Antonio, were crowded in my imagination, and left no room for rest; the finding my old lover amongst the slaves gave me some confusion, and I could not conclude what would be the event if I should chance to be discovered. In variety of thoughts of this kind I passed the tedious night upon my bed of straw, in the most afflicting manner imaginable. When the morning came, my master called me to my daily task, which was to help to dress him, and to take care of his apartment.

I was concerned that I could not understand the discourse that passed amongst my fellow-slaves; I often knew the meaning of several words, but the sense of the whole was hidden from me. This, with the convenience of understanding the language, the better to perform what I should be enjoined, made me apply myself diligently to learn it. When I considered of it farther, I found it a mixture or gallimaufry of most languages, Italian, French, Spanish, &c. I soon perfectly understood it, and by a little practice was able to speak it as well as the best of 'em; and as easy and natural to me it became as my mother-tongue. I was obliged one day to wait upon my master to his country-seat, where he had a curious and charming garden.

He intended I should root up some of the weeds that had mingled themselves amongst his finest flowers. Here I found Charles, who, was employed in transplanting some trees which his master would have removed, to make an agreeable shade in a part of the garden, too much exposed to the heat of the sun. When the patron had given what orders he thought necessary, he returned to the town, and left me alone with my fellow-slave Charles, My first lover thinking the opportunity propitious, threw down his garden-instruments, and embracing me in his arms, gave me a thousand surprising kisses.

'Pardon me, my fellow-slave,' said he, 'for being so impertinent to disturb you with these testimonies of my friendship; this manner of address I know is not customary amongst men, but you must excuse me, since every time I look upon you, I have a secret inclination that makes me covet you in my arms, so perfectly does your figure represent the most dear and faithless mistress of my heart. And though the thoughts of her perfidiousness should more reasonably provoke me to despise and detest her, to vilify and rail at her undeserved behaviour, my heart melts in her favour, my language softens in her praise, and I cannot conceive a thought or utter a syllable in her prejudice. 'Tis natural to hate what has been the occasion of our ruin, but my tenderness for her, my weakness is so great, to my shame I own it, that in lieu of detesting her, I have a warm love and fervent passion for anything that bears the least resemblance of her.'

At these words the tears trickled from the eyes of my poor fellow-sufferer. I have often wondered how I was able to support my disguise, and not join with him in his complaints and lamentations; but when he began to blame me for my perfidiousness I was the most put to it, and could hardly forbear returning him an answer in my vindication: but my prudence was sufficient to guard me from such a slip, which otherwise might have been attended with a train of inconveniencies. When the first shock of this passion was passed, he took me by the hand, and desired me to come and sit down by him upon a bank of camomile, under a shade of orange-trees, so thick that the sunbeams could scarcely enter, where he chose me as a confident to unburden his breast, as to an indifferent person, of what he had suffered for his fair and faithless mistress from the beginning of their first amours.

'The famous town of London,' said he, 'was the place of my birth, where my parents still inhabit, and are esteemed the richest merchants of that place. There lived over against us a merchant who had gathered great wealth by traffic; he had only one daughter, who, as it was generally thought, would be heir to all his riches. The fame of this and the beautifulness of her person made her the admiration of the whole town: I had two sisters about the same age; and receiving by chance their first education at the same boarding-school, they contracted an acquaintance and intimacy that continued after they came home. They used to be frequently together, and this afforded me an opportunity of beginning an acquaintance with Lucinda—the name of the only daughter,—and I already began to have that innocent affection for her which such tender years were capable of producing, the seeds of a future passion that was to be ripened by time.

'Neither was I now unhappy; for the fair one made me an equivalent return, and we were so far advanced as to promise each other perpetual love and affection. Our passions encreased with our years, and would have ended no doubt to both our satisfactions in a happy marriage, had not the father and mother of Lucinda been so exorbitantly covetous of riches as to break all our measures, and destroy our hopes. The fair one gave me herself an account of what was the obstacle to our desires, that a rich old fellow called Roderick had by the power of his riches so far gained the good liking of her father and mother, that they had promised to give him their daughter in marriage; that in vain she opposed these resolutions, the paternal commands were too positive to be disobeyed, and all the consolation she was able to obtain was the respite of eight days to fix her resolutions, to comply with what was so rigorously commanded.

'In this time she acquainted me with the great aversion she had to be married to this dotard, how officiously she was teased to yield, to her continual vexation and discontent (the opportunity we had of meeting by means of the back gate of the garden, when the servants were in bed, brought this to my knowledge.) This unwelcome news so much afflicted me, that I was even ready to terminate my misfortune by ending my own life, since nothing could be more grievous to me, than to see my charming mistress in the possession of another. But not to trouble you with numberless circumstances, we resolved to take with us what we could conveniently carry, and fly from our relations, to compleat our marriage in some other place, and to remain there till our friends had reconciled us to our parents.

'The day was appointed to make our escape, the place assigned, and the manner agreed upon, that Lucinda with her servant, who was her confident in this affair, was to meet me at the waterside, where I was to provide a boat to receive her. I was punctual to the assignation, and everything was provided to put our design in execution: but, alas! long did I expect her there in vain; and I passed the whole tedious night in the most exquisite torments between hope and despair. I doubted not, but her father had discovered our intentions, and had been the occasion of my disappointment, for I could not suspect the perfidiousness of my Lucinda, who had given me such proofs of her affections by discovering to me the design of marrying her to another, and had thus kindly contrived and agreed with me how to prevent it. But by sad experience I quickly found that the promises and vows of frail woman are not to be depended upon.

'In this condition I remained the whole night; in the morning I went to a friend's house in the town, some distance from my father's; I sent spies about to get intelligence of what had passed in the family where Lucinda lived. I was soon informed that the whole house was in great confusion upon the missing of Lucinda, not knowing what was become or where to find either her or her maid-servant, that her father and mother were in the utmost despair, and had sent men with horses and messengers to every part, in search after her, with assurances of great rewards to those who should first discover her. This news encreased my grief, and wounded me afresh. I reflected upon the demonstration of love which I had always received from Lucinda; but on the other side I could reasonably conclude no other than that she had some secret lover whom she preferred before me, and was fled away with him. I blamed her infidelity, and wondered to what purpose she should take such pains to deceive me.

'I laboured with the sharpest pangs of pain, and was tore to pieces with the inquietude of my thoughts; but, finding this served only to increase my afflictions, I resolved to return home, that I might not be suspected for the person who had fled away with Lucinda, whom I now really believed in the arms of another lover. I had told my relations that an affair of consequence required me to be in the country for four or five days, and they were surprised to see me return so soon, especially when they perceived in my face some tokens of melancholy, the occasion whereof I would not upon their demands discover to 'em. The messengers who were sent in search of Lucinda, were returned without being able to make the least discovery of which way she had taken, or with whom she was gone.

'My melancholy and despair increased; no diversions or variety of company could afford me the least satisfaction, and therefore I resolved to end my grief by seeking an honourable death in the wars that were then depending between Holland and Great Britain, I entered myself a volunteer on board one of the largest frigates in the fleet, where, by my undaunted courage and desperate behaviour, pushed on by my desire of death, I performed such daring actions, that not undeservedly I was accounted one of the stoutest young fellows in that dreadful navy. But a peace soon ensuing, with this acquired applause I returned to my relations, who being pleased with the reputation of my character, received me with unspeakable joy.

'They enjoyed not long my company, Lucinda still continued the constant subject of my thoughts; for her I went to die, and thought myself unhappy in the disappointment; my heart was never at ease, the idea of my loss troubled my soul, and 'twas impossible to live without her. I therefore resolved to end my wretched life in some honourable way; and since the danger of the fleet had crossed my hopes, I was resolved to see if the hazard of the camp would be more prosperous to my wishes. And there being wars in Turkey, I intended for the Christian Camp, in hopes that some keen scimitar might in some action cut off my miseries with my wretched life.

'To this intent, I went a passenger in the first Venetian ship that sailed, in order to prosecute my design; but fortune who had not yet paid me all the store of misery she owed me, threw us into the hands of a Turkish rover, before we reached our intended fort. We had a brisk gale, but our vessel was a sluggish sailer; on the contrary, the rover had been lately careened, built for speed; and having all her sails out, made such way that she could overtake us when she pleased. We were but forty hands in our ship, our condition was desperate, 'twas to little purpose to refill; there was no hopes of escape, and fear had disseminated the whole crew: I was the only undaunted person; for since death was the boon I fought, it was indifferent to me in what manner it should happen.

'Our captain, though he saw this disparity of force, and the vain expectation of success from his defence, was obliged in honour to make some resistance, and therefore all was prepared for an engagement. He encouraged his sailors, and told them how much better it was to die an honourable death, than tamely submit to inglorious slavery, and lead a miserable life among heathen and barbarians. We had engaged for four hours before the rovers could boast of any great advantage; when, by a broadside of cartridge-shot, they made a great havoc of our sailors who were upon the deck, and we found that our number of fighting-men was decreased to sixteen; this was a presage of our approaching ruin, we were now unable to defend ourselves, the rover boarded us with a number of his men, became masters of our deck, and we were compelled to retire into the gangway of the quarter-deck; where we turned two small guns upon them, which we discharged to clear the deck.

'But we were soon mastered, and the captain, as well as myself, being wounded, the ship was taken by the enemy. They soon plundered the ship, changed our, habits for the worse they had, and putting heavy chains upon our legs, huddled us together under the hatches, to lament our unhappy condition. It was not long before we were put to sale for slaves, and I have been three tedious years in the service of this master, without giving my father or mother any notice of my misfortune; but have bid *adieu* to my country forever, in hopes that a sudden death will deliver me from the 'cruciating torments of this world. The reason therefore why I offered to you those embraces and endearments, was, for the likeness that you bear to my beloved; though faithless, Lucinda; and it is impossible to behold you without renewing the idea of the charms of that dear mistress who always possessed my breast. And did not your habit and expression convince me of the contrary, I should believe you the very same person that has been the occasion of all my troubles, and at whose remembrance with pain I restrain my watery eyes from shedding their usual tribute.'

At these expressions, he applied his handkerchief to his face, to hide his shameful tears; the mournful story had so inclined my heart to pity, that no less than the fear of a discovery of myself and sex to the destruction of us both, could hinder me from shewing the same signs of compassion: but I found it necessary, and by my endeavours mastered my inclination, very much concerned that it was not proper for me to alter his opinion of my perfidiousness, which troubled me extremely. I did what was in my power conveniently to comfort him, advising him to think as little as possible of his absent mistress, that whilst she was in his mind it would give fresh nourishment to and augment his affliction.

'Oh my fellow slave,' said he, 'were you not every day before my eyes, perhaps in time the remembrance of her might lessen in my heart; but you are so perfectly her figure, that when I see you it occasions all these irregular transports which so disorder me.'

I bid him be of comfort, that time perhaps which brings the most unexpected things to pass, might by some unaccountable event procure his happiness; and that in the meantime, he should bear his yoke with patience. By this time, the servant came to fetch us home from the garden, and I applied myself to my daily work.

My patron was a widower of about fifty years of age, he was very rich, and all his estate was designed for an only daughter, who was not yet twenty years of age. I thought no Turkish woman could be so beautiful as she appeared to me; I do not remember to have seen any European of a fairer complexion, of more delicate skin, or a more agreeable mixture of white and red. In fine, I think she was the handsomest woman I ever saw. She called to me one day as I was passing, by her chamber; I stopped, and with all the humility of a slave, desired to know what she would please to command. She bid me sit down by her; I with excuses of my duty refused, but she again commanded me, and I was obliged to obey. She asked me of what country I was, what was my name, my age, and whether I was ever married.

I told her that Great Britain was my country, that my parents were something above the degree of common citizens, that I was about twenty years of age, and that I had never been married: she afterwards demanded of me if I had ever advised my relations of my slavery, and if I had not the hopes of being quickly ransomed? I told her that having been so wicked to leave my parents, in opposition and defiance to their commands and desires; the powers above had justly rewarded my undutifulness, by exposing me to this misfortune; that I had little reason to expect a deliverance, but yet was not without some hopes of having my liberty purchased in some time. She appeared with some concern when I mentioned my hopes of redemption, but seemed to endeavour to conceal it from an antient female slave in the room, that was there as her watch and guardian; yet in a low voice she gave me to understand that she was to go the next day to the garden, and ordered me to be there at the beginning of the afternoon. I made her a low reverence, and promised her I would not fail, when she put four *sultanoes* into my hand, and bid me I should acquaint her when I had occasion for more.

The reception she gave me, her commands to meet her in the garden, and the money she put into my hand, made me believe she was fallen in love with me. On the one side I pitied her fruitless passion, since nature had made me uncapable to give her any satisfactory return; and on the other side, I compassionated my own condition, apprehending left this amorous conversation should raise a jealousy, to which the Turks are so subject, to my infallible ruin. I knew the effect and resentment of a passion that met not with a suitable return, which I thought must infallibly be my case with Sabina (the name of the young Turkish lady, when she found I returned her not those warm endearments which she expected; her injured passion would turn to a mortal hatred, and what must be my fate from such a merited revenge? This made me curse the moment that first brought me to her sight, I could not hope to allay the fury of her desires with soft words and innocent caresses; she ran too great a danger for her satisfaction, to be rewarded with such trifling joys: but where was the possibility of returning more substantial bliss?

Alas! I was unable, I detested my face, I loathed my pleasing form that had raised her passion, and drew me into these inevitable hardships. These reflections so disturbed my rest, that I could not close my eyes for the whole night; I passed the morning as usual, in pain for the event of the day; I wished that some lucky accident would have happened to have drawn me with honour from this appointment. I knew the women of that country were not framed of the coldest mould, that opportunities were dangerous and scarce, and therefore usually turned to the greatest advantage. I am, thought I, a fit hero, and likely to oblige a young blooming wishing beauty in her first passion, full of curiosity and desire; in what manner is it possible for me to acquit myself without provoking her hatred and revenge? should I not go, the disobedience and contempt would be unpardonable; besides, my duty draws me there, my patron commanding me to free those precious flowers he so delights in from the baneful weeds.

I therefore went, though with an aching heart, the first thing I saw in the garden was Sabina, attended by two old women who were to take care of her; I was glad to see she was not alone, and thought I should be the better able to act my part. She soon perceived me, and employed the old women to gather some flowers in a compartment a little distant, that she might have the better opportunity to talk with me alone. She commanded me as before to sit down by her; she was well dressed, appeared extremely beautiful, and there was a charming sweetness in her eyes, that shewed the passion of her heart; nothing but love could make her looks, so agreeable. Her first question was, when I expected to be redeemed; I returned her the same answer as before.

'But,' said she, 'suppose you should here at Constantinople have an opportunity to make your fortune, would you not rather chuse to stay here and enjoy it, than run the hazard of your life, by taking so long a voyage as the return to your own country? I know something that may perhaps prove very much to your advantage.'

This so amazed me, that I knew not what answer to make; Sabina looked upon me with such attention, that it encreased my apprehensions: nevertheless after a little pause, I returned her this. 'Not knowing in what other place, except my own country, to make my fortune, I thought it most advisable to return thither: Yet notwithstanding, if I could meet with anything here, that would be to my certain and future advantage, I should willingly yield to the temptation; and in gratitude, acknowledge that I should owe my life to the goodness of those who should procure me that unexpected happiness.'

There was hypocrisy in my answer, my sentiments were not conformable to my words; but I was obliged to dissemble, rather than provoke her hatred. With eyes glowing with love, she returned, that I must first get myself instructed in the Turkish religion, and that then she would herself inform me in particular of that which, considering the condition I was in, would no doubt be to my greatest satisfaction, and I should forever bless the lucky moment that first brought me to her sight. I made her all the obeisance of a slave, and returned her thanks for the favours she was pleased to promise me; I found not the danger of this present rencounter so terrible as I imagined, for Sabina, whom I assisted in the most humble manner, raised herself from the green bank where she sat, not to give her old guards too much occasion of suspicion, and by that opportunity gave me a purse which I received with signs of a profound respect; and opening of it at my leisure I found it crammed with *sultanoes*, and amongst them these verses.

From the sharp pains of love, she hopes you'll ease
Her panting heart, who kindly sends you these;
Slave to a slave she will no longer be,
If all her powerful gold can set you free.
No chains but those of Hymen shall you wear,
Where the kind nymph an equal weight will bear;
That state must needs be happy, all will hold.
Wherein lies duty, blended love, and gold.

Although I was very much pleased with the gold, I received a greater dissatisfaction at the verses; the thought how this affair would end, afforded but a dismal prospect; I knew not how to proceed, or how I could disengage from Sabina's affection. I resolved rather to die the most miserable death, than turn to the Mahometan religion; and how could I give my consent to marriage, when I was so uncapable of performing the greatest part of the ceremony? This brought a fresh river of tears into my eyes, and I heartily prayed to Providence to deliver me by some means or other from these afflicting circumstances.

I know not whether my prayers prevailed; but it is certain that two days after this, my patron fell sick, and his distemper so far encreased, that he began to be apprehensive of his death. Whilst the family was in these troubles, Sabina had not the opportunity to speak to me alone; for being the only person that attended my master in his chamber, I could not leave him for a moment. At the seventh day of his sickness there came to him a *talisman*, (who is a kind of priest among the Turks) to dispose him to the thoughts of another world, and to set the affairs of his family in order. My patron immediately caused an inventory of what he owed, to be made, and laid under his pillow, that they might be discharged in case he should die.

The Turks being of opinion that they would otherwise be put to their account in the other world, and if they know not to whom to make restitution of what they have unjustly acquired, they bequeath it by their last will to the endowing of hospitals and other pious uses, and part for the maintaining lamps in their mosques, with salaries to *talismen* and other religious priests to pray for their souls after their decease. After the *talisman* had exhorted the sick to reflect seriously upon his past life, and to repent of all his enormities and evil actions, finding that life continued longer than he expected; he called for the *alcoran* or the Turkish law, and read seven times successively the chapter which the Mahometans call *Chabereth Flozy* wherein are contained the actions of Jesus Christ, for which I could hear no other reason than that it was a constant custom among the Turks.

On the tenth day my patron died, with appearance of great penitence; his body was immediately laid upon a carpet, extended in the middle of the floor of the chamber where he expired; where his nearest relations came, and standing in a circle about him, with crowns made of the wood of aloes in their hands, made their prayers much after the manner of the Roman Catholics. After this, they laid the dead body upon a table, stripped off his linen; they washed first his privities, and after that his whole body with water and soap, drying of it with clean linen clothes; when this was performed, they washed it with rose-water,. and anointed the body with perfumed oils and fragrant ointments to give it an agreeable smell. After this they clothed him in his richest vestments, putting on his head a *turbant* adorned with flowers, and when the body had lain thus for some time upon the table, it was carried away to be buried in the place he had designed when he was alive.

It is not the custom either for the wife or daughter to attend the corpse at the burial; they stay at home to prepare a sumptuous banquet for the priests when they return fatigued by continually crying, as they pass along the streets, *Alla Alla Mehemeth Resul Alla*, that is, God is God, and Mahomet is his Prophet. After the interment is thus solemnized, they erect a mausoleum suitable to the condition of the person; they fill his grave with the choicest flowers, and throw into it an oval box, in which is enclosed the elegy of the deceased.

But to return to the priests, when they have buried the corpse they comeback immediately to the house of the deceased person, to partake of the banquet, and to receive each five *aspers* as a reward for their prayers and trouble.

Many Turks have small mosques, or chapels built near their burying places, for the convenience of praying for the departed souls; and there is scarcely one of these without an inscription expressing the good deeds and life of the dead person. Those of a meaner rank have for their monuments a long chest of stone in depth about three foot strewed about, and filled with flowers, in order to oblige those passengers who go that way, and partake of their sweet odour, to pray for the souls of those who lie there, that they may be as sweet, and of as agreeable a flavour in the nostrils of Mahomet, and their great creator.

After my patron was thus interred, all his slaves had their freedom presented them according to the last will and testament of my late master. His brother who was his executor gave us besides some money to bear our expenses in the return to our countries. Sabina was upon her father's death carried to her uncle's house: and thus I was happily delivered from the apprehensions I feared from my amorous engagement with her.

I was two years in this slavery, before I lost my master, and during the whole time I had nothing remarkable happened to me, except the falling into the same slavery with my first love Charles, and Sabina's falling in love with me, each of which gave me many uneasy thoughts. I had no reason to complain of the hardships of my slavery, since my patron was, as I had good reason to believe, one of the best men, not only in Turkey, but even in the compass of all Europe. His temper was civil and obliging, free from that cruelty which the Turks generally shew towards their Christian slaves, and which as an eyewitness, I saw too often practiced by other masters.

We no sooner received the happy news of our being at liberty, but everyone endeavoured with all haste to leave this place of their confinement. Charles was the only person that amongst the general joy shewed sensible signs of grief. It was difficult for me to leave him in these troubles and discontent, and yet I was resolved not to discover myself to him till a luckier opportunity should present; when accompanying me, at my request, out of town some day in the afternoon (for now we were at full liberty to do what we pleased, and the executor obliged to furnish our expenses until we could conveniently go) my old lover with pain consented to what I had so earnestly desired. He was grown so melancholy, that conversation was hateful to him, or anything that had the least appearance of assuaging his grief, when with much ado I had prevailed with him to go with me out of town.

When we were in a solitary place, out of the danger of being seen or heard, 'I wonder, Charles,' said I, 'that you should appear so afflicted and concerned at a time that demands our greatest joy; for what can be more acceptable to a generous soul than to be delivered from the base and servile Bonds of slavery, and whose oppressive weight we have felt by sad experience? You boast yourself to be of no unworthy family, that they abound in riches, and love you to despair; your absence doubtless loads 'em with endless grief, corrupts the joys of life, and turns all their comfort into sorrow. How can a noble soul, whose delight it is to do merciful and generous actions, be pleased in giving misery and pain? When you act thus you are thoughtless of a parent's care, or of a filial duty, a return unworthy for the life they gave you.

If an unfortunate and unruly passion has forced you almost upon the brink of madness, they are not in the fault; and if perhaps you had acquainted 'em with your unbounded passion, they would have contrived some means to have favoured your design.

'Without any trial of their inclinations, or discovery of your disconcert, you have the cruelty to leave 'em, to abandon them forever, and not to ease their doleful hearts by knowing where you are, uncertain whether they ought to mourn your fatal death, or grieve for your unhappy miserable life. 'Tis strange that you should rather chuse to be a slave and serve abroad, than live at home and give command to others! Rather discard this baneful love, throw off the weighty chains, banish the fair one from your breast, return to your country, be a blessing to your parents, and take this glorious opportunity to free you from the bondage of your mind as well as body. Fortune perhaps may favour your good intentions; and who knows, but that you may in time find another Lucinda to ease your complaints, and reward your constancy with endless happiness?'

Charles, who had all this time kept his eyes fixt upon the ground, began to look up at the sound of Lucinda; he cast his eyes upon me, sighed and spoke in the following words.

'I must acknowledge, my friend,' said he, 'that what you say is very reasonable; I have behaved myself so unworthily, I must confess, to my relations, that I have justly forfeited all their esteem and value, having given 'em such continual occasion of grief and affliction; and 'tis for this reason that I wish never to see 'em more, or to return to the unhappy place that gave me birth. I will always remain a stranger to my country, banished from those I have injured, and waste a lingering miserable life in a remote and foreign climate. You wonder at the confusion of my thoughts, and why this liberty, so acceptable to most, should be received by me with such indifference, such little signs of joy; but I must own the constancy of my love, the violence of my passion debars me of all content, and in time will make me die the most wretched, the same unhappy creature I have always lived.

'To return to my relations would but produce fresh troubles, and occasion of afflictions; my impatient temper would quickly hurry me from thence; predominant passion would force me from my duty, and make me rove again about the faithless world, in hopes to find at last a welcome death. That I am unfortunate, you find; know my folly in continuing to love a person for whose sake I have endured so many hardships, doubtful of a suitable return. I know not where to find her whether alive or dead; and if by chance my unwearied diligence should luckily discover her, the same ill fate, that always has attended me, perhaps will lead me to my destruction, and shew me the faithless fair one dying with pleasure in the embraces of another lover.

'This I own proclaims me a doating incorrigible fool: but the power of love forbids me to reform. It is in vain to strive to end the charm, my life and passion bear an equal date. Oh my Lucinda! my dear beloved Lucinda! (said he, with a sigh) notwithstanding the reason you have given me to suspect your fidelity, I'll adore you with an endless passion to the last. Could I but see that pleasing form, those killing eyes that have enslaved me, my fatigues and cares were well rewarded; and to end my life upon that panting bosom, would be my utmost wish: a happiness the immortal Gods would die for! But why do I talk thus? perhaps you are now in the cold arms of death, and all that beauty crumbled into earth: I will not long be absent from you.

'I, sure, at last shall find that wished-for end which I have ransacked all the corners of the world to meet: but, as for you, my friend, if ever it be your chance to see my lovely Lucinda, whose image you perfectly represent, tell her that you have seen her constant lover, who, after he has had the unexpected fortune of being freed from Turkish slavery, is for her sake so careless of his liberty, as to hazard the loss of it by further attempts; and, being not able to live without her, is searching opportunities to sacrifice those trifles to her shrine.

So many moving sighs, and mournful tears, accompanied these expressions, that I could no longer bear to see him in this lamenting condition. There is no occasion for your rambling any farther, 'my dear Charles;' said I, 'to seek your loved Lucinda; she holds, she holds you in her longing arms, presses you with her warm embraces, and with her balmy kisses stops your fleeting soul; which if it have a tenderness like mine, would otherwise quit its mansion with excess of joy. I am the happy object of your constant passion, the fair one you complain of, the very she whom you unjustly call your false Lucinda: but when you hear the variety and turns of fortune I have undergone for you, if there be a grain of pity in your breast, give it to poor Lucinda.

'Think her not faithless and unkind, but blame the treachery of a misplaced confidence, a corrupted servant, who betrayed our first design, and sold me to a villain for a bribe, from whence ensued a train of misfortunes which would have been endless, had not my kinder stars, in pity to my sufferings, brought us together in vile slavery, and unexpected freedom, which yields a prospect of succeeding joys. I durst not discover myself sooner to you, lest the fatal secret might have proved a ruin unavoidable to us both. Neither have I (I must confess) lessened my satisfaction by the concealment; it has given me the unutterable pleasure to find what most I wished, your faithful boundless passion for me, attended with a constancy to be admired, and matchless in the bounds of nature.'

I was going to continue my discourse upon this agreeable theme, when my lover, ravished with the surprising joy, fell down on his knees at my feet, trembling with pleasure; he took my hand, bathed it with tears of joy, and imprinted on it a thousand tender kisses. He begged my pardon if he had said anything that might offend me; his passion was extraordinary, and he could not account for all the irregularities of conduct it might occasion. I easily forgave him, raised him from the ground, sealed his pardon with my embraces, and began to tell him by what contrivance I fell into the hands of old Alphonsus, how I escaped out of his house; how I refused to gratify my deliverer by marriage, till I had assurances that you was faithless, and wedded to another. In fine, I concealed nothing from him that had happened to me: and to divert his melancholy, I entertained him with my intrigue with Sabina, and her passion for me.

Being overjoyed at our lucky meeting, and perfectly satisfied in each other's conduct, we took a resolution to go as soon as possible from this place; and there lying in the port an English vessel ready to sail, we laid hold of the opportunity. It was thought convenient that I should still retain my habit; it would give me more freedom amongst the passengers and mariners: we therefore entered the ship in our slavish garb, and hoped that after so many misfortunes, we should at last meet with a happy return.

We had not been a fortnight under sail before we were surprised with a violent storm. As the day began to break, the wind blew impetuously from every corner, the clouds obscured the sky; instead of daylight darkness increased, and torrents of showers, like rivers, washed our decks. The passengers were thrown from side to side; the raging billows tossed the floating ship up to the firmament, and then as soon immersed her into the watery bowels of the deep; the unruly vessel could scarcely obey her helm; her sheets and cordage were tore to rags and lint, and the creaking planks groaned as if they'd fall asunder. The captain walked pensive with his arms across, the faces of the mariners grew pale, and, as a presage of our inevitable ruin, the general sound was now, to prayers, to prayers: the trembling priest was stuttering out his lesson, when a sudden crack, as if the ship was burst asunder, encreased our fears, and filled the air with screams.

He left his book to know what was the disaster, and found the main-mast was shattered with lightening, and blown down. We fell to our prayers again, and expecting to sink every moment, every one applied themselves to their devotion, and made public confessions of their sins, without reserve. When we had been in these agonies for some time, the sky grew clearer, the winds abated of their violence, and we had hopes, though in that shattered condition, to outride the storm. The dram-bottle went briskly about, our fears lessened, and we began to recover. I looked amongst the passengers, and could not forbear smiling at the remembrance I retained of many of their confessions: some were so comical, that I could not forbear giving too much ear to 'em in the midst of our greatest danger, which was I fear to the disadvantage of my devotion; and this six hours storm made us better acquainted with each other's frailties and inclinations, than, if we had lived so many years together.

When the storm was over, the mariners applied themselves to repair the damage the vessel had suffered; our leaks were stopped, our masts splintered up as well as the opportunity would permit, and sheets which the captain kept in reserve, braced to the yards. And yet, notwithstanding we were restored to this tolerable condition, and that the sea had smoothed its rugged face, and we were out of danger, and quiet and peaceable in a grateful calm, I made a firm resolution never to trust myself more to this angry element, when it was possible for me to get a passage by land.

This good-natured weather continued till we arrived on the coast of England; we had not one rough haughty billow to disturb us: and there being a mariner on board who had spent his younger days in the schools, and had improved himself by reading, but forced by some extravagancies in his youth to take to this fort of life, he was esteemed the wit amongst 'em; and when they were a careening, or the hands lay idle in a calm, Jonathan (for such was his name) was always courted to divert 'em with his buffoonery or some pleasing story. This season was agreeable, he wanted not much intreaty, and began to shew his parts in the following manner.

FORTUNE FAVOURS THE BOLD; OR, THE HAPPY MILANESE

After the defeat of the Switzers in the Battle between the Lords Dona and Meliguan, when Maximilian Sforza had by his ill government lost his Dutchy of Milan, Gio. Giacomo Trivultio made all his endeavours to have the Gibellines banished or forced out of the State; many of 'em having sheltered themselves at Mantua, where the Marquess Don Francesco di Gonsaga gave 'em protection, and permitted them to inhabit. At that time Charles of Bourbon, that great soldier, was *governour* of Milan for the King of France; he was so mild and courteous, that several of these who had been banished, were recalled, and restored to the possession of their estates. Some of 'em were fled to Trent, under the protection of Francesco Sforza, then Duke of Bari; others to Rome, and others to Naples, according to the reception they met with amongst the princes of Italy.

Amongst those who retired to Mantua, was a gentleman of an antient family, called Gonzalo, a person well accomplished, of much honour, and whose estate was equal to the richest cavalier of Milan, His mother had had the address to have made such interest with the *governours*, that she remained in possession of her fortune, though she was of the party of the Sforzas, and one of the chiefest who endeavoured most strenuously to drive the French out of Milan. Gonzalo before he was forced to quit Milan had by his genteel carriage and behaviour gained the favour of one of the finest ladies of Milan; and he was so violently in love with her, notwithstanding she was married, that his being obliged to be absent from her was more insupportable to him than his banishment.

They kept a correspondence by letters, by the means of a servant who had formerly lived with Livia (which was the lady's name) in the house where she inhabited. The affair was so far advanced, by the management of this servant, that Gonzalo was come to Milan to enjoy and reap the fruit of his addresses at the very time when the French had discovered some fresh designs of the family of the Sforzas, of which he was esteemed the principal. And the search after the conspirators was executed with such strictness and diligence, that to save his life, he was obliged to fly from thence with all haste and secrecy.

This parting gave great uneasiness to both sides; Gonzalo lost his desired expectation, and could not bear an absence that appeared of so long continuance. The fair lady was disappointed, and what can be more grievous to a woman? but besides this affliction, she was tormented with fears and apprehensions left her gallant should fall into the hands of his enemies by ill fortune, or be betrayed for a reward by those he was forced to confide in, to the loss of his life, and the only happiness she coveted. But fortune was so favourable to his flight, that Gonzalo arrived with all safety at Mantua, To divert him from the melancholy that his banishment and the absence of his mistress occasioned, he frequented company, and paid visits to the best of the fair sex. It was not long before one of the greatest rank and beauty in Mantua was very much pleased with his manner and deportment, and her passion for him encreasing beyond the degrees of liking, she was so much in love, as to follow the warm measures of the women of that country, and not be ashamed to endeavour publicly to have a correspondency with him.

She therefore, to engage him with the more certainty, sent a confidant of her to him, who meeting him in the church, spoke to him in the following manner: 'An accomplished cavalier of honour, when he has gained a general esteem, will never be guilty of any action that shall tarnish the reputation he has acquired, or will be neglectful of taking those measures, which if not nicely followed may be attended with the most mischievous and afflicting consequences.'

He was surprised at this discourse and compliments from a person unknown to him; and after he had looked upon her for some time, he gave her the following answer: 'I never, Madam,' said he, 'that I remember, broke my word with any person, or ever committed an indiscreet or dishonourable action that might give any occasion of disgust; but, if I have, through inadvertency, and contrary to my intentions, done anything to give offence, I am more worthy of forgiveness than revenge; and therefore I desire to be acquainted with my fault, that I may make satisfaction, and ask pardon for my mistake.'

The lady was so pleased with this answer, that she was persuaded he was a man of honour, and deserved the love of the greatest lady. And upon this she discovered to him the extraordinary passion that her friend had for him, describing her beauty, and good qualities; but it was all to little purpose, for Gonzalo's morals were at this time very much out of the mode; he persevered in his constancy to his first mistress, and thought it an injury to love, and dishonourable to be so much as pleased with the idea of any other person than of the fair one to whom he had vowed perpetual constancy and love.

'I know not in what manner,' said he, 'to receive this obliging offer that this lady makes me of her affection, not being able to remember anything that I have ever done for her to oblige her to this grateful return, which would be a competent reward for all the actions of my life spent in her service, and even for the loss of that. But, Madam, I grieve, and must ask her pardon, if I am obliged to refuse the favour.

My heart is already engaged to another, and bound to her with such vows and imprecations, that it is dishonourable and impossible for me to consent to what she desires, if it had been my good fortune to have been free, she should have had the sole possession of me, and I should have gloried in the happiness. Nevertheless I beg you not to think it pride or vanity that occasions this refusal, or that I esteem it the less for being presented to me in such a manner; and if there be anything else besides the gratifying her request, which she requires of me, I will shew her the power she has over me, by a ready and punctual obedience to her commands.'

'You make indeed Sir,' says she, 'as gallant an excuse as it is possible, from a spark who refuses the last favours of a charming lady. This would have been very fashionable in the times of our forefathers, and might perhaps have gained you the name of faithful and conscientious, and have brought you into the esteem of the old matrons, but in this age, I advise you to be careful of exposing your uncommon principles, left the whole sex deride and point at you. By your outward figure one would not imagine that you should be the only person to refuse the acceptance of that which others would sacrifice their lives to obtain. I begin to suspect your endowments, that fame has been too lavish in your favour, and that your heart has been always insensible of the pleasures of love, to refuse such an opportunity of making you intirely happy; and how can you ever have the face after this to make your courtship to the ladies? Go on in the pursuit of your vanity, and you will quickly find how many fair ones of the sex will die for the loss of your pretty engaging person.'

'Madam,' replied Gonzalo, 'you give me a severer chastisement than I deserve: You accuse me for want of civility and love, when those are the only reasons that make me guilty of this rudeness. I own that my heart is already engaged to a lady in Milan, and if I should break my faith with her, you might with more justice call me insensible and perfidious; and I think this is being honourable in the greatest degree to the lady whose affections you offer me.'

'What!' said she, 'are you one of those ignorants who would be contented with a single glory, as much to be contemned in the pursuit of love as war? Would any lady of wit or sense esteem you the more, do you think, for this scrupulous simplicity? No, no, the ladies admire not this cold temper, they would have their gallants replenished with warm desire and unbounded passion; and though they wish to keep their lovers to themselves, they would rather owe it to the excess of their own charms, than to the indifference of their admirers. Take my word for it, this niceness will never recommend you to their embraces; their joys are heightened by their endeavours to outcharm their rivals; and they conclude a man incapable of a desired passion, who has so little of nature, as to confine himself to one alone. But were this fidelity, as you call it, so commendable, how are you certain that this person, this Milaneze, for whom you sacrifice the growing pleasures of your life, makes you the same return?

'Do you vainly believe yourself the only object of her heart? and, that in your absence no other warm desires heat her glowing breast? 'Tis stupid folly! Had not her tender inclinations taught her, you had never been happy in her arms. When we have once tasted of the divine and ravishing pleasures of love, our hearts are always wishing for those joys; we know no other satisfaction, and wisely in the absence of our lovers, we long for practice, and chuse some other to supply his post. The whole sex are equally subject to the fame passion; constancy is an idle and derided fancy, stigmatizes a man with coldness, and now impracticable amongst the wiser mortals. When a gallant has enjoyed, received the luscious harvest of his amorous passion, he ought not, I must confess, to abandon the kind loving creature: He should make a suitable return, and be so faithful as to gratify her amorous desires; but to forsake all others for her sake is foolish and unfathomable. And thus, my honest, virtuous cavalier, I leave you to consider of what I have said; and for the future be wiser than to refuse an opportunity like this, when fortune presents it to you.'

Gonzalo was astonished at these expressions from a woman; but it being about the power of love, he was not displeased with it; and would not have interrupted the lady, had not she left off of her own accord.

'I must confess, Madam,' said he, 'there is a great deal of reason in what you say, you seem perfectly to know the foible of your own sex, if I may call it so, and many of them 'tis true, are not renounced for their constancy; but all your rhetoric can never persuade me of the frailty of her whom I adore: and though I have never yet been so happy to arrive at the goal, at which all lovers bend their course, I nevertheless believe myself more beloved, than ever any was by that fair sex. I therefore beg you to talk to me no more of the inconstancy of this lady, or endeavour to persuade me to the embraces of another, both subjects are equally odious to me: One I cannot suffer, and to the other I can never consent.'

The confidant, finding it impossible to change his inclinations, and that 'twas labouring in vain to endeavour to supplant the beloved Milaneze; she returned to her friend who had employed her in this embassy, and acquainted her with all the discourse she had had with Don Gonzalo; that his heart was already engaged, and had vowed a constancy which appeared impregnable and beyond the force of temptation. The lady was piqued and fretted to have a Milaneze preferred before her, she thought her charms equal, if not superior to any; yet upon reflection, she could not blame the *don* for his constancy: she therefore making a virtue of necessity, resolved to be contented, she praised him for his honourable behaviour to both; she esteemed and valued him for his good though uncommon principles; and the heat and passion of desire, diminishing by degrees, it changed at length into a solid friendship, that afterwards proved of great service to Don Gonzalo in the accidents of his future years.

Whilst this past at Milan, the charming Livia was dying with impatience to see her dear Don Gonzalo, and to give him the last favours; this she concluded would rivet him fast to her heart, and was what he merited for the dangers he had run for her sake. She understood that her husband was obliged to go out of town upon some urgent affairs, and was impatient till she had sent the *don* this letter,

> Destiny has, I hope at least, abated of its rigour, and fortune begins to shew a more favourable countenance: what gives me these thoughts is, the obligation my husband lies under to go out of town for some days upon affairs of consequence. I am ravished at the opportunity: I leave you to tell me the same thing more significantly, when I see you; there can be nothing apprehended to interrupt what I have to communicate to you; therefore your speedy arrival or answer I expect with the greatest impatience.
>
> *Adieu.*

Don Gonzalo was ready to die with joy at this good news, he was equipping himself with all haste for his journey; but whether the advocate in the church, who had been so free with the constancy of the sex, had made any impression upon him, or for what other reason I know not, he began to be wavering in his thoughts. Sometimes he reflected upon the danger of being taken by his enemies upon the way, and the hazard he run of his life; it might perhaps be a counterfeit letter to draw him into a snare, or if it should come from the very Livia, how did he know whether she resented not his absence, and took this method for a secure revenge; or whether the husband, having had some suspicion of the intrigue, might not force her to this method, in order to repay the injury. Innumerable thoughts of this kind troubled his breast, and made him doubtful what to do, or how to fix his resolutions. He intended therefore to consult with a friend of his, who knew of his intrigue with Livia, and happened to be now at Mantua about this affair; he went to him, shewed him the lady's letter, and desired his advice.

His friend honestly told him his opinion, pointed to him the dangers he underwent, and the imprudence to hazard his life for such a trifle as the possession of an inconstant woman: That though the present satisfaction might be agreeable to his youthful fancy, he would in time be of another opinion, when years and sense had more matured his understanding; that the pleasure was doubtful, but the future punishment and repentance certain: In fine, he used so many arguments, and made so reforming a sermon, that the *don* deferred his journey that evening, he went to bed; the thoughts of honour, fear, disappointment, desire, and the like, had made such a combat in his mind, that he slept not for the whole night: his waking pensiveness, and the warm bed, brought his mistress afresh into his heart; and powerful love became conqueror of ail the passions, for no sooner broke the day, but he resolved to shake off all timorous apprehensions, and haste to his dear expecting Livia.

He took with him some Mantuan servants he could most confide in, and escaping the danger of being taken by the way, he quickly arrived safely at Milan; taking up his lodging at the house of a trusty friend, he soon communicated his arrival to Livia, and begged she would grant him the favour to see her. Although Livia was impatient to see the *don*, she could not forbear being concerned at his stay in Milan, knowing how much he was exposed to the jealousies and suspicions of the French, who failed not, at least once a week, to search every house, where those of the discontented party were thought to inhabit. She nevertheless writ; a billet to Don Gonzalo, wherein she expressed her love as well as fear, and desired him to come about the evening in a disguise to her house; that she would be at the door ready to receive him, and it being the time of carnival, that he should acquaint her of some particular sign or token, whereby she might distinguish him from the other persons in masquerade who thronged the streets.

Don Gonzalo punctually obeyed the lady's commands, he came into the street where Livia dwelt, whom he observed talking to some cavaliers in masks; these seeing Gonzalo advance near the door with a feather in his hat after the Spanish fashion, and believing by the lady's carriage that there was a design of conversing together, they civilly withdrew to afford them the greater liberty.

The excess of joy which Gonzalo received when he found himself alone with his dear Livia was so great, that the surprise made him incapable to express himself; he remained mute for some time, but when he began to recover his spirits, 'Oh my charming Livia,' said he, 'I adore you with that respect, that I am ready to fall at your feet a victim to my passion. No dangers could detain me from obeying the agreeable commands of my dear obliging Livia, I would chuse rather to die in her presence this moment, than taste for ever the insipid pleasures of life without her.'

'My Gonzalo,' said she, 'these are convincing demonstrations of your passion for me, and inclination will make me have the weakness at least, to receive them as such; my heart cannot be ungrateful, it pants in your favour, and my arms are open to receive you; the dangers and perils you have contemned for me, I place to your account, and all shall be repaid in boundless love. For my sake you have often run the hazard of your life, 'twould be ungrateful not to venture mine for you; but when the satisfaction, the happiness of my beloved Gonzalo is in the case, no fears of torment or a jealous husband's care, shall fright me from the gratitude I owe my dear Gonzalo.

'This minute I thought to have been happy, but an unlucky chance has robbed me of my wishes, and distanced my expected joy; with pain I discover to you the occasion of my grief, left you should think it coldness, or unkindness in your Livia: my husband, who I thought would have been absent for three or four days, will unexpectedly re-turn this night to Milan; let not this give you any hard thoughts of me, or make you repent the dangers you have run, for if you will come to this place about four hours hence, I'll use my female arts, and do all that, is possible to give you a sample of those future joys, which a better opportunity, I hope, will yield us with more satisfaction. And in case anything should happen to prevent my coming, I will send my maid to acquaint you with it.'

This unexpected return a little mortified the *don*; however, he was extremely pleased with the assignation she had made him, and thought it then convenient for that time to take his leave. The remaining time he wasted at home, armed himself for the purpose, and came to the house at the appointed hour. He was but just there, when he heard at a very little distance, clashing of swords, and a great noise, as if several were engaged in a rencounter; and one of them who was very much wounded, crying out murder, and flying towards Livias gate, where he fell down dead, at the time the maid was opening the door for Don Gonzalo, some of the neighbours who came to their windows at the noise, saw Gonzalo with a naked sword in his hand, which he had drawn for his defence in the clamour, enter the door which was open.

He was conducted into a private apartment by the servant, and everything being quiet in the street, Livia came down to invite her lover into a more convenient chamber, where there might be no interruption to their mutual satisfaction. But alas! in the midst of their tender expressions for their reciprocal joy and content for this ravishing opportunity, they were disturbed by a violent knocking at the gate; for the guard and officers of justice, (finding in their rounds a murdered body lying at the door, and being informed by some neighbours, of whom they made enquiry, that truly they knew not the occasion, but they saw a man with a naked sword go into the house) made them desire entrance, to be better informed of the affair. Livia who overheard them speaking French, doubted not but they had discovered by the means of some of their spies, that Gonzalo was at her house, and that they were come thither with intentions to apprehend him, and was ready to die with fear and confusion.

Gonzalo was nevertheless undaunted, and retained a presence of mind; and though he wished himself at Mantua safe with his friend that advised him against this attempt, he did what he thought most likely to save him in this extremity: and being a little assisted by the trembling Livia, he mounted up into the chimney with his drawn sword, where he could not long have remained had it not happened that a large nail had been drove into the back for some other occasion, upon which he relied one of his feet to support the weight of his whole body, in which uneasy condition he waited the uncertainty of his fate.

When Livia had thus provided for the security of her gallant, finding that the guards threatened to break open the door, she took the key and unlocked it herself with an authority becoming the mistress of the house, and one of her condition, asked the captain what made him dare to disturb her at that unreasonable hour, especially in the absence of her husband. The captain begged her pardon very civilly, that he was forced to this rudeness contrary to his inclinations; for there being a murder committed in the street, and being informed that the offender had taken refuge in this house, they were obliged to obey their orders.

'Upon my word captain,' says Livia, 'you have been falsely informed, for during my husband's absence I have kept my doors locked and the key always in my own possession; yet nevertheless to clear me from the scandal of harbouring anybody in my house from the hands of justice, search about I beseech you, all the chambers and doors shall be open to you.'

The concern the gallant was in when he heard the French in the chamber, is scarcely to be imagined; he began to detest intriguing and the deceits of love, and his heart told him that he was in a fair way to be punished by the justice of heaven, for endeavouring to commit so horrible an offence, to the irreparable prejudice of an innocent person. But Providence had not yet destined his death, for the guards not discovering any person in the house, retire; and the *don* with a great deal of joy leaped from his dark apartment with an intention to embrace his Livia, and to heighten the coming pleasure by the thoughts of the dangers they had escaped. But wanton fortune played him another trick, for the husband arriving just at that time, finding his doors open and a crowd in the street, knew not to what to attribute the reason.

The arrival of the husband gave Livia more astonishment than the guards had done before; fear and concern made her look pale like death; and finding by her husband that he took notice at the change of her countenance, 'Would you believe it my dear husband,' said she, 'these guards have extremely disordered me, they have had the insolence to search your house in your absence; I'll shew you the chambers where they looked in every corner, here (carrying him into the room where Gonzalo was again got into the chimney that he might hear their discourse) but alas! my dear life, they saw no more than you do now, and soon went satisfied away just as you came in.'

At this the husband went down himself to lock the doors fast, and in the meantime Livia excused herself to her lover, for being obliged to entertain her husband longer than she desired.

The house being thus secured, the husband was retiring to his apartment to repose himself, when there was a fresh alarm at the door; this gave fresh apprehension to Gonzalo and was likely to delay his torture; for there being no more than a thin iron upon which he could rest one foot only, he was so tired that he could scarcely endure his post, being all the while upon the rack. The person who had before acquainted the officers of justice that he had seen a man with a naked sword retire into Livia's house when the man fell dead at the door, was carried to prison; and being more strictly examined, confirmed his deposition with such imprecations and oaths, that the guard could do no less than immediately obey the orders to search the house again; this made them thunder so violently at the door.

The husband came down himself to open the door, and resenting in his expressions the dishonour they did his house by this disturbance; when he assured them there was no body concealed, he let fall some words at which the officers thought themselves affronted; and therefore took the master of the house and all the servants into their custody, and without hearkening to any reasons or excuses, carried them all prisoners to the castle. Gonzalo still in the chimney, knew not what to make of all this noise and confusion; and Livia seeing her husband dragged to prison, was not less concerned, but upon second thoughts she began to take comfort. Two things contributed to her consolation, one was the innocency of her husband, and the other, that contrary to her expectations she had a lucky opportunity to gratify her own, as well as her gallant's desires; and her joy ought to exceed her grief in the same degree, that a warm wishing lover is preferable to a dull indifferent husband.

Full of the delight of these amorous thoughts, she went into the chamber where Don Gonzalo was still confined to his sooty prison. 'Now my life,' said she, with great joy, 'we have time to reap a full harvest of that happiness we have so long desired; there is no ill-natured obstacle to interrupt our pleasures; the storms, the vexatious disappointments are all past, and my heaving bosom panting with love, invites you to a full possession. Fly with eager joy into the arms of Venus, she longs to clasp her warlike Mars within her tender arms. The little boy has made his quiver of me, and has stuck all his keen arrows in my wounded heart.'

'Oh my dear Livia,' cried the *don*, 'let's give a truce to words, we'll take such joys that those cannot express: fancy can scarcely reach the expectation. Then let me embrace you thus my dearest Livia, thou ample recompense for all my dangers past, and generous purchaser of all my future days.'

In these raptures they had happily passed the night, when in the morning the *don* returned to his apartment at his friend's house: he guessed by the hour Gonzalo came in, how he had spent the night; and like a friend gave him that counsel, like other advisers, which he would not follow himself, to avoid such dangerous practices. But bold love fears no danger, the satisfaction was too great to be quitted so soon, and a lucky fate contributed to the prolongation; for the husband being detained seven days in the prison before he could give a satisfactory proof of his innocence, Don Gonzalo omitted not a single moment when an opportunity presented to pay his visit: But to be sure he failed not to pass every wished-for night, notwithstanding the peril and hazard of a discovery, in the arms and embraces of his charming loving Livia.

He would have longer perhaps continued his residence in this city, had not Monsieur Mompoier (who was then Governor of Milan for the King of France) hearing Gonzalo was in town, searched his mother's house for him. It was therefore high time to be gone, and taking his way by Bergamo and Brescia, he arrived safely at Mantua, where he told his adventures to his old friend, who soundly rallied him for his folly and the blindness of his passion.

Here the mariner finished his story, which by the variety of accidents very much pleased the company. Not long after, we had more reason to be contented, for one of the seamen, with great joy, claimed the usual reward given by the passengers to the first discoverer of land; others soon climbed up the shrouds to know the truth, his opinion was confirmed, the good news spread a general joy, and in two days we were got into the downs, safe from the dangers of so perilous a voyage. This happened at the time when the English fleet in conjunction with the French, were preparing to engage the Dutch. This occasioned fresh afflictions, for there was a terrible engagement between the British and Dutch fleets; and it was fought with such courage and resolution, that both sides were very much disabled, and it remained doubtful whose right it was to boast of the victory, which each pretended to; however, the English lost so many of their seamen, that they found it necessary to recruit; and the orders for pressing all who had been at sea, were executed with such haste and diligence, that poor Charles and I were seized, almost as soon as on shore, by the press-gang, and forced into the ship for service.

This misfortune troubled me more than when I was first carried a slave to Turkey. But patience was our only comfort, and I found there was no discharge to be expected unless I would discover my sex, which would occasion a vexation not to be born, the parting me from my dear Charles, the greatest affliction that could happen to me. I therefore chose this milder fate, and without endeavouring to be released, submitted to my destiny.

We were carried on board, where we found the mariners employed in repairing their tackle, and setting everything in order with the greatest application. It was about the middle of June when we met with the Dutch fleet; their number of ships was something less than ours: Their fleet was divided into three squadrons, the first was commanded by Trump, who seeing the British fleet retiring towards their own coasts mistook it for fear, followed them, and a sharp engagement ensued, both fleets attacking and defending one the other, with the most undaunted courage and resolution. It was about five in the evening, when our ship, which belonged to the blue squadron, was engaged; and the fire continued violently on both sides till eleven, when the darkness of the night parted us. This was a much sharper engagement than any I had ever yet experienced, and I never was so sensible of fear. The misery and complaints of the poor wounded mariners moved my heart to pity their condition, and I was ready to betray my disguise by my watery eyes.

After the second engagement, many of the seamen were permitted to go on shore to refresh themselves, upon their promise of returning on board upon the first orders. Charles and I were of this number, we were very uneasy at our last disaster, and resolved. at any rate to quit the service. There happened to be about this time a considerable fair, where many Londoners came well flocked with variety of goods of all kinds, as well as fashionable clothes of all sorts, readymade, to supply the country gentry of both sexes; hither my Charles and I repaired, believing that our escape and safety could not be better accomplished, than by changing our garb; therefore, with some of the gold which Sabina the fair amorous Turk had presented me, I bought the richest attire I could meet with, and everything belonging to the female sex answerable to it.

Charles likewise bought him a genteel modish suit, and to prevent his being known, he cut off his own hair, and bought one of the best perukes the fair would afford. We quitted our slavish and sea garb, and thus accoutred, it was impossible to know us. My circumstances now forced me to rely upon his honour, we were constrained to pass for man and wife, and he gave me all the assurances of solemn vows and imprecations, that the ceremony should be solemnized at the first convenient opportunity: 'twould have been too scrupulous not to have trusted to his honour. Convenience, and a desire of being more firmly his, gained my consent. We now passed for Londoners that were come thither for our diversion, we lived as well as our stock would permit; and when what we were indebted to the house was discharged, we found only two crowns remaining.

Charles therefore resolved to enquire after his relations, to acquaint them of the accidents he had met with, and to request them that they would pardon all his former faults, and send him a bill sufficient to defray his expenses up to town. To this purpose he intended to write when he came home, for we were now diverting ourselves amongst the rest at a droll. The house was thronged, and therefore if we intended to see it, we must sit on a bench upon the stage; which is esteemed the best place, though exposed to the sight of the whole booth. I took notice that there was a person in the pit, who, all the time the droll was acting, had his eyes continually upon Charles or me; I was afraid it might have been some volunteer or officer who had been on board our ship, but I could not remember I had ever seen him, and that uneasiness vanished.

When the play was ended he came upon the stage, looked wishfully upon Charles, when approaching after a ceremonious manner, 'Sir, said he, I must ask your pardon, if I mistake you for another, though, I should not make you this address had I not some reason for my opinion: I have a cousin who has been absent from his father and mother for some time, and they know not what is become of him, and you are so perfectly like him, that I think I may be positive you are the same person; I wish you would confirm me in my thoughts, that I may not only myself congratulate you upon your return, but also be the first messenger of the news to your aged parents, who will be ready to expire with joy at the advice of your arrival.'

He had scarcely uttered these words, when Charles, who had fixedly looked upon him, perfectly remembered his figure and person, and throwing his arms about his neck, and kissing him first on one cheek and then on the other, after the mode of the *beaus*, 'Could I ever think,' says he, 'of being so happy to see you at this place! Or how is it possible that you should know me after the alteration that all the hardships I have suffered must have occasioned in my face? I concluded myself so altered, that my nearest relations would not be able to know me at my first appearance.

'Since we were educated together, you may perhaps remember

that I was desperately in love with a young lady called Lucinda, that she was on a sudden carried away, and the person who committed the fact, remained undiscovered; it was for the love of this lady that I forsook my relations, and left my country in search either of her or death: for her I have had he affliction to have wasted so many years in misery and hardship, when I was rewarded with unexpected happiness by finding her where I could scarcely wish, even in the bonds of slavery. As she was the cause of my leaving my friends and country, so she is the happy occasion of my return, which I hope will not be ungrateful to my relations, or unhappy to us.'

Richardson (which was the name of my husband's cousin) knowing me to be the same Lucinda who was so beloved by his cousin, saluted me with all respect, was extremely glad to see us, and expressed his joy in every action. He invited us to come and stay at his house, and would not receive any denial. He happened to marry a rich heiress of this country, where they were settled and lived comfortably, and possessed the affections of their neighbours, by living as hospitably as their fortunes would permit. Our treasure was very near expended, but the smiles of fortune were every day more in our favour; and. thinking this kind proffer not the least proof of it, we willingly accepted the invitation. His coach carried us to his house, where his wife received us with all good manners and civility.

The good entertainment we met with, soon recovered us from the fatigue of the voyage, and we were yet more overjoyed when we heard that my Charles's father and mother were still alive, and enjoyed a healthful old age. We therefore desired that he would write to our father, to acquaint him with our arrival, and that he would please to fend us some bills to enable him to come and pay his duty to him. I was in great pain to know the condition of my parents, but no one here was able to give me any information; I was therefore obliged to wait till I should arrive at London. In the meantime, Charles thought it not improper to write the following letter himself.

I am sensible what excess of trouble and grief my undutiful disobedience must have occasioned to the best of parents, whose unwearied indulgence deserved the greatest thankfulness and submission. But so averse is unexperienced youth to the wise maxims of riper years that they generally foolishly refuse the advice of those whose aim is solely at their establishment and welfare.

This I have reason to know by sad experience, it being sufficiently imprinted in me by the manifold hardships and misfortunes I have suffered ever since I became undutiful; and the consideration of what pains I have undergone will, I hope, the sooner move my dear father to pardon my undutiful behaviour. It was not disrespect or want of reverence for my parents, that drew me into my first crime; my tender heart fell into the first bewitching passion love. I was ashamed to own my crime, which had I revealed to my indulgent parents' considering the object, they would perhaps have thought pardonable in such tender years, and might have used their interest to make me happy in the choice that was rooted so firmly in my heart.

I durst not venture to disclose my passion for fear of being forbid what I found I could not live without, the possession of my beloved Lucinda; she had left her relations, but whether she was forced away or fled by her own consent, no one knew, and even I, who was a party in the plot, was ignorant of the event. When she was gone, I could not stay behind, I was uneasy till I had searched the world for her, left you my dear relations, my country and all my expectations, with a design never to return till I had found the powerful charmer. Fortune rewarded my constancy, and when least expected, threw her into my arms; and we are both returned from Turkish slavery with hopes of pardon and forgiveness from my much injured parents.

I hope my fault will appear the less, when you consider I have not loved below myself, neither for riches or degree. You was a witness of the first seeds, when in our childhood there was a growing inclination between me and Lucinda, the daughter of Mr. W. It was then your diversion not dislike, and now 'tis grown mature, will I hope meet with your excuse and approbation, I have many surprising accidents to acquaint you withal; but the most grateful to my remembrance, next to your forgiveness, is the reception my cousin is pleased to give its after our fatiguing voyage, and in so free and generous a manner, that I shall always think myself obliged to acknowledge it.

This tenderness from my relations stirs up my shame, and sets my heart a bleeding at the remembrance of my undutifulness; and I cannot too humbly or too often implore your pardon for all past miscarriages, with assurances of a contrary behaviour for the time to come. I dare not approach you until I have demonstrations of your forgiveness under your own hand, when upon your permission I will pay my duty to you with the greatest expedition, if the joy of the news will give me leave to live so long. Our journey has been very expensive, I need say. no more to a father I always found so indulgent. If I am so happy to succeed in the only thing I covet, the being re-established in your favour, I shall endeavour for the future by my deportment, and all my actions, to shew myself

Your most obedient
and dutiful son.

This letter was sent by the first post, and my cousin in the meantime gave us what diversion the place afforded, till we could receive an answer. Upon this our happiness depended, and made the impatience the more insupportable. This pain did not long torment us; for, in less than eight days, my spouse received an answer. Fears and hope caused such a trembling and feebleness in his hands, that he could scarcely open the letter. I observed his countenance with great attention; I found upon his reading, his aspect began to. clear, his eyes to sparkle; and a pleasing joy encreasing in his face, my heart kept time with him exactly, and it augured to me our good success. He shewed me the letter, which gave me an intire satisfaction. He forgave us both, and assured my spouse of a perfect forgetfulness of that was past, thanked our cousin for this kind entertainment, and drew a bill of a hundred guineas to bear our charges up to town, which he desired might be as soon as possible; for he longed to see a son after whom he grieved, and who according to his thoughts had been long out of this world.

We secured places in the stagecoach for the next journey they went to London; and after we had taken our leaves, and returned thanks to our cousin for all the civilities we had received, early in the morning we were ready, when the coach came at the hour appointed. They both of 'em grieved to part with us, and I was so obliged to, and had contracted such a friendship for my she cousin, that I could not restrain my tears when we separated. Three uneasy days brought us to our journey's end, and I had now the pleasure of seeing dear London again. There was a coach ready to receive us at the inn, where the stagecoach set up, with orders to carry us to my husband's father's house, I could not forbear in our way reflecting upon my present happy condition, and all the various changes of Providence; how I first left my parents, and intended to fly into the arms of my dear Charles, how fatally I was disappointed, and fell into the snare laid for me by an old decrepit lover whom I hated; that to escape from that confinement I rather chose to submit to one of more equal years; how I was afterwards taken and forced into slavery, where I could expect no other but to end my days: and that this very accident which appeared the most terrible that could happen to me, was the greatest piece of good fortune, since by my good stars I there met my dear Charles, with whom I am safely arrived beyond expectation to my own country, kindly received by his relations, and all our fatigues and troubles likely to end in a continued happiness and contentment to us both, and a pleasing satisfaction to our relations.

By this time the coach had brought us to the gate, the youngest of his sisters was expecting us, ready there to receive us. She was so transported with joy at the sight of her brother, that she threw her arms about his neck, and was ready to stifle him with kisses and embraces. The father and the mother alarmed with this joy, came with all haste to the door. My husband at their first appearance fell on his knees before them, begged their blessing, and forgiveness for all the faults and omissions past. The old father raised him from the ground, hugged him to his breast, and kissed him with all endearment, his aged eyes trickling down tears of joy. The mother's content was not less, but her surprise was so great that she had not words to express herself.

I was not yet out of the memory of his two sisters, they former playfellows; they came and saluted me, and were very glad to see me. The old couple gave me a hearty welcome, and the joy appeared so universal, that finding myself so well received by his family, and with so much civility, kindness and respect, I was not able to bear the satisfaction, but fell into a swoon with excess of joy, in which I might have died had not they taken all care to recover me. I came quickly to myself, when the supper was set upon the table. When that was ended, they obliged me to give an account of my several adventures. I gave 'em so lively a description of the misfortunes that I had suffered, that no one was so hardhearted to refrain from paying the tribute of their tears.

I was now longing to hear what had happened to my parents, who were so kind to provide a rich fortune for me when I was so undutiful to serve 'em, but, to my grief, my spouse's father acquainted me that my mother being not able to live without me, died with grief for my loss two months after I went away; that my father was discontented and melancholy, and being wasted and decayed with grief upon the same occasion, died within the space of two years: That the estate was left to my uncle, a brother of his, upon this condition nevertheless that in case I should ever return home, he should be obliged to give me three parts in four of the whole. My present joy was a little eclipsed by the loss of my father and mother, and I could not forgive myself when I thought I was accessory to their deaths. The whole family used all the means possible to comfort me; they told me that there was a time allotted by Providence when everyone should die, that the decree was not to be prevented by human means, that it was in vain to grieve for what there could be no remedy; and what reason had we to lament their quitting this world below, when they were gone to enjoy one much more transcending in happiness above?

These sort of consolations, which were administered to me every day, began to take place, and in some degree diminished my grief. I then thought it convenient to claim the fortune that belonged to me. I was apprehensive of some difficulties, being well acquainted with my uncle's covetous inclination, I therefore consulted with my husband, and his father about it, who were of opinion that I should in the first place make him a civil visit to try if I could persuade him in a friendly manner to do me justice, and that if he refused, I should use other methods to compel him to it. In compliance with this advice, I went to my uncle, who had already heard of my arrival, but would not by any means own me as a relation.

I gave him many undeniable signs and demonstrations, told him many particular actions, and events in the family which no other person could know, but it was all to little purpose: for he stormed and swore that he knew me not; that it was all a trick and cheat contrived to rob him of what he had; that I was a false impostor, for he had sufficient testimony to prove, that Lucinda, whose name and person I assumed, died in France above five years since. I replied with as much modesty as I was capable of using on this occasion, to. all he said, endeavouring to bring him to consideration; but he still grew the more out of temper, and was at last: so outrageous to bid me go out of the house, and to threaten me if ever I came there again to send me to the house of correction.

After this mortification, I returned to, my spouse, and gave him an account how my uncle received me. He promised me to go to him with his father the next day: They were as good as their promise, but their reasons were not of more force; my uncle still persisted and swore that he knew me not, and that I had not the least resemblance to his niece Lucinda. He thought by this means to keep possession of what belonged to me. Finding there was no hopes of obtaining our right in this peaceable application, we were obliged to have recourse to public justice; and though he gave us all the trouble and delay that his litigious inclinations could procure, he found himself at last so hampered and involved in this lawsuit, and so little success to be expelled on his side, when I should produce the cloud of witnesses, who could do no otherwise than testify in my favour to prove me beyond doubt the person I pretended to be, that he underhand made applications of an amicable agreement, in case I would release some part of my demand.

I considered on my side that lawsuits were tedious and vexatious, and right, though very plain, yet some time very uncertain to be obtained; that of two evils the least was to be chosen: For which reasons, with many more of the same kind, I was prevailed upon to make him an abatement, and consented to accept of the half of what was my due, in hopes that this friendly compliance might in time make me, or mine, possessors of the rest after the death of my uncle, who had no children of his own. He soon closed with my agreement, and we were very good friends and perfectly reconciled.

The ceremony of my marriage being performed abroad, was not so satisfactory to my parents; they would therefore be better pleased to have it celebrated after the custom of this country. We soon gave our consents to all they would please to command; relations were invited, and everything prepared to solemnize the wedding a second time: Grief was laid aside, and mirth and joy reigned without interruption, and I may say, that I have scarcely been sensible of a minute of affliction since that happy time, when this marriage was reiterated, which was in the year —— to both our satisfactions, as well as the joy and delight of our relations. When this was past, we retired to a country-seat, that stood pleasantly, and belonged to the family, where, tired with the vanity of this world. we resolved to live retired, and be a mutual happiness to each other.

Providence has given a blessing to our designs, by making me the mother of three hopeful boys. The eldest has a spirit of rambling, and is already gone to seek his fortune in the world; so powerful are the latent seeds of the parents: And if any judgment may be made from his temper, and those surprising accidents that have already happened to him, he will in time, I am afraid, furnish some minutes for a narration more surprising than any that have befallen his relations. Yet Providence, together with the sad example of the sufferings of his parents in this lively plan drawn by themselves, will make him, I hope, return to his duty. And had not this intention, joined with the importunate desires of some ladies, who often oblige me with their visits, prevailed with me to publish this in prevention of a false account that was coming abroad, as I understood to my prejudice, these memoirs would scarcely have seen the light, being not over-desirous of having that renewed to the world, which was the product of my younger years, and which I wish may remain forever in oblivion.

The Noble Slaves: Or the Lives and

Adventures of Two Lords and Two Ladies

Contents

Dedication

To The Right Honourable
The Lady Colerain

Madam,

The friendship my lord and you have been pleased to honour my husband withal lays me under an obligation of making some returns, and must create in me a particular veneration for you both. But there are many other reasons why I should make choice of you, Madam, to beg your protection for these Noble Slaves and myself, to screen us from the ill-natured crowd of critics, who condemn without judgment; and atheists, who deride God's Providence, which this history was chiefly designed to vindicate, and to excite men to put their trust in, at this time when they scarce know how to trust one another.

You, madam, have beauty to charm them all into silence; a look, a smile will disarm their malice, and a frown awe the whole sex. What man dares condemn what so fair a lady approves? And though our own sex generally look with envy on such excellencies as you are mistress of; yet the good nature and sweetness of your disposition disarms their spleen, and they must love, as well as admire you; and consequently favour everything that you honour with your esteem, or approve.

For these reasons, madam, I presume to dedicate this book to you; and relying on your goodness, hope you will pardon my presumption when I tell you, that I do it with the ambitious desire of being admitted into the number of those who have the happiness to call themselves your friends; of which none has a more profound respect for my lord and you, than

Your Ladyship's

most sincere friend

and devoted servant,

Penelope Aubin.

The Preface to the Reader

In our nation, where the subjects are born free, where liberty and property is so preserved to us by laws, that no prince can enslave us, the notion of slavery is a perfect stranger. We cannot think without horror of the miseries that attend those, who, in countries where the monarchs are absolute, and standing armies awe the people, are made slaves to others. The Turks and Moors have been ever famous for these cruelties; and therefore when we Christians fall into the hands of infidels, or Mahometans, we must expect to be treated as those heroic persons, who are the subject of the book I here present to you. There the monarch gives a loose to his passions, and thinks it no crime to keep as many women for his use, as his lustful appetite excites him to like; and his favourites, ministers of state, and governors, who always follow their master's example, imitate his way of living.

This caused our beautiful heroines to suffer such trials: The grand *seignior* knowing that money is able to procure all earthly things, uses his *grandees* like the cat's paw, to beggar his people, and then sacrifices them to appease the populace's fury, and fills his own coffers with their wealth. This is Turkish policy, which makes the prince great, and the people wretched, a condition we are secured from ever falling into; our excellent constitution will always keep us rich and free, and it must be our own faults if we are enslaved, or impoverished.

But to leave this unpleasant subject, let us proceed to reflect on the great deliverances of these noble slaves: You will find that chains could not hold them; want, sickness, grief, nor the merciless seas destroy them; because they trusted in God, and swerved not from their duty.

Methinks now I see the atheist grin, the modish wit laugh out, and the old lecher and the young debauchee sneer, and throw by the book; and all join to decry it: It is all a fiction, a cant they cry; virtue's a bugbear, religion's a cheat, though at the same time they are jealous of their wives, mistresses, and daughters, and ready to fight about principles and opinions.

Their censures I despise, as much as I abhor their crimes; the good and virtuous I desire to please. My only aim is to encourage virtue, and expose vice, imprint noble principles in the ductile souls of our youth, and setting great examples before their eyes, excite them to imitate them. If I succeed in this, I have all I wish.

The charming masquerades being at an end, our ears almost tired with Italian harmony, and our pockets emptied of money, which must prevent extravagant gaming, unless our private credit outlives the public; it is possible that we may be glad of new books to amuse us, and pass away that time that must hang heavy on our hands: and books of devotion being tedious, and out of fashion, novels and stories will be welcome. Amongst these, I hope, this will be read, and gain a place in your esteem, especially with my own sex, whose favour I shall always be proud of: Nor have they a truer friend, than their humble servant

Penelope Aubin.

Chapter 1

A French West-India captain just returned from the coast of Barbary, having brought thence some ladies and gentlemen, who had been captives in those parts, the history of whose adventures there are most surprising, I thought it well worth presenting to the public. It contains such variety of accidents and strange deliverances, that I am positive it cannot fail to divert the most splenetick reader, silence the profane, and delight the ingenious; and must be welcome at a time when we have so much occasion for something new, to make us forget our own misfortunes. The Providence of God, which men so seldom confide in, is in this history highly vindicated; his power manifests itself in every passage: and if we are not bettered by the examples of the virtuous Teresa and the brave Don Lopez, it is our own faults.

These persons, who are the principal subject of this narrative, were both natives of Spain; the Lady Teresa's father was Don Sancho de Avilla, a gentleman of Castile; who being a widower took this young lady, his only child, then but ten years of age, and went for Mexico, where he resolved to reside the remainder of his days; having received some disgust at his master the King of Spain, who had refused him the government of a place in Castile, which he had asked for.

He left Spain in the year 1708, and arrived safe at Mexico with all his effects and family. There he soon increased his fortune greatly, and the fair Teresa improved in stature and beauty, so that in two years time she was admired by all the men, and envied by all the women. She was moderately fair, but her eyes were black and shining, and inspired love with every glance. Her mouth and features were so sweet, so charming, that her smiles still healed the wounds her eyes did give. Her shape, her air, her voice, were all divine. Her soul was noble, full of solid sense and honour. She was affable, pious, witty, chaste, and free from pride. Her father was so fond of her, he thought his happiness consisted wholly in her life and welfare; prized her above his wealth, and resolved to sacrifice all he had got, rather than not place her nobly in the world.

But alas! Heaven smiles at our designs, and soon convinced him he could live without her. One evening the fair Teresa being at a country house of her father's, at Segura, going to take the air in a pleasure-boat, with her servants, a strong wind rose, and blew them out to sea: Three days and nights they remained tossed to and fro, in the extremest danger and despair. At last the boat over-set, and the merciless waves swallowed that, and all her attendants, except a blackamoor slave, who leaping into the sea, cried, 'My dear lady, throw yourself upon me, and I will bear you up till I die.' It was dusk, and no land appeared: But as she held him round the neck, he (swimming) cried, 'Land, land; hold fast, I tread on land'. Then getting nearer to the shore, he found his hopes answered; for they were cast on a desolate island, where no signs of any inhabitants appeared. Here the half dead Teresa fainted, and the poor black laying her upon the grass, sat down weeping by her, having nothing to give her, to comfort her or himself. She at length recovered, and with that weak voice she had left, returned God thanks for her safety.

At break of day they saw an old Indian man come down towards them drest in beasts' skins, a hat of canes, and sandals of wood upon his feet. He went to a tree, dragged a canoe of a strange fashion, that stood against it, down to the sea, and was entering into it when he perceived Teresa and the Moor: He presently made up to them, and by strange gestures expressed his surprise, seeming to admire her habit and beauty; the black who was skilled in them, by signs informed him of their distress. The Indian who proved a Japanese, cast on shore there, with his wife and three children, in the Chinese language invited them to his home: The Moor understood him, and informing his lady, they went with him. They found his wife and children in a poor cottage, or hut; she was dressed in beasts' skins, and the children were naked: The hut was built of boughs of trees, and hurdles made with canes to fill the spaces; the roof was thatched with plashes and leaves, yet so that the rains could not enter.

The Indians were humane, and treated her the best they were able, bringing out dried fish, and eggs, which the woman roasted in the embers of a fire they had made to warm them. There was only one room where they must all eat and lie; rushes and dried leaves, with no coverlid but beasts' skins, were their beds; Indian corn, dried in the sun, their bread; water their drink. This was a hard trial for so young a creature as the fair Teresa, who had been bred with such delicacy and indulgence: But her virtues exceeded her years and strength; she eat thankfully what was set before her, was wholly resigned to the will of Heaven, and murmured not at Providence. Here she and the Moor continued eight days. The poor Indian who was a Christian, converted with his family by the missionaries in Japan, and shipwrecked here as he was going with goods for the merchants to China, with a small *bark* which he was then owner of; he and the Moor went daily out to fish, hoping to get sight of some ship, or *bark*, that would carry them to Japan, or Mexico.

Meantime the lady not being able to converse with the poor Indian woman, whose language she was a stranger to, walked out as far as her weak legs would carry her, to view the island, which seemed of no small extent: Here she found fruits of divers kinds, pleasant and good, especially grapes, which, though wild, were of excellent taste; these she eat and brought home; where pressing out the juice, she mixt it with water, making a pleasant drink of it. This raised a curiosity in the black to range about the island, hoping to discover something worth his labour. He found nests of young birds, and rice, olives, honey in the hollow trees; and every day brought home something acceptable, and of great use in their melancholy condition. But Providence was determined to deprive Teresa of this comfort also; for one morning she walked out with Domingo (for so was her faithful slave called) to divert herself with the sight of some pleasant walks he had discovered in a woody place about two miles from the house; which being arrived at, they ventured into the thickest part of it.

There Domingo espied a tree with fruit he had never seen before, not unlike an European pear; he boldly ventured to gather, and taste it, though Teresa warned him to forbear tasting it till they had shewn it to the Indian: He eat two of them, putting more in his pocket; and in few minutes after found himself sick, and began to vomit. They hastened to return home; but before they could reach halfway, he fell down, and embracing his lady's knees, cried, 'Farewell my dear mistress; may God, to the knowledge of whom your dear father brought me, keep you, and deliver you hence; comfort you when I am gone, and have mercy upon the soul of your poor slave. Remember me, charming Teresa; my soul adored you, but Christianity restrained me from asking what my amorous soul languished to possess. I brought you to the wood with thoughts my soul now sinks at. I was born free as you, and thought I might with honour ask your love, since Heaven had singled me out to save your life, and live your only companion and defender; but God has thought fit to disappoint me. May no other rob you of that treasure which I no longer can protect. Angels guard you. Give me one kiss, and send my soul to rest.' Here he grasped her hand, and strove to rise, but fell back and expired.

The fair Teresa remained so afflicted and surprised, that she was not able to stand; her tender soul was so shocked, she was even ready to follow him; the generosity and love he had shewn, the desolate condition she was left in, distracted her: yet she could not but applaud the goodness of God, who had so wonderfully prevented her ruin; for though he had a soul fair as his face was black, yet Domingo, her father's slave, was not fit to enter her bed.

She was now left alone, no human creature left that could understand her language; very small hopes of ever being delivered from this dismal place, the poor Indians having lived here five years already.

These sad thoughts overwhelmed her for some time; one while she turned her eyes to the insensible Domingo, then to the distant sea, and Mexico: At length she cast them up to Heaven, and cried, 'My God, pity my youth and innocence; death would be now a favour to me. What shall I do in this sad place! How spend those wretched hours thou hast allotted me to live! Who shall close my eyes, or lay me decently in my grave? But why do I reflect on that? Who shall improve by any good that I can do, whilst living, or teach me to sustain the miseries of life as I ought? Oh! thou who madest and canst not hate me, increase my faith and Patience; or free my soul from this extremity of grief by death. But alas! do I instruct my God? Do I point out to him the way to help me? Am I fit to die, and not resigned to him? Forgive me, gracious Heaven: I rest satisfied: This lonely place shall henceforth be my Patmos: Here free from temptations that delude mankind I will live; the woods shall be my oratory: I will only eat to live, count things the most distasteful, wholesome and good, and live to die.' Here she attempted to rise, but was not able. She remained here some hours. At last, the poor Indian woman came to seek her, and after having expressed in her language much concern for Domingo, led her home.

She continued thus ten days, beginning to understand something of their language: The Indian buried Domingo, and Teresa grew very sick, yet refrained not to walk daily to the wood where she offered up her prayers to God.

One morning as she was at her devotion, she was interrupted by the voice of a woman, who was making sad lamentation in the French tongue, for the death of some person. Teresa rose from off her knees, and following the sound of the voice, came to the farther side of the wood, where she perceived a dark valley betwixt two small hills, which were so covered with trees as rendered the valley very obscure; here sat a woman with her hair dishevelled, her habit rich, but altogether negligent, upon the ground: upon a scarlet cloak lay a man, whose habit spoke him no common person, a death-like paleness reigned in his face, and he appeared as one just dead. The woman wrung her hands, tore her hair, and shewed all the symptoms of a person in despair. Teresa, who spoke French, after some time addressed herself to her in this manner: 'Madam, behold here a person, who is, perhaps, wretched as yourself, yet not quite unable to help you; tell me your grief, and if I cannot repair your loss I may yet comfort you.'

The woman looking up, discovered the most lovely face imaginable. 'Speak not,' said she, 'to me of comfort; since the too charming Hautville is no more, I am inconsolable. See here a man, who has left his country, fortune, and friends to follow me; and being cast on this cursed shore by an unskilful pilot, has perished at my feet for want of food. We have been five sad days in this inhospitable place, where the bruises he had received against the cruel sands upon his breast, bringing me upon his back to shore, made him unable to go farther. I gathered fruit and honey; but alas! he wanted other food, refused to eat enough to support life, and is now departed, leaving me the most unhappy wretch on earth.'

Here she renewed her transport of sorrow, kissed his pale lips, and beat her breast against the ground; which Teresa, who wanted strength to hold her, beheld with utmost compassion. At last the gentleman fetched a deep sigh, and opened his eyes. 'Fond woman,' said Teresa, 'sit not thus to weep, but rise and follow me; the God which grief makes you forget, sends you help by me: Make haste, I will give you food and wine, which, though but poor, will sustain life.'

At these words Teresa ran back to the hut as fast as her weakness would permit, and made the Indian woman follow her with food to the wood, where they found the lady and gentleman, both almost senseless; but pouring some of the grape juice down their throats, which was strong, though not purified like wine, they revived, and having got a little food into their stomachs, made shift to rise, and walk a little way, but could not reach the hut till evening. Teresa staid

231

by them all the day, overjoyed that she had company; and after having eat and drank a second time, the gentleman repaid her courtesy with this handsome acknowledgment. 'Blest angel, for such you have been to me, and my dear Emilia, how came you here? Such beauty and such youth, and innocence, as appears in your face, might surely have secured you from the miseries of life. What cruel accident brought you to this desert isle?'

Here Teresa recounted her misfortunes, and in return, desired to know theirs, if his strength would permit. The Count de Hautville readily consented to gratify her, and began the fair Emilia's and his own history, in this manner.

Chapter 2

'Madam, we are natives of France, born both in one province, Poicton is our country; I was the son of the Marquis de Ventadore, a man whose fortune and quality rendered him vain, and me unhappy. This lady was the daughter of a gentleman, who, though not equal to my father in fortune, was as nobly descended. He was the younger son of a general, and related to the Duke de Vendome. Emilia was his only child, whose beauty and virtues made her worthy a prince's bed. I saw, and loved her from her infancy; our affection was increased by years, and grew up with us. When I was fourteen, my father carried me to Paris, shewed me the court, and all the celebrated beauties that shine there, where art is used to improve each charm, and jewels and habit join with nature to subdue the heart; but Emilia was possessed of mine before. I viewed them all unmoved, was impatient to return to Poicton; and then my father first began to mistrust my being pre-engaged to some person there. He carried me back with him, and set a watch upon my actions.

'Soon after my return home Emilia's father died, and she was taken by an old aunt to be educated. The fortune left Emilia was about two thousand pounds, the estate was entailed, and could not descend to a daughter, so a kinsman enjoys it. This lady was a sordid, malicious old maid, who pretended to devotion and sanctity, but was really a vile Hypocrite: She used her with great severity, and gave my father intelligence of my frequent visits and presents to Emilia, hoping to gain his favour and a reward, which she did not fail of. He urged me often to address myself to one lady or other, and finding me firm to my first choice, resolved to rid her out of my way: In order to which, he sends for a captain who was going to the French Canada for to trade, and offers him three hundred crowns to carry her away with him.

'The villain accepts the offer, visits the aunt, acquaints himself with

Emilia, at last invites them to Rochel, where his ship lay, to a treat on board: She takes my father's coach, which she pretended to borrow, and with the innocent Emilia goes to the cursed entertainment, where they gave her wine with an infusion of opium, which soon bereft her of all sense; then the hellish fiend left her on board, and set out for Paris, where soon after my father went. There they contrived a story together to blind the world, pretending Emilia was retired into a monastery near Paris ; which when I heard, who was sufficiently alarmed before with her absence, I posted to Paris, searched every place to find her, and quickly learned the fatal truth.

'And now, having vented my passion, I consulted my reason, and resolved to sooth my father into giving me some fortune, and then to follow her. Providence, who never fails to punish such enormous crimes, in a short time gave me the means of executing this design. An uncle of my deceased mother died, and left me a handsome estate, being a bachelor, and my godfather; I immediately sold it, secretly put the money into the India Company's hands, taking bills; and one morning left a letter for my father on my table, and attended with one servant only went post for Rochel, where a ship lay ready to sail with me to Canada, the Company having had an account of the other ship's safe arrival at Quebeck. The letter contained words much to this purpose.'

My Honoured Lord and Father,
That you may not condemn me unjustly, or be surprised at my leaving you and my country so suddenly and secretly, I leave this to inform you, that I am gone in search of Emilia, whom I have promised to make my wife, to repair the inhuman injury you have done that charming maid. If I never return, it is the will of Heaven. Whether ever I am blest with your favour, and a sight of you again, or not, I shall never cease to honour, respect, and love you as a father, and to be your
Most obedient son and humble servant,
Francis Edward, Count de Hautville.

'I left France before those my father sent after me could overtake me, and in six weeks arrived at Quebeck, where I soon learned where the villain captain lodged, who had robbed me of Emilia. I addressed myself to the governor, and merchants on whom my bills were drawn, who all promised to assist me. I obtained an order from the governor to secure him, and search his lodgings; but could hear nothing of her.

He denied the fact, pleaded ignorance, so I was forced to let him go, and use my sword to do myself justice. I got what money I could of the merchants, discounting the bills, secured a ship to carry me off, and then one evening dogged him out of the town with my servant. So soon as he was at the fields, I came up to him; and demanded satisfaction. We drew, fought, and it was my fortune to wound, and disarm him; he begged his life, and confessed that he had left Emilia at Panama, designing so soon as he had dispatched his affairs at Quebeck, to return thither and make her his mistress, which he had in vain attempted when he had her at sea; she having threatened him with death if he offered to force her.

'But now being left in a widow woman's care, where he had placed her, destitute of money and friends, he doubted not of her complying with his desires at his return to her, since she could not subsist in a strange country without him. I was so provoked at this, that I could scarce refrain killing him in the place; however, I governed myself, my servant and I led him to town, and put him into a surgeon's hands: Then I went directly to the governor's, and acquainted him with what had past, desiring he would go and hear the villain confess the truth himself. He went with me, and now all the place rung of him, so that had he lived he must never have returned to Quebeck again: But in few days after I left it, he died of his wounds; of which a merchant sent me word to Panama, to which place I went with horses which I hired, and there found the widow's house, but not Emilia.

'The woman informed me that some days after the captain left her, she heard of a French captain's arrival, who was come to trade, and bound to New Mexico, and with him she was departed thence. I presently embarked in a small vessel I hired, and went thither, and found her on board the honest gentleman's ship, who had treated her with extraordinary civility, and designed to carry her home to France with him. What joy and transport we both felt at this meeting, you may imagine. I there married my charming Emilia, and resolved to return with her home. The captain was not long before he had dispatched his affairs here, and then set sail for Japan, where he was obliged to deliver goods; but we had not long passed the Straights of California, before a hurricane rose, and our pilot being unskilful, we ran foul of one of those islands that lie near Cape Orientes; there our vessel struck, and split to pieces, everyone shifted for their selves, my dear Emilia was my only care.

'I threw my cloak into the boat, threw her and myself into it, and fortunately got clear of the ship before she split, taking only the captain with us, whom I called to me. We had but eight hands aboard of sailors, and they doubtless all perished in the sea. The poor captain, Monsieur de Bonfoy, holding the rudder to steer the boat, was by a wave washed overboard and drowned. We were left to the mercy of the winds and seas, but by Providence preserved; for the boat oversetting, I took Emilia on my back, and seeing myself near this island, made towards it: But my strength was not sufficient, had not God caused the waves to cast me on this shore.

'We were both so spent we lay almost senseless for some time: At last we made shift to creep to the wood, being wet, cold, faint, and hungry; I being bruised, and my limbs numbed with lying on the ground, could not rise, or walk farther; so my dear Emilia strove to supply my wants and her own, and finding my cloak on the sands, brought and dried it, in which we wrapped ourselves, and found much comfort: But when God sent you to our relief, nature was no longer able to support us, and we were near dying for want of food.'

Teresa embraced Emilia, saying, 'Now I repent not my own misfortunes in being cast on this place, since it has preserved you both from perishing; we will cheerfully support the inconveniencies of it, till Heaven sends some vessel to deliver us: Come let us try to reach the homely cottage that must shroud us from the cold air, and revive you with food and firing.' They got to it, and found the poor Indian and his wife ready to receive them: They made a fire, boiled them eggs and fish, gave them boiled rice; and though they could not converse with, or understand their language, expressed much compassion for them. Here they lay this night much comforted, and Teresa much overjoyed that she had such companions to converse with; conceiving strong hopes of God's delivering her thence, who had so wonderfully provided comforts for her in that dismal place.

Chapter 3

The next morning the poor Indian went a fishing; the number of his guests being now increased, it was necessary to use more diligence than usual to get food for them. The Indian woman prepared all at home, whilst her guests walked out in search of fruits and roots, of which they failed not to bring back some, especially grapes, which were of great use to them. Thus they continued to live, though very poorly, for some days.

One night the wind blew hard, and it thundered as if nature had fallen into convulsions, and the world was unjointed. Towards morning it cleared up, and Teresa, Emilia, and the count, walked out to view the shore, desirous to see what havoc that dreadful night had made: They found on the shore several coffers, boxes, pieces of timber, &c. which shewed some vessel had been shipwrecked there. By this time the Indians came to them, and the count helped them to bring up some of the chests and vessels, which they could reach, to shore.

Meantime the ladies walked on farther, and at some distance Teresa perceived a man floating upon a chest, which the waves at length threw on the shore: His habit was Spanish, very rich; his shape incomparable; his hands were clinched on the chest, and when she took hold on him, she thought him dead. Emilia and Teresa pitying him, strove to lift him up: But how great was Teresa's surprise, when discovering his face, she knew him to be the brave Don Lopez! a young gentleman, only son to the Governor of Mexico; a youth of great hopes, quality, and fortune; who had adored her from the moment he first saw her, and one who had made an impression in her heart, which she had carefully concealed, but could not efface.

'My God,' she passionately cried, 'can I see him perish thus without regret? Must Don Lopez charm the undone Teresa no more, nor my ears hear that pleasing voice? Help me, Emilia, to save, if possible, the man I esteem above the world.'

By this time the water pouring out of his mouth, his spirits recovered, and with a deep groan he gave signs of life. Teresa calling for help, the count and Indians came up; they took the stranger up, and carried him to the hut; there they warmed, chafed, and brought him to himself, some quarts of water having first been vomited up. And now the Indian having discovered that a vessel of *rack* was amongst the things they had saved of the wreck, ran and fetched a cup made of a calabash full of it; which holding above two quarts, served to revive them all, and mixed with grape juice and water, made excellent drink for that day.

And now Don Lopez lifting up his eyes, saw the lovely Teresa, who was behind him, supporting his head with a concern that had made her forget the discovery she made of her tender affection for him to the standers-by. 'Blest God!' he cried, 'do I again see Teresa? Is life restored with such a blessing?' Here he fainted, at which she was so much surprised, that she turned pale and swooned.

They were in some time both recovered; then he clasped her in his arms, saying, 'Charming maid, I have sought you everywhere, resolving to find you, or die in the attempt. I no sooner heard of your disaster, but I procured a ship, have visited all the coast of Peru and Canada. Missing you there, I determined to go to Japan, it being the nearest coast to which you could be drove. I feared, indeed, that the cruel waves had swallowed you; but not being able to live at Mexico without you, I rather chose to range the world, and court death amongst pagans and Mahometans. I designed to visit the Holy Land, and retire to some desert, and to spend my days in fasting, prayers and contemplation: But indulgent Heaven kindly drove me here, and would not let me perish. Now I am happier than Eastern kings. This place is as paradise, where Teresa's presence makes all things lovely. Say, my good angel, did you wish me living when you thought me dead? Am I welcome?'

Teresa much confused, conscious of the discovery she had made of her passion for him, answered, 'Don Lopez, I have shewn too much concern for you, not to explain the sentiments I have for you: My thoughts of you are too well discovered by my actions.'

Here he bowed, saying, 'I thank thee, gracious Heaven, my vows are heard: If I return in safety with her to my home, I will build a church, and consecrate it to the honour of our God.'

The count and Emilia joined in congratulating these transported lovers; and now store of Salt meat, bisket, brandy, wine, and sugar, which was cast on shore, being secured, they prepared such a dinner, as the poor Indians had not tasted of some years.

Don Lopez remembered to ask what was become of the coffer he was brought to shore upon, which was not once thought of before, saying, It had much treasure in it. 'When I found,' said he, 'how great the storm was, I caused it to be brought up upon deck. The ship, though small, being not loaded, and a good sailer, held out a long time: At last the lightning fired the shrouds: We got the boat out strait, and had but just time to throw that chest and ourselves into it, before the ship was all on fire. We saw this island, and made for it; but the waves rose so high, the boat overset near the shore: We leaped into the sea, and I threw myself across the chest, the wind driving to the island. At last losing my breath, I fainted, so the water entered my mouth, and God's Providence brought me ashore.'

They went forthwith, and found the chest where they left it; but the tide flowing, had they staid much longer they had lost a great treasure, for Don Lopez had put into it much gold, plate, jewels, and clothes, designing to return no more home.

And now nothing was wanting to make this company happy, but a ship to carry them and the poor Indians to Mexico; for they were resolved to take them and their children with them, in gratitude for the assistance they had given them. Meantime, to pass away the tedious hours, they walked daily out, and found beyond the wood a ruinous pagan temple, in which were several strange images, the chief of which represented a man whose head was adorned with the rays of the sun: It was rudely cut in black marble, but the rays were gilded finely. They concluded it to be the work of some Chinese or Persians, who had inhabited that place in antient times. It was a curious building, and seemed to be founded upon vaults. Near this place were several pits and altars where sacrifices had been killed and offered. Beyond this place was a high hill over which the ladies did not dare to venture; several times they returned to this temple, and still found something more of antiquity to admire in it.

One morning the Count de Hautville and Don Lopez walked out very early to this place, resolving to go over the hill; and entering the ruined temple, to rest before they pursued their walk, they considered it more attentively than ever; and Don Lopez observed a door that went down behind the altar on which the image of the sun was placed: He boldly pulled it open, saying, 'In the name of God let us enter, and see what this place contains.'

They descended by some stairs, and entered a large room, where a lamp was burning before a hideous image, whose face was bigger than a buffalo; his eyes were two lights like torches; his mouth stood open; his limbs were proportionably large, made of burnished brass; on his breast was a lion's head; his feet were like a camel's: he had a bow and arrow in his hands, a mantle of curious feathers hung over his right shoulder: he stood upon a crocodile of stone, whose jaws seemed open to devour all that entered: skulls and jawbones, with locks of clotted hair, hung up against the walls of this dreadful vault, and skeletons of cats, wolves, and screech-owls: several grave-stones were in the floor.

As they entered the bones began to rattle, the image shook, the crocodile's teeth gnashed, and distant thunder seemed to roar. The Christian heroes, though surprised, went not back, but falling on their knees, besought God to assist and keep them. As they prayed the lightning flashed from the image, the graves opened, and voices were heard in the Chinese language, which they understood not. At last the lion's mouth opened in the image's breast, and a voice pronounced these words in French: 'Christians, you have conquered: Adored by pagan Indians, long I have been worshipped here, and human sacrifices offered to this hideous idol, by which I was honoured. But now my power is taken from me; the God you serve has silenced me. Depart, through this room you will find a way leads under the great hill, by antient Persians made. There are Christians will assist you to depart from this sad place and isle. Avoid the Indian shore, and men. It will be long e'er you will see your native country, and friends again. My fatal hour is come, and I am henceforth dumb.'

Here the image fell in pieces, the graves shut, the lamps in its eyes went out; and by the light of the lamp before it they departed, full of wonder, and past through another door which led to a long passage, at the end of which they found themselves on the other side the hill, in an open country; there they saw the open sea, and on the coast a small stone building, which coming nearer to, they found to be a house. At the door of it stood a venerable man in a Persian dress: He observed them as one amazed; when they came near, he came to meet them, and speaking Spanish, asked whence they came, and who they were: Don Lopez informed him.

He embraced him, saying, 'Welcome Christians, in God's name; enter, and refresh yourselves.' They came in and found a house neat, and well furnished, with carpets, porcelain, quilts, painting, screens, and such furniture as the Persians of distinction use; with three well dressed slaves, who brought wine, sherbet, and fowl, and boiled rice. Being seated with much ceremony, the Persian staid not to be in-treated, but said, 'Eat, gentlemen, and I will tell you how I came to this place, and why I dwell here.' They bowed, and respectfully kept silence, much desiring to know who he was, which he thus informed them of.

Chapter 4

'I was born in Persia, my father was a general in the emperor's service. I was made a captain of his guard at 20 years of age, much esteemed by him, and in great favour, and knew no greater happiness than to be great, or religion but Mahometism: I had a noble house and a *seraglio*, where five women of great beauty served my pleasures, and sweetened all those hours that I dedicated to my diversions. It happened that a Turkish captain brought some slaves to sell at Ispahan; amongst which was a Spanish girl, a virgin of but thirteen years of age, fair as nature ever made: Her complexion exceeded art, her eyes were dark blue, her hair light brown, her features soft and charming; she had an air so innocent, so modest, so engaging, that she attracted the eyes of all that past along: It was my fortune to be going to the palace that way: I saw her, and stopping to admire her beauty, I presently asked the price of that sweet girl; the captain asked me a hundred crowns: I paid him down the money, and sent one of my slaves home with her.

'It is impossible to describe to you how uneasy I was to go home; my impatience was so great, that I thought each hour a year whilst the emperor detained me. He was going to ride in the Almaidan, which would have obliged me to stay with him all day; I therefore feigned a sudden indisposition, and begged leave to retire; he consented, and I flew to my charming slave: The eunuch that kept my women had placed her in a chamber to wait my commands. I hastily asked for her; they told me dinner waited: But I neglected eating, and entering the chamber, found the charming Maria, for that was her name, seated upon a couch, pale as death, her head gently reclining on her lovely hand, her face all bathed in tears. She rose at my coming up to her; I took her in my arms with a transport I had never known before, and bid the eunuch bring in wine and meat, and I would eat here.

'He withdrew: I kissed, embraced, and shewed her all the most tender marks of esteem: she trembled, wept, looked down, and sighed as if her heart would break. Dinner brought in I courted her to eat and drink, but she refused. Unable to delay my bliss, I took her by the hand, led her into the bedchamber; but then she fell upon her knees, still silent, not answering one word, and shewed such fear and grief, that I was shocked; my blood cooled, and I resolved to court her to my arms, and stay till she would make me happy. I took her up, wiped away her tears, and asked her in Spanish, why she treated me so cruelly? having asked what nation she was of, when I bought her.

'"You are," said she, "an odious Mahometan, and I a Christian: I am your slave, by Heaven's permission; but my soul is free, and cannot consent to such a hateful deed. Leave me or kill me; for I prefer death to a disgraceful life. Force me, and I will hate you, loath you, ruin your joys, and fly you with scorn and coldness: but spare my virtue. Oh! spare my shame, and I will adore you, do anything that you command."

'In short she melted my soul; I treated her as if I had been her slave, and used her so, that she promised if I would turn Christian, she would yield to be my wife. In few days the emperor was informed what a beautiful virgin I had purchased: He asked me gently, "Tanganor, may I not see the fair Spanish girl you have at home? Pray bring her to me this day: I have heard much of her."

'I remained silent, as one thunderstruck for some time; at last recovering, "My mighty Lord," said I, "she is not what fame reports, but I will fetch her to you."

'I departed from court that moment so distracted, i knew not what course to take; I acquainted Maria with what happened, who appeared as disordered as I: I resolved not to part with her, yet dared not keep her: The emperor was not to be trifled withal: If he were disobliged, death and ruin must follow. Whilst we were debating, my eunuch entered the room trembling; "My Lord," said he, "the emperor has sent Bendarius his chief eunuch with a guard to demand the fair slave."

'E'er he had finished the eunuch entered, and taking her by the hand, who was all in tears, "Weep not, fair virgin," said he, "for such I hope you are; an emperor's bed courts your acceptance; you are too fair for any subject to possess." He gave her no time to reply, but took her away in a *sedan*, leaving me in the utmost distraction and despair.

'I knew my ruin was decreed, and was too well satisfied of Maria's virtue, to believe that she would yield to the emperor, without such reluctance as would inform him she loved me; and then my death was certain: I therefore resolved to convey into some secret place what money, jewels, and plate I could; and disguising myself, retire to some place, where I might lie concealed. Achmet, my eunuch, generously offered to attend, and conduct me to his mother's house, which was far from Ispahan, near Mount Taurus. I accepted willingly his offer, and loading two horses with what was most valuable, departed that night, and travelling all night and the next day, got clear of all pursuit.

'So soon as I was arrived at Mount Taurus, I blacked my face and hands, and changed my dress for that of a slave; buried my treasure, and resolved to continue here till Achmet returned to Ispahan, and learned what Maria's fate was; charging him to procure a sight of her, if possible, and to return and tell me; resolving if she had yielded, and was content, to cross the mountain, and retire to the deserts, and there spend my days.

'Achmet departed, and it was many days before he returned; during which you may imagine the anxious thoughts that possessed my soul; but just God, how great was my surprise when I saw him enter the house with Maria in his hand! She had a vail on, which I throwing up to salute her, saw that she was blind. "My Lord, said she, start not at the sight, my eyes are sacrificed to virtue, with the loss of them I have procured your happiness; I would have done more, had Christianity permitted, and would have died, but I have cheaply bought my repose with the loss of one sense."

'"Thou glorious woman," said I, clasping her in my arms, "what words can express my wonder, and affection? Thy virtues shine more than their lovely eyes did, and shall procure thee an immortal name."

'I led her into my homely chamber, refreshed her with wine, and food, and there she told me what had befallen her.

'"I was," said she, "brought to a noble apartment, which you, no doubt, have seen in the palace: There the eunuch brought two female slaves to me, with a habit suiting a queen, and departed. The maids dressed me, whilst my soul was tortured with a thousand apprehensions. I fancied myself preparing to be sacrificed, and almost wished I had not been a Christian. When they had decked me as they pleased, they withdrew; and soon after the emperor came in, a man whose person and mien was noble and agreeable. He gazed upon me some time, then took a ring of great price from his finger, put it upon mine, and said in Spanish, 'Fair Maria, you are worthy a monarch's bed: Fame has done you wrong, and Tanganor was a villain to his prince and you. I'll make you mistress of queens, and shew you what a Persian monarch can bestow on her he loves. Come to my arms, and let your soul welcome mine.'

"'Here he embraced, and almost stifled me with kisses; I gently strove to loose myself, and, falling down at his feet with tears, begged to be heard: 'My mighty Lord, said I, look not upon me with desire, I am unworthy you, I am a wretched maid, torn from my friends and country, by a villain, a robber, and by his means now made a slave; but I am a Christian, and a virgin, and e're I will yield to your desires I will die. Tanganor is by promise my husband, he has vowed to be a Christian, and to marry me; Oh! let your bounty give me back and make me happy, or resolve to see me die here at feet: I will be only his, and never yield to gratify another.' 'Fond maid,' said he, 'I have heard too much, all that my slaves possess is mine, and you are, and shall be so; your virtue charms me more than your eyes. Now I am resolved never to part with you: Force must I find procure me now what your consent shall afterwards secure me of.'

"'Here he took me in his arms, and carried me to a rich bed, on which he threw me. My soul was shocked at this, and so surprised, I soon resolved what to do; "My eyes shall never see my shame," said I, "nor more inflame mankind: These I offer up to virtue, and they shall weep no more in ought but blood."

"'At these words I tore my eyeballs out, and threw them at him."

"'I saw no more,' but heard him say, 'Ah cruel maid, what have you done? Tanganor, you are happy: Had I been so fortunate to be beloved like you, I had been more than mortal. Maria, I would give all Persia to restore your sight: By Mahomet you are more than woman, and I will never presume to sue again for what you must deny. Tell me what I shall do to expiate my crime.' 'Restore me to my Lord, I beg only that grace,' said I, 'and I will pray for you with my last breath.' He answered, 'I will resign you to my rival; but it is hard. Blind as you are, you charm me, and to keep my word I must not view your face again; go, and take care I never see you, nor Tanganor more, lest I forget my promise, and relapse.'

"'Here he called Bendarius, kissed my hands, on which I felt his falling tears, and left me. I was carried strait back to your house, where Achmet found me sick of a fever, which recovering I came with him; and now am happy, if you keep your faith with me."

'Thus Maria finished her sad story; and after this I need not tell you I adored her, and there sought, and found a Christian monk who first baptized me, and then married us. I then considered what course it was best for us to steer; and resolved to retire with her into this island on this side where the Japanese vessels often call for fresh water. I carried her through the great mogul's dominions down to Goa, and there we took ship for this island, where my slaves which I brought with me repaired and fitted up this house. Here I have now lived fifteen years, and have three children by my dear Maria, who keeps much in her chamber, because of her being blind. Once a year we receive letters from my friends, and returns from my estate of fruits, spices, clothes, and what is wanting. The emperor never enquired more after me, nor molested my house or friends; my brother manages, and lives upon my estate. And thus, gentlemen, I have related to you my unfortunate life; and if I can assist you, command me. The ship we expect soon, it shall carry you where you please.'

They returned him many thanks, and he desired them to bring the ladies. 'I have,' said he, 'a priest, my chaplain in the house, whom I brought from Goa with me, he shall supply your spiritual wants, and my dear Maria shall with joy entertain the ladies. My house is large enough to receive you all, and it will be a great happiness for us to be all together. I have often wondered there were no inhabitants to be seen when I have walked over the hill, but never thought it worthwhile to search farther.' Don Lopez and the Count de Hautville took leave, being impatient to inform Teresa and Emilia of the strange discoveries they had made, and promised to return to the noble Tanganor's the next morning.

Chapter 5

It was noon before Don Lopez and the count reached the cottage, where they found the ladies, to whom they related all the surprising adventures they had met with. 'And now, my charming Teresa,' said Don Lopez, 'we may quit this dismal place; Providence has directed us to a better, where we shall have company and entertainment suiting our desires and wants. And you,' said he to the poor Indians, 'our generous hosts, shall be received, and if you like of it, entertained at ease, or return to your own country in that ship that will, I hope, carry you to Japan, and us to Mexico.' An universal joy now spread itself through this little family; dinner was got ready, and nothing spared of what provisions they had got. The poor Indian got out his canoe in the evening, to put aboard it what wine, brandy, and salt meat they had left. They lay down at night to sleep, but Don Lopez slept not at all; his soul was transported, having nothing in view but the possession of his dear Teresa: He knew a Christian priest was at Tanganor's, and resolved to press her to make him happy.

At break of day they all rose, and set out for Tanganor's; the poor Indian and her children followed, loaden with the mean furniture their cottage afforded; which they could not consent to leave behind them. Don Lopez and the count emptied the rich chest that belonged to Don Lopez, and fearing to venture it in the canoe, carried all the plate, money, and clothes that were in it, with them, the ladies assisting. In some hours, resting often in the way, they arrived at Tanganor's, who received them courteously, with Father Augustine, his chaplain, a man whose humble appearance, and affable behaviour spoke his virtues; he embraced, and welcomed them with great tenderness, and taking the ladies by the hand, said, 'Come, my children, I will lead you to a lady, who though blind, shall welcome you; and one whose virtues you may be proud to imitate.'

Tanganor conducting the gentlemen, they all went to his lady's apartment, whom they found sitting in a chair with her three children seated on little stools by her: Her son who was then about eight years old, was reading a holy meditation for the morning; whilst the two little girls, Maria and Leonora, were at work.

Tanganor informed her of the ladies being there, whose story he had told her the night before. She rose to salute them, saying, 'Ladies, excuse me, if I pay respect to the younger first, since I cannot see you. My soul rejoices at the arrival of such company; though I cannot see the light, yet I can relish the charms of conversation.' Here Teresa and Emilia embraced her, admiring her beauty, which could not be altogether eclipsed by the black ribbon that covered her eyelids; her shape, her features and complexion were incomparable.

'Madam,' said Teresa, 'I wonder not that an Eastern monarch adored you; you are still so lovely, that your lord may justly account himself supremely happy in the possession of such a wife. The want of sight adds to your charms, and causes us to love and admire you, even before we converse with you.' Emilia joined in her praises; and, in fine, the lady put an end to the discourse, by begging them to accept of a breakfast with her, which was brought in. They passed the day with much pleasure.

In the evening, Don Lopez, who had privately acquainted Father Augustine with his design, taking Teresa by the hand, led her aside into a room, where he thus addressed himself to her: 'Charming Teresa, God has been pleased to preserve and bring us together, in a wonderful manner; I know that you are not insensible or ignorant of my passion for you, nay, I even hope that you love me; do not longer, charming Maid, defer to make me happy. Here is a priest to join us; give to my arms and care, that person that my soul adores and loves above all earthly things. It is I must guard and carry you to Mexico again. Though you are very young, yet you are of years to marry. Fate has decreed you mine, keep me no longer languishing; but crown my hopes, and yield to Heaven's will, who brought me safely to you.'

Here he embraced her tenderly; she blushed and answered, 'Don Lopez, you shall be happy. 'Though with much confusion I consent to make you master of Teresa's heart and hand, do as you please: If we must perish on the sea, or wander in strange lands, it is better we should be married, and my honour so secured, than to be still but friends. I own your merit, and confess I love you.'

He clasped her in his arms transported, led her to the priest, who that joyful night performed the ceremony, making Don Lopez blessed as man could be. And now for some days they past the time in pleasure; Tanganor diverted them with hunting, fishing, and shewed them many curious caves, and pagan oratories which yet remained on the island. At last the ship arrived from Japan, bringing much goods, as rich Persia silks, cotton, linen, spices, fruit, sugar, Tea, chocolate, liquors, live fowls of several kinds for breed, tame beasts, and all things wanting. Tanganor with these treated and made presents to his guests of what they wanted: And the ship being to return to Japan, he proposed to them what to do. They resolved to go for Mexico with the ship, which being now unloaded, might easily go thither before it returned to Japan; so taking their leaves, the count and Don Lopez, with their wives, departed, leaving the poor Indians, who chose to live with Tanganor.

The wind sitting fair they soon arrived at Mexico, where they found the governor, Don Lopez's father, gone for Spain, being recalled, and Don Sancho de Avilla, Teresa's father, they found very sick; her loss having thrown him into a deep melancholy, and lingering fever, of which he never perfectly recovered, but in less than a year's time died, leaving a vast estate to his daughter Teresa. In short time after, the governor being gone, his son Don Lopez resolved to go home to Spain, in order to which he sold off all his effects, and lands, taking bills on merchants at Barcelona; and with Teresa, the Count de Hautville, and Emilia who desired to accompany him, designing to go to France from Spain, went on board a Spanish ship with much riches, and set sail for Spain.

They had good weather and a prosperous voyage many days, but when they came near the entrance of the Straights of Gibraltar, the wind began to blow hard, and drove them on the coast of Barbary. Here two pirates of Algiers came up with them, and soon gave them to understand who they were, by firing at them, and summoning them to surrender; they made all the defence they were able, but, alas! the ship was heavy laden, their hands and guns few: howsoever, the captain was very brave, and Don Lopez and the Count de Hautville assisting, they resisted the Turks, till such time as the grappling irons having hold of the vessel the cruel *infidels* boarded it, and entered in such numbers as obliged the poor Christians to retire into the great cabin, which the Turks broke into sword in hand. The captain was killed before upon the deck, both the young lords wounded, the seamen mostly dead, or dying, so that none were left but the two helpless ladies, and their wounded husbands, whom they held bleeding in their arms, and a poor boy who stood weeping by.

The poor affrighted ladies fell on their knees, imploring the *infidels* pity: Their beauty pleaded more than all they could say in their favour. The Turkish captains raised them from the ground, gazing on their charming faces; and having given orders to their men to plunder the ship of what was most valuable, and bring her into Algiers, they ordered them and their husbands to be brought on board one of their ships, where Achmet Barbarosa who commanded the biggest received them, ordering the lords' wounds to be dressed by his surgeon; and entertained the ladies with much civility, and seeming compassion. Teresa was big with child, and so disordered with the fright, that Don Lopez was in the utmost concern for her.

In few hours they landed at Algiers, and were conducted to Barbarosa's house together, and lodged in an apartment, where he left them to go to the Governor of Algiers, to acquaint him with the rich prize he had taken, and to offer him what share he pleased of the slaves and plunder. Our unfortunate travellers thus left alone, Don Lopez was the first who broke the melancholy silence, that till then reigned amongst them. 'Charming Teresa,' said he, 'my joy, my love, my all, soon shall we be parted; all my hopes of happiness are ended; your youth and beauty now will cost my life and your repose; you will be ravished from me by some powerful *infidel*, who will adore your charms, and force you to his cursed embraces.'

Teresa, drowned in tears, fell on his neck, and could not speak. Then the count, whom loss of blood had rendered faint, and scarce able to speak, looked on Emilia; 'My dear,' said he, 'do you hear this unmoved, what may your wretched husband hope? Can you consent, and live another's?'

'No, my dear Lord,' said she, 'you know me better; my soul is prepared for all events, and I will die rather than live a vassal to a vile Mahometan's unlawful lust.'

'And so will I,' answered the reviving Teresa. 'Fear nothing, brave Emilia, we will go together, trusting in that God who is able to preserve our souls and bodies. Slaves we are doubtless doomed to be, but our minds cannot be confined; our lives we must not end with our own hands, but may resist all sinful acts till life and sense be lost.'

At these words a servant entered the room, a *renegado* Spaniard, wicked as hell, and one who renouncing Christianity, had endeared himself to the Governor of Algiers, and was by him made rich, and used by him for his beastly pleasure; he told the ladies in Spanish, they must go with him to the governor; 'and you, gentlemen,' said he, 'must prepare to go in a litter that will presently be here, to carry you to his Country seat, where you may recover your health, and write to your friends to send what ransom shall be required for you.'

At these words, the brave Don Lopez rose, and clasping Teresa in his arms, replied, 'Vile slave, depart before these hands stop your damned voice, and rend you in pieces: I will die, apostate villain, before I will part with her; my arms shall grasp her even in death, and bless the hand that kills us together.' The Count de Hautville stood before Emilia; they had no swords or arms of any kind to defend themselves.

The slave, as if amazed, departed the room, shutting the door fast after him, but soon returned with a band of soldiers, who rushing in, seized the ladies and lords, giving them no time to speak to one another. They led, or rather dragged, Teresa and Emilia through the streets to the governor's palace, and there secured them; their arms pinioned, they tied them to two pillars in the hall, and so retired to the gate. Meantime the lords were bound hand and foot, thrown into a cart, and drove to a country house of the governor's, forty miles from the city; there they were carried into a spacious room, and chained to the floor by the leg; a mattress and quilts lay there upon the boards, on which they might lie down. Here they had food and wine brought them, for the Turks guessed by the vast treasure they found in the ship, and their habit, that they were persons of quality, and therefore feared to lose their ransoms if they killed or starved them. They refused to eat two days, but the third, hunger compelled them to it. Thus they remained some days, in the most disconsolate condition that ever men were in; where we must leave them to enquire what became of Teresa and Emilia.

The *renegado* Roderigo giving an account to the governor of what was past, and of the ladies arrival, he soon entered the hall with Capt. Barbarosa, to whom he had promised to give her he least liked; but he beheld them with admiration, seemed divided in himself, not knowing which to choose. He was a man of an excellent shape and stature, his mien great and majestic, his vest and tunic were made of cloth of gold, his *turbant* glittered with jewels, diamonds, rubies, and emeralds, which seemed to emulate each other; in fine, he was not much above thirty, and was one of the most beautiful and accomplished men of his nation, which I mention out of respect to those unfortunate ladies, whose virtues are to be the more admired in resisting the passionate solicitations of such a man. Teresa's youth, and the charming innocence that blooms in virgins faces at fourteen, which she had not lost by being a wife wonderfully struck him; grief added to her charms, her downcast eyes received new fires when lifted up. He gazed upon her with such transport, that had not the captain who was inflamed with her beauty reminded him of Emilia, he had fixed on Teresa; but turning to the other, he was doubly wounded: Her riper charms, with the heroic soul that sparkled in her eyes, a second time inflamed his soul, and he could part with neither.

'Barbarosa,'said he,'I must have both these lovely women, name the price, and make some other choice, these must be mine.'

The captain murmured, but seeing he was obstinate, he dared not tempt his fate, but told him they were at his service. The governor pleased, strait ordered him two hundred pieces of gold; so he departed horribly vexed, and meditating revenge. Then the governor ordered the ladies to be unbound, and placed in two different chambers, with slaves to watch and attend them. Here the trunks of rich habits they had brought from Mexico, were, to their great surprise, brought and presented to them; nothing being taken from them by the governor's order.

Nothing was more dreadful to these ladies than this separation; they both refused to eat or drink, and by night were so faint, that they were scarce able to stand. About ten o'clock in the evening a supper was brought into Teresa's chamber; and soon after the governor entered, the *renegado* waiting on him, retired to the door, which he shut, and stood without: The governor seeing her look pale as death, sitting unmoved, approached her with much tenderness, fearing she had taken some fatal resolution to destroy herself: He kissed her hands, kneeled at her feet, and intreated her to rise and eat. He courted her with all the eloquence love can inspire, to which she gave no answer but sighs and tears; at last she looked upon him earnestly:

'Governor', said she, 'you plead in vain; I am deaf to all intreaties, and can never yield to gratify you. I am married, and with child by a noble husband, whom I am bound to love, and for whom I will preserve my person, nor will I ever consent to your desires; nor will I ever eat again, till you have freed me from this place: Resolve therefore to see me die, or generously set me at liberty. Do not attempt to force me, lest I do some dreadful deed, and fill your soul with endless remorse.'

Here she fell at his feet, and let fall a shower of tears, then fainted.

This touched his soul, and made him relent; though a Mahometan, he was generous, and compassionate. He took her in his arms, poured wine into her mouth, and with much difficulty brought her to life again. Then she renewed her complaints; to which he replied, 'Charming, matchless woman, where virtue, beauty, wit, and every grace conspires to captivate my soul! too happy he who calls you his. Fly not from me to death; but give me leave to wait upon, and merit your esteem, by all a lover can perform. I will never use base force, but prayers and sighs shall thaw your breast, and Selim will be your eternal slave. To prove I am so, this night I will leave you to repose, and not presume to urge you farther.'

He kissed her hand, and, opening a door, withdrew into another room. Then a blackamoor maid entered, and folding down the bed, made signs to her to undress; which she fearing to do, though in great want of sleep, refused, and only lay down upon it. The maid left a candle burning, and withdrew, shutting the door after her. Soon after Teresa heard Emilia's voice in the next room, with Selim; and hearkening, heard him say, 'Are you then cruel like Teresa? You are more experienced and more ripe for joy: Come, come, trifle not with me; I am resolved to possess you, and will not be denied.'

She heard a noise, and then Emilia said, 'Villain, I fear you not, I will sacrifice you to preserve my virtue; die *infidel*, and tell your blasphemous prophet, when you come to Hell, a Christian spilt your blood.' Then she heard a dismal groan, and soon after Emilia entered the chamber, with a look that spoke the terrors of her mind, and the strange deed her hands had done. She had Selim's habit on, and in her hand a woman slave's. 'Disguise yourself in this,' said she, 'my dear Teresa, and follow me, with this I will free us both or die.' Here she drew forth a bloody dagger Selim wore. Teresa trembling put the habit on, and followed her: They passed through the chamber Emilia came out of, for Teresa's chamber door was locked, and there she saw Selim lying on the bed, weltering in his blood.

They found another door; opening which, they descended a pair of back stairs, and entered a garden, in which the *renegado* Roderigo was diverting himself with one of his master's fair slaves: He started, and came boldly up to them, doubtless suspecting something; but Emilia stabbing him, prevented any noise; the woman he was sporting with, having retired the moment they appeared. They forced open the garden gate, and not knowing where to go, hasted out of the town, nor stopped till they had reached the fields. Here they wandered, ready to die for want of food and rest.

At last unable to go farther, they sat down under a tree in a wood, and consulted what to do; they supposed they should be pursued, and if taken, surely put to death. Teresa, whose courage was not equal to Emilia's, was almost ready to despair; and she seemed so dispirited, that Emilia used all her eloquence to comfort her. 'My dear Friend, said she, look up to Heaven that never fails to succour the distressed: 'The God that this day strengthened my feeble arm to deliver us, will, I doubt not, send us help. Death is the worst that can befall us, and that is only what we are born to suffer, and what no human power can shield us from; nay, what we ought to meet with joy, since we have an eternal state in view, that shall compensate for all the miseries we suffer here. Since no guilt does wound our consciences, we need not fear to die, or dread all our inhuman enemies can inflict upon us. Come cheer up, and strive to go yet farther from that hateful city, which we are fled from; perhaps some hospitable cottage may receive and shelter us.'

At these words Teresa cast a dying look upon her. 'Alas,' said she, 'my dear, my faith is stronger than my body, though not so great as yours; I cannot rise, my trembling limbs are now unable to bear my weight; and if no help be sent us soon, then I must lay down the tedious burden of life in this sad place, and leave you.' Here she fainted. At this instant Emilia heard a rustling among the trees, and looking behind her, saw a young man of about twenty years of age, whose handsome face and shape surprised her; he had on the habit of a slave; he came down from the tree they were sitting under; he approached her with much respect, and in French, which he had heard them converse in. He was by birth a Venetian, as the sequel of this history will inform us, and addressed himself to her in this manner:

'Madam, be not surprised that I have overheard you: I am joyful to tell you, it is in my power to serve you. I am servant to a widow woman who lives not far from this place, to whose husband it was my good fortune to be sold; she by my means has embraced the Christian faith, though we keep it a secret: She gets her living, and mine, by making *turbants* and embroidery, which I carry home to our customers, and the shops. We live very comfortably, and I am certain if you will give me leave to conduct you to her, she will receive you kindly, for she is a person of great goodness.'

Emilia gladly accepted his offer, and they lifting up Teresa, who was scarce alive, led her along to the widow's house, which was just behind the wood. The slave, whose name was Antonio, gave his mistress a brief account of their condition: She embraced and welcomed them, bringing out meat and drink; with which being much refreshed, they related to her the cause and manner of their escape from the city; upon which she advised them to change their clothes, since they would surely discover them: But when Emilia came to pull off her *turbant* and vest, she was amazed to see the rich jewels it was adorned with: In the pocket of the vest she found 100 *sultanas* of gold, the buttons were diamonds. They blessed God for this treasure, which would enable them to live here, and procure them means to escape hence together.

They immediately cut the clothes in pieces, which served to make the caps of the *turbants*; and the jewels they ripped off, and hid in a box in the ground, resolving Antonio should dispose of a few of them at a time, as they had occasion, to the Jews, many of whom the widow woman worked for in embroidery, particularly in rich belts which they traded with to Spain and other parts of Europe. The good widow, whose name was Saraja, brought them mean Turkish habits, such as she wore, saying, 'Ladies, you must now conceal your quality and beauty with this homely dressing, and pass for young maids whom I have bought to assist me in my work.'

Teresa, who was much joyed at this unexpected good fortune, replied, embracing her, 'I will assist you,' said she, 'in working with all my heart; we both know how to use our needles.' A bed was laid for them in Saraja's chamber after the Turkish manner, that is, a carpet was spread upon the floor, on which were laid a quilt, blankets, sheets, and coverlids: And now had they known what was become of their lords, they had been tolerably easy.

Antonio set out for the city the next morning, to learn what news he could, and returned at night with this account: 'I am, said he, acquainted with a Christian boy, who is slave to the governor: I walked two or three times before the house to watch his coming out; at last I saw him come sweating up the street with a surgeon; I winked upon him as he passed by, he returned the sign and entered: I waited not long, before he came out again, "Lorenzo," said I, "cannot we drink a dish of coffee together this morning? I am obliged to wait for some money, one of my mistress's customers owes her, and therefore have an hour to spare; which if you can, we will pass together."

'"Lord, said he, our house is all in confusion; my master bought two Christian women yesterday, one of whom has this night wounded him cruelly, and left him weltering in his blood upon the bed; our *renegado* Roderigo they have likewise killed, as we suppose, for we found him dead in the garden, and they are escaped. Hearing some dismal groans in the night, I entered the room, and found my master in this condition; so I raised my fellow servants, and we have brought him to life, and the surgeon has some hopes of his recovery. We informed him the women were fled, but he commanded us to make no search after them. He praised their virtue, and seemed to pity them, saying, he wished their happiness, and commended their courage."

'I asked Lorenzo whom these women belonged to? He said, he did not know. So I suppose none but Roderigo knew anything of your lords.' Thus ended Antonio.

Here the ladies remained undisturbed seven months, never stirring abroad but in the dusk of the evenings, when they walked only into the wood. Meantime Antonio often enquired of Lorenzo for news, but heard none. Several ships failed for Europe in this time; but the ladies resolved not to leave Barbary till they heard of their husbands. We shall therefore leave them at the widow's, and proceed to give an account of what befell the unfortunate Don Lopez. and the Count de Hautville.

Chapter 6

The two lords being chained, as has been before recited, had no hopes of getting their liberty: They had writ, the one to France, the other to Spain, to their friends, of whom they knew not who might be living: but alas! the sum demanded was very great; and the time they must wait, before it was possible for them to receive any answer from either of those places, so long, that there were little hopes of their living to receive it. But these considerations were nothing grievous to them, in respect of those relating to Emilia and Teresa; their ignorance of their condition, and distracting apprehensions of their ruin, almost overcame their reason and Christianity: They were both sick with grief, and incapable of comforting one another. But Providence, that saw their wrongs, at length provided a way for their deliverance.

A fair virgin, who was a slave to the governor, waited on a mistress of his, whom he having enjoyed slighted, and had sent to this his country house, where she had now been two years. This girl, who was then but twelve years old, often came into the chamber where these poor gentlemen were confined, to bring them tea and coffee from her lady; who, having had a sight of them, admired Don Lopez, and therefore ventured to do something to oblige him. This pretty girl they asked some questions of; as what country she was of, what religion. She told them, she was a Venetian, that her mistress was the same; that they both were brought there by misfortunes but seemed shy of saying more.

One evening she entered the room, followed by a lady, in a Turkish dress exceeding rich; she was about five and twenty, her shape and mein was enchanting; her face so lovely, that it would have charmed the most insensible: A cloud of blushes overspread her face, and her disorder was such for some minutes, that she could not speak. The count and Don Lopez, whose weakness and chains hindered them from rising, to pay her the civilities due to her sex, bowed their heads and kept silence also, expecting her to tell the business that brought her there. At last she spoke to them thus in French: 'Is it possible, that the cruel governor can be so void of humanity to treat you thus barbarously? Can he see such noble persons as you appear to be, perish in chains, and not relent? Though I risque my life to do it, charming strangers, I will free you. But,' continued she, addressing herself to Don Lopez, 'may I hope to find you grateful? Will you give her a place in your heart, who gives you life and liberty? Will you preserve her life, who is determined to save yours? With you I am resolved to live or die. Speak then, for time is precious, and deserve my love, or hate.'

Don Lopez was too well skilled in the fair sex, not to perfectly understand this lady's meaning; and since no other means but this was left to free them, wisely concealed his being pre-engaged. Nay, doubtless he was not altogether insensible of Eleonora's charms, for so was the lady named; he was a man, and though he was intirely devoted to Teresa, yet as man he could oblige a hundred more: Life is sweet, and I hope my reader will not condemn him for what his own sex must applaud in justification of themselves: For what brave, handsome young gentleman would refuse a beautiful lady, who loved him, a favour? He bowed with a look full of love and gratitude, saying, 'Liberty, which in itself is the greatest blessing man can possess, joined with so great a good as your favour, who would refuse? Your charms would even render confinement supportable; a dungeon with such a companion would be pleasant: Shew me the way to freedom, and it shall be the study of my life to make you happy: I will defend you to the last drop of my blood.'

At these words he grasped her knees and sighed. Poor Eleonora suffered herself to be deceived, and thought of nothing but being happy with the man she loved. The Count de Hautville was amazed at Don Lopez's proceedings; his soul was constant and noble, and would have refused a life offered on so hard terms as the breach of his faith to his lovely Emilia. But his years were more than his friend's, and his temper more sedate. The sweet girl Anna fetched wine and sweetmeats to them. Eleonora sat down by them, eat, and suffered Don Lopez to kiss her hands, and say a hundred tender things to her. They appointed midnight for their escape, when she promised to bring them files to take off their fetters, and disguises to put on to prevent all discovery. She had provided a place for them to retire to also, near the seaside: She had by this means, when she was first a darling mistress to the governor, prevailed with him to free a slave whom she fancied; it was a young black whom her father had purchased when a child, of a captain, and given her, and being taken with her in the ship she was taken in, by an Algerine pirate, lived some time with her at the governor's, his name was Attabala. The governor at her request gave him a little house and garden, which he used in the summer to repair to for his pleasure, to fish on the sea coast, and take the evening air on the water with his pleasure boat.

This place he gave to Attabala to live in, and take care of, and it being now winter, there was no fear of his going thither. In this slave she could confide; to him she had declared her design the day before, when he came, as he often did, to see his dear mistress, bringing her little presents of fish and fruits, as grateful acknowledgments of the favour she had done him. From this place it would be no difficult matter for them to escape to some Christian ship or port. Having staid with them two hours, she retired; and then the count entered into talk with Don Lopez in this manner: 'My dear friend, Heaven seems now to smile upon us, a gleam of hope appears to comfort us; but, tell me, was it well done to dissemble? Are you changed? Is your wife forgot? And the sacred matrimonial vows no longer valued? Excuse me if I blame you; let nothing make you buy our liberty by a crime; it is better to die here, than live with Heaven's displeasure.'

Don Lopez blushing replied, 'Forgive my weakness; I do not mean to proceed farther than an innocent deceit, Teresa is always present with me: But had I refused this lady's offer rudely, we had, perhaps, been here detained and murdered; and then Teresa and Emilia never can be rescued from the villain that robbed us of them. Be satisfied therefore, that I have acted prudently, and not designed amiss.'

The count was then contented, and now the joyful hour approached when darkness and sleep had lulled the busy world to rest; Eleonora came with Anna loaden with jewels, gold, and clothes; they quickly filed their fetters off, and found the faithful Attabala at some distance from the house, with three horses, swift Barbaries, that run fleet as the wind; on two of these the lords mounted, Don Lopez taking the lady, and the count the girl behind him; the black riding the other horse led the way, with which he was perfectly acquainted: In few hours just at daybreak they reached the house, and being safely lodged, began to taste the pleasures of liberty.

Next day the governor, who was recovered, was informed by the servants, that remained in the country house, of the lords' flight: But he had that night received an order from the emperor to repair to Fez, to take a command in the army, to which he was determined to send him. This took up all his thoughts, so that he took little notice of their escape; and, as they afterwards learned, he never returned to Algiers, but died in the army of a fever. And now Don Lopez had an opportunity to enquire who Eleonora was, and the fatal accident that brought her to this Place. He treated her with such respect and affection, that he could ask nothing of her, but what she was ready to grant. One morning as the count and Anna, whom Eleonora now treated as her friend, letting her lie with her, as became a person who was indeed her equal, were conversing together, Don Lopez intreated her to relate the adventures of her life.

'Yes, my Lord, said she, I will, provided Anna, and you gentlemen, will do the same; for she would never let me know who she is, though a Venetian as well as I.'

Anna replied, 'Madam, whilst I was a slave I was not willing to be known: Now I shall take pleasure to entertain you with a story full of strange adventures.'

Then Eleonora began in this manner.

Chapter 7

'I was born at Friuli, a place situate on the Adriatic Sea, in the Venetian dominions; my father was a wealthy merchant, in the city of Aquilegia; he had no child but me by my mother, who was his second wife, and the daughter of a noble Venetian. He had two sons by a former wife, who loved me not, because my father seemed to prefer me in his affection before them; all his ambition was to see me well disposed of during his life. I was also very apprehensive that my brothers, if he died before I was married, would clap me up in a convent, to get my fortune, and be revenged upon me. The great portion he offered with me, with that tolerable person the world thought me, procured me many admirers, as soon, or indeed before I was of an age to marry.

'Amongst these, there was a kinsman of my mother, the eldest son of a Venetian senator, whom the custom and laws of that state will not permit to marry out of a noble family, became much enamoured with me: His name Seignior Andrea Zantonia. He secretly courted me, my mother and father giving encouragement; my heart soon yielded, and I gave him the preference above all others. I was now almost fourteen, and it was resolved that we should be privately married at a country seat of my father's. These proceedings could not be kept so secret, but that the servants were some of them privy to them. Amongst my lovers, there was a rich captain of a ship, who had cast his eyes upon me in my infancy, and was one of the first that entertained me with discourses of love; he was in years, and I treated him with ill nature, and indeed could not indure him: Yet he persisted, till at length I used him so ill, that he concluded I had made choice of another, and made it his business to find out who was the fortunate man.

'In order to which, he gained my maid, who waited upon me, by bribes to discover all to him. She informed him from time to time of Seignior Andrea Zantonio's courting me, and all that passed. His business obliged him to be often absent on voyages to Spain, and elsewhere; and he arrived but the day before my intended wedding, of which being informed, he resolved to prevent it if possible. He therefore went to Seignior Andrea's father, and acquainted him with the ill news, promising if he would assist him, he would prevent it; which he soon agreed to do, being much enraged at his son. The captain desired three or four men to aid him, which he immediately procured him, sending four ruffians disguised along with him; with these he lay in ambuscade, in the way which we were to pass to my father's country house, where Seignior Andrea was to come to us the next morning, not thinking it proper to go with us.

'There were none in the coach but my father, mother, and me; two men servants rid before the coach, and my poor black was behind it: As we past by a wood, the captain and his crew bolted out upon us, with vizards upon their faces, and pistols in their hands; they stopped the coach, and tore me out of it, whilst my mother shrieked, my father stormed, and one of the servants going to lay hold of me, was shot dead. They fled with me into the thickest part of the wood, where they bound and gagged me. The poor black Attabala, who has now helped to deliver you, being very nimble of foot, pursued me, and running after them, came up crying just as they were binding my hands. They seized and bound him also; then they placed us before two of them on horseback, and made for the sea side; where being soon arrived, we found a boat ready, into which one of them entered; we were next lifted in by the seamen that rowed it, and then the four villains that assisted in taking us, cried, "Farewell," and rode off. The captain taking off his vizard so soon as we were put from the shore, discovered to me the author of my misfortune.

'"Madam," said he, "I have you see done a bold deed to manifest my love, and secure you to myself; fear nothing more, you are now in the hands of a man that adores you, and it is your own fault if you are not happy."

'I could not answer, being gagged; but the disorder of my mind cannot be expressed. I saw myself in the hands of a man whom I hated, and no way left to escape. I was ten times more sensible of the loss of him I loved, than I could have before imagined. My soul shivered at the thoughts of what was to follow. I could no more hope to see my country and friends, for thither it was not to be supposed this villain would ever venture to bring me again, at least not in some years. I was tortured with a thousand such dismal apprehensions, when I saw the ship which laid by to receive us. He took me up in his loathed arms, and with the seamen's assistance, though I struggled, put me on board. Attabala and I were presently unbound, and now I began to expostulate with Alphonso, for that was the captain's name. "What do you propose," said I, "in taking me thus by force against my inclination? Do you vainly imagine to be happy with me, whilst I hate and detest you, and view you as the only cause of my being wretched? Never will I pardon or love you, unless you carry me back to my father's. I will make you as miserable as myself, and never suffer you to rest whilst I am with you. I always disliked you, but now my aversion is confirmed, and I would prefer the most vile wretch on earth before you."

'"Rage on," said he, "fond girl; whilst I possess you, you shall be mine, and only death can free you from me."

'Here he suddenly kissed and embraced me. "You shall," said he, this night marry me, that I may have a lawful title to you, and you have nothing to reproach me. I will not be a ravisher, but having secured your person, and your honour, take what will be then my due."

'"No, villain," I replied, "my tongue shall never call you husband; I would sooner suffer hot pincers to rend it from the root than speak those words, or answer to such a question." "Silence," said he, "does give consent, and I shall not want witnesses to prove our marriage."

'Here he went out of the cabin, and left me in the extremest grief and despair. Poor Attabala comforted me the best he could, offering to risque his life to kill him; but I regarded nothing he said to me.

'It was now night, and very dark; I heard the winds blow, and a mighty disorder and noise upon the deck, the captain stormed and called loudly to the seamen in terms I did not understand; he came twice down into the cabin, kissed me, and said, "Madam, it is a rough night, but fear nothing:"

'Yet I read a concern in his face that spoke our danger. I cannot say that I was much terrified with the thoughts of death, because at that instant I was apprehensive of something worse. I recommended myself to God, and calmly expected. Before day the ship had lost her masts, and most part of her rigging; she was so shattered that nothing but getting to some shore, or meeting with some ship, could save us. We were now drove in sight of Barbary, when a ship coming up our ship's crew hailed her. She soon came near, and lay by, hoisting French colours. The captain sent his boat aboard, but to their surprise they were all clapped under hatchets, it proving a pirate ship of Algiers.

The captain wondered the boat staid, but at last seeing the ship bear up to us, he suspected the truth. He would have made some defence, but the ship was disabled; so he hastily catched up his sword, and mounting the deck was there met by a crowd of the pirates, who had boarded the ship: He was soon dispatched, and his men all killed, or taken. I remained with poor Attabala in the cabin all this while, and was so lost in thought, I was scarce apprehensive of my danger: When the Algerine captain entered the cabin with his men, they took me, and conveyed me into the pirate ship, rifled ours, and then set her adrift. They put me into the great cabin with Attabala, and in few hours we came to Barbary, landed at Algiers, and the next morning Ibrahim the captain presented me to the governor.

What my thoughts were, and how I expressed my sorrows under all these misfortunes, would be too tedious to tell you: In fine, the governor treated me kindly, pretended to love me passionately, and forced me to his bed; after which he denied me nothing, purchased and freed Attabala at my request; and for eight years, though he had many other new mistresses, gave me the preference, and loved me with the same ardour as at first. He reproached me often that I brought him no child, which Providence no doubt did not think fit to give us: At last a French lady, of incomparable beauty, was presented him, and she brought him a son the first year of their acquaintance.

This caused him to grow cold to me, which I resenting, we quarrelled; so he sent me away to the place you found me in. There I mourned my misfortunes with a Christian sorrow, and never thought to see the world again. Here I and my dear Anna came together; she was purchased by him a month before I left him, and I begged her of him to keep me company. Thus have I given you a true narrative of my misfortunes; and now Don Lopez, if we reach a Christian shore again, and you prove grateful, I may yet live to be happy.'

'Madam,' said he, 'it shall be my study to make you so.'

'Fair Anna,' said the count, 'we will refer your story to the afternoon, it being now dinner time; and I doubt not but we shall hear something as extraordinary as what Madam Eleonora has related to us.'

They rose, and Don Lopez led Eleonora to the table; they dined, and then returned to her chamber, which was a pleasant room, having the prospect of the sea. Here they sat down, whilst Attabala made their coffee, and then they importuned Anna to keep her word; which she with a sigh consented to do, saying, 'My story is little worth hearing, and were it not to oblige Eleonora, I would beg to be excused.'

Chapter 8

'I am the daughter of an unfortunate prince, who was once a lieutenant general in the Venetian Army. My mother was a lady of great birth; but the family being ruined, had no fortune; my grandfather, being one of those who headed the Hugonot party against his sovereign Lewis XIV. lost both his life and estate. My mother, then an infant, was bred up by an Hugonot sister of my grandfather, who spared no cost upon her education, but could give her no fortune proportionable to her quality. She had beauty, wit, and was certainly a very charming person. My father, who was the eldest son of one of the noblest families in France, saw and loved her; he visited her in secret, often made her large presents; and knowing his father and family would never consent to his marrying her, he resolved if possible to debauch her; but her virtue made her resist him, though she loved him: So that he was forced to have recourse to stratagems to accomplish his desires. He used to walk with her often in her aunt's garden alone, she thinking herself secure from all attempts there.

'He had procured a key to the garden-gate, pretending it was more convenient for him to come in that way, because it was most private; and therefore her aunt gave him one she had used to carry in her pocket, to let her niece and her in when they thought fit. He sent three of his servants in the night, who going in, hid themselves in this garden. His page, who conducted them where he ordered, brought back the key to him. In the morning the prince comes himself in a travelling coach to the garden-gate; there alighting, he enters the house, calls for my mother, and pretends he was going in haste on a journey on some extraordinary business for the king. After some talk with madam her aunt, he takes her into thc garden, to say some little tender things to her alone, as she supposed.

'As they were walking in a close walk, his servants disguised started

265

out upon her, and stopping her mouth, bore her to the coach, into which he entered, drawing up the canvasses; and the coach driving swiftly, he carried her thirty miles off to a remote old castle which belonged to his father, but had not been inhabited by anything but servants a long time. When he entered, the gardener and his wife, who had lived there to look after the furniture and gardens many years, made haste to open the rooms, and asked no questions. Here he accomplished his ungenerous design, and here he kept my disconsolate mother some years: Her aunt concealed her loss, and, as she thought, her own dishonour, as much as was possible, concluding she was gone with him by her own consent; she therefore pretended she was retired farther into the country to some relations.

'Yet it reached the ear of my grandfather, who only laughed at it, calling it a piece of gallantry in his son to receive a lady who fled to his arms. He often pressed my father to marry, but his affection to my mother, and conscience, which now began to awaken him, made him always decline it. The lady her aunt loved her so tenderly, that she soon after the loss of her, fell sick with grief, and died. And now the war being broke out between the Turks and Venetians, my father resolving to marry my Mother, who was young with child, and with her charming affable behaviour and tears, had entirely gained his heart, he proposed to the duke his father to go to Venice a volunteer, with an equipage suiting his quality, to make a campaign or two. To which his father readily agreed: All things were got ready, and my mother, concealed in men's clothes, went with him.

'So soon as they arrived at Venice, the *doge* presented him with the command of a regiment of horse. Here he acquainted a bishop with the engagements that were betwixt my mother and him, together with the reasons why it must be a secret: The good bishop married them, and placed my mother with a widow lady of great quality and worth, who was his own relation. Here my mother was brought to bed of me, and unfortunately died in childbirth; so that my father returning from the army at the end of the campaign, found my mother just dead, and me at nurse. His grief was very great, and his fondness of me so extreme, he begged the bishop and lady to take all the care imaginable of me. The next campaign he was made a lieutenant general, and was killed, dying in the bed of honour, leaving me a helpless orphan, whose greatest happiness at that time was, that I was too young to be sensible of my loss.

'My father had deposited into the lady's hands a great sum of money, as a provision for me in case of his death. The generous Angelina, for that was her name, bred me up with as much care and tenderness as if I had been her own child. She had a lovely youth, her only son, who was seven years older than me; for him she declared she designed me, provided we loved one another: His name was Carolus Antonio Barbarini: We lived together, and his name was one of the first things she taught my infant tongue to pronounce.

'At seven years of age I found how dear he was to me, and he being fourteen, began to feel the glowing passion he had for me warm his breast. I was caressed and loved by all his family, and had a prospect of being one of the happiest women in the world. The Turks gaining many unfortunate victories over the Venetians, I was not thought safe at home, but sent with some young ladies of Angelina's family to a monastery. There, with a world of others, I was taken captive by the cruel *infidels*, and carried to Constantinople, where my tender years preserved my virtue. A sea captain bought me, and carrying me to Algiers, made a present of me to the governor, whom he used to supply with mistresses, for which he was doubtless well rewarded. This is my unhappy story. I suppose the governor reserved me for his use, when I was older; but God has been pleased to deliver me out of his hands, for which I bless his name, and I hope to see Venice once again with his assistance.'

Here she finished, and Eleonora rising up, embraced her, shedding some tears. 'Are you then,' says she, 'the charming girl the noble Angelina bred up? Fair Anna, forgive my ignorance that made me treat you as a servant: My Mother was Angelina's sister; you are dear to me by the ties of blood, and far my better in your noble father. May Providence restore you to my kinsman, and bring us safe to Venice again.'

Here the two lords related part of their adventures; Don Lopez concealing that part only that related to Teresa, whom he mentioned as his sister: They related the manner of their being cast on the dismal island, their escape thence, and unfortunate meeting with the Algerine pirate, with the ladies being ravished from them for the governor. At last they declared they would not leave Barbary till they were found and rescued. Attabala undertook to go to the governor's, and learn what was become of them, which he faithfully performed in few days after. He went to enquire after his master's health as usual, found none but servants, who informed him of the ladies escape thence, and how the governor had been wounded by one of them, and that Roderigo was likewise killed; in fine, of all they knew, but where the ladies were retired to, that they could not tell.

So Attabala returned with this account; upon which the lords resolved to disguise themselves, and go together in search of them in all the villages near the city, to one of which they supposed they must have fled for shelter. They dressed themselves in the habit of Grecian merchants, which habits Attabala bought for them at the city, and both speaking Greek, they doubted not to pass for such if questioned. Thus metamorphosed they went daily out, and ventured to enquire if any ladies in European dresses were arrived in that town or village which they passed through. Thus they did in every place they could think of; but finding all their search in vain, they began to imagine they were hid in some wood or cave, and therefore concluded to visit all lonely woods and places least frequented: This they did for several days also, but without success.

One evening as they were returning home, they passed by a small wood, into which it was difficult to find an entrance: They stopped, and having viewed it well, they perceived some footsteps and beaten ways over the grass. They entered into the thickest part of it by this path, and there found a dismal sort of hut made only with boughs of trees, and a piece of sail-cloth; under which, upon some straw, lay a woman, whose face, though very beautiful, expressed the greatest want and misery. She had a canvas waistcoat and petticoat on, was barefoot, had a silk handkerchief tied about her head, and a piece of flannel wrapped about her shoulders; she was young, fair, and finely limbed, but her eyes were sunk: She was meagre, pale, sick, and so weak she could not rise. The lords viewed her with such compassion, that they were ready to weep. 'In the Name of God,' said the Count de Hautville in French, 'what are you? And how came you to be left in this dismal place?'

'I am not able,'said she, 'to tell you; If you are Christians, give me something to eat or drink, for our Saviour's sake.'

They had nothing with them; but Attabala, who went with them as a guide, hasted to the next village, and soon brought some bread and wine, with some of which they a little revived her. She drank a good draught of the wine, but had not strength to chew or swallow the bread. As they were assisting her, a man came up, whose face, shape, and mien engaged their attention: He was dressed in a jacket and drawers of canvas, his red cloth cap upon his head with fur, barefooted, and so pale and lean, that he appeared the very image of death; in a ragged handkerchief he held in his hands, he had nuts and wild sour grapes with a few dirty bones, such as seemed to have been flung out into the streets for dogs. He retired back when he saw the lords; at which the woman called to him in a sort of ecstasy: 'Come here, my dear lord, God sends us friends and food.' He then bowing, approached them. Their surprise was such, when they saw him nearer, they could not speak. His feet bled, his sinews and nerves were all open, his bones stared upon one another; in fine, he was the most miserable object their eyes ever saw.

They put the bottle of wine and bread into his hands, at which a flood of tears poured from his eyes; and going to lift the bottle to his mouth, he staggered and fell down; at which the woman shrieked, and fell into strange convulsions. Don Lopez who caught the bottle when the man fell, endeavoured with his friend's assistance to get some wine down his throat; but his teeth being set fast, it was very difficult. Meantime Attabala was employed to hold the woman, who beat her breast, gnashed her teeth, rolled her eyes, and appeared to be in the agonies of death. In some time both recovered a little, and Don Lopez ordered Attabala to run back to the town and hire horses to carry them to Attabala's house. This was soon done, and the lords mounting, took the man and woman up before them, and so posted home: Where being arrived, they put them into warm beds, not being certain they were man and wife, Attabala having first washed their feet.

This with some burnt wine, and bread sopped in it, threw them into a profound sleep till the next morning; when Eleonora, Anna, and the lords visited them to enquire who they were, and how they did: They first entered the man's chamber, who no sooner saw them, but he raised himself up in the bed, and lifting up his hands broke out into these passionate expressions: 'To thee, first, my merciful Creator, I return my thanks; it is to thee I owe this great deliverance, and all the good things I have received in my whole life. I bless thee for the miseries I have suffered: It is most just, my God, that I should be punished with cold, hunger and thirst, who broke my faith with thee, and fled thy altar for a sensual satisfaction. It was I seduced the virtuous Clarinda from her blessed retirement, for which she suffers both in mind and body; but no more will I offend my God. Now pardon us, and as thou hast delivered us from death, so grant peace to our souls.'

Then bowing to the lords, 'To you blessed instruments of Heaven's bounty,' said he, 'who have saved the life of her whose life is dearer to me than my own, you who saved both from certain death, I return unfeigned thanks, and will make all the grateful returns my present circumstances will permit.'

They embraced, and congratulated him with much tenderness, and promised to return to him so soon as they had visited the lady. To her they went, and found her waking. She was very faint, and the ladies welcoming of her, desired she would drink chocolate with them, and not spend her spirits by talking; yet she uttered many affectionate thanks and acknowledgments to God and them. The breakfast was brought in, and soon after the gentleman being risen and dressed in a shirt, a thing he had not on before, waistcoat, breeches, cap, nightgown, stockings, and slippers of one of the lords, entered the room, and appeared like what he really was, a man of quality, of excellent parts and person.

Anna had likewise supplied the lady with shift and nightclothes; she appeared to be about two and twenty, and the gentleman upwards of thirty. Being refreshed with eating, the gentleman handsomely, without asking, addressed himself to the company thus: 'Gentlemen and ladies,' said he, 'I am positive you are very desirous to know who this lady and I are, and what strange misfortunes reduced us to the deplorable condition you found us in; I will therefore as briefly as I can satisfy your curiosity, and you must excuse me, if I do not relate every particular with that exactness it ought to be done in, since my strength is but little at present.'

They assured him they would rather deny themselves that pleasure, than trouble him; and begged that he would proceed.

Chapter 9

'This lady and I, said he, were both born in France, in the same province; Dauphiny gave us birth. My father—whom it is necessary I should mention first, because I am but ten years older than she, which occasioned my misfortune, in being destined to the Church, before she was grown up to inspire my soul with that fatal passion that has undone us—was the king's lieutenant for that province, and Marquis of Harcourt. I was his third son, and therefore designed for the Church, in which I could not miss of preferment, being descended of so great a family; nor did I want the qualifications requisite to render me capable of that noble profession. I was not inclined to any vice; nor, I thank God, wanted sense to learn, and retain, all that was taught me. In fine, I was very dear to my father, and much esteemed by my friends and family. I passed through my study, and was ordained a secular priest at twenty.

'I was soon dignified with being made a canon of the royal Cathedral of Cambray. My brothers were greatly preferred in the army, and we were all very great and very happy: But Providence did not think fit I should continue so. I got an ague and fever, which rendered me very weak; the physicians advised me to the country air. Upon which I retired to a village, where my father had a little summer seat. In this town was a monastery of Benedictine nuns; this place I visited, having two young ladies my relations there. Here I saw the charming Clarinda, who was then about fifteen; she was daughter to the Count de Villeroy, who having ten children, four sons and six daughters, sent three of his youngest daughters to this monastery, of which the lady abbess was his sister.

'He gave a thousand pounds sterling with them, and all possible persuasions and means were used to persuade them to embrace this holy way of living, as is customary in France, because great fortunes and families should not be impaired and ruined, by portioning many children; therefore they commonly dedicate some of them to the church, which prevents their impoverishing estates, and too greatly increasing the family. Thus they were enabled to give such great portions with their eldest daughter, and making settlements on the second sons, as may marry them into noble and rich families suitable to their own. But though this be an excellent piece of policy, yet it often causes the children to be very unhappy, and the church crowded with those, whose inclinations do not suit the habits they wear, but tend to the world, and sigh after the pleasures of it; nay, too often do, as I have done, forget the sacred vows they have made, and follow the dictates of their passions.

'Clarinda was fair as an angel, witty, free, affable, and in all things so engaging, that I soon lost my heart to her; I struggled with the growing passion, sometimes resolved to see her face no more, but love overcame all my resolutions, and I at last resolved to possess her or die. I soon found means to reveal my passion to her, and she in short time yielded to fly with me to any part of the world, for in France we could not stay. I had a great deal of money by me, and now I thought only of amassing such a sum, as might provide handsomely for us in Holland or England, to one of which places we were determined to go: In order to this, I made bold with some very rich jewels, which were laid up in a reliquary, of which I kept the keys; to prevent discovery I employed a Hugonot jeweller to set false stones in the room of the true, which I picked out before he saw them, pretending to him that I was desirous to repair and beautify those sacred things; and that time having reduced them to this condition, I could not bestow diamonds and rubies, and was willing to make them decent, at my own expense.

'And indeed I thought there was but little use for diamonds, to adorn dry bones and relics, which we were not certain belonged to those holy persons whose they were pretended to be; and that the money bestowed on the poor would have been much better employed. Though in me this was sacrilege, and a great crime, yet having given the reins to my passion, I ran headlong to destruction. All things being ready, I provided a boat to carry us down the River Rhosne to Arles, from whence I doubted not to get passage to England, in some ship from Marseilles that was going home through the Straits. Clarinda failed not to be ready at the appointed hour, which was midnight. I brought a ladder of ropes, which throwing over the wall of the garden, which was not very high she mounted, and turning it over on the other side descended. I received her with open arms, and all the transport a man may be supposed to feel, who has rigorously lived to his duty, denied himself all the pleasures of sense, and gives a loose to his desires. The sad prisoner, who has lived long confined in a dark loathsome vault, feels not a greater joy at the sight of day and liberty than I did then. I hasted with her to the boat, into which I had already conveyed habits for us both, with all things necessary. The jewels I had hid about me in a purse, and my pockets were stuffed with gold, besides all I had put into the trunk I had got aboard with our clothes and linen.

'As soon as we were come aboard, and alone in the cabin, we dressed both in gentlemen's habits. I threw our others into the river. And now it is needless to tell you that I enjoyed the maid I so much languished for, promising to marry her so soon as we were arrived in a place of safety. When we came to Marseilles, which we soon did, we discharged the *bark*, and went ashore with our things and lodged at an inn. And now grown distractedly fond of Clarinda, I longed to perform my promise of marrying her; and in few days after, having purchased some woman's apparel for her, we stepped out one morning early, and going to a country village two miles from Marseilles, were lawfully joined by the Parish priest: And now had I not been before engaged to live single, I had been one of the happiest men on earth. We waited not long before an English ship arrived homeward bound. I agreed for our passage; we went aboard, and soon after set sail. And now my fears were all over, I fancied myself going to a country where I should rather be applauded than condemned for what I had done, where I should be free in all respects; and though I never had a thought to change my religion, yet I fancied I should be extreme happy in a place where I should live free from all constraint: But God, whom I had offended, soon convinced me of my folly.

'An Algerine pirate met us, and after a sharp dispute took the ship, and made us all prisoners, carrying us into Tunis, where he sold us for slaves. It was Clarinda's fortune and mine to be bought by a merchant's widow, who sent her steward to market to buy a man and a maid servant. When he brought us home the lady viewed us, seemed pleased with his choice of us. She asked me many questions, as what nation I was of, what I could do, who Clarinda was, and such like; to which I answered, that she was my sister, that we were born in France; that I could write, cast accompt, play upon several sorts of music, but neither of us had been bred to work: I said my sister could work finely at her needle. She told me it was our own faults if we lived uneasy, and that she would use us kindly. In short she liked my person, and in few days gave me to understand what she expected. She was old, and very disagreeable; yet having given the reins to passion, the fear of being parted from, or of Clarinda's being ill used, made me resolve to oblige the lustful hag, which I accordingly did.

'And now I was treated as the master of all, I sat at table with her, and Clarinda with us; I was denied nothing, but managed her affairs and fortune as I pleased. I had still left of my own the purse of jewels, which I had hung about my neck with a string; and when the pirates took us, they staid not to strip us of our shirts, so they found not what was concealed next my skin. This I always kept about me; but I wanted two things which are the greatest blessings of life, liberty and a good conscience. I continued to please Admela the widow some time; but one fatal evening she being walked into the garden, I stole to Clarinda's room, where she was working, as I often did undiscovered, and taking the privilege of a husband to enjoy my virtuous wife, was by a malicious slave watched, and betrayed: He envied my good fortune in being beloved by his mistress.

'He was an Irishman, a sort of people who never want a good opinion of themselves, and are generally successful with the women. He thought he had now a good opportunity to ruin me, and insinuate himself into her favour. He gave her an account of what he had seen; and when I came into the garden some time after, and gave her my hand, she looked upon me with such rage and disorder in her face, that I quickly apprehended what was to follow. I entertained her as usual with pleasant talk; we supped, and I went into her chamber, when her servants withdrew, as I was accustomed to do; but when we were alone, she explained herself in this manner. "Malherb," said she, for under that name I concealed myself, "Clarinda is more than a sister to you, and I have nursed a viper in my bosom, that steals your affection from me. You adore her, and doubtless care not for me. I thought to have provided nobly for her and you; but since she makes me wretched I will remove her from my sight, and yours forever."

'Here she wept. What different passions rent my divided soul at this dreadful moment words cannot express. I stood for some minutes immoveable as a statue: At last I endeavoured to pacify her, begging her not to credit what a villain said, who conspired my ruin, envying my good fortune. At last I gained so far upon her, that she received me to her arms; and then I made her promise to put the villain away

274

that abused us, which the next morning she performed, ordering him to be sent to a country house she had near the sea side, twenty miles distant, to look after the gardens. He uttered a hundred curses and imprecations against me; but they did not hurt me, or serve him. And now I was obliged to caress Admela in an extraordinary manner, and be more circumspect than ever with Clarinda, on whom she kept a watchful eye.

'We continued thus some time; but Admela observed the tender regard we had for each other so well, that she was convinced I had imposed upon her: And being very cunning, she took no notice to me; but taking Clarinda with her into the garden one morning, when I was gone out to receive some money of the merchants for her, she had her seized, and put bound into a cart; where being covered over with some sacks, she was drove to the country house, where the Irish villain was, and there locked into a chamber, where they chained her by the leg, and only one old hag, who had been Admela's nurse, left with her. Here she remained a long time: At my return home I missed her, and asking where she was, none answered; at last my devil-mistress told me she was where I should never see her more. I raged and stormed in vain; nay, I used tears and prayers, but jealousy had rendered her soul obdurate and inflexible; in fine, none would inform me what was become of her.

'From this hour I resolved to shun Admela's lustful arms and bed; at last she threatened me with Clarinda's death if I treated her so ill. Thus I lived two whole years in perpetual torment, and anxiety of mind; my health decayed, and I was no longer the same man. Admela grieved, and being old, fell into a lingering illness that at last ended her days, but not my sorrows. And now having got much riches of the widow's into my power, I resolved to find out where Clarinda was, though I spent it all; but all my designs were vain. Mustapha, a Mahometan captain that was nephew to Admela's husband and his heir, comes home, and seizing upon all, cast me into prison where I lay three months, and then was turned out to be used as a slave, with a clog chained to my leg, to prevent my escaping. I was forced to carry burdens as a porter about the city to earn a morsel of bread.

'Whilst these things passed, my dear Clarinda remained a prisoner very sick; the Irish villain, and old woman lived rarely, and grew great friends; they feasted and lay together, he meditating how to revenge himself upon me, and having always viewed Clarinda with desire, prevailed on Dimas, the old hag, to let him sometimes visit her. He always brought her something, as fruit, coffee or wine, to revive her poor decayed spirits; and though grief had much altered her face, yet her beauty charmed the villain. One day when Dimas was gone to Tunis for money for their salary, which Admela allowed them, he thus addressed Clarinda: "Madam, said he, I am touched to the very soul with a tender sense of your sufferings. I adore and love you equal with him you are parted from; grant me the enjoyment of your person, and I will free you. Malherb is dead, the revengeful Admela poisoned him three days after you were brought here. Dimas has orders to poison you, but I keep her from it. I am an European and a Christian; give yourself to me, and I will procure a safe passage for us to Ireland, where I will marry you."

'At these words she lifted up her eyes, and with a flood of tears replied; "Is my dear husband dead then? Can I no more hope to see him? Then why do I live?"

'At these words she swooned. Macdonald, for that was the villain's name, held her up in his arms, till she recovering, poured forth the most passionate expressions of grief. He then departed, fearing to hear her reproaches and subtlety, considering, that after the first efforts of her passion was over, reason would take place, and she would reflect upon the misery of her present condition, and the impossibility of being freed from it by any other means but by him; and so concluded, she would at last comply and fly with him, which was the thing he designed to compass, by this invented story of my death. Dimas returning, wondered to find her so afflicted, and asked her the reason of her grief; but Clarinda feared to tell her, and discover what had passed betwixt her and Macdonald, and so gave her no answer. And now Heaven kindly inspired her with a thought, that this story might not be true: "Why, said she, am I kept here if he is dead? Admela has no need to fear me if the man we love is dead; if she would have taken my life away, she might have done it long since; no, doubtless, this villain tells me this to make me despair of any help but his. My God, continued she, who can bring Good out of evil, direct me what to do,"

'Thus she passed the sleepless night, and at last resolved to dissemble with Macdonald, and if possible, get her liberty without injuring her virtue. The next time he came to her alone, when Dimas, who was jealous of him, was absent, she pretended to hearken to his proposals, and told him, if he would contrive a way for them to escape, she would gladly go with him. He seemed transported; and the next night, whilst Dimas slept, whom he had given a large potion of opium to, in some coffee they had drank together, he rises, and packing up what money and clothes he could get in the house, he came into Clarinda's Chamber, filed off her fetters, and they hasted to a neighbouring wood, where they sat down, fearing to lose themselves, it being a very dark night; resolving to stay till the daybreak, and then he proposed to go down to the sea side, in hopes to find some ship's boat to go off to sea in; if not, he had made an acquaintance with a poor fisherman, of whom he used to buy fish, in whose cottage he doubted not they might safely stay. And now the villain began rudely to press her to yield to him.'

'"Macdonald, that you are a villain," said she, "I am sensible; I have used you to obtain my liberty, I never design to gratify you; therefore desist, or expect to die by my hand, or kill me, for I prefer death a thousand times before a life of infamy. If my husband still lives, I may be happy; if he be dead, I have no more business with the world, and shall gladly die: But this be assured of, I will resist to death."

'Macdonald's surprise was very great, yet he persisted in his wicked design, and when he found persuasions would not do, proceeded to use force, saying, "Clarinda, it is in vain you strive; the happy Malherb ruined me, and I will revenge myself by robbing him of you."

'At these words, she caught a bayonet from his side, which he had armed himself withal, and stabbed him, before he suspected her design. And now guess but the terrors of her mind, alone in a dismal wood, she knew not where to go, a dying man lying by her. She withdrew some little distance from the place, and there falling upon her knees begged of God to deliver her from the miseries of life by a speedy death. At last day breaking, she looked round her, and rising walked through the wood in a pathway which led to a hill. This she ascended with much pain, being very weak. In a shady valley on the other side the hill, she saw an antient man of a venerable aspect, his beard reached to his waist, his habit was a coarse gray cloth, very old, his feet were bare; he had a little pitcher in his hand, and was going to fill it with water at a small spring that rose at the bottom of the hill. She approached him trembling, and fell at his feet, crossing her breast. He lifted her up, saying in French, "God save you, woman; what would you have?"

'"A place to conceal myself, Father," said she;"I am a Christian, fled from those that sought to ruin me; I am faint, sick, and friendless: Oh, assist me in what you can: If not, I must perish, for I cannot go much farther."

'He led her down the valley, and brought her to a poor cottage, there he gave her some bread and boiled roots, which was what he lived on; and here she recounted to him how she was with her husband taken and made slaves, with the cause of her confinement at the country house; how she escaped thence, and had killed, as she supposed, the villain that would have forced her. Then the old man, she having finished her story, began thus: "Daughter, I am a man who have long since retired from the world; I am a priest, born in France, I was chaplain to an India ship; and being desirous to see the world, chose that way to travel, in hopes to be useful to the ignorant. We were taken by the Algerines, as you have been, and I was seven years a slave to a merchant at Fez, where I learned to live hard; he at last freed me, and being well acquainted with the place and people, I resolved to live here the remainder of my days.

'I never eat flesh, nor drink wine, but content myself with bread and roots, to which you are welcome. I get my living by practising physick amongst these poor Barbarians, and so have frequent opportunities of baptizing infants, unperceived by them, and sometimes converting poor souls to the Christian faith. Sometimes I paint small pictures of holy persons, for which they give me bread and roots. Thus have I lived these forty years, daily visiting the sick in the adjacent towns and villages. And now, daughter, if you can content yourself to work, I will procure you a cottage and business, for with me it would be indecent for you to stay. You say you have killed a man, a thing you ought to mourn for all the days of your life. Alas! could you find no way to touch his soul, but to cut him off in that dreadful moment when he was least prepared for his eternal state? Why did you not rather call earnestly to God to deliver you? Are you certain he is dead"

'"No Father," said she, "but I believe so."

He rose hastily, saying, "Stay here and I will go, and see if God has mercifully spared him to repent."

'He run to a cupboard, took out a bottle of cordial, and with his staff in his hand departed, going as nimbly as if he had been young, though he was so old and feeble. This sight filled her soul with an unusual strain of devotion: "My God," said she, "What a lively devotion glowed in the face of that good man! How vigorously he performs his duty, and how careless have I been of mine? How have I distrusted God, how lamented for a mortal man, and how little for his and my sins? I will henceforth resolve courageously to support all adversity. Why did I imbrue my hands in blood, and rashly ruin the soul of him whose hands gave me liberty but some few hours before? I should have strove, and reasoned with him; God would have strengthened me no doubt, and touched his heart. Well might the psalmist cry out to be delivered from the guilt of shedding innocent blood."

'Here she melted into tears, and truly repented her rashness. Not long after, as she sat pensive, the good Father Clementine returned, for that was his name, and with much joy told her, Macdonald was sitting under a tree when he came, so weak with the loss of blood, he could not rise. "I viewed his wound," said he, "after giving him some cordial; it is in his thigh, deep, but not mortal. I mentioned nothing of you to him, but admonished him seriously to prepare for death, not letting him know that I thought his wound not dangerous. He viewed me earnestly, and at last said, 'Are you a Christian priest?' I assured him I was, he seemed overjoyed, made his confession to me, expressing great sorrow for his sins. I went to a poor man's house, and we have got him thither. There have I left him in bed; at night I have promised to return: He says your husband is living at Tunis."

'Poor Clarinda blessed God and him for this good news; he conducted her to a widow woman's house where she was to live till news could be got of me; there she helped to embroider belts with this good woman, who maintained herself with that work. It was a great way from Tunis to this place, and it was some time before somebody could be found to go thither with her, which the good Clementine could not do himself, because he could not leave his sick patient. Poor Macdonald died, before her departure, of a fever, occasioned by his great loss of blood, and was very penitent. The clothes and money he had were by the good priest taken care of; who having paid the countryman for lodging and diet for Macdonald, gave the rest to Clarinda. She took leave of the generous Father with tears, promising to return to him soon with me; he said he would provide for us to live.

'The good widow loved her much, and invited her to live there again: The woman's son went with her, they came safe to Tunis, lodged at a poor woman's who was kin to the widow. Here they learned the news of Admela's death, my imprisonment and poor condition. Clarinda got the young man to enquire me out; at last he found and brought me to her, but when she saw me in so miserable a plight, a clog chained to my leg, my beggarly habit and altered face, no words can express her concern; yet our souls leaped for joy. We kissed, embraced, and wept; so moving was the scene, the poor countryman and woman of the house could not refrain from tears. She told me what a retreat was provided us; but I feared being pursued, and thought it was better for me to stay at Tunis.

'We took a lodging in this woman's house, she promising to procure needlework for Clarinda, to help maintain us. In few days the honest countryman went home, carrying a letter from us to the good Father, full of our acknowledgments. And thus we lived for ten months, in which time Clarinda found herself with child. We lived very poorly; and no hopes of freedom appearing, at last I resolved, she importuning me, to file off my fetter and steal away to the widow's house, where she could lie in more conveniently, and with Clementine the pious priest's assistance, be better supplied with necessaries. We had little money, no guide, and travelled on foot mostly in the night, fearing to be observed and questioned in the day. We soon lost our way, and wandering about, came to the wood where you found us.

'Here poor Clarinda fell into the pains of childbed, and was delivered of a dead chid, which was doubtless lost for want of help. I did all I was able to assist and comfort her, but she was now in so weak a condition as rendered her unable to go from this dismal place. All I could do was to wander in the neighbouring villages to seek for food to sustain our lives. In this condition God sent you to us; and now if he assists us to get safe to France again, Clarinda and I are determined to do penance for our past sins, and if a dispensation cannot be granted, part for ever: I will return to serve my God at the altar, and she to her peaceful Convent, to wash away our stains and oversights with tears, to obtain a happy death, and rise again to everlasting peace and glory.'

Thus he ended his moving relation, which drew tears from every eye. The lords and ladies caressed them both in an extraordinary manner, and the praises of the good Father Clementine were confirmed by every tongue. And now the Count de Hautville called for wine to refresh the gentleman, whose name they now knew to be Monsieur de Château-Roial. Soon after, dinner being ready, they repaired to the parlour, and the ladies charmed with Clarinda, strove to entertain her as well as they were able, and to recover her health, she being very weak, and much indisposed. We must now take leave of them for some time, and return to Emilia and Teresa, whom we left at the widow's.

Chapter 10

Teresa was a month after her arrival at Seraja's delivered of a dead son, and lay some time sick; but recovering, and both the ladies working with their needles all day, gained a great deal of money, whilst Antonio went frequently abroad, to make inquiry after Don Lopez, and the Count de Hautville. At last going to the city with work, he met Lorenzo, who told him how the lords were escaped with a lady and girl from the country house; but he knew not whither, and that the governor was gone for the army, from which he had sent him two days before on business. This was all Antonio could learn, and enough to fill the ladies with new hopes of seeing them again. Sometimes they imagined they were got to some ship, and returned home; yet it seemed not very probable they would leave Barbary without having found them: Then they concluded they lay somewhere concealed, and would not fail to enquire them out.

This, with the knowledge of the governor's being gone for the army, made them more venturous than before, and they walked out sometimes into the adjacent towns, and often in the open fields, in hopes of meeting their husbands. But it so happened, that Muley Arab, youngest son to the emperor of Fez and Morocco, who was used to hunt often near this place, it being now winter, riding by one evening with few attendants, saw these unfortunate ladies, attended by Antonio, walking home to the widow's. Their beauty surprised him, though their habit was mean; he ordered one of his slaves to follow them, which he did, and returned to the prince, who the next morning sent one of his chief favourites to the house. He talked with the woman in the Turkish language, asking her who these women were. She told them they were poor maids, captives, whom she had bought to work with her in embroidery.

He presently demanded what price she would part with them at, saying he would purchase them. At these words the poor woman was confounded. She replied, trembling, 'I love them so dearly I cannot part with them.'

Then, said he, 'You shall go along with them; my master the Prince of Fez will provide nobly both for you and them; he will be here this night.' He instantly departed, and left the widow and ladies, to whom she explained what the Mahometan had said, in the utmost distraction: Whither to fly they knew not, and to stay there was certain ruin. They therefore resolved immediately to pack up their money, clothes, and jewels, and be gone towards the sea side. Whilst they were doing this, Antonio enters the house quite out of breath. He had been out that morning with some goods to a merchant's near Attabala's house, and returning, saw the two lords and Attabala walking in a field near it. He concluded it was them by the description Emilia and Teresa had given of them, and therefore hasted to bring the good news, having never rested in the way, though it was ten miles from the good Widow Seraja's. 'Ladies,' said he, 'I have fortunately found your husbands; now we shall be happy, and only Antonio will remain wretched.'

Teresa and Emilia transported, replied, 'Blessed be our God who ever helps us when distressed, let us go hence, with them we shall be secured; and though you our good angel have not yet informed us who you are, yet I doubt not but we, or our husbands, may be instrumental to make you happy also.'

Here they informed him of Muley Arab's message, and the necessity of their removing thence: 'I will then,' said he, 'return to the house where they are, and give your lords notice of your coming: Meantime delay not to haste to us, we will meet you on the way; but if you meet any company on the road, conceal your selves behind some trees, or stay in the great wood till we come to you.'

Teresa put the box of jewels into Antonio's hands, saying, 'Take you these into your care, and give them to our lords to secure, before they come to us: We will follow your directions, and be soon with you.'

He drank something to refresh him, and departed; it was not long e'er they followed, making what haste they were able to get to the place appointed; but alas, fate has otherwise decreed. The Moorish lord returning to his prince, related to him the disorder Seraja was in at his proposal, and advised him to be quick in securing the women. 'My Lord, said he, they are the fairest creatures my eyes ever saw, and, if I mistake not, Christians, and of noble birth.'

The prince more inflamed with this relation gave orders to some of his attendants to follow him, and mounting a swift Arabian horse, set out for the widow's, Ismale the Moorish lord leading the way. They found the house empty; and all things being left in disorder, shewed the inhabitants were fled in the utmost haste and confusion. The prince raged, commanding his vassals to divide themselves into parties, and pursue them with all diligence.

The cunning Ismale advised him to make for the sea coast; 'They are doubtless,' said he, 'fled thither, in hopes to get off in some ship or boat to some of the European forts or consuls, to Tripoli or Ceuta.' Muley Arab followed his counsel, and soon overtook the unfortunate travellers, who being loaded, unused to walk fast, and afraid of every passenger they met, were not got halfway to Attabala's. The Moors seized upon them; and it was needless to ask who they were, for their charming faces betrayed them. The prince viewed them with transport, descended from his horse; and speaking to the affrighted widow, who spoke his language, bid her tell them, they should not fear, he was passionately in love with them, would make them great, they should live in his palace, and smile in his arms. To all which she answered not, but with low curtsies, and downcast eyes.

At last she too well explained his meaning to the almost despairing ladies, whose prospect of approaching happiness rendered this cruel disappointment insupportable: Nor was their terror less that their lords should come up to them at this fatal juncture, and be exposed to the cruel *infidel's* fury. This is the uncertain condition of man's life, that we scarce know what to wish for, or to fear. These poor ladies but a few moments before impatiently longed to see their dear husbands, and now they dread their presence worse than death. Thus the fruition of our wishes is oft our punishment; and we ought to desire nothing earnestly, but leave all to Providence. Emilia, Teresa and the widow, were placed in the middle of the band of Moors, and led by three of them, who quitted their horses, to take care of these unfortunate ladies.

It was with much difficulty they got them to the next village, where the prince ordered they should stay to rest, till one of his coaches came to carry them to his summer palace, which was not many miles distant. Here he entered the house of a *bassa*, who was much overjoyed at this fortunate opportunity of obliging his prince. Here the ladies and widow were conducted to a chamber, where two eunuchs waiting on them, hindered their conversing together; for they dared not discover their thoughts to each other, for fear of being understood, and betraying their lords. They sat looking dejectedly, tears and sighs only expressed the state of their minds: wine, sherbets, sweet-meats, cold-meats, and the most delicious things that please the taste, were presented to them; but they respectfully refused to eat or drink.

Muley Arab was magnificently treated by the *bassa*, and his coach being come, departed, the *bassa* waiting on him, with many of his slaves, to guard the coach into which he was entered, with the two ladies, out of respect to whom the rich curtains of the coach were drawn. Seraja was presented with a horse to ride on, which a slave leading, she went next the coach; for the prince used her very kindly, designing to make her assist him in gaining the ladies affections. And now he had an opportunity of viewing the charming Teresa and Emilia at leisure: The first having lain in but some months before, and been long sick, looked pale and thin; but her youth, and the innocent sweetness that bloomed in her face, rivalled Emilia's majestic charms, where the heroine appeared, and every look drew admiration and respect.

Muley Arab gazed, and burned; his eyes sparkled with desire, and he languished to possess both: He was divided in his choice, yet gave Teresa the preference; he longed to speak his passion; and having learned the Spanish tongue, addressed himself in that to them, asking, if either understood it. Teresa replied, 'I do, my Lord.' He was transported that she understood him, and began to speak the most tender and passionate things to her that love could dictate; for the Moorish nobility, and indeed the whole nation, are much inclined to love, very amorous and gallant.

At length casting down her lovely eyes, with a modest blush, a look, where virtue, fear, and resolution were all blended together, 'Prince, said she, being so greatly born, as you are, and so generous in your deportment to us strangers, I presume to implore your pity, and promise myself success, since you appear so humane and princely in your speech and mien; we are both Christians of noble birth, already disposed of to two gentlemen, who were unfortunately brought to this place by pirates, and made slaves. None ought to have the honour of sleeping in your arms but virgins, whose hearts and persons have not been sullied with another's embraces, or love. We are already pre-engaged, and cannot oblige you without horror and dislike, or meet your love with mutual warmth and satisfaction; nay, we must rather choose to merit your utmost displeasure and die, than yield to gratify your lawless love.'

While she spoke, the prince listened as if he had heard some siren sing, and grew more mad in love. Her wisdom charmed him, every look, each motion fired his blood, and he thought every moment was an hour till he reached home.

He answered with a bow, and said, 'If man can make you happy, Muley Arab will: By Mahomet I swear, you shall command my very soul, and I will make you blessed as woman can be.' This he spoke to make her easy, and in mysterious words concealed his meaning, which was never to part with her; nor did he think Emilia less worthy of his favour, though he did not love her equal with the other.

They at last arrived at his palace, where he took Teresa by the hand, the Moorish Lord Ismale leading Emilia. They were conducted to a noble apartment on the top of the house, where the prince took leave of them, leaving a female slave to attend them. Teresa begged him to permit Seraja to come to them, which he immediately granted: So saluting both with passion, he retired, the reason of which was this: He had received from the emperor his father's hands, six months before, a wife, who was the daughter of an Arabian prince, who had assisted him in reducing a powerful rebel and his party, who had rebelled against him, and dethroned him, had not Abdela the brave Arab come to his assistance.

This lady was very handsome, and of a haughty disposition, very proud and revengeful; she loved him passionately, and was so jealous of all women that he but seemed to like, that she had poisoned several of those fair unfortunate creatures she found in his *seraglio's*, whom he had purchased or received as presents. He therefore dreading she would serve these ladies so, if he omitted to visit her immediately upon his return home, left them, and going to her apartment, appeared very pleasant and obliging, sat down to dinner with her, a particular favour in that nation; and after dinner proposed to her to return that night to Fez, to the royal palace, because he should go forth very early the next morning to hunt, and should disturb her, and designed to return to Fez in the evening: To this she willingly consented. And now he thought he had secured himself one happy night, in which he pur-posed to enjoy the two loveliest women in the world: But the prayers and tears of the virtuous Teresa and Emilia had reached Heaven; God who disappoints the wicked, and preserves in a wonderful manner those that fear and love him, had otherwise decreed.

Ximene the haughty princess was quickly informed by a slave whom she favoured, that the prince had brought home two European women, fair as angels, in the pursuit of whom he had spent that day; that his hunting was but a pretence to procure her absence. In fine, this officious woman told her all that could excite both her curiosity and revenge; which she was spurred on to do by a secret reason, which was, that she had been in her youth vitiated by the prince, and afterwards neglected: This made her distracted whenever she saw him fond of any other, and study to make him wretched, which she could no other way bring about but to continually incense Ximene against him, who always rewarded her for these cruel malicious services.

The prince, who had been those unlucky moments absent, whilst the treacherous Dalinda had whispered this fatal secret to her lady, returned to give her his hand to the coach, which was then ready with her attendants to set out for Fez, but found her much disordered: 'I am not well,' said she, 'and I cannot go tonight.' At these words she pretended to faint, and fell down on her bed. The prince was sufficiently vexed at this cross accident, but did not suspect his secret designs were betrayed to her. He seemed much concerned (as no doubt he was) kissed, embraced, and used all possible means to please her. She seemed to recover, said she would lie alone that night; though she had a secret design, and not sickness, made her choose to do so. In some time he asked her to take the air in the gardens; but she refused, and chose to let him go alone, for that was what she wanted.

He longed to consult Ismale, having perceived a change in Ximene's face and humour, that made him fear somebody had told her of the ladies. Whilst the prince and his favourite walked in the garden, Ximene conjures the slave to shew her Teresa and Emilia: She leads her lady to the room; Ximene only passed through it, and returning to her chamber, was so surprised at their beauty, and fired with jealousy, that she resolved to poison them that night, and commanded Dalinda to make a China bowl of delicate sherbet mixed with a deadly poison, which she always kept ready prepared for such wicked purposes. Dalinda failed not to execute her mistress's orders, and having mixed the deadly potion, left the bowl upon a table in the next room, designing to carry it up to the ladies as a present from the prince, whilst Ximene detained him with her, which she resolved to do that night, knowing the ladies would not live till the next morning after drinking that fatal draught.

No sooner had Dalinda left the room, but the Prince returning from the garden enters it, and being very dry takes up the bowl, concluding it was sherbet made for the princess; and going into her chamber drinks to her. She, not imagining Dalinda had been so indiscreet to leave the poisoned sherbet there, refused not to pledge him, taking a good draught of it. She seemed very obliging to the prince, to engage him to stay with her, asking him to drink tea with her. They sat down together, and Dalinda being called for, soon missed the bowl, and perceived the fatal error, yet dared not speak. In less than an hour the prince and princess began to fall into strange convulsions; which Dalinda perceiving, and fearing to be tortured and put to death, for being the fatal cause of theirs, packed up what she could, as jewels and gold, and fled to the woods, where she was seen to enter, but never came forth again, being (doubtless) that night devoured by the wild beasts, of which Barbary is very full.

A great distraction reigned in the palace; the physicians were called, and used all their endeavours to save them, but in vain. Dalinda was believed the author of this mischief, but none could guess the reason why before five in the morning Muley Arab and Ximene expired, she confessing what she designed, and acknowledging God's justice in her end. And now the slaves and favourites of the dead prince walked like silent ghosts, looking upon one another. A messenger was sent to acquaint the emperor with this dismal news of his son's death, whom he was very fond of: Ismale the Moorish lord bare the fatal message, and soon returned with a troop of soldiers, who by the emperor's order discharged such of the attendants as he thought fit; took all the women in his *seraglio*, and conducted them in coaches, being all vailed, to an old *seraglio* where the wives and concubines of the deceased princes are kept, some all their lives, and others are disposed of to the favourites of the emperor, or prince who succeeds the prince to whom they belonged.

To this dismal place was Teresa and Emilia carried; yet they in their hearts praised God for their deliverance from Muley Arab, whose surprising death, and the manner of it, they looked on as an earnest of God's favour, and were the more encouraged to confide in his merciful Providence. The good widow was offered her liberty to return to her home; but she chose to attend the ladies: They had in this decayed palace the liberty of walking in the gardens, lying together, and hoped soon to find an opportunity to escape, resolving to fly to Attabala's, if it were possible to find the way: But alas, it was more than sixty miles thence, and almost impossible for them to reach it without falling into new misfortunes: The widow advised them rather to make to the sea side, and endeavour to get a passage to Spain or France, promising to go herself to Attabala's, which she could do safely.

This counsel they approved of, and though they were very unwilling to part with her, yet they at last consented to her going; she easily obtained leave of the governess of the *seraglio*, and chief eunuch, and so left them, setting out for her own home, where she doubted not to find news of Antonio, and the lords. And here we shall leave the ladies for a time, and relate what happened to Don Lopez, the Count de Hautville, and the rest of Attabala's guests, since Antonio parted from the ladies, and the good Seraja's house.

Chapter 11

Antonio soon reached Attabala's house, and found the two lords, Monsieur de Château-Roial, Clarinda, Eleonora, and Anna, at dinner: He asked for Attabala, who coming to him, he desired to know if two gentlemen were not there, whose names were Don Lopez, and Count de Hautville. 'I come, said he, from their ladies, Emilia and Teresa, who are now on the road, coming to them.' Attabala ran into the parlour, and told this good news: All the company rose from the table. Antonio was called in; but what words can express the transport he and Anna were in, when she knew him to be her lover Carolus Antonio Barbarini, the generous Angelina's son, that noble Venetian lady who had bred her up? They flew to one another's arms. He gazed upon her, wept for joy, at length swooned upon her bosom; joy so disordered his soul, that every faculty stood still, and his heart and pulse forgot to move.

Don Lopez held him up, and all the company stood looking on surprised. At last awaking, as it were from a long sleep, he lifted up his eyes, and cried, 'Anna, thou dearest thing on earth, behold the man that has followed you to this barbarous place, and for your sake ventured to brave both death and slavery: We will part no more whilst we do live; I will perish by your side, or carry you safe to Venice again. And now, gentlemen,' said he, 'arm yourselves, and set out this moment to meet your wives; as we are on the way I will tell you more: We must not delay one moment to go to them; here is a box of jewels of great value which they gave me for you, and I will give to Anna's care till we return.'

At these words Eleonora casting her eyes upon Don Lopez, cried, 'Ah! faithless Spaniard, you then are married, and another claims your heart; you have deceived me cruelly.'

He was too much in haste to answer more than in these few words,

'Forgive me, Madam, I dared not tell you truth, nor did I know whether Teresa were still living; had she been dead, the charming Eleonora had a juster title to my heart than any woman: Yet you shall be happy, I will esteem, respect and love you next Teresa, keep you still near me, and make your interest always mine.'

They hastened him to depart, and the three gentlemen, Attabala, and Antonio set out well armed, to meet the ladies. They came to the wood, hollowed, called, and ran to every corner of it, but in vain: At last they went quite to Seraja's house, and finding all in disorder, concluded they were fallen into Muley Arab's hands; in which opinion they were confirmed by the report of some passengers whom they inquired of. Nothing could be more afflicted than the count and Don Lopez; they were even inconsolable, and Monsieur de Château-Roial and Antonio had much ado to prevail with them to return home. They would have pursued the Moorish prince, but Antonio told them the attendants he had with him were so numerous, and well armed, that it would be the action of madmen to attempt an encounter with them.

The lords seemed quite abandoned to grief, and returning home, appeared so cast down, that at last the charming Clarinda spake to them in this manner: 'My Lords, are you men and Christians? Have you been both delivered from perishing in the merciless seas by God's Providence, from a desolate island, where he supplied you not only with bread, but with friends, and a ship to carry you thence in safety, and land you at the port you desired? Has he preserved your lives from the pirates sword, and freed you miraculously from chains and slavery? Preserved your wives from the vicious governor? And have you now forgot his mercies, and doubt his power? Is there one of us here who are not living monuments of the Almighty's goodness, and shall we despair? Suffer not then your reason to be silenced by passion; but call to mind the great things God has already done for you, and put your confidence in him, who will never leave nor forsake us, whilst we trust in and love him. He will give his angels charge of the virtuous women you so mourn for, and restore them safely to you if he thinks fit; if not, by your submission to his divine pleasure, endeavour to obtain his favour, an happy end in this world, and eternal joy and repose in the next, where your wives will be restored to you; and all your sufferings here converted into joy and glory.'

Here she ended her admirable discourse, and the Count de Hautville returned her this answer: 'Madam, your advice is good, and I will endeavour to take it. Come, my friend,' said he to Don Lopez, 'shake off your weakness, and let us leave all to God; this life is short, and full of disappointments, let us behave ourselves like men and Christians. He that made us and our wives, will preserve them.'

Here fair Anna interrupted them, saying, 'My Lords, look upon this young gentleman and me, and learn to trust in Providence. I have not yet had time to ask him how he came here, nor by what miracle conducted to this place.'

'Charming Anna,' said Antonio, I will with pleasure satisfy both you and the company; but first my advice is, that Attabala 'should go to Seraja's house, and see if any person be there, and leave word in the village which she and the ladies, if they escape, will probably go to, to enquire after me: And let Attabala leave word with Johanna Benduker, her dear friend, that her slave Antonio waits for her and her friends at the place they were coming to, when he left them. Attabala may likewise enquire after the prince, and what else he can. In the meantime let us continue quiet; for should we remove hence before we hear from them, they would never be able to find us, nor can we be so safe elsewhere.'

They all approved of this advice, and Attabala went to Seraja's that afternoon. And now the company sitting together, Anna fetching the box of jewels, gave them to the lords, saying, 'Here is the rich treasure given to my charge, which I deliver to you, to whom it belongs: Upon my word it would fell for a sum great enough to provide for us all handsomely.'

The lords were amazed at the number and richness of the diamonds, and Antonio told them how the ladies came by them.

Don Lopez said, 'Since Providence gave them thus, they shall serve us all, and provide for all our necessities: Since God has made us companions in adversity, we will mutually strive to make one another happy.' Now Anna proposed the hearing Antonio's story since he and she parted, and he related it in the manner following.

'Gentlemen and ladies, said he, my name and birth I find fair Anna has already informed you of, and how our affections grew with our years, and the manner in which she was ravished from me. I must then begin my narrative from the most unfortunate hour of my life. The day that we were parted, I was with my dear mother Angelina, at our house in the city, to which we were retired for safety, when the dismal news was brought, that the Turks had landed and ravaged all the coast, and entered the monasteries, and carried away a great number of the nuns and inhabitants round about, destroying and plundering the most sacred places; and that Anna was amongst those the *infidels* had carried away captives.

'This news filled all the city with grief, and nothing but sighs and lamentations were heard in the streets, ladies of the first quality ran about distracted, tearing their hair, and wringing their hands, for the loss of their daughters, and death of their sons, killed by the cruel *infidels*: Every family had lost one or more out of it, and every tongue was employed in aggravating the public calamity. But though my grief was not so clamorous, yet I believe none more severely felt the loss of those they loved, than I, when I heard Anna was gone, my soul was shocked, and all my faculties failed me, I could neither eat nor sleep. In few days I resolved to follow her, and rather choose to die in slavery, than live free, and without her.

'I concealed my desperate design from my mother, who was highly afflicted at Anna's loss and my melancholy, and pretended I would go to travel only to Rome, Spain, and France. She was very unwilling to let me go, telling me with tears, "My dear child," said she, "God has been pleased to take your noble father from me, and my sweet Anna, whom next you I loved, you are all that are left me, in you are all my hopes placed; do not leave me then alone."

'Touched to the soul with her tender expressions, I delayed to go, and confined myself to her presence. But seeing me every day decay and pine away, she resolved to send me abroad, in hopes to divert me; and commanded me to go. I yielded, and all things being prepared, as habit, horses, and two servants, with bills for money at the places I passed through, I took leave of my dear mother and friends; and with her blessing departed, promising to return soon. Now my reason for going to Spain was, because had I gone from Venice, which was then at war with the Turks, I should have been liable to be taken, and made a prisoner of war; but if I went from Spain or France, in a vessel belonging to either of those nations, I might be safe, and have the protection of their consuls at Constantinople, by whom I might procure Anna's freedom, paying her ransom. And I resolved, though she had been ravished by the Turks, and sold or presented to the *seraglio* of some villain, for that her beauty would doubtless occasion her to be, yet I would take her to my arms, with as much Joy and affection, as if she had been ever mine: Yet this her tender years made me hope to prevent.

'In fine, I posted through Italy, and arriving at Barcelona in Spain,

I sent back my servants with a letter to my mother of my true intention, got a letter to the Spanish consul at Constantinople, from a great Spanish merchant, to whom I declared my design, and who had money in his hands for my use remitted to him from Venice; and with his assistance got passage in a Spanish ship, with the fleet arrived safe at Constantinople, and was well received by the Spanish consul, who soon got me information that Anna was bought by a Barbary captain, who was bound to Algiers, to which he used to carry slaves, and rich goods. I presently resolved to go thither, from which he endeavoured to dissuade me all he was able, but in vain.

'I left some money in his hands, and the next ship that was going to Algiers, I went on board as a passenger, paying for my passage before-hand; but the villainous Mahometan, so soon as he came into the port, chained and sold me at the common market for a slave. I was bought by an old Jewish merchant; and in one year, keeping his accounts, for he put me to no drudgery or servile employments, became his chief favourite. I endeavoured all I was able to learn news of Anna, but could get none. And now another misfortune befell me; my master's wife, a handsome Portuguese woman, whom he had married, and extremely doated upon, cast an amorous eye upon me, and gave me several invitations to be great with her: But I constantly avoided her, and seemed to be ignorant of her meaning: This so highly provoked her, that one day, when I was alone in the counting-house, and my master abroad, she came in, and shutting the door, said, "Antonio, must I be forced to tell you I love you to distraction? Are you blind to your own interest, and determined to refuse me? Am not I fair, and cannot I reward you? See here."

'At these words she threw down a great purse full of gold: "Take this," said she, "and take to your arms a woman who loves, and can make you happy."

'At these words she clasped me round the neck, and almost stifled me with kisses; I put her gently from me, in great confusion. At this moment my master entered the room; some officious slave who sought my ruin, had observed my mistress and me, and given him intimation of her love to me; and he had thus contrived to surprise us, having only pretended to go forth, and staid concealed in the house: She swooned, I stood confounded, though guiltless: He took me by the hair, beat and kicked me unmercifully, and swore he would poison her, and sell me the next day. He had so bruised me I could scarce crawl to a hole under the stairs, and there I laid me down, expecting to rise no more. I too late repented my rashness in leaving Venice; yet would have died contented, had I but once seen my dear Anna safe and free.

'In the evening of this unpleasant day, the good Tamosa, Seraja's husband, came to the house with embroidered caps and belts, as usual; he staid in an outer room, and as Providence decreed, espied me in this sad condition, my face was bloody, and my clothes all torn: He seemed much surprised, having always seen me well dressed, and caressed by my master; he asked me what was the matter; I told him the truth: He said he would willingly buy me. I had catched up the purse of gold when my master entered the counting-house, I put some of it into his hand to purchase me, when my master called him into the counting-house, to pay for the embroidery: He asked him for me, to give me something, as he pretended, and sometimes used to do, when my master paid him; my master exclaimed against me: The good Tomaso persuaded him that his wife and I might be innocent, at least that I was very young, and might be seduced. In short, he asked to buy me, and my Jew master, glad to be rid of me, sold me for a trifle.

'With him I went, and he hired a horse for me to get home to his house, where I was maintained, and looked after as if I had been their own child. In short time the good man died, and since that I have converted Seraja to the Christian faith, and assisted her in all I was able; and getting acquainted with many great *bassas*, and merchants servants, still desirous to find my dear Anna, I continually enquired for her, and never could learn anything but this: Lorenza the governor's Christian slave told me, his master had bought a girl, much resembling her I described; but he had sent her into the country, and I could not see her. This kept my hopes alive, but till this fortunate morning I was never assured of my happiness; but now I regret nothing I have suffered, and trust in God we shall be happy together, and return in safety to our dear mother, whom I long to see again.'

All the company admired the strange adventures these two young lovers had met with, and they all resolved to go away together from Barbary, the first opportunity after Teresa and Emilia were found; for now such an entire friendship was contracted betwixt these unfortunate persons, that not one of them would consent to abandon the rest, till all could be happy together. Villainy and base designs often unite men for a time, but end generally in their ruin, and hatred to one another; but when religion, and virtuous noble designs are the basis of men's friendships, they are lasting and successful.

Chapter 12

Attabala returned home at night, and related what he had learned of Muley Arab's carrying away the ladies; he had left the message with Johanna Benduker. And now they were obliged to remain in suspense for some days, in which the lords passed their time very unpleasantly; and Eleonora secretly rejoiced that her rival was more wretched than herself: She now behaved herself with much reservedness to Don Lopez, who treated her with great respect and tenderness.

At last Seraja arrived, and gave them an account of the ladies wonderful deliverance, by the tragic end of the prince and princess; as likewise of their being removed to the old *seraglio*, from whence she said it would be no hard matter for them to escape. This news transported the lords, and filled them with new hopes of happiness: They entertained Seraja with the story of Antonio's good fortune, at which she much rejoiced. They made her promise to go with them to Venice, and to live with Anna, who called her mother, and caressed her extremely for being so kind to her lover. Seraja lay there that night, and the next morning they consulted what to do. They at last resolved, that the two lords should accompany Seraja back, that she should go into the *seraglio*, and acquaint the ladies where they staid to receive them, they designing to lie at some village near.

So putting on their Grecian disguise, like merchants, they sat out with her, having bought a horse for her to ride upon, which Antonio got at the village where he and Seraja had lived. They took some money sufficient for the journey, and left the company, with many good wishes attending them. Monsieur de Château-Roial and Antonio would have gone with them, but it was feared it would render them suspected to be seen travelling so many together. It was but threescore miles they had to go, and in two days time they reached the nearest town to the *seraglio*. Here Seraja advised them to stay, and lodge, till she returned to them from the ladies: They did so. Entering the town they went to an inn, pretending they came to buy goods, and took a lodging. Seraja entered the *seraglio*, but was told the ladies were not there, but gone. She enquired whither: They told her Ismale the Moorish lord had begged them of the king, and fetched them thence the night before. The governess said, 'Seraja, they are fortunate, he is a generous lord, and will use them nobly; here are many young virgins in this place would rejoice to be so preferred.' The widow hid her concern as much as possible, and took leave, returning to the expecting lords with this sad news, which they took heavily, and returned to Attabala's house, more sorrowful than ever.

And now it is necessary we should enquire what befell these unfortunate ladies, whose unhappy beauties occasioned them such great misfortunes. Ismale having been charmed with their persons when he saw them at Seraja's, studied how to obtain them, and asked the emperor for them. He readily bestowed them upon this favourite, who made haste to fetch them from the *seraglio*, fearing their being seen by some person more favoured, and greater than himself, who might prove a troublesome rival.

When he came there, and told his business, you may imagine how surprised the ladies were; but he expecting such treatment immediately put them into a close coach, and carried them to his palace, where he locked them into a chamber, which was in the upper floor of the house, out of which a door opened upon a lovely terrace walk made on the top of the house, to take the evening air upon. Here the two wretched ladies walked a while ruminating on their sad condition, and considering what to do. At last Emilia, whose presence of mind was always extraordinary, and was at this time doubtless inspired by Providence, looking down into the garden below, said thus: 'My dear friend, shall we fear to tempt death, by venturing some way or other down this place, into the garden, from whence God may find us some means to escape; or shall we stay here and meet our ruin?'

Teresa thought a moment, and then running into the chamber, looked about to see if she could find any cord or string to help them: It was just the close of the day; they found no strings but took the window curtains, and sheets, tied them fast together, and fastening one end to the rails on the house top, Emilia slid down first as low as she could, which was some yards from the ground, which she ventured to leap down; Teresa followed, and both escaped without much hurt. Recovering their legs, they ran down the garden, and finding a door open, went out, not knowing where to go. They wandered through some fields, and at last coming to a wood, sought a place to hide themselves till morning, resolving at break of day to be gone farther off. Here they sat trembling, full of dreadful apprehensions of being taken again, or devoured of wild beasts. They knew not what part of the country they were now in, nor how far from honest Seraja's house, where they had so long lived secure: At last they resolved, if possible, to climb up into some low tree, which with some difficulty they did, and sat there in much fear.

Meantime Ismale, who had been engaged by some company who waited to speak with him at his coming home, which occasioned him to leave Emilia and Teresa so soon, having in some time got quit of his visitors, went up to the chamber, ordering supper to be brought thither, designing to enjoy himself in their company all that night: But when he found the room in such disorder, and the ladies gone, his surprise cannot be expressed: He soon discovered how they had escaped, and calling for his servants bid them light *flambeaus*, and search the gardens and fields adjacent, and if possible bring them back. The amazed slaves ran up and down the fields, and some of them entering the wood searched here and there, but saw them not. What concern the poor ladies were in is easily guessed. At last the servants returned home; Ismale fretted and raged, but in vain, and then went to sleep in an old mistress's arms, at which the servants rejoiced, and went to rest.

The ladies passed the night in prayer, and so soon as day broke came down from the tree almost faint, and hasted over a high hill, from whence they saw a lovely river at some distance: They hasted to it, and in a boat that lay there to ferry passengers over, passed safely to the other side; and asking where they were, the poor man told them the river they had passed over was called Omirary, a river that parts the kingdoms of Fez and Morocco; that they were not far from Mount Atlas, which if they passed over, they would come into Numidia, a country inhabited by Mahometans and pagans, governed by no king, but ruled by some chief men, heads of tribes, chosen by the rest. 'They are a people,' said he, 'inclined to thieving, Turks and pagans in religion, dwelling in tents, living chiefly on dates, feeding their goats with the stones, which make them very fat, and yield good store of milk; a country but ill inhabited.'

The ladies thanked the poor man, and went on towards the mountains, not knowing which way to go, ready to faint for want of food and rest. They had no money, their habits were fine, such as are given in the *seraglios* to the women of condition; the day was far spent, they had no food. At last they came to the foot of a great ridge of mountains; there, unable to go farther, they sat down: Teresa, who was of the weakest constitution, laid her head on Emilia's bosom, and sighing, said 'Surely now, my dear friend, my unfortunate life draws to a period, if God sends us no help soon, we must perish here: Our husbands know not where to find us, nor are we able to go to them. For my part, I have only this satisfaction, that having done my duty to God, and my dear lord, I have no reason to fear death. You, my dear friend, will, I hope, not only survive me; but, by some Providence preserved, live to be happy with your lord. Tell Don Lopez I died only his, virtuous and chaste, as when he took me to his arms, and hope to see him with joy in the other world.' Emilia wept over her, and strove to comfort her.

Now night drew on, and darkness rendered the place more dreadful. About midnight Emilia saw a light at some distance, in a house, as she thought; and looking steadfastly, she saw a man kneeling at the door, with a candle in one hand, and a book in the other, as if at prayer: She shewed him to Teresa. 'My dear (said she) let us try to get to that place, perhaps he is some Christian; but if not, we must venture: To stay here is certain death, and therefore it is better to ask help of *infidels.*' Teresa attempted to rise, but could not stand, the cold and fasting had so debilitated her limbs, they were useless. Emilia was unwilling to leave her, but at last was forced to it: She hasted to the place, and approaching near, saw a man of a middle age, tall, well shaped, and would have been very handsome, had not abstinence, sickness and hardships altered his face: He had a coarse *frize* coat, like a Turkish *dervise* or hermit, a fur cap, short boots like an Arabian. He was so intent at his devotions, he saw her not, though now very near him.

She listened, and hearing him pray in the Latin tongue, was encouraged to speak to him. She threw herself on her knees before him, saying, 'Generous Christian, help two unfortunate women, almost dead with want and travelling, fled from a vile Mahometan's house who would have ruined us: My companion lies yonder on the cold ground; give us shelter in your house, and a little food or drink to save our lives.'

The hermit being risen viewed her with amazement: 'Lovely creature,' said he, 'you may command my life; who would refuse to receive such a guest? Let us haste to your companion, and fear not to live with a man, in whom you shall find a protector and friend.' He fetched a lanthorn, and putting a candle into it, went with her, carrying a bottle of rum in his hand. Emilia's care for Teresa was such, that she staid not to drink; but forgetting her own weakness, ran to her, whom they found almost senseless. Emilia gave her some of the cordial, and with their help she was got into the house.

And now the hermit shutting the door, hasted to kindle up a fire of leaves and sticks, setting before them bread, meat, and wine; of which having eat a little, they began to revive, and the hermit, who waited on them with much seeming pleasure and respect, appearing very courtly in all things, said, 'Ladies, you are highly welcome to a man who has lived many years in a manner sequestered from the world. I believe we are of one faith, and equals in birth; my homely cell begins to look pleasant with such company: May I ask who you are, and beg to know your misfortune, that I may be the better enabled to serve you.'

The ladies had by this time observed the room, and man: The house was very poor and mean, containing below two rooms, and (as they supposed) no more above: The furniture was suitable; but the master of the place appeared to be noble, and of great birth and education. Emilia answered him, 'Sir, I think it is but reasonable that we should first know who you are, and your adventures, since our want of strength, and disorder of mind and bodies, may well excuse us from so tedious a task, as the relation of ours.'

He bowed, saying, 'Madam, forgive my curiosity, which made me forget my duty, and be too bold in asking so great a favour, as to know you. Rest is fittest for you; my poor bed and chamber waits to receive you. Here is the key, I shall not presume to wait on you to the door; this place will serve me to wait your commands in tomorrow morning, when I will freely, and with pleasure, tell you all the adventures of my life past.' The ladies were charmed with his behaviour; he presented a candle and the key to them, and would not admit their staying below any longer. They went upstairs, and found a bed and chamber, neat as those in palaces; there were some chairs, a carpet on the floor, with quilts, sheets and coverlids neat and good; in a closet were many watches, and tools of all sorts belonging to the art of watch making.

Many pictures of fine painting without frames, adorned the walls of the chamber. They shut the door, undressed, and having returned thanks to God for this signal mercy, went to bed, and slept sweetly. At break of day they wakened and rose; the hermit heard them, and prepared a fire: They came down, and he received them with a cheerful countenance; he was preparing coffee for their breakfast: And now they desired to hear his story, which he thus related.

Chapter 13

'I am by birth a Venetian, my father was a noble man, and I was his eldest son; my name is Andrea Zantonio Borgomio. I was related to a lady, who having married a wealthy merchant, had one daughter, with whom I fell passionately in love; but the custom of my country forbidding me to marry with any woman whose father was inferior to my own in quality, I resolved to marry her in secret. The day was appointed when I was to meet her at a country-house of her father's to espouse her; but the evening before, she being in her father's coach with her mother and father, attended by three servants, was forcibly taken out of it, and carried away with a black boy who followed her. The ravisher was a captain of a ship, who was an old man, very rich, and had loved her from her infancy. She was then about fourteen; he carried her aboard his vessel, set sail with her, and was taken by an Algerine pirate who carried her to Algiers, as I have since been informed; but how she was disposed of, I could never yet learn.

'It is almost eleven years since we parted. Her father sent a messenger to inform me of our misfortune the same night she was taken away. We soon discovered by what means we lost her, and I that minute resolved to hire a vessel to follow the villain's ship. Her mother, being my father's relation, flew to him for redress, but his behaviour soon informed me that he was consenting to the hateful deed: He treated her very coldly; and when I importuned him to procure an order from the senate to arrest the villain and his ship, offering to go myself to execute it, he looked upon me, and said ironically, "I do not doubt your readiness to follow him; you are too much concerned about what ought not to concern you at all, mind your duty; your kinswoman is fitter to be his wife than yours, speak no more to me about her."

'I understood him perfectly, and was so enraged, that I almost forgot he was my father. I went out of the room from him immediately,

301

took a great sum of money with me, and attended only with one servant, went directly to the port, where I hired a light brigantine and went after her. I guessed he was gone for Spain or France. In few hours we met a ship bound for Venice, who told us he met Captain Alphonso's ship; they saluted one another, Alphonso came aboard him, drank a bottle of wine, and said he was bound for Spain, taking some sweet-meats and wine this captain had brought from Leghorn. This made us steer our course that way.

'A great storm rose that night, and shipwrecked us upon this coast. I know not what is become of the captain and his men, but I was saved on a piece of the rudder, and cast on the coast of Barbary near Tunis. Here I was taken up almost dead by a peasant, who was very kind to me. So soon as I could walk abroad, I began to enquire where I was, what the manners and customs of the country were. But I was soon taken notice of, and sent for by the Turkish governor of Tunis, who examining me, took a fancy to me, and said if I would live with him, he would use me kindly; if not, I should be sold to somebody else. It was my best way I thought to accept of his offer, by which I might have an opportunity to get off for Spain. He employed me in the managing many of his affairs, sending me with letters and presents, to several ministers of state and friends: He was very gentle, and familiar to me, and, in fine, clothed and kept me so, that I began to apprehend he had an ill design upon me, and liked me for an use the Mahometans often keep young men for.

'As I suspected, it proved; one evening he called for me into his closet, and gave me a rich vest, *turbant*, and an entire Turkish dress of satin embroidered with silver, with linen suitable. He bid me take it and go and dress me, for I must cease to be a Christian and a servant, and live at ease. Then he kissed me eagerly; I turned pale, bowed, took the clothes, and went out trembling, determining in myself to fly thence whatever was the consequence. Whilst I dwelt with this Bassa Solyman, for that was his name, he had a *renegado* slave, by birth a Hollander, who indeed had not more religion than honesty or conscience. This man's name was Cornelius Vandunk, he was a watchmaker by profession, and having, as he owned to me, being extravagant, and run in debt, he fled his own country, and went with a merchant to Constantinople, to work there with him.

'His unconstant temper made him uneasy there, so he wanted to be gone elsewhere, and went aboard a French merchant ship, which was taken by an Algerine pirate. There he was sold to a Jew merchant who used him ill; coming to Tunis, he resolved to free himself by renouncing Christianity. He did so, by which he ingratiated himself with the Bassa Solyman, and became a favourite, working for him in curious work: He was certainly a great artist at his trade, and of him I learned so much, as to be able to put a watch together, and mend one tolerably; I took much delight in it; and painting in water-colours I was also a tolerable master of.

'Being now resolved upon quitting my service, I was considering how I could provide for myself, and enjoy my religion, the thing I valued far above my life. I thought now if I had a good sum of money with me, I might escape to some place far distant from Tunis, and retire to an obscure place where I might work and sell what I did make, till I could hear something of Eleonora, for that was my adored mistress's name; and having learned from a merchant that arrived from Algiers, who came to bring a rich present to Solyman, that Alphonso's ship had been taken and plundered, and the crew and passengers brought in and disposed of there, I was determined to stay in Barbary, till I got farther news of her. I had some money by me, but not sufficient for such an undertaking. I was now perfectly acquainted with the customs of the country, and under the religious disguise I have now on, I knew I could pass undiscovered and live safe.

'I at last resolved to take some jewels of Solyman's, which I had by his order laid up in a cabinet: This I did, and at midnight departed, having provided myself of an excellent Arabian horse out of his stable. I staid just without the town till break of day, when I set spurs to my horse, and rid towards Algiers, where in short time I arrived safe. I went to a merchant's house, with whom my master was acquainted, knowing he could not send after me so far, not knowing which way I went, at least till I had dispatched my affairs; and I designed to stay here no longer than till I had sold the jewels, and made a full enquiry after Eleonora. With the assistance of this merchant, the jewels were sold in three day's time; a Jew gave me five thousand crowns for them. I was informed the Algerine pirate had presented a lady that was in Alphonso's ship to some Turkish governor, but it was not known who; and that the captain was dead.

'At last despairing to find her, and fearing to be discovered and taken, I left Algiers, and went through Fez, which being too populous I quitted, and retired to this lonely place, having worn this holy disguise seven years, which I have lived in this place. I bought this poor cottage of a merchant for whom I work, I pass for a religious man, a hermit; the people reverence me as I pass. I mend watches for several merchants in the adjacent towns and cities. I sell my little pictures likewise to Europeans, and live comfortably, bringing home what I want. I receive no visits but at my door. I am called Ismael the Holy Hermit. I give what alms I am able to the poor; sometimes clothe the naked, and secretly assist Christians who are in distress. I have made myself a rule to live by; I dedicate every third hour to devotion in the day, and rise once in the night to prayer, and am now so reconciled to this retired kind of life, that I am indifferent whether I ever return to Venice or not, unless I could be so happy as to have Eleonora with me, or be assured she were dead; and then I would mourn her here, and die in this place.'

Here he ended his relation; Emilia said, 'What was the black's name who belonged to the fair Eleonora?' He answered, Attabala. 'Then, said she, I shall tell you wonders; blessed be our God who has brought us here together.' She then began the relation of their adventures, and in conclusion told him of the Lords being at Attabala's house, which she had learned from Antonio, but whether the lady is there or not, said she, I cannot tell. The hermit, for so we must call him till he leaves his cottage and habit, was filled with admiration at the things he heard: And they mutually acknowledged God's goodness in preserving them all in such an extraordinary manner. And now they were very cheerful, and fell to considering what was best to be done.

They were above an hundred miles distant from Attabala's House; and the hermit knew not whom to trust to send thither: At last he proposed that they should stay there whilst he went, though it was dangerous for him to go so far. The ladies were very unwilling to be left behind, but it was altogether unfit for them to go. The hermit said he would buy a good Arabian horse to ride on, and be soon back; to which at last they consented. He gave them money, shewed them where he kept it hid, and counselled them to put on such habits as he wore. He went and bought them such, with food and all things necessary; and in five days time, having put all his affairs in order, pretending to his customers some extraordinary business at Algiers, departed, having first taken leave of the fair hermits with much tenderness and many blessings; they praying fervently for his safe return. And here we must leave them till we have learned what is become of the lords and the rest of Attabala's guests.

Chapter 14

The lords being now at home in Attabala's house with Antonio, and the charming Anna, who wanted nothing but a safe passage to Venice to be completely happy, as likewise the fair Clarinda and her Lord Monsieur de Château-Roial, who were passionately fond of each other, yet determined to part, if they could not obtain a dispensation for them to live together lawfully; and the fair Eleonora, who liked Don Lopez so well, that she thought no more of her first lover, Signior Andrea Zantonio Borgomia : All the company began to importune Don Lopez, and the count to think of returning to their homes: 'Consider, said they, the dangerous consequences that attend our staying here longer; if any one of us is discovered, it will be the ruin of the rest.'

The good Seraja likewise pleaded for their going: 'My Lords,' said she, 'Ismale knows my house, you are sensible; and should he have the least Intimation of your being here or any Strangers, he would doubtless have you all taken, and examined. You must submit to the will of Heaven; if God pleases he can send your wives to you into Spain or France; but I am sorry to tell you, it is very unlikely, for being now in Ismale's hands, he will probably keep them too safe; Force cannot fetch them thence, you are in a strange country, and have none to assist you. It is now the season of the year for ships to come, and go to Europe: Let Attabala look out for a ship to carry you hence to Venice, or any part of Europe, from whence you may go to your several countries, and stay not here to be made slaves, and the poor ladies who have escaped hither torn from you again.'

In fine, all arguments were used to persuade them to go thence; but none was so prevailing as the generous regard they had for their friends, who could now be happy if they were not detained there by their respect for them. The lords begged them to go and leave them to

Providence, offering to divide all the money and jewels amongst them, and desiring to be left with none, but a servant of Attabala's, and in his house; but Eleonora opposed that strenuously, and all the rest refused to hear of leaving them alone. But now an accident happened that in few days obliged them to come to a resolution: The incensed Ismale, mad to be thus disappointed, and resolving in his mind that Seraja was the only friend the ladies had, and that it was most probable they would fly to her, resolves to go to her house with his slaves, and force her to discover where they were.

He accordingly comes to the house, enquires for her, but could learn nothing. He levels the house with the ground and departs, threatening to return again, and search all the adjacent towns and villages. He likewise offered a great reward to any person that should find and discover her or the young women, or her slave Antonio. No sooner was he departed but Johanna Benduker, Seraja's friend, runs to Attabala's, and warns them to be gone: 'If you are discovered, said she, as you certainly will, because of the reward Ismale offers, you are ruined.' This news both surprised and pleased Don Lopez, and the count; they were transported that the ladies had escaped Ismale's hands, yet feared to stay his coming:

At last, Seraja persuaded them to leave Johanna the care of the ladies, if they came; 'For,' said she, 'the slave here left and she will conceal, and get them off if they come, with less trouble than you can, who will be watched and questioned.'

Attabala hasted to the sea side, and going off in the honest fisherman's boat, went aboard a Spanish ship which lay there, and agreed with the captain to carry them to Venice. Returning home, Attabala hastened them to get off; they packed up all, leaving with Attabala's servant money for Teresa and Emilia to get home; Johanna promising to take care of them. But when the count and Don Lopez entered the boat, their concern appeared; they both turned pale, and the big drops rolled down their cheeks: 'My God,' said Don Lopez, 'pity me, and preserve Teresa, whom I am now forced to leave behind me: Ye angels, guard her, and conduct her to me safe.'

The count only lifted up his hands and eyes, and sighed deeply. Thus come on board, they were by the Spanish captain well received. They rewarded the fisherman, and he departed. And now joy filled every face, but the two lords, and they were extreme sad. The ship lay that night at an anchor, and the wind being contrary, they were obliged to wait its turning. This doubtless Providence ordered; for towards the close of the day Attabala's servant comes in the fisher-boat with the hermit, who entering the great cabin with him, saw Eleonora, whom he immediately ran to, catching her in his arms with such transport, that she had not time to discover who he was; but his voice soon informed her, it was Seignior Andrea Zantonio. She seemed equally glad, and if she was not so transported, yet she was doubtless pleased to see the man she had once loved so well. After some passionate expressions to her, he turned to the company, saying, 'I know not which of these gentlemen are the fortunate husbands of the virtuous Emilia and Teresa, for to them my business is.'

The lords soon informed him; he told them how he had saved and left the ladies safe at his house at the foot of Mount Atlas. The lords embraced him, and made him welcome, with repeated acknowledgments for his generous treatment of their wives, whom they were impatient to see. Eleonora also was curious to know his adventures after they were parted, which he related to her and the company. Then she presented Anna and Antonio to him, telling him who they were. He embraced them tenderly, glad to find some of his own nation there, Antonio being his kinsman. They now deliberated what to do; Venice being the nearest Place, they resolved to call there first. Antonio and Anna, Eleonora and Seignior Andrea Zantonio our hermit, feared not to be welcome to his father, if he was yet living, after so long an absence.

He had always resolved to marry Eleonora, who now told him, with much confusion, what had passed between her and the governor, which force excused; so that his passion being sincere as ever, he took her to his arms with as much joy as if she had been a virgin, and the chaplain of the ship performed the ceremony that evening; which gave Antonio an opportunity of pressing the charming Anna to make him likewise happy. Her youth and innocence made her hard to be persuaded to yield; but all the company joining, she gave him her hand, which he received with transport; and the next morning the whole company meeting in the great cabin, resolved what to do farther. The two lords determined to go with the hermit to Emilia and Teresa; the rest of the company were to stay aboard; and it being unsafe for the ship to lie there long, they agreed it should weigh anchor, and put out to sea for two or three days, and then return and stay at an anchor till they came back with the ladies, which could not be sooner than five or six days, because they could not travel so fast with them.

The hermit taking leave of his bride, who looked with confusion upon Don Lopez, and was concerned both for him and her new husband, not being able to quite stifle the passion she had conceived for that charming Spaniard, parted with them with much uneasiness.

The lords took a tender farewell of the whole company, and so departed, going ashore in the ship's boat. They staid that night at Attabala's house, where none remained but the faithful Abra, a Turkish boy Attabala had bred up and made a Christian of in secret, to whom he had given his house and effects. The next morning he went and hired horses for the two lords, on which they set out for the hermit's house; and travelling thither, we must leave them, and give an account what befell the ladies in the hermit's absence.

Chapter 15

The second night after the hermit's departure, Teresa and Emilia, having recommended themselves to God, went to bed, and composed themselves to rest. About midnight they were waked with dismal groans and lamentations, which seemed to proceed from some person near the house. They listened a while, and heard a woman's voice, who expressed her grief in these words, in the French tongue: 'My God, where shall I find shelter? Who shall assist me in this barbarous place? When shall my sorrows end? Why is my wretched life prolonged? And to what end dost thou preserve me yet on this side the grave, to suffer farther miseries? Has not thy vengeance yet overtaken him that ruined me? And can thy justice suffer me, who am innocent, to be thus miserable? Must I live still to be the slave of cruel lustful *infidels*? Oh, shew me some hospitable cave or cavern in the rocks to hide myself, and die at peace in.'

Here she sighed, her voice seemed to decay, and groans succeeded. Teresa and Emilia, whose hearts melted at these moving sounds, were both fearful to propose what both desired to do, which was to open the door and take the stranger in. They were alone, and in a lonely place, unable to resist whatever violence were offered. It might be some imposture. At length, compassion forced Emilia, whose courage was extraordinary, as she had before manifested, to speak thus to Teresa: 'Shall we deny that charity to another, which we were saved by in this place? Shall we not relieve a Christian and one of our own sex in distress?'

Teresa answered, 'Do what you please.'

Emilia went to the window, and called, but none answered. Then she struck a light, and they went down stairs, and opening the door saw at a little distance from it, a woman fallen down upon her face. They dragged her into the house, and fastening the door, set her in a chair, and poured some cordial down her throat, upon which she revived. She was richly dressed in an Arabian habit of silk embroidered, her hair was hanging loose, very fair, and in great quantity. She had a small wound in her left breast, a necklace of brilliant diamonds about her neck, ear-rings of great value, and her face and person delicately handsome. She appeared to be about five and twenty, and extremely frighted. At last having recovered her reason, she looked round her, and then perceiving the charming Emilia and Teresa in their odd hermits dress to be women speaking words of comfort, and very earnest to help her, she broke out into these passionate words, 'Am I with Christians? Are angels provided to take care of the unhappy Charlot? Has my God heard me at last? And brought me to a place, where virtue and charity reside? And am I freed from impious *infidels*?' Here she kissed Emilia's hands, who was putting balsam to her wound. And now the ladies asked her who she was, and her misfortunes that brought her there.

She willingly informed them: 'I will recount to you, said she, a story full of wonders, so moving and so strange, that you will be filled with admiration.' They made a fire, and having given her wine and meat sat down by her, she desiring them to put out the light for reasons she would tell them.

'I am, said she, a native of France, born in Paris. My father was a celebrated painter. He had by my mother, who was the daughter of a French colonel, a woman of great beauty and fortune, no child but me. Our house was frequented by a great many of the nobility, who came to have their pictures drawn, or see my father's curious paintings, he having a collection of the choicest pictures, both antient and modern, of any painter in Paris. He was very rich, and designed me a great fortune. I was tolerably handsome, and this caused me to be extremely courted, both for a mistress and a wife; but my father's ambition was so great, and he thought so well of me, that he refused to give me to several good tradesmen and merchants, hoping to match me to some great officer or count.

'In fine, a young nobleman coming to have his picture drawn by my father, saw and loved me, courted and visited me often in private, fearing his father's displeasure, who was of great quality. I was so foolish to imagine his designs were honourable; and being charmed with his agreeable person, behaviour, and bewitching conversation, grew insensibly to love him passionately. He too well perceived my weakness, and made his advantage of it. He made me many presents of value, caressed my father and mother highly; so that they entertained and gave him all the liberty imaginable with me, suspecting nothing of his base design, which was to ruin me, which he thus effected: He had gained my maid to be his creature, she filled my ears with his praises daily, and increased my distemper. One day when my father and mother were invited to dine abroad with some grave company, where it was not proper for me to go, my lover who had information of their being absent, comes in a hackney coach, and after some amorous discourses, as gallant and pleasant as usual, asks me to go abroad with him, taking Phillis my maid with me. "We will go to a friend's of mine, said he, whom I can trust, and be merry."

'I was proud that he would shew me to his friends, and thought myself very safe, having Phillis with me; nay, I thought him so noble and sincere, that I had not the least distrust of him. I dressed myself richly, and went into the coach with him, leaving my parents and home, which I fear I shall never see again; he carried me ten miles from Paris, there we alighted at a house, hired for his fatal purpose, as I was too soon sensible; I saw none but two servants, a man and maid, who received him as their master. The house stood in a garden, and no house within call. Here he gave me wine, and a dinner, which was ready prepared. I began to be much surprised, and apprehensive of what followed. He told me after dinner he was tired, and must lie down upon the bed: In fine, I trembled, and saw too late I was betrayed.

'And to dwell no longer on the dismal subject, here he forced me to bed, and though I used prayers, tears, and resisted all I was able, he at length overcame me, swearing he would marry me. Here he staid all night, and left me the next morning in the hands of my betrayer, Phillis, and his two servants, who watched me as a prisoner. I knew not where to go; I loved the villain that had undone me, was ashamed to be seen, and was so well watched, that if I would have gone thence I could not. He came frequently, kept me nobly, and used me tenderly. My poor father and mother too well guessed their misfortune, and mourned for me in secret. My lover went no more to visit them. My father attempted to speak with him, but the servants used him rudely.

'The neighbours laughed and ridiculed him, because he had disobliged many of them, whose sons and brothers had been refused when they addrest me: In fine, he fell sick, and in less than two months died, leaving my mother a rich but disconsolate widow. I was kept no longer so very strictly, being big with child, and my father dead. I was permitted to visit my poor mother, to whom I related my misfortune; we wept together, but could find no remedy. I was kept thus five years, in which I never appeared abroad, but with a mask. I had three children. My dear mother often came to me privately, and passed some days with me, my two sons died at nurse, my girl, grew, and my betrayer was very fond of me and the children.

'I still flattered myself he would at last marry me, but his father, who had took little notice of his keeping a mistress, thought it was time for him to marry, and give an heir to his family; he proposed a young lady of quality and fortune suitable; and having now glutted himself with me, my lover made no difficulty to oblige his father and himself with a new dish. He married the lady, who was handsome and a virgin; he grew fond of her, and slighted me, I never saw him, but I reproached him with my wrongs, so that he not only continued to slight me and came seldom to see me, but used me so unkindly that we never met but we quarrelled. This, with the torments of his conscience, doubtless made him resolve on being rid of me.

'He comes to me in his own coach as usual, for now he made no secret of our converse, which made him not very easy with his lady; he appears very sad, and treats me with unusual tenderness, sups, and goes to bed with me, and there with all the marks of affection and penitence, says thus to me: "My dear Charlot, I have wronged you cruelly, my conscience is wounded, I have not had a moment's quiet since I married, and now I am resolved to make you reparation; I am yours, and not hers whom I sinfully married. I am determined to leave her, and have provided a ship to carry, and money to maintain us in England, whither I mean to fly with you and my dear child."

'You may imagine, loving him as I did, how easily I was persuaded to credit him: In fine, I agreed to all he proposed with joy, and a few days after he came, took me and would have had the child, but my mother would not be persuaded to part with it: He carried me to Calais, where we went aboard a merchant ship. I had carried only my clothes and maid, and he pretending he had remitted his money to England, brought only two large portmanteaus on board. He led me into the cabin, where we supped, and lay all night. He left me dressing in the morning to go talk with the captain, I suspecting nothing. In some time I sent Phillis to call him to breakfast, and she staying long, I called, but nobody came: At last I looked out, and saw the ship under sail. The captain came, I asked for my lord and maid; he told me they were gone on shore in the boat. I wrung my hands, and wept; he told me it was all in vain, he had orders for what he did. In short I fell sick with grief, kept my bed, and was brought to Tripoly before I knew where I was. Here I was brought to shore, carried to a house, robbed of my clothes and jewels. The portmantuas brought aboard by my villainous lord, were empty, as I satisfied myself before.

'In this place I was sold to an Arabian captain, or chief of a tribe. He carried me with him, and what became of the Christian dog that sold me I know not. Abenbucer the brave Arab used me kindly, loved, and preferred me before all his women; but, alas! what joy could I take in this dismal course of life? A thousand times I have wished to die. I was carried up and down with the rest of his women, in a covered waggon, when we moved our habitations, which we did twice in the sad year. I lived with him three days since we came near this mountain. A brother of Abenbucer's, great as himself in power, of a humour different, resolute and revengeful, some time since saw and liked me, and studied how to take me from his brother. Yesterday Abenbucer being gone with his band to forage, Abdelen comes with his band of soldiers to the tent, and takes me away.

'Just as he was going off, Abenbeucer comes by, in short I screamed, a bloody dispute ensued, in which I was the victim to their rage, being dragged by the hair from one side to the other; here I received my wound: At last seeing the two brothers sharply engaged, I ran from them, and escaped over the mountain, where I wandered the rest of the day, fearing to be pursued, till darkness, loss of blood and weakness obliged me to stop; at last my senses failed, and had not God sent you to assist me, I had perhaps perished on the cold ground.'

The ladies admired, and wept at the sad story; and then lighting a candle, got her to bed, where they spent the remainder of the night in discourse, telling her part of their adventures. Towards morning they slept, and rising late, found Charlot so ill she could not rise; and now she expressed her fears to them: 'Ladies,' said she, 'I fear it will not be long before the incensed brothers, at least he that survives, will come in search of me over the mountains; it is my advice therefore, that we remove to some town of strength for some days, lest you are discovered and ruined by protecting me. Your beauty, which far excels mine, will perhaps cause them to bear you hence with me; you are very unsafe here.'

This alarmed the poor ladies, who finding but too much probability in what she said, were now afraid to remain here; Emilia therefore goes to a neighbouring village, where the hermit was known, says they were his kinsmen whom he had left in the house, and desires a lodging, and some lad of integrity to stay in the house for some days till Ismael their kinsman returned, because they had been frightened with a band of robbers, who were roving on this side the mountain; which was not very frequent, they not often venturing to come on that side.

The honest Moors reverencing their habit, offered them a house to live in till the good Ismael came home. Emilia gave the poor of the place a large alms, which highly increased their respect for her: And so she returned with a lad with her, the son of one of the principal men of the village. She had before she went packed up their money, and dressed the sick lady in an old habit of the hermit's, packing up her rich habit and jewels in a bundle. They led her betwixt them, and left nothing of much value behind them, ordering the lad to bring the hermit, and whoever came with him, to them. The boy did not fear the robbers, when nothing was left in the house worth their taking: But the fourth night of his stay the poor lad was murdered by some robbers, who entered the house in the night, and plundered it, and fearing discovery, killed him in the bed as he slept; which some days after was discovered by the thieves being taken, one of whom being put to death, confessed this fact, with many others.

The next morning after the boy was killed, the hermit and the lords arrived, and entering the house, were entertained with this dismal spectacle: The door was open, the house plundered, and the strange lad lying dead, the hermit concluded the ladies were murdered; and now the lords' grief cannot be expressed. The hermit found all the money gone, and believing it to no purpose to stay there longer, persuaded the lords to go back. Said he: 'My Friends it is in vain to stay here and mourn, it is Heaven's pleasure: If the ship sails without you, you will perhaps perish here also. The virtuous ladies are, no doubt, happy and at rest; God has permitted it to be so, and we as mortals must submit: If we stay here one night, it may be our fate to be murdered also, or carried by the robbers into slavery.'

They yielded to his advice, and returned in great affliction to Attabala's house; and the ship coming again to an anchor, they went aboard, and set sail for Venice, leaving word with Johanna, if the ladies were ever heard of, to send them word, and to assist them, if they came, to get to them; resolving to stay some time at Venice before Don Lopez and the count went to Spain, where the latter resolved to stay with Don Lopez the rest of his days, both determining never to marry again: Clarinda and the Count de Château-Roial having agreed likewise to go with them to Spain, and to stay there till interest could be made for them by their friends in France for a dispensation from Rome, for him and Clarinda to be man and wife, by discharging him of his vows; he fearing to be punished if he returned home without permission, and a pardon for the crimes he had committed. They all passed their time very agreeably in the ship, except the two lords, who sincerely mourned the loss of their ladies; and the ship arrived safe at Venice the 10th of March, 1715.

Chapter 16

The ladies waited some days, in expectation of hearing by the lad of the hermit's arrival: At last the father of the boy went to the house, and returned with the melancholy news of his son's death, and the house being plundered; and having enquired of some poor goat-herds who were upon the mountain, they informed him, that they had seen three men, two of whom appeared Grecians, and the old hermit, alight at the cottage door and go in; but they staid not long, but mounted their horses, and turned back by the way they came. From this account the ladies concluded, that they finding the house rifled, a strange lad dead, and nobody left to inform them what was become of them, departed, imagining them dead, or fled thence.

They therefore resolved to set out immediately for Algiers, and to go to Attabala's house, where they supposed their lords would wait, in hopes to hear of them, at least till they were better informed what was become of them. They took their money, clothes, and jewels; and having given some alms to the village, and a present to the man whose son was killed in their service, departed the town in a covered waggon they hired to carry them, it being the most easy and private way for them to travel, leaving a good name behind them. The poor villagers having conceived a high opinion of their sanctity, accompanied them on the road a great way, praying for the good *dervises* welfare, as they called them; and in four days time they got safe to Johanna's house, where they first stopped to alight, for they lay in the waggon all the three nights on the road, and went not into any house, only walked sometimes in the lonely places they passed through, to stretch their limbs.

Here they discharged the waggon, taking their things out, and sent it back: And here Johanna informed them of their lords being gone for Venice, and advised them to go early the next morning to Attabala's house, which she thought more safe than hers. The poor woman entertained them kindly, and they rejoiced at the good Seraja's being gone to Venice, hoping to find her well and happy there. Johanna entertained them with the adventures their lords had met with, and the fortunate meeting of the hermit and Eleonora, at which they were much pleased. This night they rested sweetly, being in great want of sleep.

The next morning early they went to Attabala's, there Abra made them very welcome; they were obliged to stay here till an opportunity of a ship could be found to carry them to Venice. And now poor Charlot, whose wound was not perfectly cured, fell very sick; the disorder of this long journey threw her into a fever, of which she was so dangerously ill, that her life was despaired of: Emilia and Teresa used all their endeavours to save her. Whilst she lay in this condition, Emilia walked frequently down to the sea side with Johanna, who came and staid with them, to wait upon, and keep them company, till they got off; and as they were musing one evening on the shore, they saw a man lying upon the sand, who appeared so miserable that it moved their compassion and wonder together.

They drew near to him, he was young, but his face was so pale, and disfigured with dirt and want, that it appeared frightful; his hands were so lean that the bones and nerves were visible, the skin being shrivelled and withered, his clothes were miserably torn and ragged; he had no shirt on, only a poor coat and breeches, with shoes and stockings suitable; he had three wounds in his stomach and breast, which appeared not to be fresh, but foul and rankled, and not covered with any plaisters: Emilia was so touched with this dreadful object, that she wept.

The man looked steadfastly upon her, she being in her hermit's dress, and that made him silent, believing her a Turk. At last he said in French, 'Why do you stand staring upon me, am not I a man? What do you see to wonder at? If you compassionate my miserable condition, relieve me, or kill me, for I am weary of living.'

Emilia answered, 'Are you a native of France, and a Christian?'

'I am,' said he, 'one, who being cast on this barbarous shore, am reduced to this misery.' 'Follow us,' said she, 'and we will relieve you.'

He looked eagerly upon her, and scrambling up, made shift to crawl to the house after them: Being entered the door, she desired Johanna to give him wine and meat, which he devoured with great greediness; and a few minutes after fell into strange convulsions; they

gave him some cordial water, and Abra ran and brought a quilt, coverlid, sheets and boulster; and on a carpet spread and made a bed: The
lady withdrawing, Johanna and he washed his face and hands, put him
on a shirt, and laid him in bed: Then they put balsam to his wounds.
He seemed almost insensible of all they did to him; but nature, which
struggled hard to digest what he had eat, at last threw him into a sweat,
and then he fell into a slumber; upon which they retired, leaving him
to rest. Emilia going up to Charlot's chamber, who was now on the
mending hand, related to her and Teresa the strange adventure she had
met with, which drew tears from their eyes also.

The stranger slept all night, as they supposed, for Abra who lay in
the next room heard nothing of him, only sometimes a deep sigh or
groan. About eight in the morning Emilia sent Johanna to ask how he
did: When she entered the room, she was surprised at the change of
his countenance, and concluded he was a person of quality, and very
handsome when in health: He made the most grateful acknowledgments imaginable, begging to know who the charitable person was,
to whom he owed his life. She answered, that she was commanded by
that person to ask his name and quality, if it were not improper, that
they might know how to treat him.

'Alas!' said he, 'the gentleman's curiosity will not be much more
satisfied, when I tell you that I am the son of a Marshal of France, and
that my name is Victor Amando, Count of Frejus; born to a plentiful
fortune, and by one unfortunate action ruined. I was going to Rome
in a ship from Marseilles, and by a storm cast on this shore: Here I have
been robbed in a wood, wounded and left for dead; and not knowing
where to go, or who to apply to, being unable to go far, I wandered
about the wood for these ten days past, eating nothing but wild fruits
and nuts, which threw me into a bloody flux. I at last crept to the sea
side, and there sat down, unable to go farther, having no other design,
but to lie there and die, which God prevented by your generous master's hands.'

At these words Abra entered the room with a Grecian habit for
him which Don Lopez had left behind, and waited to dress him: At
which Johanna retired, and went to her ladies with the account of
what he had told her: But who can express the surprise poor Charlot
was in when she heard the stranger's name, and knew him to be her
faithless lord, who had ruined, and basely sent her here? 'My God,
said she, how wondrous are thy ways, and how miraculous thy power?
Has thy justice then found him out, and brought him here to suf-

fer? I thank thee my God.' Being very weak she fainted; the ladies were much amazed at her words, and soon guessed who the stranger was: They revived Charlot with cordials, and begged her to compose herself, lest her fever should return with this great disorder of mind, and consider with them, whether it would be proper for her to see him now, or stay till they had sounded his inclinations, and learned whether he were single, and inclined to repair the injury he had done her, by an honourable marriage. She thought that best: So Emilia and Teresa went into the parlour, and sent for him to breakfast; they were both in their hermit's dress, as men.

When the Count de Frejus entered the room, they gave him a good morning with great gravity; he returned the compliment: They treated him now with ceremony: He much admired the beauty of these young men, and soon perceived by their voices and mein that they were women disguised. At last Emilia entered into a serious discourse with him, in this manner: 'My Lord, I am no stranger to you, nor the actions of your life; nor am I surprised at the misfortunes that you have met with, which I hope the Almighty will sanctify to you, and turn to your advantage. Where is the unhappy Charlot and her child? Oh! my lord, how could you expect prosperity to attend you, till you had expiated by repentance the cruel injury you did that lovely maid?'

At these words the count was even thunderstruck, to hear a stranger in Barbary reproach him for a crime he thought a secret to the greatest part of his own acquaintance. He at last lifted up his eyes, the big drops rolling down his face. 'My God,' said he, 'I own thy justice.' And falling at the ladies feet, 'Bright angels,' said he, 'for such doubtless you are, who pry into the hearts of men, and know our secret actions, pray for me to the Almighty: I have sinned so greatly that an age of penance cannot expiate my crimes. Oh! teach me what to do to appease Heaven.'

The ladies raised him, saying, 'Rise, sir, we are frail mortals like yourself, and living monuments of the divine mercy, preserved in this inhospitable land by miracles. But tell us, were Charlot living yet, would you repair her injuries?'

'Witness,' said he, 'that God in whom we trust, he who has seen my tears, and heard my prayers, that I would marry her that hour I were blessed with her dear presence; nay, I would choose to beg with her, and suffer every ill, nay death itself, rather than wrong her any more, or marry with a queen: Long have I mourned my sin, nor can I e'er deserve so great a blessing, as to see her face again.'

'Are you then single?' said Teresa, 'is your lady dead? And may we credit what you say?'

'Oh! what a wretch am I,' said he, 'that cannot be believed.'

Here Charlot, who had listened, entered the room. 'I would believe you, my lord,' said she, 'but have so suffered for my credulity already, that I hardly dare trust you.'

He fell at her feet transported, all he said was confused, he embraced her knees, gazed on her face, and at length fainted falling down on his face. Her tenderness for him revived; she strove to raise him, but through weakness and surprise swooned, falling by him. This sight was extremely moving: The ladies calling, the servants entered, and took them up; in some time they recovered, were laid together on the bed the count had lain on. And now looking tenderly upon her, he said, 'Charming, much injured Charlot, can you forgive me? I am now single, our dear child is well, and is my heir; God has cast me on this shore to bring me to myself and you; this happy place has brought me peace of conscience. Do you but pardon me; and consent to marry me, I will bring you home to France with triumph, with God's leave.'

She gave him her hand, 'Tell me,' said she, 'what has befallen you since the fatal day you left me.'

'I will,' said he. The ladies being seated, he thus began.

Chapter 17

'The unhappy day,' said he, 'when I basely left you, a day I ever must repent of, I went ashore with the treacherous Phillis, whom God has already punished, having struck her soon after with madness, in which she died insensible, and I fear unrepenting. I returned to Paris to my fine wife, and thought myself happy, vainly fancying I had secured my peace for the future. Your mother inveighed against me, saying, I had trepanned you: But I dissembled with her, pretending you had by misfortune fallen over board, and was drowned to my inexpressible grief, which I was forced to stifle for fear of my father, and my wife's reproaches. This Phillis justified to be true; and my great fondness of our child, and the large presents I made your mother, prevailed with her to credit this story; so I remained quiet from all clamours but my conscience, which hourly reproached me: I had no rest, my soul was on the rack; I grew surly and morose to all the world; my wife grew to hate me, and we lived miserably. A thousand times I wished for you again.

'At last I discovered that she did me justice, in dishonouring my bed with one of my pages: I exposed her to the world; we parted, and in a short time after she died in childbed of a child, which I did not believe mine: And that dying with her, put an end to all disputes. And now being little esteemed by my friends, and conscious to myself of my wickedness and shame, I left France in that cursed vessel which brought you here, being forced to be civil, and keep a correspondence with the villain who commanded it. We were bound to Italy, where I designed to see Rome, and pay my devotions at all the holy Places there. I asked him when he came in sight of this coast, if he thought it was possible to find you, resolving to purchase your freedom with all I was worth; but he told me it was in vain to attempt it. Soon after this discourse a tempest arose that tore our ship in pieces, and cast me on this shore; the captain perished in my sight. I was half dead when I reached the shore; and was scarce able to walk: I saw a small coffer on the sands, and taking hold of it, I made shift to drag it to the wood.

'Considering I was in a strange place, I thought it must contain something that would be useful to me, having neither clothes, food, nor money. I sat down, and rested that night, having nothing to eat to refresh me. At break of day I found my limbs stiff, and a great faintness over all my body; I broke open the coffer, and found money, clothes, and many rich things in it, by which I judged it belonged to the villain captain. As I was looking into it, three Moors appeared, who coming up to me, one struck me over the head with a sabre, which stunned me quite; they gave me three stabs in the stomach and breast with a knife; and emptying the chest, fled, leaving me for dead. It was long before I came to myself; but when I did, you may guess my condition: I bled much, I sought for some dust to stench the blood, and that performed it; but being unable to walk far, and not knowing where to go, I remained there destitute of food and help. Here I examined myself as I ought, prepared to die, and, I hope, made my peace with God, whose mercy has been signally manifested in my deliverance, and our wonderful meeting.'

The ladies admired, and blessed god for their good fortune, and his conversion; and wished nothing more than to see them married, which they could not accomplish till a Christian ship arrived, which was in less than a month's time; when a French ship came to them, sent from Venice, to enquire after them; which no sooner arrived, but Abra went aboard in the fisherboat: Monsieur Robinet the captain welcomed him. When the ship was ready to depart, he gave notice, and they came aboard, bringing their money, clothes, and jewels; and taking leave, with much affection, of the good Johanna, whom Emilia and Teresa offered to take with them, but Abra and she had agreed to marry, so she chose to stay in Barbary.

The captain entertained them nobly, as became the Generosity and good breeding of a Frenchman, and a Christian. They related to him all their adventures, excepting the occasion of Charlot's misfortunes, which they concealed in respect to the Count de Frejus . And here he and Charlot were married by the chaplain, a good Carmelite, who made them an excellent discourse upon the subject of the deliverances they had all met with in that barbarous place, from whence God had been now pleased to free them. They were bound for Venice, where they expected to find their lords.

It will now be proper that I should inform you what reception the lords and the rest of our travellers met with at Venice. Antonio and his fair bride invited all the company, at their landing, to go home with them to his mother, the noble Angelina's. At their arrival, the servants seeing their lord and the beautiful Anna, were so transported, they scarce knew what they did: They wept for joy, and so great a noise was made in the house, that Angelina, who had been long sick in her chamber, imagined the house was on fire, and crept out to the stairs-head, to see what was the matter: But when she saw her son and Anna coming up to her, she was scarce able to express her joy. They threw themselves at her feet; she blessed and raised them, clasping them in her arms and weeping on their bosoms. They informed her, that they had brought other persons of worth and quality with them, whom they would recommend to her favour. She composed herself a little, and her son led her down, where she received them with demonstrations of respect: But when she saw her niece and Seignior Andrea Zantonio, she was amazed: 'Just Heavens,' said she, 'Kinsman! who thought to have seen you together?'

'God had decreed it so, madam,' said he, 'and therefore seas and Barbarians could not prevent it.'

Angelina called for supper, saluting Clarinda, welcoming the lords, the Count de Château-Roial, and the good Seraja at supper, which was splendid, as the company and occasion merited. Great part of the company's adventures were related, and Angelina informed Seignior Andrea, that his father was dead, very much afflicted for his son's loss: 'But my brother and sister, niece,' said she to Eleonora, 'are well, and tomorrow we will go and see them.'

Beds were made for all the company, and no excuse would pass but the lords, Clarinda and her lord, must all stay there while they continued at Venice. The next day the whole city rang of this strange story, and all the noblemen and ladies, who were friends or related to Angelina, crowded thither to see, and welcome Antonio and his charming lady to Venice. A messenger was dispatched early in the morning to Eleonora's father's, who by noon arrived at Angelina's, with her mother. Poor Attabala was likewise much caressed for his faithful service to his lady.

In fine, a month was past in nothing but feasts, balls, and enter-tainments, to welcome these noble Venetians home; in all which the Spanish and French lords shared. Yet Don Lopez and the Count de Hautville were deeply melancholy: They had related the story of their misfortunes, and Emilia's and Teresa's loss; and a French ship lying in the harbour, Angelina proposed to them to send for the captain, and agree with him to cast anchor and call at Attabala's house, to which they should direct him, and make enquiry after these unfortunate ladies. They did so; and this was the ship that Abra went aboard of at his coming to an anchor. And in this vessel they came safe to Venice, but not before the lords had left it; for Don Lopez desirous to see his father and native country again, having little hopes of Teresa's being found, or escaping if alive, growing uneasy at the multitude of company he was obliged to be engaged in every day, and wanting to be alone with his friend, whose melancholy humour suited best with him at the time; he therefore proposed to the Count de Hautville to go thence soon.

However, they were detained two months longer; in which time Monsieur de Château-Roial fell sick of a fever. And though all possible means were used to save him, yet all proved ineffectual, and the physicians gave him over. He behaved himself in this his last scene of life so like a Christian and a hero, that it charmed all that attended him. At last the pangs of death being on him, he took a solemn leave of every one there present, but particularly of the two lords who had preserved him and Clarinda from perishing. He at last having received the last sacraments, concluded all with taking leave of the disconsolate Clarinda, who had not for many days gone into a bed, or left his bedside: He grasped her hand, and fixing his dying eyes upon her, said, 'My dear Clarinda, the hour is now come when we must be parted, though not for a long time; God does not think fit to continue us longer together. I have unfortunately occasioned you many misfortunes, we have known little satisfaction in the enjoyment of one another; now human passions will cease to fire my soul, and my reason will govern.

Believe me, sensual pleasures are bitter in reflection, and in death afford no consolation; I hope my peace is made above. I am glad to leave the world, and can advise you but two things: The first is, to be contented with our separation, submit to God, and acquiesce in all things he decrees: Nor murmur at misfortunes, which are the holy fires that must purge our souls of vice, and make us fit for glory. And next, I beg that you would quit the world, and in a convent spend the remainder of your life, where you may be no more in danger of being again unhappy. Nor give that lovely person to another, who may involve you in worldly cares. Alas! my dear, life is well spent in learning how to die; live so that we may meet again to part no more.'

'Yes, my dear lord,' said she, 'I will obey you, and never venture into the world again.'

Here his agonies increasing, his confessor began the prayers, and in few hours he departed. Clarinda, after he was handsomely interred in the Benedictine's Church near the altar, was invited into the Convent of Nuns adjoining; to which she went, attended by Angelina, Antonio, Anna, Eleonora, Seignior Andrea, the two lords, Seraja, and all Angelina's relations and friends, who loved her much, and left her there to enjoy uninterrupted peace, where no worldly cares can enter to disturb her.

After this Seraja choosing to stay at Angelina's, the lords took leave, and went for Spain in a Spanish vessel. They arrived safe at Barcelona, from whence they went to Madrid; and there at his seat near that city found Don Lopez's father, Don Manuel de Mendoza, who was astonished to see him. He and the Count de Hautville entertained him with a faithful account of all the strange adventures they had met with, which filled him, and all his friends to whom their story was related, with admiration. But no part of their history was more wondered at than that of Tanganor and Maria; the heroic action she did, in pulling out her eyes to save her virtue, charmed all that heard it related.

And now Don Lopez was worse fatigued than ever, being obliged to receive visits from all his, till then, unknown relations, and all the Spanish nobility that heard of him; so that he had scarce an hour to himself, or to give to his friend alone. At last he retired to a seat of his father's in the country, where he past a few days to the satisfaction of his mind, but the prejudice of his body; for here he and the count talked, and thought of nothing but Emilia and Teresa, and that melancholy, which company and noise before diverted, seized their spirits; so that in few days they both grew altered, forgot to eat or sleep as nature required; and nothing but leaving the world, and retiring to a convent was thought of.

One morning about ten o'clock, a coach stopped at the gate, with an elderly lady in it, who much desired to speak with Don Lopez. The servants brought her in, and Don Lopez being informed of her being there, readily came to her, hoping to hear something of the ladies, but it proved otherwise: 'My Lord,' said she, 'I have heard with amazement your adventures, and your noble Venetian friends; it is the subject of all people's discourse in this province: But there is one story in particular, in which I am nearly concerned, which relates to a lady whose name was Maria, lost from her country, and me her afflicted mother long since. I beg to hear from your own mouth what I have heard from others, that being informed of each particular circumstance, I may be able to judge whether the lady you have seen be my dear child or not.'

Don Lopez sitting down by her, related all the story of Tanganor, and his lady, and then begged to know how this excellent lady came into the hands of the Turks. The lady much transported, being now positive that it was her daughter he had seen, wiping away the tears, which joy had filled her eyes withal, proceeded to satisfy his request in this manner: 'My lord, my husband Don Fernando Valada was a merchant at Barcelona; it had pleased God to give us a very handsome fortune, but it was many years before he blessed us with a child, which was the only thing we wanted in the world to make us completely happy. At last I proved with child, and was delivered of this lovely girl, which we bred up with the utmost care and tenderness. When she was turned of twelve years old, my husband having a ship very richly laden returned from Goa, which lay at anchor in the road, invited a great many of his relations and friends on board, to give them a treat: I was at that time unfortunately indisposed, and therefore sent my daughter with her father to supply my place.

'It was autumn, and late at night before the company broke up: The pinnace carrying part of them ashore, and returning to fetch my husband, Maria, and the rest, it grew dark, the wind rose, and my Husband was afraid to let her venture to go so late, and apprehending a storm, thought it best to stay aboard till morning: But alas! the storm increased, and about two o'clock the ship was drove to sea, having lost her anchors, and running before the wind, was drove on the coast of Barbary: There the ship was beset with three Algerine pirates, and after a sharp fight, in which my dear husband was killed, the ship was taken and carried into Algiers. A Turkish captain, who was come there to purchase fair slaves for his villainous masters to make sale of, bought my dear child; but where he carried, or how disposed of her, I could never be informed till now.

'What I tell you, I got information of by means of a friar, who was chaplain to my husband's ship, and being a very sickly man, and unfit for slavery, the pirate captain dismissed him, and put him on board a French ship they made prize of, in their way to Algiers; and having plundered it, put on board it all the wounded and disabled persons, and some provisions, and bid them go home. But alas! they were unable to manage the ship, and had not God sent an English ship, who met them at sea, they had perished: The English captain putting some hands aboard, brought the ship to Barcelona, to which place he was bound. Thus, my Lord,' said she, 'I have informed you what you desired to know; and now I beg only one favour more of you, which is to direct me how I may send to my dear Maria, whose virtues have now made her ten times dearer to me than she was by the ties of nature.'

Don Lopez told her the only way was to send by some East-India ship, as he would direct. After many thanks she took leave, and having a brother who was a captain of a merchant ship, got him to go to that island, and had the satisfaction of having a message from Maria's own mouth, with a letter from Tanganor, promising to come to Spain the next year, so soon as he had got another return from Persia. In the meantime he sent her his eldest daughter, the lovely Leonora, whom she received with the greatest joy imaginable. This was a year after she was with Don Lopez, whom we shall now leave at his country seat, and return to enquire after the ladies.

Chapter 18

Three months after Don Lopez and the Count de Hautville's departure from Venice, the charming Emilia and Teresa arrived, with the Count de Frejus and his lady, the now happy Charlot, and were by Monsieur Robinet conducted to Angelina's house, where they were received with great joy and civility: And here they put on habits suiting their sex and quality, and were obliged to stay some days both to refresh themselves, and in compliance with the importunities of their friends, Seignior Antonio Bargomio and the engaging Anna, and Seignior Andrea and Eleonora his lady, who mutually strove to divert and treat them; rivalling each other in the magnificence of their feasts and balls: And all their relations visited and invited them to entertainments; so that a month was past before they could handsomely take leave.

They forgot not to pay a visit to Clarinda, whom they dearly loved and honoured, lamenting Monsieur de Château-Roial's death, whom they much pitied whilst living; fearing no dispensation would be granted him to live with Clarinda. And now Monsieur Robinet, who obligingly staid for them, prepared for their departure, taking aboard wine and fresh provisions of all kinds, to accommodate them in the way. And now taking leave, though with some uneasiness, being much pressed to stay longer, they went on board, accompanied by all their generous friends, who waited on them to the ship. The good Seraja, who was overjoyed at their arrival, gladly went with them, being amazed and charmed with the treatment, and fine things she met with, and saw in Europe. Abundance of fine presents were made to Emilia and Teresa by the Venetian ladies, of rich Venetian brocades and some jewels, to be the monitors to remind them of their absent friends; rich wines, lace, perfumed gloves, sweet-meats, and all sorts of things useful and ornamental.

Nor did Emilia and Teresa omit to make such returns as became them to do, promising the noble Angelina and Anna never to neglect an opportunity of writing to them, and to keep their friendship alive with frequent converse of letters. And thus embracing one another they parted, and the ship setting sail, arrived at Barcelona. The captain took a lodging for the three ladies and the Count de Frejus at their landing, and then making inquiry for Seignior Don Manuel de Mendoza, Don Lopez's father, was soon informed where he was; and going the next morning to his seat, which he rid to in few hours, he informed that noble lord who was arrived in his ship.

He received the news with much joy, and curious to see his daughter-in-law and Emilia, of whom he had heard so much; as likewise desirous to bring the lady, and good news to his son himself; he ordered his coach and six to be got ready against the next morning; when he set out with the captain for Barcelona, where he found the expecting Emilia and Teresa, whom he tenderly embraced, and welcomed the Count de Frejus and his lady, admiring the ladies' youth and beauty, especially Teresa's, which he had expected to see much changed. He carried them to his seat the next day, having entertained them at a relation's house the day of his arrival at Barcelona, and the night of his stay there: Then he paid Captain Robinet nobly, making him promise to call on him at his next return from France. He treated his daughter and company in such a manner at his seat that even amazed them; and then set out for the country seat, where those they most longed to see were. When the coach came near the gate, he begged the ladies to abide in it, till he went in and prepared his son and the count to see them; 'lest,' said he, 'the surprise of seeing you on a sudden may hurt them.'

They consented.

'Ladies,' said he, 'I assure you your husbands are much changed for the worse, that is, they are pale, lean, and dispirited, but you will be the best cordial to revive them.' He quitted the coach, and attended with two servants only, entered the gate, and asking for his son, was informed the count and he were in the gardens. Thither he went, and found them sitting together in a deep discourse: They started at his coming up to them, like men lost in thought. 'Gentlemen,' said he, 'why do you pass life thus in solitude, unactive, and lost to the world? Son, I blush to think the loss of a woman—though a wife—should rob you of your reason, make you forget your duty to your prince and country. Come, wake, shake off this lethargy, rouse at the call of glory and honour, and let your ancestors souls no longer mourn, to see you waste your youth in pining for a woman, which should be employed in doing deeds worthy your birth, and to perpetuate your name.'

'Alas! my honoured lord,' said he, 'you cannot comprehend what I have lost: Consider the amazing proofs Teresa gave me of her virtue, and the sad condition I have left her in. See here, my friend, a man brave as the world can shew, he droops like me, for such another woman. Why should we be censured if we leave the world, and live retired? Are not our convents filled with such, and do not they merit our esteem.'

'My son,' replied the old lord, 'they leave the world by choice, you only because you are disgusted; suppose your wives are dead, must you rebel and murmur against Providence?'

'Ha!,' said the Count de Hautville starting, 'Dead! what are you going to prepare us for? If they are so, tell us at once, our resolutions are already made, a cloister shall secure us from all future mischief; we will not make a second choice. Let glory and the idle ambition that deludes mankind tempt them to venture in a crowd, and end life in a tumult; we will study how to die, and wait our maker's pleasure, till he rids us of a tedious life, and calls us to eternal rest.'

Here the cold sweat trickled down his face, and the old lord admiring their constancy and affection, took him by the hand, and said, 'Come friends, revive, God has heard you; I have some good news to tell you; I have heard from your wives, they are not far off, follow me.' Here turning about, he went to the gate, they following in such disorder they scarce knew what they did: But when they saw the ladies, they forgot all ceremony, and rushing into the coach, regardless of Charlot the stranger, they fell on their knees before their wives, embracing them, who were so transported the tears flowed from their eyes, and they mutually blessed God, and said so many passionate things, that the old lord, Charlot and the Count de Frejus wept. In some time they began to remember who waited, and Don Lopez recovering himself, begged pardon of his father.

'My son,' said he, 'it is a laudable error; you have a wife worthy the affection you bear her, she merits all your care, and God has blessed me beyond my desert in such children.'

The ladies alighting, entered the house. And now an universal joy spread itself through all the family, and ten days were past in nothing but balls and entertainments.

They departed thence for Madrid, where fame had spread the news of their adventures before their arrival; and there they saw the splendour of their glorious monarch King Philip's court, where the French gallantry has taken place of the Spanish gravity, and wisdom and good manners seem to walk hand in hand; where solid sense and generosity, greatness and goodness, appear united; where men are statesmen and courtiers together.

For six months they passed the time agreeably, and then the Count de Hautville having received news from France, that his father was dead long since, and the title and estate his due; though his supposed death had consigned it to another, who was ready to resign it to him with pleasure; communicated this news to the company: But Teresa and Emilia knew not how to think of parting, they were both with child. At last it was resolved the Count de Hautville, now Marquis de Ventadore, should go to France, settle his affairs, and return to them; Teresa begging Emilia might lie in with her.

The Count de Frejus and the *marquis*, with Charlot, who longed to see her mother and child, went together to France over the Alps, Emilia making her lord promise never more to go upon the faithless seas. They arrived safe in France, where they were greatly welcomed, and Charlot's lovely daughter received by her parents with great transport.

The Marquis de Ventadore quickly returned to Spain, and was not long after blessed with a son, which Emilia brought him on the 10th of August, 1719, and the charming Teresa made her transported lord father to a son and daughter, on the 13th of September the same year: The two lords stood godfathers to each other's sons, and Don Lopez's father and Emilia to Teresa's daughter, who bare Teresa's name; and Don Lopez in performance of his vow built a church, and dedicated it to St. Teresa.

And now one would suppose, that having past seven years in an almost continued scene of misfortunes, and thus fortunately arrived in their native Country, the happy Don Lopez and his charming wife might expect to pass the remainder of their days in peace. It is true, the fair Teresa was but nineteen, and that fatal beauty that had occasioned her so much sorrow, was rather improved than diminished: But her known virtue would have awed any bold admirer from once daring to disclose his flame, and secured her from all attempts of love, one would have imagined. But alas! it was otherwise decreed: A young nobleman of Spain, son of a duke, and favourite of his young prince, the Prince of Asturias, whom he was bred up with, nephew to Don Manuel Father of Don Lopez, coming frequently to visit him and Teresa, who was now up again, and seemed to rise like the glorious sun to bless the world, with new charms in her face and fire in her eyes, content adding smiles to her natural sweetness; the unfortunate Don Fernando de Medina gazed away his liberty, and grew so mad in love, that he forgot all ties of blood, honour, and Christianity; and resolved to possess her, or die in the attempt.

He knew her virtue rendered all means but force impracticable, despairing to gain her any other way; and therefore subtly contrived how to effect it, without her being aware of it, or her husband able to find out where she was, who had stolen her. In order to this, he hires four desperate Catalonian gentlemen, Sons of Fortune, who had been employed before in such, or as bad undertakings: These he promised a great reward to. One of these hired a house next a wood, about five miles from Fernando's country seat, and placed in it two old hags, proper for such a wicked design. Here they made a chamber strong as a prison, furnished it with a bed, and all necessary things. Thus prepared he goes to his kinsman's, invites him and the *marquis* to a hunting-match, with the ladies.

They willingly consented to go, and the next morning went to his house, where after being magnificently treated, they went into the field; and the ladies loving the sport, excellently mounted, pursued the frighted stag, till the heat of the day made them retire to this fatal wood, where Don Fernando had prepared a treat for them. Here they dined in a tent pitched for that purpose: And then he proposed to the lords, to leave the ladies there to repose, whilst they hunted another deer, and so return to conduct them home in the evening. Two servants were left to attend the ladies. About an hour after their lords were gone, the four villains who lay in ambush, with vizards on their faces, and pistols in their hands, rushed into the tent, and seizing upon Teresa, carried her away before the servants, who were fallen asleep upon the grass behind the tent, awaked with the alarm of Emilia's cries.

Fernando kept the lords some hours, and then returning to the tent, they found Emilia almost distracted with grief, and the servants standing mute as statues: The cunning Fernando shewed a mighty concern for his kinsman's misfortune. Don Lopez raved, and stormed like a man in despair, but all in vain. They searched all the wood, and passing by the lonely house, saw one of the old hags, who stood at the door on purpose. The lords enquired of her, if she had seen any man with a lady pass by that way: She told them, yes; about two hours before, she saw four men ride by, with a lady bound hand and foot before one of them, and supposing them thieves, shut the door.

'They turned to that road,' said she, shewing a contrary way to that they had really taken: Emilia and the lords went on that road the woman directed, but to no purpose. At last night approaching, they went home. Don Lopez was inconsolable, and the dissembling Fernando, who inwardly triumphed at the good success of his cursed plot, staid with him all night. Next morning he took leave, pretending he would make it his endeavour to find Teresa, and bring the villains to justice: But alas! he burned to possess her, and flew with the utmost speed to the place, where he knew she was. And now I must inform my reader, that the villains did not carry her directly to the house by the wood; but rid twenty miles farther through unfrequented places, having put her, bound hand and foot, into a horse-litter, which they had placed just beyond the house. Here they stopped till it was dark; then lighting torches they had brought in the litter, they returned by the same ways to the house, and left her in the horrid room where the old hags attended to watch her.

Here they laid her bound upon the bed, ungagged her, and strove to pacify her, but in vain: She wept and lamented her misfortune, in terms so moving it would have melted the hearts of Barbarians: But these vile relentless women derided her, asking, what she feared from a man who passionately loved her. Thus poor Teresa passed the remainder of the sleepless night and morning, taking no sustenance, but refusing to eat or drink, they feared to unbind her. About noon the base Fernando arrived so disguised, it was almost impossible to know him; he put a vizard upon his face before he entered the Chamber, then shutting the door, he came to the bedside, and used all his rhetoric to persuade her to yield fairly to him. Then he proceeded to threats, yet she remained inflexible, used prayers and tears to dissuade him from so horrid a crime: 'Heaven,' said she, 'will find you out, and pour its vengeance on your head; my lord will discover you, or some thunderbolt dispatch you, and bring your soul to the dreadful tribunal, where your sentence will be given.'

He seemed deaf to all she said, rudely kissing and embracing her. At last summoning all her reason, she changed her behaviour: 'Well then,' said she, 'since love makes you deaf to all entreaties to dissuade you from this dreadful deed, unbind me, give me something to drink, and let me find some humanity in the treatment you give me; if I must be yours, shew that you love me.'

Fernando transported at her seeming so consenting, readily called for wine, unbound her hands and feet, having first locked the door, she drank, and watching an opportunity, threw a glass of wine in his eyes, then flew to the door, broke the lock, and attempting to run down the stairs, her foot slipt, and she fell down, and unfortunately broke her right leg short at the instep, so that she could not rise. By this time he had recovered himself, and hearing her groan, ran down stairs, where he found the old hags standing as amazed. He took her up in his arms, carried her up to the bed, and seeing the blood running on the floor, soon discovered what had happened; she swooned, and the shinbone was shivered, so that it had cut through the skin and sinews, and appeared. This sight dashed his amorous fires, and awakened his care to preserve her.

He ran down, took his horse, and went to a village for a surgeon; who came, and was doubtless surprised to see so fine a woman in such a dismal place. But Fernando had told him, it was his wife, who was lunatic, and had broke loose, and endeavoured to escape, and so came by this sad accident; pretending himself to be a gentleman who belonged to the court, and could not keep her in his own apartment there. The surgeon dressed her, not regarding her complaints; and Fernando, who was obliged to unmask, lest the surgeon should suspect something, took care to hide his face from Teresa. No sooner was the surgeon gone, but he put on his vizard, and approaching the bedside, said many kind and tender things, to which she gave no answer: excessive pain, and the fright, with the fatigues of the foregoing night, having made her almost unable to complain.

At last he left her, it being necessary for him to appear in sight, to prevent his being suspected of the villainy he was guilty of. One of the old hags watched by her that night, and in the morning when the honest surgeon returned, he found her light-headed, with a strong fever which had seized her, in which she talked of Don Lopez, Emilia, her child, and of being stole. This made him begin to suspect something. She remaining dangerously ill for some days, in which time Fernando came often to see her, he was much concerned, and took care to let nothing be wanting but a physician, whom he durst not send for, for fear of discovery. In this time great inquiry being made after Teresa, the surgeon heard of it, and immediately took horse, and went to the lords, informing them of what he knew. Don Lopez and the *marquis* desired much to know who the villain was, but that the surgeon was ignorant of.

They took horse immediately, attended by five servants well armed, and conducted by the surgeon, went to the house; it being midnight before they reached it, the door was made fast, a horse being tied near it, and a light in the chamber: They consulted what to do, fearing if they knocked, it might alarm the old hags, and the ravisher, who might by some back door or window escape; so they concluded to wait till he came down to take horse. They did so, and towards daybreak one of the old hags opened the door. The lords, who were dismounted, and stood ready, rushed in, and running up stairs, found Fernando in the room masked. Don Lopez staid not a moment to deliberate, but shot him through the head: He fell dead at his feet, not uttering one word.

Thus he perished in a moment, unprepared for death, and got a just reward for his villainy. Teresa, who was almost dying, and delirious, looked up, and knew her lord; she strove to rise to reach him, but fell back: He laid his cheek to hers, and strove to stifle his tumultuous joy, and hush her to repose. The hags were seized, and some of the servants dispatched for a horse-litter, in which Teresa was carried home to her lord's, and the vile women sent to prison. Fernando's body being known, was sent home: And though Don Lopez had received so great an injury, yet he feared a trial, or private injury, from Fernando's family, revenge being very natural to the Spaniards; he therefore absconded, resolving to retire to France with the Marquis de Ventadore. And now able physicians being sent for, in some days Teresa got rid of her fever, and began to recover: At last she got up again, but went lame, and never expects to do otherwise whilst she lives: She rewarded the honest surgeon nobly.

Don Lopez got safe to France first, and the *marquis*, with the ladies, children, and servants, followed; Don Lopez's father having taken care to make a noble provision for his son to live in France. They travelled gently, and arrived safely at Poicton, where they are all happily seated together.

And now it is fit that we make some reflections for our own improvement, on the wonderful Providence of God, in the preservation and signal deliverances of these excellent persons in this narrative.

A great number of Christian slaves are at this time expected to return to Europe, redeemed from the hands of those cruel *infidels*, amongst whom our noble slaves suffered so much, and lived so long; and no doubt but amongst these, if we enquire, we shall find some whose misfortunes, if not their virtues, equal these lords and ladies. It

335

is in adversity that men are known: He is only worthy the name of a Christian who can despise death, and support even slavery and chains with patience; whom neither tortures nor interest can shake, or make renounce his God and faith. How frequent is it for us, who boast so much of religion, to sacrifice our consciences to interest? How impatient are men for small injuries or disappointments?

The gentlemen in this story well deserve our imitation; the ladies, I fear, will scarce find any here who will pull out their eyes, break their legs, starve, and choose to die, to preserve their virtues. The heathens, indeed, shewed many examples of such heroic females; but since the first ages of Christianity, we have had very few: The nuns of Glastenbury, who parted with their noses and lips to preserve their chastity, are, I think, the last the English Nation can boast of. It is well in this age if the fair sex stand the trial of soft persuasions; a little force will generally do to gain the proudest maid. But I forget that to give good advice, and not to censure, is at present my business; I shall therefore sum up all in few words.

Since religion is no jest, death and a future state certain; let us strive to improve the noble sentiments such histories as these will inspire in us; avoid the loose writings which debauch the mind; and since our heroes and heroines have done nothing here but what is possible, let us resolve to act like them, make virtue the rule of all our actions, and eternal happiness our only aim.

LEONAUR

ALSO FROM LEONAUR

AVAILABLE IN SOFTCOVER OR HARDCOVER WITH DUST JACKET

THE COLLECTED SUPERNATURAL AND WEIRD FICTION OF J. SHERIDAN LE FANU: VOLUME 1 *by J. Sheridan le Fanu*—Contains Two Novels 'The Haunted Baronet' and 'The Evil Guest', One Novella 'Carmilla',One Novelette and Ten Short Stories of the Ghostly and Gothic.

THE COLLECTED SUPERNATURAL AND WEIRD FICTION OF J. SHERIDAN LE FANU: VOLUME 2 *by J. Sheridan le Fanu*—Contains One Novel 'Uncle Silas', One Novelette 'Green Tea' and Five Short Stories of the Ghostly and Gothic.

THE COLLECTED SUPERNATURAL AND WEIRD FICTION OF J. SHERIDAN LE FANU: VOLUME 3 *by J. Sheridan le Fanu*—Contains One Novel 'The House by the Churchyard', and One Short Story 'Dickon the Devil' of the Ghostly and Gothic.

THE COLLECTED SUPERNATURAL AND WEIRD FICTION OF J. SHERIDAN LE FANU: VOLUME 4 *by J. Sheridan le Fanu*—Contains One Novel 'The Wyvern Mystery', One Novelette 'Mr. Justice Harbottle,' and Nine Short Stories of the Ghostly and Gothic.

THE COLLECTED SUPERNATURAL AND WEIRD FICTION OF J. SHERIDAN LE FANU: VOLUME 5 *by J. Sheridan le Fanu*—Contains One Novel 'The Rose and the Key', One Novelette 'Spalatro, From the Notes of Fra Giacomo', and Two Short Stories of the Ghostly and Gothic

THE COLLECTED SUPERNATURAL AND WEIRD FICTION OF J. SHERIDAN LE FANU: VOLUME 6 *by J. Sheridan le Fanu*—Contains One Novel 'Checkmate', and Six Short Stories of the Ghostly and Gothic

THE COLLECTED SUPERNATURAL AND WEIRD FICTION OF J. SHERIDAN LE FANU: VOLUME 7 *by J. Sheridan le Fanu*—Contains Two Novels 'All in the Dark' and 'The Room in the Dragon Volant', Two Novelettes 'The Mysterious Lodger' and 'The Watcher' and Four Short Stories of the Ghostly and Gothic

THE COLLECTED SUPERNATURAL AND WEIRD FICTION OF J. SHERIDAN LE FANU: VOLUME 8 *by J. Sheridan le Fanu*—Contains One Novel 'A Lost Name', One Novelette 'The Last Heir of Castle Connor', and Six Short Stoies of the Ghostly and Gothic

LEONAUR

ALSO FROM LEONAUR
AVAILABLE IN SOFTCOVER OR HARDCOVER WITH DUST JACKET

MR MUKERJI'S GHOSTS *by S. Mukerji*—Supernatural tales from the British Raj period by India's Ghost story collector.

KIPLINGS GHOSTS *by Rudyard Kipling*—Twelve stories of Ghosts, Hauntings, Curses, Werewolves & Magic.

THE COLLECTED SUPERNATURAL AND WEIRD FICTION OF WASHINGTON IRVING: VOLUME 1 *by Washington Irving*—Including one novel 'A History of New York', and nine short stories of the Strange and Unusual.

THE COLLECTED SUPERNATURAL AND WEIRD FICTION OF WASHINGTON IRVING: VOLUME 2 *by Washington Irving*—Including three novelettes 'The Legend of the Sleepy Hollow', 'Dolph Heyliger', 'The Adventure of the Black Fisherman' and thirty-two short stories of the Strange and Unusual.

THE COLLECTED SUPERNATURAL AND WEIRD FICTION OF JOHN KENDRICK BANGS: VOLUME 1 *by John Kendrick Bangs*—Including one novel 'Toppleton's Client or A Spirit in Exile', and ten short stories of the Strange and Unusual.

THE COLLECTED SUPERNATURAL AND WEIRD FICTION OF JOHN KENDRICK BANGS: VOLUME 2 *by John Kendrick Bangs*—Including four novellas 'A House-Boat on the Styx', 'The Pursuit of the House-Boat', 'The Enchanted Typewriter' and 'Mr. Munchausen' of the Strange and Unusual.

THE COLLECTED SUPERNATURAL AND WEIRD FICTION OF JOHN KENDRICK BANGS: VOLUME 3 *by John Kendrick Bangs*—Including twor novellas 'Olympian Nights', 'Roger Camerden: A Strange Story', and ten short stories of the Strange and Unusual.

THE COLLECTED SUPERNATURAL AND WEIRD FICTION OF MARY SHELLEY: VOLUME 1 *by Mary Shelley*—Including one novel 'Frankenstein or the Modern Prometheus', and fourteen short stories of the Strange and Unusual.

THE COLLECTED SUPERNATURAL AND WEIRD FICTION OF MARY SHELLEY: VOLUME 2 *by Mary Shelley*—Including one novel 'The Last Man', and three short stories of the Strange and Unusual.

THE COLLECTED SUPERNATURAL AND WEIRD FICTION OF AMELIA B. EDWARDS *by Amelia B. Edwards*—Contains two novelettes 'Monsieur Maurice', and 'The Discovery of the Treasure Isles', one ballad 'A Legend of Boisguilbert' and seventeen short stories to cill the blood.

Lightning Source UK Ltd.
Milton Keynes UK
UKHW010804090223
416681UK00002B/759